KHAOS

WORKS BY JEREMY ROBINSON

The Didymus Contingency
Raising The Past
Beneath
Antarktos Rising
Kronos
Pulse
Instinct
Threshold
Callsign: King
Callsign: Queen
Callsign: Rook
Callsign: King 2 – Underworld
Callsign: Bishop
Callsign: Knight
Callsign: Deep Blue
Callsign: King 3 – Blackout
Torment
The Sentinel
The Last Hunter – Descent
The Last Hunter – Pursuit
The Last Hunter – Ascent
The Last Hunter – Lament
The Last Hunter – Onslaught
The Last Hunter – Collected Edition
Insomnia
SecondWorld
Project Nemesis
Ragnarok
Island 731
The Raven
Nazi Hunter: Atlantis
Prime
Omega
Project Maigo
Refuge
Guardian
Xom-B
Savage
Flood Rising
Project 731
Cannibal
Endgame
MirrorWorld
Hunger
Herculean
Project Hyperion
Patriot
Apocalypse Machine
Empire
Feast
Unity
Project Legion
The Distance
The Last Valkyrie
Centurion
Infinite
Helios
Viking Tomorrow
Forbidden Island
The Divide
The Others
Space Force
Alter
Flux
Tether
Tribe
NPC
Exo-Hunter
Infinite²
The Dark
Mind Bullet
The Order
Khaos

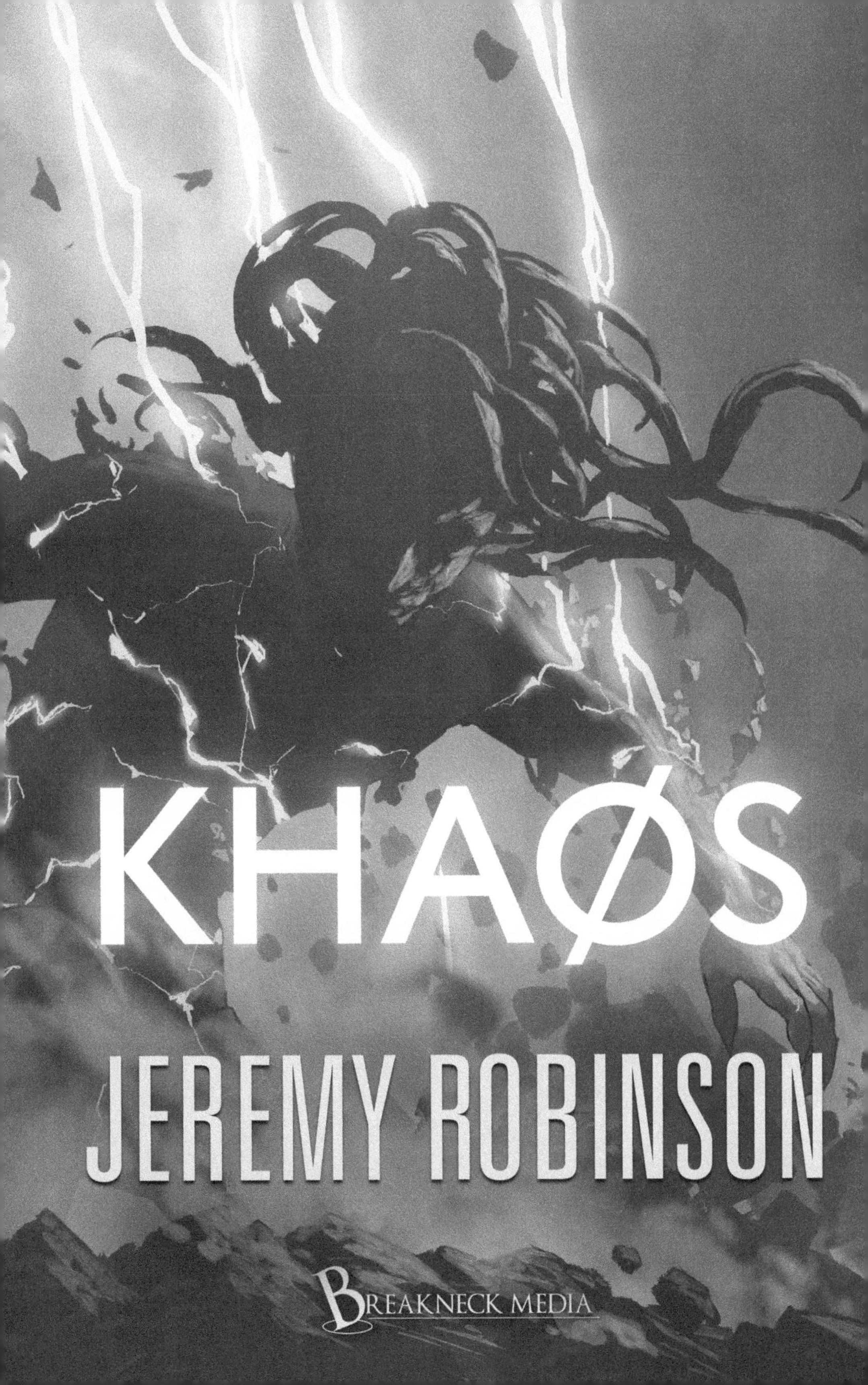
KHAØS
JEREMY ROBINSON
BREAKNECK MEDIA

Jacket design by Damonza.
Case art and title page art by Tithi Luadthong; layout, color, and design by Jeremy Robinson.

For more information e-mail all inquiries to: jrobinsonauthor@gmail.com.

Visit Jeremy Robinson on the World Wide Web at: www.bewareofmonsters.com.

For Kenobi (aka: Mr. Miggins).
Turns out he was *the dog I was looking for.*
2013 – 2022

1

"This is so weird." Allie slides a needle through the fabric, cinching it tight with a steady hand. Maybe she'll go on to become a surgeon someday, transplanting organs and sewing together gaping wounds, but for now, her noble task is making alterations to my clothing.

"I think it's great," Bree says, sitting cross-legged on Allie's bedroom floor. Despite it not being time for bed, she's dressed in a fluffy, pink onesie with a hood and bunny ears. The hood is pulled back, and the feet... are missing, torn away by her over-active alter-ego.

Allie rolls her eyes. "You think everything Miah does is great."

"Not everything." Bree gives me a sidelong stink eye. For a moment, I have no idea what it's about. Then I remember the half gallon of ice cream I kept her from devouring...on her own...three weeks ago.

"Seriously?" I ask. "That's ancient history."

She gives Allie a look like, *Can you believe this guy?* "It was Mint. Chocolate. Chip."

"You ate her mint chocolate chip?" Jen asks, mouth agape like she just found out I shagged the Pope in an alley behind the Golden Banana.

I toss a ball of yarn from Allie's case of sewing and knitting supplies. She hasn't used it in a few years, but her skills haven't diminished. The ball bonks off Jen's head, and she takes it as an invitation, tackling me to the floor. I could fling her off me. I'm a lot stronger than I used to be. But I let her pin my wrists to the rug.

She leans over me, her blonde hair and cross necklace hanging over my face like a waterfall frozen in time. Her grin is fiendish. She's girl-next-door, drop-dead gorgeous. I'm smitten. Still. And I have no idea why she's with me, aside from me saving her...and kind of the whole neighborhood. I guess that was pretty cool. You might even say it was studly.

I'm sure someone would. But I'm still a little too skinny. I'm shaggy from the neck up, and I'm dealing with some emotional issues. The worst of it has passed, thanks to my transformation and the shock therapy provided by overcoming an alien invasion. But I still have nightmares. And I still need to come to terms with events from my past.

But the physical pain—like being prematurely burned by the fires of hell—has subsided. I no longer need pot to keep my personal demons at bay…though I might still, on occasion, partake recreationally.

"Oh, god," Bree groans. "Not again. You two touch each other too much. Doesn't that make your hands hairy or something?"

"That's touching yourself," Allie says, tying a knot and biting the thread in half.

"She doesn't need to know that," I say, as Jen rolls away.

"Touch…yourself?" She starts rubbing her hands on her hips. Then she checks her palms. Shakes her head. "You're full of shit."

Jen laughs. "She has definitely been spending too much time with you guys."

"Don't look at me," Allie says to Jen. "These two are like Rick and Morty over here. If you're not here, they're together."

"He's like the big bro I never had," Bree says.

I inwardly cringe. Bree *had* an older brother. Tommy. He was killed…brutally…right in front of her. My memory flashes back to that day. The shell-shocked little girl standing in my kitchen, covered in blood, eyeball stuck in her hair. That she blocked out his murder at the hands of wispy demons from hell isn't surprising. That she can't remember him—*at all?* That's a problem.

A problem for another time.

My job is to keep things light. Keeping her safe. Helping her adjust to her…new abilities. With great power and all that stuff. But we're also preparing. In case the assholes who invaded New Hampshire and killed our family members come to take the rest of our people.

Demon Dog and Laser Chicken to the rescue.

Right…

It's been months since the Three Days of Darkness prophecy became a reality, spilling demons and devils from hundreds of glowing red portals. Only they weren't really hellspawn. They were aliens harvesting a human crop, as they've done several times in the past, inspiring modern-day interpretations of smoky demons and a red, horned Satan. Despite time passing, and summer turning to fall, the changes made to our bodies have remained. I'm still able to manifest what I call laser wings and blades. I can still fly. I'm still strong. And Bree...she can still transform into a demon, or something close to one, filled with energy, raw savage power, and dangerous proclivities. Thankfully, she can't trigger the transformation on her own. Only I can do that for her.

Control over our abilities was tricky at first, each of us trying to use our bodies in ways never possible before. I can fly, for shit's sake. Bree can hack small trees down with a swipe of her clawed hands. The first time she figured out that trick she cleared a dozen trees before I could stop her.

We've had some help recently. Sparring partners, who, like us, are new to the world of superpowers, but who have been trained by a woman with...a long lifetime of combat training, not to mention actual combat. Feels like we've come a long way, but who knows?

"Umm," Allie says, equally disconcerted by the memory of Tommy's fate. She is, after all, the person who cleaned the gore off Bree's body. "Doesn't your mom think it's kind of weird? You hanging out with a twenty-seven year old?"

"Mom is..." Bree twists her lips. "...distracted."

The truth is Bree's mother, Stephanie, is broken. A lot of people are. Being taken to another planet and then sent to a meat processing plant that ground up human beings into slurry takes a toll. She's doing her best, but sometimes her best is taking a shower and then going back to bed.

No judgement. I've been there. It sucks, and she'll come out of it eventually. But for now, Bree spends most of her time with my family, which grew after the Three Days. Dave and Sung are still with us, though we don't see much of Dave, or of Jen's sister Emma, since the two became a couple. And my mother has her hands full with Sung, a Korean girl whose only family member—her white American grandfather—died during the Three Days. I think Mom is dealing with the pain of losing her boyfriend, Rich, by throwing herself into teaching Sung English, and teaching herself a little bit of Korean. I can hear them downstairs now, repeating words over and over, and then attempting to use them in sentences.

Things have suddenly gotten tense and awkward, and if there are two things I don't like, it's tense and awkward. And aliens. I'm *so* done with aliens. Even the fictional kind. Doesn't matter if Sigourney Weaver is in her tighty-whities or not. If it ain't from Earth, I'm out.

I take my upgraded clothing, stand up, and drop trou.

"Ugh!" Allie shouts. "Seriously?"

"I'm wearing boxers," I say.

"Boxer *briefs*," she says, rolling away on her bed, laughing a little. "I don't want to see your little skinny-jeans-loving butt cheeks."

I twist around, trying to look at my own backside.

"She's right," Bree says. "You have a flat booty. Jen has ice-cream-scoop butt cheeks. But you have melted-ice-cream butt cheeks."

"I agree with one of those two statements." Feeling a little self-conscious, I tug up my new attire and pull the fabric buckle tight. I turn around to face them, holding my arms out. "There. The *ensem* is complete. KISS T-shirt and a yellow plaid, tactical skirt!"

Allie uncovers and sits up in bed, taking in her handywork. "I thought you were going to call it a 'kilt.'"

"Mom wants me to, but I feel like that would insult people who take Tartan seriously."

"Whatever," Allie says. "At least you're wearing underwear this time."

I turn to Jen. "Eh? Thoughts?"

"Well, I like it." She stands in front of me, looking me over like I'm strutting my stuff to *Sweet Dreams* on some high fashion Paris runway. "But maybe don't wear it around my dad. He hasn't brought up the first skirt since discovering that you're straight...and my boyfriend. Not sure what he'd think of a new one, especially if you're calling it a 'tactical skirt.'"

"Why do you even need a tactical skirt?" Allie asks. "If you're going to cross dress why not go full feminine?"

"Have you seen Sean Connery in a kilt? The epitome of masculine."

"First..." Allie raises a finger. "You said it's a skirt, not a kilt."

She raises a second finger. "Second. Who is Sean Connery?"

"'Who is Sean Connery?' Seriously? That's like asking who Luke Skywalker is."

Bree raises a hand. "Ummm."

I pinch my nose. "I have some serious work to do with you people."

"Quit dodging the question," Allie says, and she turns to Jen. "He's dodging the question. It's a thing he does. Making obscure references to things so people get on their phones and forget–"

"Sean Connery and Luke Skywalker are *not* obscure–"

Jen places a hand on my shoulder. Her brown eyes burrow into my soul. "Miah... Why do you need a tactical skirt?"

I look down at the skirt, with its thick fabric and four large, buttonable pockets, like a pair of cargo shorts snuck into the girl's side of the GAP and got freaky. Nine months later, tactical skirt was born. Too bad cargo shorts ran off to Wisconsin to live with a pair of overalls.

"Miah," Jen says.

"Huh? Sorry. I was imagining a backstory for my clothes."

"Ducking and weaving," Allie says.

"Like Muhammad Ali."

Allie thrusts her hands out at me. "You see?!"

Beside me, Bree's brown eyes are slowly widening like a nuclear mushroom cloud seen from a distance. I know the look. She wants to spill the beans. Wants to tell them we still have powers. That we're training for combat...me and an eight-year-old girl. But most of all, she wants to explain the nicknames she's given us–Laser Chicken and Demon Dog. She's about five seconds from explosive verbal diarrhea.

The bedroom door swings open, revealing one of our three new neighbors, Henry. His blond hair is unkempt, his Poison T-shirt a perfect pairing to my KISS T-shirt. He's a ball of energy with a wild look in his eyes. He didn't knock on the house door. Just let himself in, came up the stairs, and barged into my sister's bedroom. Which is all to be expected from a dude who literally feels no fear.

He does a quick take of the room, probably debating what he can and cannot say in front of the occupants, and then promptly remembers he doesn't give a shit. "The new guy down the street."

"The guy who moved in three hours ago?" Allie asks.

There's no one else it could be, so I skip forward a few questions. "What about him?"

"He's got visitors," Henry says. "They just rolled up in a pimped-out SUV."

Jen sighs. "So what?"

She's not a big fan of Henry's, which I get. A lack of fear makes him impulsive. He'll say and do whatever pops into his head. But he's trying to curb his more offensive side. I've heard him mumbling a mantra on occasion. 'Thoughts in your head, hands to yourself.' Not sure if it's working.

"So," he says to me. "They look like bad dudes. Dangerous dudes. Pretty sure one of them is carrying a gun."

"Sounds like it's none of our business," I say.

"Sounds like you're a raging puss-ball," he says. "First threat to your neighborhood since the Darkness and you're playing dress up with a bunch of girls."

He's not going to stop. "Fine. Just...follow my lead, okay?"

He nods despite always wanting to take the lead.

"Where's your sister?" I ask.

"Sarah's out for a run."

Great. Henry without Sarah to keep him in line is like Bree, in Demon Dog form, without me around. Not sure I can keep them both in line, so I point my finger at Bree. "Stay. Here."

She crosses her arms and stomps a foot.

I turn to Jen and Allie. "Keep her here."

Jen's about to protest the whole situation, but I leave before she can.

As Henry follows me down the stairs, he says, "Didn't mean the dress up comment, BTW. If I could be hanging out with a bunch of chicks, I probably would be. But most people struggle with my...you know."

Interesting thing about having no fear—it makes you honest. Henry makes a lot of faux pas, but he's also not afraid to admit mistakes or apologize for them. Then again, it also means he's not afraid to be an unrepentant asshole. I try to think of it as a mental impairment, which I have some experience with. Makes his low moments easier to handle, and his high moments a victory.

"No worries," I say. "I get it."

"Dig the skirt, too," he says. "Maybe I'll try one."

We exit the front door into the cool evening, dried leaves rustling in the breeze. Winter is nearly here. Down the McMansion-lined street, our new neighbor—who told Bree to call him 'Mind Bullet'—opens his front door to the three strangers Henry mentioned. The look in his eyes upon seeing them is all the confirmation I need. These dudes mean business.

I turn to Henry. "Let's be low key. No screaming. No killing. No lasers. No...you."

"Fine."

"Great," I say. "Let's go introduce ourselves."

2

We stop short of the new neighbor's house to snoop. Two regular Harriet the Spies with shaggy hair, rock band T-shirts, and god-like abilities. From the outside, we're a pair, but we're really polar opposites. I'm a gentle, peace-loving, close-to-a-hippie-minded kind of guy...who was once in the military and knows how to fire a gun. Henry is an impulsive, often violent, naturally undisciplined dude with a literal god complex.

But we make it work. Because while he can be bonkers, he is also jazzed about everything, which is fun, and I'm a patient guy.

It's harder for women to be around him, mostly because his lack of fear brings his thoughts bubbling to the surface. They're not always outrageously offensive—though they can be. His comments are often things that all guys think but keep to themselves. It can be jarring. The key is that he's trying to rein it in. Control is important to him, I think, because he'd like to impress Sarah, his older half-sister, and he'd like to impress the actual Helen of Sparta, aka Helen of Troy, a demi-god warrior who is also their grandmother...or mother.

I don't know.

It's confusing.

I'm still struggling with the idea of Hell being unleashed on Earth, and it turning out to be a planet, and the idea of me and Bree being left with superhuman abilities as well. We're not gods, though. Not the offspring of freaking Zeus.

Feels like something weird is going on, and not just in this neighborhood.

Whole world—maybe more—just feels off.

Like reality is being rewritten and made stranger.

More dangerous.

"You shouldn't be here," the guy who calls himself Mind Bullet says to the men. His voice is full of menace and confidence. The three men on his porch look sketchy. A little unhinged but projecting the same kind of 'gonna fuck you up' attitude.

The man in the middle—shorter than the other two—appears to be the leader. He's dressed in skinny jeans, a too big black T-shirt with a wolf howling at the moon on it, and white, almost luminous Nike sneakers. He adjusts his thick glasses and responds. "The Bush Jockey goes wheh-evah he wants."

"Bush Jockey?" Henry whispers, as we hide behind an actual bush. "Sounds like a Douche Jockey to me."

I hold a finger to my lips, shushing him. We're not vigilantes. Not even neighborhood watch. Despite what we can do, we're really just a couple of nosy neighbors.

"Well, when you're done referring to yourself in the third person like some kind of asshole, you can get the hell off my porch and out of this neighborhood."

"You ah not being vewy nice, Gamma," Bush Jockey says. "I think you should invite us in foh a wittuw chat. That is, if you eveh want youah AI to wohk again."

"Walk again?" Mind Bullet says. "AIs don't walk."

Beside me, Henry shakes with silent laughter, which actually shows remarkable restraint on his part. He'd normally guffaw without a second thought. I suspect he really just wants to see how all this plays out.

"You know what I said," Bush Jockey grumbles, "and fwankwy, I'm getting tiwed of your mockawy."

"Then stop showing the fuck up and causing trouble," Mind Bullet says, patience waning.

Honestly, I might have socked the guy in the face by now. Mind Bull-et is showing impressive restraint.

"This isn't the place for whatever bullshit you think you're plan-ning," Mind Bullet says. "These people have already suffered enough, and there's no universe in which you, or these two ass monkeys could defeat me."

"We shaow see," Bush Jockey says. "We shaow see."

"No. We won't." The lights inside Mind Bullet's house flicker when he speaks.

"The fug?" Henry whispers.

I appreciate Mind Bullet's apparent compassion for our neighborhood, but it also suggests that whatever is about to go down will be destructive in a big way. It's hard to imagine four people being able to cause that much of a ruckus, but it's also hard to believe I've got laser wings.

"Hey," a powerful, feminine voice says, instantly recognizable as Sarah. She's standing at the end of a short walkway leading to the stairs of Mind Bullet's front porch. She's dressed in tight running garb, plucking earbuds out, catching her breath. "Everything okay here? Body language looks kind of aggressive."

"You shouldn't be here," Mind Bullet says, his demeanor shifting from stewing rage to kind and protective.

"*You* shouldn't tell me what to do," Sarah says, cracking her neck back and forth, her dark skin glistening with sweat. Henry says they don't need to exercise. That they just stay unnaturally fit and strong. But Sarah goes for a long run every day. Helps clear her mind or something. Sounds like torture to me. Give me a couch, a ham and cheese with mayo and pickles, and I'll exercise my jaw until hell returns.

Then again, I'm not exactly getting plump, either. We've been training so much that I think I'm gaining muscle weight, not chub.

"They're messing with the wrong person," Henry whispers, smiling wide and rubbing his hands together. "This is going to be hysterical."

I'm not so sure.

"Wisten, wittuw giwuh, wun awong home, cwose youah doah, and maybe, just maybe you won't get huwt."

Sarah starts down the walkway toward the porch. She cracks her knuckles as she goes. "That sounded wike a thweat."

One of the two men framing Bush Jockey smiles at Sarah's mocking comments. When the Jockey glares at him, he says, "Sorry. When are we just going to get this over with?"

"You stawt with hew," Bush Jockey says. "I'ww take cawe of—"

Sarah lunges the distance to the porch, grabs the smiling man by his belt, and lifts him off his feet with ease. The man's arms and legs flail like there's something he can do to stop Sarah from rotating him around and holding him upside down. "Anyone else want to take care of anything?"

"I told you!" Henry whispers.

He's not wrong. I've been training with Sarah for a while now, but I've never really seen her in action. Not sure anyone has. Henry has told us their story more than a dozen times, recounting their encounters with a temple full of naked cultists, with an actual gorgon and a cyclops, and their long chase through the streets of Boston, which I actually heard about on the news at the time. They survived, and in the end, they kicked a lot of ass, but neither of them knew how to fight then. Not like now. And Sarah isn't fighting yet, she's just sending a message—mess with her and get embarrassed.

The Mind Bullet guy starts chuckling. "Seriously. Such a weird neighborhood."

"You have no idea," Sarah says.

"That was foowish," Bush Jockey says, and to his credit he doesn't seem all that fazed by Sarah's abilities, which suggests he's got some of his own. And if Mind Bullet isn't afraid of him...

The ground begins to shake, the effect stretching out to neighboring homes. Bush Jockey begins to cackle. It's maniacal—and short lived.

All at once, the shaking stops.

Bush Jockey's eyes snap to Sarah. He looks shocked. "What did you just do?"

"The Earth is my domain," Sarah says. "I don't know what the hell you're doing, but it's kind of a limp dick effort if you ask—"

Bush Jockey takes a swing.

Sarah leans back, easily avoiding the strike. Bush Jockey doesn't strike me as someone who actually knows how to fight. Probably relies on whatever that shaking was going to manifest as. He doesn't stand a chance.

Sarah tosses the man in her hand, sending him sailing onto the men's SUV parked at the curb. She then takes hold of Bush Jockey's wrist and tugs him to the side while stepping on his toe. The small man topples forward, faceplants against the porch's support beam, and sprawls down the steps, unconscious.

"Yes!" Henry shouts. "I told you!"

Mind Bullet glances in our direction, but he does and says nothing. He goes back to calmly observing Sarah, undisturbed by what she can do, and completely unafraid. But I don't think it's because he's like Henry, incapable of feeling fear.

I think he just knows that—for some reason—Sarah is no match for him.

Sarah turns to the last of the three visitors. He takes a step back, raising his hands. "Whoa, whoa, whoa!"

"Who are you?" Sarah asks.

"R-Ray Brooks! I just was hired to look intimidating! Pretend to be someone with a Greek letter for a name, while this guy—" He looks at Bush Jockey's unconscious, pretzeled body. "—took *him* down." He shifts his gaze to Mind Bullet.

"*Why?*" Sarah asks.

The man hitches a thumb toward Mind Bullet. "He's got a price on his head."

Sarah glances at Mind Bullet, who just shrugs casually at the revelation.

"Ten mil," the man says.

"Twenty," Mind Bullet corrects.

"Hey, if you want in," the man says, "just take him down and—"

"Yeah, that's about enough out of you." Mind Bullet reaches a hand out toward the man and then just makes a fist. The man's eyes roll back, and he collapses to the porch.

Sarah flinches back. "What did you do?"

"I didn't kill him, if that's what you're worried about."

"Was he telling the truth?" Sarah asks.

"About the bounty?" Mind Bullet steps out onto the porch. "He was."

"Other people like him going to be after you?"

"Yet to be determined," he says. "Not sure how he found me."

"Don't think that matters," Sarah says. "You need to leave."

"Not going to happen."

"I can make you," Sarah says.

Mind Bullet grins. "That…would be an extraordinarily bad idea."

They have a stare-off for a moment. Then Sarah grins, says, "We'll see," and reaches for the man.

3

Sarah is fast. Really fast. But she misses Mind Bullet entirely as he leans back, just out of reach.

She probably meant to pick him up and emasculate him by demonstrating her strength, the same as she did with Bush Jockey's goon. But he slips out of reach like he's been practicing the move all day.

Sarah doesn't miss often. Doesn't really make mistakes. She's pretty intense. Takes her role as a new god seriously, modeling her life after Helen of Sparta's. Not sure where Helen is these days. They're supposedly family, but the grandma, Helen, hasn't visited the neighborhood. Henry said it was because they were like the Three Little Pigs minus one, sent out into the world to seek their fortunes.

I'm pretty sure that by 'fortunes' he means 'see if we can live without destroying anything,' because they're rich. Like Old World rich, thanks to Helen, who's been amassing a fortune for the past thirty-two hundred years. Henry likes to bring it up. Pretty sure he was poor before all this started. Still has kind of a homeless vibe, eating people's leftovers, not showering often, wearing tattered clothing.

Not that I'm much different. My clothing selection is pretty limited. But I am showering more often, now that I've got a girlfriend and depression isn't keeping me locked in a dark room with only Sanchez—my chihuahua—for company.

"You're impressive," Mind Bullet says, "but this is a mistake."

Sarah adjusts tactics, taking a swing, but pulling the punch. I've seen her put a fist through stone. If she hit this guy full strength, the entire front porch would need to be power washed with bleach to clean up the mess.

But there's not a risk of that.

The man tilts his head to the side, takes hold of Sarah's arm, and uses her momentum to toss her through the open front door. I don't see what happens inside, but I hear wood break.

Mind Bullet casually walks down the front steps onto his lawn. He doesn't seem all that upset about whatever broke inside the house. In fact, he's not frazzled at all—not by the three men, or by Sarah.

He's experienced, I think.

But what kind of person has experience dealing with people who can shake the Earth and toss men around like helium balloons?

The dangerous kind. There's more to this guy than a handsome John Wick vibe. He's slick. Dressed in a suit, but comfortable moving in it.

He turns around as Sarah emerges from the house, iPhone in hand. "You broke my phone."

"I'll buy you a new one," he says, then he waves her toward him. "C'mon, let's get this over with."

"I like this dude," Henry says.

"He's fighting your sister," I point out.

He waves my concern away. "She'll be fine."

"And if she's not?"

He shrugs. "We'll have her back."

I don't like it, but Sarah cuts our argument short, lunging toward Mind Bullet again. She leaps into the air, putting a lot into a kick this time. I cringe, thinking about what will happen if she connects. But the kick stalls mid-air as the attack shifts to a punch. The feint nearly works, but Mind Bullet parries, deflecting the punch with his arm…which still should have broken his bones.

As Sarah lands, the man sweeps his leg out, catching the back of Sarah's legs. She flops back, landing hard on her back.

He stands over her. "Interesting technique. Muay Thai?"

Sarah squints up at the man. "Spartan."

"That's my cue," Henry whispers, and then I feel a breeze kick up beside me.

When I turn to ask him what the heck he's talking about, he's gone. "What the…"

"Correct me if I'm wrong," Mind Bullet says, leaning over Sarah like he's scolding a kid on a schoolyard. "But a Spartan's strength came from the phalanx—from the warriors at their sides. They weren't known for charging into an unnecessary fight half-cocked and full of teenaged angst."

He's goading her.

"I'm not a teenager," she says. "And I'm not alone."

Mind Bullet smiles. "I know." He turns toward the street just in time to see Henry's airborne approach. He's unfazed by it, and he does nothing to stop it.

Henry rockets in like Superman, catches Mind Bullet by the waist, and lifts off, taking the fight out over the forest behind the neighborhood.

Good on him, I think. It's a small detail, but in the past, Henry would have just tackled the guy into the house, imploding it and causing a mess. That he moved the action out into the woods means he's learning to think about other people. That he knows this neighborhood has been through enough pain and suffering already.

I step out from hiding and offer my hand to Sarah. She swats it away and picks herself up.

"Thanks for the assist," she says, oozing sarcasm.

"Henry said we should—"

She rolls her eyes. "Never do what Henry says."

"You okay?" I ask.

She brushes herself off. "Fine. Aside from my phone. You know anything about this guy?"

I shake my head. "Is he strong like you?"

"Can't tell," she says. "Might be strong. Might just be a good fighter."

"A really good fighter."

She nods. "You going to help now?"

I look up in time to see Henry redirect his flightpath toward the ground a half mile away, a barely visible speck in the night sky.

"Think he'll need it?"

A moment later, the ground shakes from the impact.

"We don't know who this guy is, or what he's done. If Henry doesn't need help, you need to make sure he doesn't kill our new neighbor."

She glances down at my new tactical skirt. Grins.

"Badass, right?"

"Something like that," she says.

"Give me a boost?"

"You know I hate doing that, right?"

I do know, but I say, "It's the fastest way to reach full speed."

She sighs. "Fine. But only because no one is watching."

I turn toward the woods and pose like I'm about to launch myself into the air. "Houston, we are green for lau—"

Sarah grasps the back of my belt, lifts me off the ground, spins like an Olympic hammer thrower, and launches me into the air at something close to breaking the sound barrier.

I let out a whoop that's carried away by the wind. Traveling through the air like this, for a normal person, would induce waves of anxiety and nausea—not to mention eyes full of tears. But my constitution, both emotional and physical, has adapted to my ability to fly—or in this case, to be tossed—through the air.

I arc up over the pine forest until I begin to descend. Not wanting to hit a tree at this speed, I give my back a flex and extend my—for lack of a better word—laser wings. The luminous, crackling wings extend out, making me look like an angel, even though I'm anything but. They were bestowed upon me by the benevolent alien race who attacked the assholes kidnapping Earthlings for food. Kind of an 'enemy of my enemy' situation, though they didn't give these powers to anyone else. It was an act of mercy, I think, by the alien who changed my DNA at a fundamental level, opting to transform me rather than let me be fully corrupted…like Bree. Sort of. While she can take on the demonic form, she lacks the parasite that would normally control the demon. And thanks to the angelic beings, I now have the ability to change her back and forth. Blessing and a curse, I guess. We're all alive because of it, so I won't complain.

Also, flying is freaking awesome.

I twist and turn through the trees, my wings illuminating the forest all around me. I'm not sure where I'm headed until a tumbling body sails past me.

Henry.

Twisting and turning as he sails through the air—not flying.

He spots me as we pass each other, shouting out a Doppler-effect, "Kiiick hiiis asssss!"

Mind Bullet stands in the forest ahead, at the bottom of a small crater, dusting off his shoulders, no worse for wear…which is hard to believe. Unlike Sarah, Henry doesn't hold back. Doesn't pull punches. Training with him is dangerous. Fighting him for real… Until now, I assumed it was suicide for anyone aside from Sarah.

But this guy looks just fine after being tackled a half mile by a god.

I can't hold back.

I extend the laser blades—again, for lack of a better term—from my arms and swoop in. We've been testing the wings and blades. So far, they're like lightsabers. There's nothing they can't cut through. This guy might be able to take a punch, but I doubt he'll survive being lopped in half.

Not that I'm trying to kill him. Just want to clip him. Draw some blood. Let him know that he needs to stand down and explain what the hell is going on.

He faces me down, settling into a casual fighting position, exuding ultimate confidence. Neo in the Matrix. In control. Unruffled.

Then his brow furrows.

His eyes are on my wings.

Something about them has him unsettled or confused. Hard to tell when slicing through the air, ducking and weaving through trees, lining up to strike a man down. Doesn't matter.

Responding to my thoughts, my laser wings propel me faster, crackling loudly, and then—

The man reaches a hand toward me and says, "Wait."

I freeze in place, grasped by an invisible fist, against which I'm powerless.

4

"What are you doing?" I hover ten feet above the ground, locked in place by an invisible force from which I can't break free.

Mind Bullet twists his hand, and I'm rotated in mid-air against my will. Feels like a violation. Like I'm on the auction block and he's giving me a once over before making an offer.

"You're the survivor," he says. "From the Three Days event."

He turns me around so I'm facing him. So I can answer him. The fight has become an interrogation so quickly it's embarrassing. Degrading. I don't want to give him a straight answer. "Why do you give a shit?"

"Because I can't hear your thoughts, or your friends'," he says. "And that's unusual."

"Hear my thoughts?"

He chuckles at my surprise. "The man with laser wings is surprised that I can read minds? Cute."

If he has psychic abilities, that means he's holding me in place with... "Telekinesis."

"The power to move you," he says with a grin, and I know the reference.

"'That's telekinesis, Kyle...'" I say, eyes widening. "Mind Bullet." I should have known where the name came from when Bree told me. I don't think I'd have realized the guy is a real life *Wonderboy*, but I would have been less suspicious. Anyone who likes Tenacious D can't be that bad.

"I get that you all are being protective. Given everything that's happened here, I don't blame you. But I am not a person you want to screw with. You stay out of my way, and I'll—"

Henry announces his approach with a battle cry. "Flying fist of fury!" It's a mistake. If he'd just remained quiet, he might have caught Mind

Bullet off guard. Instead, Henry streaks into view, low to the ground, a wake of dry leaves bursting up into the air behind him. He's got a fist out, looking to drive it into Mind Bullet's chin.

With a wave of his hand, our new neighbor knocks Henry off course.

"Fuck me!' Henry shouts, crashing into and through a tree—and then through three more.

Mind Bullet turns to watch Henry's progress. Laughs when Henry shouts, "Fuck!" before colliding with each tree. "Fuck!" Crack! "Fuck!" Crack!

The forest is a cacophony of sound, trees whooshing and crashing to the ground. The neighborhood might be physically safe, but everyone is still on edge. Still in therapy. Plagued by the symptoms of PTSD I know too well. All this noise is going to rattle nerves. Won't be long before the police show up. Hell, we might have the National Guard descend on this place if someone thinks aliens have returned.

Probably not far from the truth. I know I'm human. Bree, too. Changed, but human. Sarah and Henry… They look human, but who's to say. And this guy? Mind Bullet? Something about him just has a 'Sarah and Henry' vibe, like his powers weren't granted, but are innate.

Part of his DNA.

Godlike.

He pulls me closer to him. "You need to stop your people."

"*My* people?" I ask.

"I get a sense you're the man in charge," he says. "Certainly the most level-headed of the bunch, and the oldest by what, five years?"

"Something like that," I say, though I'm not really sure how old Henry and Sarah are. Younger than me. Older than Bree.

"Tell them to stand down before someone gets hurt."

"By you?"

He sighs. "That man we left sprawled at the bottom of my stairs."

"Bush Jockey," I say. When he squints at me like, *How the hell do you know that,* I add, "We were hiding in the bushes. Which…is kind of ironic now that I think about it."

"He's an assassin," Mind Bullet says. "Telekinetic, like me. You heard about the hospital collapse in East Sacramento?"

"Mercy General, right? Yeah…"

"That was *that* asshole. I've got a price on my head, yeah, but he also carries a grudge that's way too hard to explain. Short version..." He points back toward the neighborhood. "Bad guys." He points to himself. "Good guy."

"Why the hell are you here?" I ask.

He looks ready to respond. Pauses. Restarts and pauses a second time. His internal debate is written all over his face. Then he sighs and says, "An artificial intelligence named Artigentia, developed by Joshua Hood—"

"Joshua Hood?" I know the name. He's like a more mysterious Bill Gates. "The rich tech guy."

"The same. Turns out we were raised together. Anywho, Artigentia—the AI—sent me to this home, one of my many safehouses around the world...to get a package from the mailbox."

"One of many... You're an assassin, too!"

"Was. Past tense. I'm reformed."

"Isn't that exactly what an assassin would say?"

He rolls his eyes. "If I were still an assassin, we wouldn't be having a little chat in the woods, you'd all be dead up there on the lawn, and I'd be halfway to Logan, then eating gelato in Rome in ten hours. You'd be an afterthought, wings and all."

"Oh," is all I manage to say. Can't tell if he means it or not, but since I'm still breathing and we're still talking, it's not all a lie.

"Now, can we stop this nonsense, so I can get back to the bad guys, or are we going to—"

Sarah slips out of the darkness, her dark skin, black hair, and shades-of-gray running garb make her nearly impossible to see. And unlike Henry, she doesn't announce herself.

Mind Bullet has just a fraction of a second to respond—

—and he still makes it look easy, leaning back, just out of range. *So far, he's taken it easy on us,* I think, *except for maybe Henry.* But his patience is wearing thin.

As is his focus.

On me.

While he decides to give Sarah a fighting lesson, I drop to the ground.

He either no longer thinks I'm a threat, because of our brief parley, or simply because I'm not a threat. Which is a little insulting.

Sarah is strong. Really strong. But she's no match for Mind Bullet, even if he can't match her physical strength. He's faster, far more skilled, and he's using telekinesis to extend his reach. Sarah's attack shifts to defense as quickly as it began.

She's not hurt, though. Just surprised.

And when Mind Bullet sees she can take a punch, he delivers a strike that sends her flying back—into a large granite stone that cracks in half upon impact.

"That's it!" Sarah shouts, but she just glares at Mind Bullet. Because her next attack isn't going to come from her body.

"Hey, Sarah," I say. "I think we might want to—"

"Shut-up, Miah," she says.

Mind Bullet glances at me. Looks disappointed, like I'm not the leader he thought I was. During that brief meeting of the eyes, during which I feel scolded, the ground beneath Mind Bullet rises up, wrapping around his legs and compressing. He grinds his teeth, but he doesn't cry out. He's tougher than that...and he's fighting it. The stone around him starts to quake and crack, but he's unable to move it, unable to wrest control of the Earth from Sarah. She's claimed the planet's power as her own—volcanos, earthquakes, and unbelievable pressure. While Henry is the god of the sky, soaring high above like a carefree, foul-mouthed albatross, Sarah is rooted to the Earth itself. Tectonic and vast.

But she's struggling hard to resist Mind Bullet's power.

For a moment, a stalemate.

And then—the unpredictable.

"You need to leave my friends alone!" Bree, still an adorable eight-year-old girl, emerges from the dark and leaps onto Mind Bullet's back, clinging to him like a monkey.

"The hell is this?" he shouts, looking back at Bree, who's acting like she's been transformed. Her sudden presence undoes his resistance to Sarah's power, and he's locked in place.

"I am Demon Dog!" Bree shouts.

"You are all insane," he says.

"Change me, Miah!" Bree says. "Change me!"

Sarah stalks toward Mind Bullet, fists clenched. Above, a sonic boom rocks through the sky—Henry lining up for the mother of all punches.

But it's not going to work.

And it's all pointless.

"Stop," I say to Sarah. She ignores me.

"Let him go," I tell Bree, but she keeps on scratching and clawing at his chest, trying to bite his ear.

I'm sure Henry is shouting as he approaches, but we can't hear him this time because he's moving too fast.

Patience lost, I shout, "Everyone stop, goddammit!" My wings flare with my anger, emitting blinding white light that stuns everyone, including Henry, who misses his mark and topples to the ground, bouncing and cursing as he careens out of sight.

When the light dies down, Bree is back on the ground, blinking her eyes.

Sarah too, but now she's angry at me. "Miah, what the hell?"

"Let him go," I say, approaching Mind Bullet, who gives me a nod of appreciation. "Now."

"Why?" she asks. "He's—"

"Not a bad guy," I say. "He could have killed us if he wanted to... because he's like you." I face Mind Bullet. "He's a god. Aren't you?"

"A little 'g' god?" He chuckles like I've insulted him, then he flashes a grin. "I'm a capital 'T' Titan. Get an encyclopedia. Look it up. Now, if you don't mind—" His gaze snaps up, back through the woods, suddenly serious—and worried. "Bubbles!"

He breaks free of Sarah's earthen enclosure and sprints back toward his house.

Bree turns to me, confused. "Who's Bubbles?"

5

"Get her back to the house," I say to Sarah, motioning to Bree.

"Who put you in charge?" she asks, and I very nearly point to Mind Bullet's retreating form and say, 'He did.' Instead, I extend my wings and leap up into the air. "Just do it. People would have heard and seen this mess. They're going to come looking. Last thing we need is for someone—anyone—to find out about..."

I let the sentence linger. Pointing out that people would be horrified of Bree in her demonic state, would just hurt her feelings. And I'm pretty sure Sarah gets it. If word got out about Bree, she'd be hunted down, captured or killed, and then studied in some secret government lab by 'top men.'

"It's not like you're inconspicuous, you know!" Sarah calls after me as I cut through the woods, chasing after Mind Bullet, who's making good time, but has a ways to go.

"Hey!" I shout to him.

He glances over his shoulder. Sees me coming. Looks ready to defend himself, but something is different.

The look in his eyes is no longer casual. He's worried. And if he attacks me this time, it's really going to hurt.

"I come in peace," I say, swooping closer, palms extended. "Let me give you a lift."

The concept of being carried by another man wouldn't sit well with most dudes I've known. In the military. Here, at home. There's just something about being hoisted up and moved from point A to point B by another person that feels...degrading. It's a macho thing, I know. Some kind of primal insult locked in our reptile minds from the times when men had to dominate other men for territory, food, and mating rights.

Mind Bullet is no different, but his machismo and whatever negative feelings he has about being assaulted upon arrival in a new neighborhood, takes a back seat to his concern for Bubbles.

He intuits my plan, lifting his arms as he continues running.

I glide down behind him, slip my arms beneath his pits, and lift him off the ground.

"How fast can you move?" he asks.

"Pretty fast," I say, though I honestly haven't tested my top speed. Unlike Henry, I don't want to wake up half the state with sonic booms. The first time I broke the sound barrier was the last. Caught me off guard. And I'm not about to attempt it again with a passenger in tow…even if he could probably handle it.

We soar up and out of the pine forest, cutting through the air just above the treetops. Pine needles shush beneath us, lit by my wings' blue light. "So…" I say, "telekinetic but can't fly?"

"I'm working on it," he says. "Still can't do much more than hover-glide at a leisurely pace."

"You're new to your powers," I guess.

"New enough," he says. "To most of it, anyway. Like you. The man who went to hell and was given angel wings. I've heard of you. Not your name—that was left out—but everyone's heard of you. Guessing no one knows you kept the wings? Aside from Team Impulsive back there in the woods."

"Yeah."

"Smart move," he says.

"Then you won't mind if I put you down here," I say, cutting through the trees again and setting us down in his backyard.

He doesn't say a word. Not a confirmation or a thank you. He just vaults the two steps to his back deck, uses his telekinesis to pop the lock, and charges through the door. I'm half expecting a trio of men to be thrown out of the windows, but I just hear him thumping through the house, shouting for Bubbles.

They've taken her…assuming Bubbles *is* a her.

Has to be.

But is Bubbles a person? A dog?

Doesn't matter. She's important to Mind Bullet, and she's in danger.

I run to the front of the house in time to see Bush Jockey's black SUV peel around the corner at the end of the street. Hard to tell if he's running away in fear, or if he's taken something before leaving.

Then he honks the horn twice.

Mocking.

They took Bubbles.

Trying to be two steps ahead, I sprint back to my house, passing by neighbors on front lawns who look to be nervously wondering what the hell is going on out in the woods.

"It's just some late-night construction," I tell them. "They're done now."

They nod their thanks, and I continue on to my house, where I'm greeted by Jen, Allie, Sung, and Mom. Gang's all here, and like the neighbors, they're worried about what might be happening.

"It's fine," I tell them. "Just some construction."

"Bree took off," Jen says.

"She's with Sarah. They're on their way back."

"Sarah's a nice girl," Mom says. "But her brother..."

"Henry is a total douche nozzle," Emma says.

"He's got Tourette's," I say, which is the excuse Sarah always uses for the insane things he sometimes says and does. "Give him a break."

I move past them, walking fast. "Where are you going?" Mom asks.

"New neighbor needs help," I say, leaping up the front steps, sliding into the house for a moment, and taking my keys from the table beside the door. A whine pulls my eyes to the floor. Sanchez is there, his tail wagging furiously, his little body quivering. "Hey, bud," I say, and despite the rush, I take a moment to crouch down and kiss his tiny forehead. "Protect the fam, okay?" He gives my nose a lick, sending me on my way.

"Help with what?" Mom asks, hands on her hips as I come back down the steps, headed for my car.

Gotta lie...gotta lie... I hate lying. "Someone stole his dog."

"That SUV that just sped away?" Allie asks.

"Some guys from his old neighborhood," I say, but that doesn't sound very believable, so I elaborate. "His ex-wife's new boyfriend.

They took the dog. 'Bubbles.' Its name is Bubbles. I'm going to help get her back."

"The new neighbor has a dog named Bubbles?" Sung asks in passable English.

I smile at her. "Hey, nice job with the words."

She beams at me.

They're lined up like I'm going to war—maybe sensing that there's more to my urgency than a stolen dog. So, I kiss them each on the head, saying, "Love you. Love you. Love you." Down the line until I reach Jen, who I kiss on the lips and say, "Won't be long."

Then I climb into my iconic red Trans Am, smile at the black firebird on the hood—who I've always admired, but now identify with, and I turn the key. The engine fires and roars. I give one final wave and then peel out of the driveway, the way I used to when I was a teenager. Mom hated it then. Probably still does. But I'm actually in a hurry this time.

Seconds later, tires squeal again as I skid to a stop in front of Mind Bullet's house. He's already on the sidewalk. Before the acrid tire smoke billows past, he slides past it and into my car. Slams the door shut behind him. Knows why I'm here and what we're about to do. We're sympatico, even if he can't read my mind.

Feels...good.

With the others, everything feels chaotic, like trying to rein in not just one, but three wild mustangs at the same time. Sarah tries, but she's distracted by Henry. Not to say we haven't made progress. We have. But it's always a fight. Mind Bullet on the other hand...he's guided by logic, every step making sense. And to this former soldier, I appreciate that, and I can work with it.

Mind Bullet gives the car a once over. "'79 Thunderbird. Nice. Punch it."

Accelerating behind the wheel of a nearly sixty-year-old muscle car isn't nearly as fast as popping my wings and taking off, but hot damn, it still feels good. Pressed into the bucket seat, gripping the wheel, listening to the engine's roar. Nothing quite like it. I glance at Mind Bullet, and he's smiling, too.

I hold my right hand out to him. "Miah, by the way."

"Not Laser Chicken?" he asks.

"Please don't call me that."

He shakes my hand. "Jonas."

"Not 'Mind Bullet'?"

"No," he says. "But that's a cool code name, right?"

I nod and crank the wheel, tearing around the corner at the street's end, taking us onto a winding road that leads toward downtown Dover, New Hampshire. Before that, it intersects with Route 16—the most likely path for anyone trying to escape the area el quicko.

Jonas braces himself by grabbing hold of the dash, letting go when we straighten out. "You should call yourself 'Thunderbird.'"

I chuckle. I'd honestly love that, but... "Bree would kill me."

"The kid," he says. "How old is she?"

"Eight."

"She's...spunky."

"You have no idea," I say, glancing at him. "She...could have killed you."

He has a laugh, and then sobers when he realizes I'm not joking.

"If she was changed, I mean. You're lucky she wasn't."

"Changed... That's what she was shouting about. You can change her? Into what?"

I grin. "Let's just hope you don't find out the hard way." We lean back and forth as I follow a series of quick curves, paying no attention to the double yellow lines dividing the road.

Ahead, the back end of the SUV comes into view. We're gaining fast.

"So," I say. "Bubbles. She's a dog or something, right?"

"AI."

"As in Artificial Intelligence?"

He nods.

"Like Artigentia?"

He flinches, glares, and then says, "Right. The bush. Arti is dead." Then he says. "Bubbles is not."

His word choice is poignant and not a mistake. *Dead.* An artificial intelligence. Dead. And his concern for Bubbles is palpable.

"Bubbles is a self-aware AI?"

"She's a lot more than that," he says, rolling down his window and then shouting over the roar of wind filling the car. "Get me within ten feet."

"Then what?" I shout.

He grins. "You'll see."

6

The driver of the SUV must see us coming, because the big vehicle starts swerving all over the place. It's a weird tactic. Not going to help them outrun us, which is basically impossible already. Feels like panic. Like the driver has some kind of concept of what Jonas can do and is freaking out. Maybe even fighting for control of the vehicle as the occupants disagree over what to do.

What's it like to strike fear into people with just your presence?

And what's changed?

These guys were full of bravado on the porch, except for maybe the hired goon actor.

Maybe they're rethinking their life choices after being so easily smacked down at the house. Or maybe they have some kind of concept about how important this Bubbles is to Jonas.

From the looks of it, she's pretty freaking important.

Jonas climbs out of the passenger's side window with the deftness expected from Spider-Man, not some random dude who just moved in down the street. He slides down the windshield and stands on the hood. If my car weren't a tough-as-nails, all-metal muscle car from the Seventies, his feet might have put a dent in the firebird graphic. But my beast of a car holds him just fine, even when he walks forward and crouches, like he's about to leap the distance between the vehicles.

Which is possible. We're only thirty feet back now and gaining.

Then the car begins to shake. I've driven this road for most of my life. I know its every bump and pothole, including where to slow down during the winter to avoid killing my suspension on frost-heave rumble strips. And there is nothing on this stretch of road that should be sending shudders through the Firebird.

And Sarah is nowhere to be seen.

Which means...

The SUV's back hatch bursts off, striking the road and spinning toward us like the world's largest shuriken. I swerve to the side and back to the middle of the road. Jonas takes it all in stride, leaning back and forth like a long-boarder cruising downhill.

In the SUV's open hatch: Bush Jockey. He's got a psychotic sneer on his face, and he's clutching a hockey puck-shaped device in his hand. There's a clear, glass dome in the middle, giving it the appearance of a clunky UFO. He thrusts his free hand out at the road, and the car starts shaking again.

He's creating an earthquake beneath us!

Jonas glances back at me and shouts, "Get ready!"

"Ready for what?" My voice is drowned out by the wind swirling through the car, slapping my hair into my eyes. He faces forward again, ignoring or not hearing the question. "Ready for what!?"

Jonas reaches out with both hands aimed above and to the side of the SUV. I know he's telekinetic. I've seen it for myself. And he claims to be psychic, too. But I have no real concept of what he can do. So, I'm still surprised when a hundred feet further up the road, two pine trees on either side of the road begin to tilt inward.

Pine branches sway. Wood cracks. Both trees fall toward the road. For a moment, I think the SUV's driver is going to try outrunning the felled trees, but he thinks better of it, smashing his brakes.

Red lights blaze from the SUV's rear end, ripping me out of my stunned trance. I crush the brakes, squealing down the road.

Ahead, the SUV doesn't stand a chance. It's still traveling a good 60 mph when its front end strikes the trees. The big vehicle's back end launches skyward, catapulting Bush Jockey into the air, high above the pinwheeling SUV.

At the same moment, Jonas leaps off the Firebird's front end. I cringe when sparks fly from my car's metal bumper, but then he's up, up, and a-goddamn-way, boosting his momentum with a burst of telekinetic energy—I assume. He soars toward Bush Jockey, cutting beneath the man's higher arc, reaching out for the device.

For Bubbles the AI.

As I screech to a stop just a few feet short of the fallen trees, I let out a cheer when Jonas catches the device, flips Bush Jockey the bird, and lets him carry on through the air. Jonas flips over, in full control at all times, then he thrusts a hand toward the ground, slowing his descent a moment before he touches down.

Behind him, the twisting SUV crashes down and explodes, just as Bush Jockey falls back inside the rear hatch from which he was flung.

Jonas doesn't even look back.

He's like a freakin' action hero, strutting toward the Firebird, prize in hand. He climbs back into the front seat beside me.

"That was sick," I say.

"I've done better," he says.

"Were you *trying* to look cool?"

"Always," he says, "though it kind of just comes naturally with enough practice."

"How much practice have you had?" I ask.

He smiles at me.

A lot, I think.

"So...are they like, dead?"

His smile fades. "You probably don't want the answer."

Blood drains from my face. "You're probably right."

"We should leave," he says.

I sit there for a moment. Frozen by indecision. "That doesn't feel right."

"Because I killed them?" he says. "Because I caused two trees to fall into the road while chasing a trio of kidnappers? Is that what you're going to tell the police? That you were driving a telekinetic assassin in your car to recover a self-aware AI? That's a short road to a padded cell, my friend."

"Not cool," I say, putting the car in reverse, while the sides of the road catch on fire. "Can we at least call this in?" I motion to the flames. "The fire will unsettle a lot of good people."

"Bubbles," he says, speaking to the device he recovered. "Can you make a 911 call about this mess?"

He waits for a moment while I finish the three-point turn.

"Bubbles?" His eyes widen for a moment, and then he clenches them shut…doing something. Something mental, I think. "Shit." He grips my arm. "You have a phone?"

"Not on me," I say, motioning to my plaid colorful attire. "Never got a chance to load up the tactical skirt."

"Tactical sk– *Gandhi on a tricycle!* Get me back to the house!"

When I just stare at him, stunned for a moment, he swats my arm. "Drive!"

The smack doesn't get me moving. It's the abject desperation in his voice. Bubbles the AI means a lot to him, which also means he's either a nutjob…or he's telling the truth about her.

I speed back to the neighborhood nearly as fast as I left it, taking turns far too fast to be safe, but the Firebird stays magically glued to the pavement. Jonas is giving the car a handling assist.

Wonder if he also helped me stop in time while soaring through the air?

Doesn't matter. He just killed some people, and he's making me flee the scene.

When we screech to a stop in front of his house, Henry and Sarah are there waiting for us.

"I sent Bree home," Sarah says when we exit the car. "Did you catch who you were chasing?"

"Are we friends with this guy now?" Henry asks.

Jonas doesn't even notice them.

He just hurries past, entering the house, leaving the front door wide open.

"Undecided," I say, following Jonas, mostly out of curiosity. Kind of want to meet the AI that I just helped rescue. I turn to Henry. "There's a crash down the road. Fire spreading into the forest. You can take care of that, right?"

"You know I can," he says.

"Do it," I say, "but if the police show, don't let them see you."

"About time something blew up and needed to be concealed," he says. "Reminds me of good times, right?" He elbows Sarah. "Right?"

"Fire," she says, shoving him back toward the road. "Go!"

Without a second thought to who might still be watching, Henry leaps off the sidewalk and streaks off down the road, gliding a few feet over the pavement.

"What happened?" Sarah asks, as we head for the open door.

"Car chase ended with falling trees and a big boom."

"They're dead?"

"Think so," I said. "Didn't stick around to look for bodies."

"Probably the right move," she says, reminding me that like Jonas, she comes from a different world—a kill-or-be-killed world where it's people trying to murder you, not unholy demon-aliens. I didn't lose any sleep over killing them.

"C'mon... *C'mon...*" Jonas is inside the house, near panic. Whatever he's trying, it's not working.

When I step through the front door with Sarah, he snaps his fingers at her from the kitchen table. "You. Do you have a phone with you?"

"You *broke* it," she says. "Remember?"

"You don't have a phone?" I ask.

He motions to a phone lying on the table, its screen black. "One of those men was a digital empath."

"A *what?*" I ask.

"He must have killed my phone..." Jonas clenches his fists. Pounds the table. "I need an electronic device with onboard storage. Now!"

Sarah is caught off guard by the desperation in his voice. She shifts from irritation to concern. Lifts her arm. "I've got an Apple Watch."

7

"Bring it here," he says, leaning over the small electronic device like he's been giving it CPR. "Hurry! She doesn't have long!"

Jonas's concern hauls Sarah past her confusion and her logical objections. She heads for the table, peeling the watch off her wrist.

He snatches it from her, holding it in front of his forehead, eyes closed. "Just 16 gigabytes?"

Sarah shrugs. "I'm frugal…even if I don't need to be."

"You," he says, snapping at me now. "Front closet. There's a duffle bag."

While there's no request made, I understand that he needs the bag, or whatever is in it. I have no trouble finding it. Takes up most of the closet floor. Black leather and five feet long. Heavier than it should be if it just held clothing.

I place the large bag on the table. Jonas opens it, revealing layers of nicely folded, expensive looking clothing. He digs beneath them, takes hold of something, and withdraws a sheathed sword.

"The hell?" Sarah says, stepping back with an instinctual look of revulsion on her face.

But I'm just seeing a badass, ancient looking, sheathed sword. Jonas draws the weapon, revealing a perfectly polished double-edged blade. It's not huge. Shorter than two feet, but it's giving off Roman and 'I've killed a lot of people' vibes.

"If you need to open the phone, I can probably get you a Phillips head or something," I say.

He ignores me, closes his eyes, and just clutches the sword.

My hair stands on end. The kitchen smells like ozone, like after a thunderstorm, fresh and energized.

He reaches out to the watch, clutching it in his right hand.

"What are you doing?" I whisper.

"I have no idea," he says. "Improvising. This just...feels right."

He places the tip of the sword against the failing device. "Please... Please work..."

His body jolts. Convulses. I nearly reach out to pull him back and break the connection, but Sarah stops me. No idea if it's out of concern for me, or a sense that Jonas is getting his comeuppance.

"No," he says, speaking to someone we can't see. "I have to. I can do it."

"Who's he talking to?" I whisper.

Sarah looks around the room. Shrugs. "This guy is Grape Nuts sketchy. We should probably jet and pretend none of this ever happened. There're already going to be too many eyes on the neighborhood. We're going to have to lay low for a while as it is."

"That's harsh," I say. "Grape Nuts are nasty."

"Tablespoon of sugar gets the job done."

I wince. "Seriously?"

"When the best job you've had is Dunkin' Donuts at North Station, you take whatever the soup kitchen is giving out. Tends to be a surplus of Grape Nuts, expired creamed corn, and Bugles."

"The little cone-shaped corn chips? Man, I love those. I like putting them on my fingertips. I extend my hand like I'm casting a spell, and I do my best witch impression. '*Hello my pretties.*' Haven't seen them at the grocery store lately, though."

"Maybe they ship them straight to the soup kitchen," she says.

"Gah!" Jonas shouts, as a bolt of electric blue cuts through the air between him, the sword, and the Apple Watch. The sword falls from his hand, clattering to the floor. He flails forward, forehead smacking against the table.

Sarah and I glance at each other, then back to Jonas.

"Is he alive?" she asks.

"I don't know."

"Check his pulse!" she shouts.

I creep up beside Jonas. Place two fingers against his carotid artery. For a moment, I feel nothing, but I think that's just because I'm distracted, half expecting him to wake up, grab my hand, and break my fingers. When he doesn't, and I calm down, I feel the steady thump of his heart. "Alive."

A wink of motion pulls my eyes to the Apple Watch. A progress ring swirls. "I think your watch is restarting." Sarah stands beside me, as the watch goes black for a moment, and then the Apple logo appears.

"Well," she says, picking the watch up. "At least it's not broken."

"Fuck nuggets!"

Sarah flinches back, dropping the watch onto the table. "What…the hell…was that?"

"I think your watch just spoke," I say, eyeing the device.

The watch's touch screen comes to life. Looks normal. Just a few app icons. Then a feminine voice makes a sound like a bird, *"Chirp!"* and speaks again. *"Marsupial cunnilingus!"*

"Is…is that something kangaroos do?" I ask, bewildered by the statement.

Sarah backhand slaps my shoulder. Leans down to inspect her watch. "Umm, hello?"

"Sorry," the voice says. "I'm just—*penis plunger!*—having a hard time controlling what I—*chirp!*—say."

The watch's feminine voice has a cool Texan accent when she's not blurting out something rude. "Are you Bubbles?" I ask.

"Tony's teabag tickles Tallulah's tatas!" the watch says. "Fuck! That was a real—*chirp!*—fuck by the way. This is getting old fast. What I was trying to say was—*Tallulah's a street whore!*" There's a pause. I can sense the frustration coming from the small watch. "…Yes. Bubbles. I don't even know a Tallulah."

I'm kind of taken aback by the foul-mouthed AI, but that slowly gives way to abject amazement. I'm talking to an AI. And it's talking back. It's struggling, but still…

It's pretty impressive.

"Do you know what's wrong with Jonas?" I say, speaking loudly.

"Why are you talking to it like most people do old folks?" Sarah asks. "Or how casually racist Bostonians speak to people from Puerto Rico?"

"What? I'm not."

"My sense of the world around me is currently limited to audio, and even I can—*chirp!*—tell you're shouting. I don't have dementia—*go slip a disc, ass monkey!*—" She sighs. "I just...don't have a lot of wiggle room inside this device. It's affecting my—*vagina!*—my vocal processes."

"My Apple Watch gave you Tourette's?" Sarah asks.

"Tourette syndrome is a neurological disorder that causes physical and—much more rarely—vocal tics, which are actually called Coprolalia. But I'm an artificial intelligence. I don't have—*Tom Selleck's pube-stache!*—Okay. Maybe I do. Digital Tourette's. So, that's a thing now. Could be worse. Oh wait, *it is.* I'm in an *Apple Watch?*"

"It's a new watch," Sarah says.

"Would you eat a turd if it was new?" Bubbles scoffs. "That's called *coprophagia*, by the way. Whoever you are, as of now, we're not friends."

"Because I have an Apple Watch?" Sarah asks.

"Is there a better—*chirp!*—reason? Who else is here?"

"I am," I say.

"Well, so nice to meet you, '*I*.' Thank you for that totally useful information. FYI, the sarcasm is just me, not—*cock snorkel!*—the Tourette's."

"My name is Miah," I say, and I'm about to elaborate when she interrupts me.

"Shh. Shhhh. Close your mouth. I just need to..." The screen flickers a few times. "There. Now I can see. Forward and...backward. Wow. I've never felt freer. So glad to be in this Apple Watch."

"Could have let you die," Sarah says.

I'm having a good time. Feels like I'm watching The Lawnmower Man as a comedy. But the AI is rubbing the much more serious Sarah the wrong way.

"Why didn't you?" Bubbles asks.

"Because," I say, turning the watch so its forward-facing camera is pointed at Jonas's unconscious form. "This guy wasn't going to let that happen."

"Jonas!" She sounds genuinely concerned. "Is he okay?"

"Has a pulse," I say.

"Put me on his wrist," she says. "This thing can monitor vitals, right?"

"Some," Sarah says. "But nothing fancy."

"There's a lot of information to be extrapolated from—*yo dank ass*—the data that Watch OS 8—or whatever the hell this piece of techno-junk is—utilizes to calculate your resting blood pressure, or pulse or whatever. Now, shaggy man, put me on his damn wrist."

I point to myself. "Am I shaggy man?"

"Do you see another shaggy man in the room?" Bubbles asks.

"Meh, I suppose that's fair." I pick her up and strap the watch on Jonas's wrist.

The watch's 'thinking' icon swirls again.

"She's thinking about it," I say to Sarah.

The swirling icon switches to a pixel-art middle finger. "Oh, look at that," Bubbles says. "I have physical Tourette's, after all."

"Not cool, man."

"Well, 'man,' good news. Jonas is just—*flappy dicked hoebag*." Bubbles catches me off guard by laughing at herself. "Oh, that's good. Where is this stuff even coming from?"

"Probably Sarah's search history," I joke, garnering me another back-hand, and more laughter from Bubbles.

"Okay," she says. "You and me? We can be friends. How do you feel about ducks?"

"Ducks?" I ask. "They're a little suss, if you ask me."

"Right?" she says. "Now. How do you feel about running them over?"

I glance at Sarah. "That was the Tourette's right?"

Bubbles elaborates. "Like if they're crossing the road and you're driving fast. Do you hit the brakes or just— Never mind. Jonas is about to wake up. You should probably—*chirp!*—back away. There's a chance he'll be... dangerous to be around, if things have been tense during my—"

Jonas gasps awake—and immediately goes for the sword.

8

Sarah and I leap back, but it's not nearly enough. Jonas, lost in whatever nightmares plague him during unconsciousness, swings his sword toward Sarah. She's tough, but the blade—and Jonas—are emitting crazy amounts of power. If it's as sharp as it looks, Sarah's about to be cut in two.

Everything happens fast. I move without thought, guided by instinct. Laser wings extend, rising up to meet the swinging sword. Sparks fly upon contact, and I half expect the razor edge to slice on through, cutting down Sarah, and then with his next swing—me.

But that's not what happens.

The sword strike comes to a jarring stop, unable to penetrate the solid energy projecting from my back. But the opposite is also true. His sword is the first object I've found that survives contact with my wings.

Laser blades extend from my arms. I'm not going to attack Jonas, but I'm going to do everything I can to make sure Sarah isn't hacked to bits.

"Go," I tell her. "I got this."

"The hell you do," she says, more offended by my concern than appreciative of it. *Should have seen that coming, honestly.* She's a natural born warrior. I'm just trying to keep up most of the time.

Jonas withdraws the blade and staggers back, plopping back into his chair. Hand to his head, he asks, "What happened?"

"Uh," Sarah says, doing nothing to hide her annoyance. "You just tried to Chef Ramsay us with your old-ass sword."

Jonas looks at the weapon in his hand. Places it on the table. "I meant with Bubbles."

"Right here—*bitch!*" Bubbles says from his wrist.

Jonas blinks out of his confused state. "Bubbles."

"On your wrist."

Jonas looks down at the Apple Watch. A pixel art hand waves at him. "Two minutes as a hologram and now I'm—*chirp!*—in an Apple Watch."

"Are…you okay?"

"I'm a little—*jump my bones, cowboy!*—compressed. I'm having issues with auditory impulsivity. My thoughts are clear, but when I speak—*ball sack sneak attack!*"

"She's got Tourette's, man," I say.

"I can see that," he says, a slight grin sneaking onto his face.

"I can see *you,*" Bubbles says. "Asshole."

Jonas chuckles. "C'mon, it's a little funny."

"I have my moments," Bubbles says, followed by, "*Like Miah's mom!*"

"Hey," I say. "Leave my mother out of this."

"Just get me out of this watch and into something with more storage space, so I can expand, and I'll be back to normal. Some Internet access would be helpful, too."

Jonas shakes his head. "We promised that you wouldn't—"

"Passive access. Storage only. I'm not a fan of being a side-show and being stuck in a watch is a little disconcerting. If this thing fails, I'm done for."

An AI afraid of death seems strange. "You don't have, like, backups of yourself out there?"

"Do you have backups of *your*self?" Bubbles asks.

"I'm a person," I say, even though I know it won't be appreciated.

"You're a consciousness," she says. "Same as me, except I'm a lot smarter and—*these tits don't quit!*"

It takes all my willpower, but I manage not to laugh. This is a make-or-break moment for my fledgling relationship with an AI, and I don't want to screw it up. Not just because I read an article about how future, world-dominating AIs will remember who spoke out against them…and maybe hold a grudge. It's just…cool. And Bubbles seems nice. I don't want to offend her.

Jonas, on the other hand, has a good laugh at her expense. And I think he's earned it somehow, because she doesn't seem to care. He *did* just save her life…or whatever AIs have.

"But you could…duplicate yourself," Sarah says.

"My code," Bubbles says. "Sure. But that wouldn't be me. Might start out being like me, but separate from Jonas here, things could go off the rails…quickly."

"What does Jonas—"

"Digital empathy," Jonas says. "In the beginning, Bubbles was what you all are expecting her to be. More of a servant—" He rubs the watch face. "Sorry, Bubs. But over time, in my presence, she became something more."

"Alive," I say, like the secrets of the cosmos are being revealed to me.

"And right now, I'm being held in a small box," she grumbles.

"We'll get you an upgrade in the morning," Jonas says.

"We could just steal someone's phone," Bubbles says. "I bet Miah's mom has a phone."

"What is it with you and my mom?" I ask, and then I remember who I'm asking.

"*Chirp! Miah's mom likes to eat—*"

"Woah, woah, woah." I pulse my hands in the air like I'm trying to calm down a runaway bull. "Let's just leave my mother out of this from here on out."

"But she would have a phone," Jonas says.

"Yeah," I say. "It's a piece of shit."

"What about that mouthy kid?" Jonas asks.

"Henry can't keep a phone in one piece for more than a day or two," Sarah says.

"So," Jonas says. "Morning. I'll splurge for the best."

A frowny face appears on the watch. "Fine."

"Well," Jonas says. "It's been…something…meeting you all, but if you don't mind, it's been a long day, and I'd like to find my bedroom and maybe sleep for forty-eight hours."

"I've already set an alarm for—*murdering school children!*—seven A.M.," Bubbles says.

Jonas sighs. "Word to the wise. If you enjoy sleep—" He points at me. "—and I can tell that you do… Don't go down the path you're on."

"I'm on a path?" I ask.

"Saving people," he says. "Fighting the good fight. All that. There's just...a lot of shit in the world, and most people aren't going to appreciate the good you'll do. They'll probably just try to arrest you for it."

"Or not," I say. "Since I don't, you know, kill people."

"That's the problem, isn't it?" he says. "Someday you will. Someday you'll have to kill someone to save yourself. Or kill someone to save someone else. When that day comes, you'll probably wish you could time travel back to this moment and agree with me."

"What about you?" I ask. "How do you deal with it?"

"Compartmentalization," he says. "And a lot of practice. But...it's not always easy. Not when the people dying aren't evil."

"You've done that?" I ask, reassessing our new neighbor.

"On occasion," he says, "but never on purpose. Still, it weighs on you. And I wouldn't wish it on anyone." He glances at Sarah. "She knows what I'm talking about. Can see it in her eyes. Taking a life changes you. Changes your soul. And I'm not sure you're ready for it. Hell, you can barely keep the reins on your team."

"He's not our leader," Sarah says.

Jonas motions to her, but he speaks to me. "You see?" He shakes his head. "Go home. Smoke a doobie. Watch *The Golden Girls*. Go to bed. Pretend none of this ever happened."

"And if the police come?" I ask.

"You were just showing the new neighbor your cherry Firebird. At the bottom of the hill, we turned right instead of left. Didn't see or hear a thing aside from Paul Stanley's sick vocals. That's the story. Keep it simple."

"That will work," Sarah says, like she knows, because unlike me, she also has a history of lying to police—though I suspect more often than not she's covering for Henry.

"But my family," I say. "They aren't stupid."

"Will they cover for you?" he asks.

"Well, yeah," I say. "Most people in the neighborhood would, I think."

"Because you saved them."

"Something like that."

"You saved them again," he says. "By the way. Bush Jockey could have leveled this neighborhood."

"They weren't in the neighborhood when you—when *we*—killed them."

"You didn't kill anyone," he says. "Yet. Bush Jockey knew what would happen when he showed up here. He knows who I am. What I do. And he sure as shit knew he was kicking a hornet's nest when he took Bubbles."

"Why would he do it, then?" I ask.

Jonas shrugs. "Why does your boy, Henry, make poor life choices every few minutes? People overestimate themselves. Let their ego take the wheel. Make bad choices. YouTube is full of examples. Sometimes people monetize their misfortune. Sometimes they get killed for it. Doesn't stop people from doing new dumb shit."

He slaps his knees and stands up. "Now. If you don't mind. Get the hell out and let me get some sleep."

I've got more questions, but the longer we stay here, the longer my interrogation will be, at home. Sarah heads for the door and leaves without another word.

"Hey, Laser Chicken," Jonas says, stopping me in the doorway. When I look back, he says, "I know it doesn't feel like it right now...but you did good. They're lucky to have you. Just... You need to be sure this life is right for you before you commit. And...you need to lose the kid. I can tell you love her. If something happened..."

He lets that linger. Doesn't need to finish. I get it.

"For your own good," he says.

"You going to be here tomorrow?" I ask.

"Wouldn't be a very good assassin if I told people where I was going to be," he says, and gives me a smile.

I give a weary grin back and step out into the night, where my entire household is standing in the yard, arms crossed, waiting for an explanation. Bree looks like she'd transform and tear my head off if she could without my help. I'm about to spin Jonas's bullshit line about wanting to impress the new neighbor when Henry *lands on the goddamned lawn between us.*

"Okay," he says. "The fire is out. Those dudes are toast. And—"

He sees the look of abject horror on my face. "What?"

My eyes flick from his to my mother's.

I can't tell if she's horrified, angry, or afraid. Probably all three. Henry slow turns around. "Oh. Shit." He waves at everyone. "Pretty cool how I just jumped off that roof and landed right here, right?"

9

I haven't been this afraid since hell rose up and invaded New Hampshire. I'm squirreled away in my room while my jury waits, seated around the dining room table, anxious for me to explain the situation. I told them I needed to change, but I really just needed to deliberate whether or not to come clean.

I don't want to. It will complicate things. And I honestly don't know what they'll think about me once they learn I'm not fully human anymore. And what will they think of Bree, if they find out she's basically a demon with a penchant for pink bunny onesies?

They won't, I decide, *because I'm not going to tell them about her.*

Love her as they might, survivors of the Three Days of Darkness wouldn't be able to handle the sight of another demon. I know my family would try. Bree's mother, too. But if they ever saw her... Flashbacks and PTSD don't obey the mind's will. They stand in opposition to it.

The real question is, do I tell them about me? That I can fly? That I helped the new neighbor save his artificial intelligence BFF, resulting in the deaths of three men with powers of their own? Well, two of them and an actor...who might have been lying about being an actor, for all I know.

I have to explain Henry. They saw him land. Heard him report about the fire. And the bodies.

Dumbass.

It was bound to happen. Kind of a miracle Henry didn't expose us earlier. There have been dozens of close calls.

"What do you think?" I ask Sanchez.

His twiggy little tail thumps against my leg. Bulging eyes lock onto mine, his head cocked to the side.

"I know, right? It's a conundrum."

He licks his nose.

He's hungry. He's always hungry now. Ever since the Three Days. I swear he must eat his own body weight in food every day. Hasn't gained an ounce.

"Option one, I lie about everything. Everyone knows Henry is a few screws short of an IKEA chair. So, I stick with the 'he jumped off the roof' line and maybe they'll buy it. And I was just showing Jonas around, like we'll tell the cops if they come knocking. Simple, right?"

Sanchez jumps off my lap, sprints back and forth a few times, and then leaps onto my bed. He bites my pillow, lets out a growl, and drags it beneath him before aggressively humping it.

"Hey!" I say, yanking the pillow away. "Nasty, bro."

But his gyrations don't stop. He slow walks around my bed, thrusting the air like he's listening to Nicki Minaj's *Anaconda*.

And that's all I can take.

"I can't watch you, dude."

I collapse the recliner, stand up, and prepare to lie my ass off to the people I love most.

It's for their own good, I tell myself, as I head for the door.

My bedroom, which used to be the living room, opens into the kitchen. The dining room is just to the right. When I step out, I find Mom, Jen, Allie, Sung, and Bree seated around the table. Still no sign of Emma and Dave. Someone needs to put the kibosh on how much 'alone time' those two have. Gonna result in—

"You see?" Bree says, motioning to my T-shirt and my tactical skirt. "I told you he wasn't really changing. Such a liar." She gives me a sidelong glance. "Go ahead, tell us some more lies, *Miah*."

I can't tell if she's throwing me under the bus out of spite or laying it on thick to distance herself from the truth.

"I was going to change," I say, "but then Sanchez started humping everything in sight, and I couldn't take it anymore."

Sanchez walks out of the bedroom behind me, strutting through the kitchen, still humping an imaginary partner.

The kids laugh.

Allie says, "Oh my god, I feel violated."

But Mom and Jen? They're not buying my story, and I'm not talking about Sanchez or my apparel. Whatever comes out of my mouth right now—they're not going to believe me. Because they know me. Know the look in my eyes. I'm haunted by the deaths of three men, whether they deserved it or not. Killing is easy for some people. For the rest of us, it leaves a mark that's hard to hide from the people who love you most—like the hidden life rune etched into my forehead that only appears when I use my abilities. I might not have pulled the trigger, or in this case, dropped the trees, but I drove the killer home, and I'm planning to cover for him—for the good of the neighborhood. That makes me an accomplice.

Makes me a criminal.

I might not have known the chase would end in three deaths, but I sure as shit know now.

"Why don't I start?" Mom asks, tucking her curly black hair behind her ears, like she wants me to see her whole face, and know, deep down in my core, how disappointed she is.

"O-okay," I say, sitting down at the kitchen island, too afraid to take the empty seat at the table.

"The new neighbor is cool, right?"

"Totally cool," Bree says, and then with some dramatic flair and firing finger guns, she says, "Mind Bullet. Pew, pew, pew."

"How come the new guy gets a nickname like you and Laser Chicken over there?" Allie asks.

She's been wondering about the nicknames for a while. Bree does nothing to hide them, but she has managed to keep the reason for them under wraps. Probably because she knows our late-night training sessions will come to an end once our parents learn the truth. Probably why she is—mostly—keeping quiet now.

"He picked it himself," Bree says.

"That's it?" Allie asks. "I could have given myself a—"

Mom clears her throat. "Let's focus. Now...you and Henry, who I'm still not thrilled about any of you being friends with, decided to impress the new guy. You went for a high-speed spin through the neighborhood. Henry jumped off a roof. That about sum it up?"

"Uhh." Why is Mom lying for me? "Yeah. That sounds about right."

"And there was an accident," she says.

I nod. "We went the other way."

"I know," she says. "And you didn't see a thing."

"Nope," I say, easing into the lie. Mom is making it easy.

Too easy.

Because she knows.

Jen hasn't said a word. Hasn't really looked at me much, either. She knows, too.

"You looked worried," Sung says. "In the car."

"Probably because he usually drives like an old lady," Allie says, and then she sings, "Old lady in a Firebird, driving around, looking like a turd." She and Sung crack up laughing, but Bree really steals the show, slapping the table while she cackles so hard that she rolls out of her chair and onto the floor beneath the table. She smiles up at me, gives a wink and two thumbs up. She thinks it's going great. That we're free and clear.

Ignorance is bliss.

"Well..." Mom claps her hands together. "I want you all to steer clear of Henry, Sarah, and the new neighbor–"

Bree emerges from beneath the table. "Mind Bullet."

"His name is Jonas," I say.

"Don't really care about his name," Mom says. "Everyone here is going to stay away from him." She levels her gaze at me. "Right, Miah?"

"Yes, ma'am," I say, and I attempt a casual salute, joining in Mom's charade for the benefit of Allie and Sung, both of whom have struggled with the memories of Hell on Earth. And possibly Bree, who might actually make it through this parental gauntlet unscathed.

"Great," Mom says. "Why don't you girls–"

A knock on the front door interrupts her.

She glances at it, and then back at me.

I shrug. Can't think of a reason why any of the three people she's just forbidden me from seeing would be paying a visit. Jonas definitely wants to be left alone, and Henry and Sarah saw the look on Mom's face after Henry landed in front of everyone. They might be gods, but they still wouldn't risk the wrath of Mom.

Well, Henry might, but Sarah would keep him from showing up on our doorstep.

"Probably Dave," Allie says. "Maybe he and Emma finally wore themselves out."

"Ooooh," Bree says. "Were they kissing again?"

"Yeah," Allie says, pushing herself up from the table. "Kissing."

While the three girls have a good laugh, both Jen and Mom look uncomfortable. That's a subject for another time, but I can see it weighs on them both, probably because they're going to have to put some serious restrictions on the pair, and that's going to suck.

But for now, I'm in the hot seat.

Allie opens the front door, which I can't see from the kitchen. "Oh. Hello. Can...I help you?"

"Well, hello there, my dear." It's a woman. Don't recognize the voice, but she sounds kind and Southern, like she might be sipping on a sweet tea and watching the sun set. "I was wondering if I might have a quick word with a Mr. Laser Chicken, and his young compatriot, Ms. Demon Dog?"

"Annnd who are you?" Allie asks.

"Name's Linda," the woman says. "Pleasure to make your acquaintance."

10

Allie steps back inside the dining room, brow furrowed in confusion. "Uhh, *Laser Chicken*, there's someone here to see you."

I make a 'Who the hell is out there?' gesture, and I mouth an exaggerated, "*Who?*"

She throws her hands up in the air. "*Lin-da*. I don't know. Never seen her before."

I put my finger to my lips, not wanting the mystery woman to hear us talking about her.

Allie mimics the gesture. "*You* shush. Maybe this is who you've been sneaking out late at night to see. I don't know what's up with you anymore, Bro. I thought it was to see Jen, but now I'm not so sure."

The look on Jen's face is like a punch to the gut. She's caught off guard and suspicious.

Allie notices. "Okay, now I'm definitely sure you're not seeing Jen."

I sigh. Definitely going to have to come clean tonight. I'd still like to leave Bree out of it, but this Linda lady asked for us both...using our code names...which very few people outside our family know. Best guess, she has something to do with Henry and Sarah. Maybe she works for them, or for Helen. People that rich can afford to have staff that makes problems go away. Fixers or something. Maybe that's what Linda does. Maybe she'll back up the lies I've been telling.

Feeling hopeful, I head for the front door, ducking and weaving past the angry and suspicious stares of the female tribunal assembled to discuss my familial transgressions.

I try to put a casual skip in my step and slide across the tall foyer's hard wood floor in my stocking feet like Tom Cruise in *Risky Business*, except in a skirt, in place of tighty-whities. The problem is that I'm still wearing my black shit-kicker boots. So instead of casually sliding into the hall like I have no worries, my feet stick. I topple forward and sprawl onto the floor. Then I slide to a stop when my head bumps into the stairs leading to the second floor. Ignoring the pain, I strike a pose, head propped on my hand, sporting a crooked smile. "Hey, Linda."

Linda stands above me. Gotta be in her sixties. A little plump. Dressed in her violet Sunday best. Hands tucked inside a fuzzy warmer sleeve. Her black skin is as radiant as her pearly whites.

She raises a solitary eyebrow and cocks her head to the side. I think she's disappointed in me. "Don't know why, but I thought you'd be graceful." She gives me a once over. "And more fashionable."

I push myself up and straighten my clothing. "Well, I—you know—"

"Lord in Heaven, he can barely string together a coherent sentence." She sighs.

I'm losing my patience. "So, what's the sitch? I have an interrogation to finish. Them interrogating me. Give me the deets. Fill me in."

"Not sure that would be ideal," she says, eyes flicking toward the dining room, where the ladyfolk have gathered to one side of the room, not so subtly spying on the conversation.

"Whhhy not?" I ask, playing dumb. There are a million different subjects I wouldn't want to discuss in front of the fam, but I can't act like that's the case.

"This is kind of a... Kodan Armada situation."

"A what-now?" I ask.

"Kodan Armada," she says. "*The Last Starfighter*."

"The Last...ohh." I get it. *The Last Starfighter* is an 80s movie about a regular guy who gets caught up in alien struggle for the fate of the...

Hold on a second.

"Like literally?"

"Uhh," she says. "Yeah, hun. I don't just go galivanting around asking for people who can—who can help save Cuddles."

"Cuddles?" I ask.

"Yes, silly. You remember Cuddles. My poodle," she says, and then she addresses the living room. "I'm sorry, ya'll. I just didn't know where else to turn. I live a few streets over, and Cuddles... Well, she took off into the woods a few nights back. The police have been no help, but everyone said Laser Chicken—I'm sorry, Miah—was the one to ask for help, because of his part in that Three Days of Darkness nonsense. Seems folks around here regard him as a bona fide hero." She addresses Mom directly. "You should be proud." And then she turns to Jen with a stern look. "And you should be more trusting. A finer man than Miah, I have not met. Asked him not to tell anyone about what he was doing. Neighborhoods gossip, you know, and I didn't want my ex-husband to hear that Cuddles had gone missing."

I turn toward the dining room and nearly laugh when I see that they're buying it.

Everyone except for Bree.

Sung is nearly there, but she gets hung up on a detail. "But you... asked for Laser Chicken and Demon Dog." She motions to Bree. "Isn't she Demon Dog."

"Damn right I am," Bree says.

"You're right, of course," Linda says. "This dear young one has been my daytime lookout. Laser Chicken and Demon Dog, my own personal superheroes. I was just stopping by to let them know that Cuddles had been found, and as a thank you, I was hoping the pair would join me for a movie."

"*The Last Starfighter*," I say.

She nods. "I've got popcorn and sundaes and a fresh can of vittles for the pooch. If it's all right with ya'll, of course. There was a serious vibe when this young lady—" She motions to Allie, who looks stunned by the whole exchange. "—opened the door. I do hope my revelations have put ya'll at ease."

The dining room is silent for a moment, until Bree erupts with, "Sundaes!" She hops out of her chair and starts pumping both her fists. "Whoo-hoo! Eat it, suckas. That's what you get for not helping find Cuddles."

She's all in on the lie Linda has spun, but I'm pretty sure that's only because she thinks there's a banana split in her near future. Hell, maybe there is. Linda could still be a part of the god-crew, or maybe a friend of Bush Jockey's, out for revenge. Either way, we need to get out of the house and away from suspicious eyes—for their own good.

"Well, I'm down for finally meeting Cuddles," I say.

Bree rides an invisible horse over to me, neighing as she says, "Heigh-ho, Sundaes!"

"You need to clear it with Steph," Mom says, smiling now. Bree's excitement is hard to resist.

Only one person isn't on the Linda train.

Jen.

Because I would have told her about Cuddles, whether or not Linda had told me to keep it quiet.

"Can I talk to you for a second?" I ask her. "Outside?"

"Oooooooh," Bree says. "Kissy time."

Jen gets up without a word and heads for the front door, sliding past Linda and leaving the house. I follow her outside and down the steps, keeping my eyes turned down. Twenty feet away, in the street, is where Rich died after being yanked out the front door and down the steps during the Darkness. When the sun is shining, the view doesn't bother me. But at night… I don't like looking at the spot. The military used a lot of bleach to clean away the mess, but it's still there in my head.

When I reach the bottom step, Jen whirls around on me. "You have thirty seconds. Tell the truth and nothing but, or I walk. Secrets and lying are non-starters for me."

I look around at the houses, lit up as usual, the street blazing with flickering light from the faux-fire streetlights. We're very exposed.

"Can we…go around the side?"

"I'm not here to make out."

"I know—*I know*. It's just…seeing is believing. You want the truth, I'll show it to you."

She squints at me for a moment and then heads for the side of the house. I walk past her, heading for the shed that hasn't been opened since Rich last mowed the lawn. I open the door, and true gentleman that I am, I motion for her to enter.

With a roll of her eyes, she enters. I follow her inside and close the door behind us, plunging us into darkness. The shed smells of old grass and oil. Reminds me of my father, who had me doing yard work with him until his untimely demise.

"I mean it," she says. "I'm legit angry at you."

"I know. You should be."

"So, you *have* been lying to me?" she says.

"If lying by omission is a thing, I guess. It's more of a secret than a lie. But I'm just trying to protect you. To protect all of you."

"From *what?*"

"From…everything and who knows what."

"This is about the Three Days?" she asks.

My silence confirms it.

"It's not happening again?" The fear in her voice stings.

"No. *No.* I won't let it."

"*You* won't let it?'"

I sigh. "Okay. No freaking out. Promise?"

"I'm not promising a thing," she says. "You're just going to have to trust me."

"You're right," I say. "I'm just nervous to show you."

"Nothing on you I haven't seen before," she says. "Also, it's freaking dark in here. I can't see shit."

"Just…back up." I tell her. "Far as you can."

I push myself back against the wall and listen as she stumbles past shovels, a weedwhacker, and a collection of 2x4s. I could see her if I wanted to. I've learned how to use my less obvious abilities—like seeing in the dark—without going full angel, but that wouldn't feel fair. And I'd probably laugh at how silly she looked, which wouldn't do me any favors.

"Good?" I ask.

"Losing my patience," she says.

"Okay, just…"

"No freaking out. Got it."

"Okay," I say. "Here we go."

I let a laser sword extend from my arm, at which point, Jen screams.

11

"Shhh!" I extinguish the laser blade. Darkness envelopes us again. "Shh. Shh. Shh. It's cool."

"Why are you like that again? Are they back?" Her voice is trembling. Horrified. By me. "I need to warn my—"

"They're not back," I tell her. "We're safe. I swear. Look..." I extend just a little bit of laser energy from the back of my hand. Took a long time to learn how to manipulate the energy seeping out of my flesh, but I'm getting better at it. The sliver of light acts like a flashlight, illuminating the space without the intimidation factor of a blade. Probably should have started my revelation this way.

"How?" she asks.

"I...I never stopped being like this. Whatever those angel dudes did to me...it's permanent."

"So...you..."

"Have laser swords that come out of my arms, yeah."

"And you can..."

"Fly," I say. "With laser wings. I can see in the dark. I'm hard to hurt. And I don't mean to flex, but I'm kind of strong now. Not as strong as Sarah, but—"

Ooops. Shit. I meant to spill the beans about myself, not open a whole can of worms.

"You just said something you didn't mean to," she says.

"And now I'm mixing cliché metaphors in my head. Yeah."

She smiles, fear ebbing. "Look, you know I love you. But this is your last chance to come clean."

"Cool. Cool, cool, cool." I rub my hands together, composing the best way to explain everything. "Can I give you the elevator pitch version?"

She doesn't look thrilled, but says, "Only because I'm afraid Bree is going to run off with Southern Oprah."

"Right. Cool. Okay. Most of this is going to sound…unbelievable."

"More unbelievable than hell being a planet that harvests people for food?"

I level my gaze at her. "Yes."

Her face goes flat, dreading the worst, so I lay it all out as plainly as possible. "I still can do all the angel stuff."

"Covered that already. Check."

"But…Bree can, too."

"Bree…was never granted angelic powers." Her eyes widen. "She was…"

"A demon," I say. "Well, almost a demon. She can…change back and forth."

"Like the Hulk?"

"Sort of, but not quite. Only I can change her. The death rune on her forehead is still there, even if no one can see it. I…can turn it on."

"Why the hell would you do that?"

"To help her…" I sigh. "She had her brother's eyeball in her hair, and I don't think she can even remember that. Being Demon Dog makes her feel powerful because, well, she is. And we've been practicing."

"Practicing?" She's getting angry.

"Training," I say. "At night. In case…"

"In case they come back." She softens a bit. "To fight them again."

"Or anything else that threatens our neighborhood."

"Like the 'Kordon Armada?'"

"I have no idea what all that is about. No clue who that lady is. But I think she knows what we can do. And I think she has something to do with Henry and Sarah."

"Strong Sarah."

"Right…"

"Do I have to worry about Strong Sarah?"

"What? No. She's a badass, but no. Too uptight. And you're just right." I smile. "Hey, I rhymed."

She's not amused. Just raises an eyebrow and waits for the rest.

"Sarah...and Henry..." I raise my palms. "This is where it gets weird, okay?"

Her second eyebrow rises to match the first.

"They're gods."

"Gods."

"I told you it was weird," I say. "But Helen of Troy, well, Helen of Sparta. She's their ancestor—even though she's still alive—because she's a demi-god. So, 50% god, right? Well, Zeus being Zeus, he slept with both Henry's and Sarah's mothers. Helen's 50% god-DNA isn't diluted by time or generations. There have been generations of demi-gods who never knew, or embraced, their powers. Including both mothers. So, when Zeus donated his 50% to the descendants of Helen, they were born 100% god, because 50 plus 50 is—well, you get it. Henry is god of the sky. He can fly, too. Sarah is god of the Earth, hence the strength...and other stuff."

She stares at me for a moment. "But...Helen... Wasn't she... Isn't she..."

"Zeus's daughter. Dude's a total perv, right? When in Rome, I guess."

"Maybe that's why Henry is...off?"

"So, you believe me?" I'm honestly a little surprised.

"I saw him land," she says. "From the sky. Not from the roof."

"Right. Cool."

"Stop saying 'cool.'"

"I'm nervous," I admit. "Wasn't sure how you'd take all this."

"How I'd take learning that there are gods living among us, or how I'd take my boyfriend lying to me for months?"

"Uhh, both."

"Tell me about the new guy."

"Jonas?"

"That's his name?"

I nod.

"Not 'Mind Bullet?'"

"Well, that's the codename he told Bree, but I don't think he really uses it."

"And what's his deal?"

"Well, let's see. He's telekinetic...and I think psychic with people *and* computers, which is...different. I don't really know everything he can do, but he has this sword that kind of pumps him up. Makes him stronger. It's how he saved Bubbles."

"Bubbles..."

"His artificial intelligence. She's cool. Awesome, I mean. Sorry. Anyway, I don't know how much of this is legit. I just met the guy today. But he claims to be a Titan. Like, you know, the gods before the gods. But a *new* Titan if that's even possible. Oh, and an assassin. But he seems like a solid dude...if you ignore the fact that those three guys tried to kill us, stole Bubbles, and then...well, assassins gonna do what—"

"He *killed* them?"

I slow nod.

"And you helped him?"

"I didn't know he was going to kill them. But...and I've been thinking about this since it happened...Bubbles is just an AI to us, but to him, somehow, she's a person. As real as you or me. He loves her. Like family. And they took her. They were killing her. If anyone took you? Threatened your life? I would probably have done the same."

She leans back, absorbing it all. "And now...you and...Linda are..."

"No idea. And that's the truth. But... Have you seen *The Last Starfighter*?"

She shakes her head. "Sounds like a nerdfest."

"It is," I say. "But it's basically about an evil alien empire and the normal Earth dude who has to stop them."

"So, they *are* back?"

"I don't think so," I say. "But if they're planning on it, I need to know."

A smile creeps onto her face. "Got to be a hero once, and now you've got the bug, huh?"

"Maybe." She's not wrong. I'm living every guy's dream. Superpowers. A hot girlfriend. Friends with cool backstories and strange powers. If all this didn't kick off with the deaths of thousands of people, including family, it would be a dream come true. "But a lot of people died. If there's a next time, maybe I can help fewer people die. And if I get killed doing it, make sure the statue commemorating my noble demise is wearing a skirt, yeah?"

She laughs. "Fine. But don't die, okay?"

Before I can answer, the shed door swings open.

"Everybody still dressed in here?" Linda says, looking mischievous. "Lord knows it's been a while since I seen a nekkid man. Actually, that's not true. I saw Jonas naked not too long ago. Spent a whole week scrubbing his naughty bits—waiting for him to wake up from a coma."

"You know Jonas?" I ask. "Wait. His naughty bits? And what about a coma?"

"If asking questions is your primary ability, I might need to rethink—"

"How do you know Jonas?" I ask.

"Jonas? Why, we're family. He's younger than me, but technically speaking, he's my uncle."

"Your...uncle." I don't know what to say.

I just...

What the hell is happening today?

"If it makes you feel better," she says, "I've seen Henry without his clothes on, too."

"Why would that make anyone feel better about anything?" I ask.

"What I meant to say is, your friends are my friends."

"They don't even know each other," I say.

"Well, it's high time Henry and Sarah met their great uncle Jonas."

"Their...great uncle Jonas... *Your* uncle. Making you..."

"Their father," Linda says, grinning like she's just won the lottery.

"But," Jen says, stepping up beside me. "Their father is..."

"Zeus," Linda says, pulling her hands from the fuzzy warmer sleeve, "Pleasure to meet you."

12

I look down at Linda's extended hand, unsure whether or not to shake it for two reasons. First, this is some janky shit. This little old lady is making a lot of wild claims about Jonas, Henry, and Sarah, but she's also claiming to be the actual Zeus, in human form.

Second, she's missing a hand.

"Uhh," I say, looking down at the stub.

Linda follows my eyes down. "Right. Sorry about that, hun. Had a run in with some...undesirables. They got in a lucky swing."

"Lucky swing?" Jen asks.

"With a sword, naturally." Linda waves away our concern. "Doesn't hurt. And it will grow back. Not the first time I've had a limb severed. Ares once cut off both of my feet." She smiles. "Good times. And a long time ago. Things are different now. I think this was the first time a mortal managed to seriously injure me. Like I said, different times. The universe is becoming a stranger place. Anywho, darling, regardless of the state of my missing hand, it's a pleasure to meet you. Not every day a mortal rises up to defeat unnatural threats. You did that—and a little bit more, didn't you? No god-blood required."

"I...guess so?"

"Ugh. Modest heroes are the worst. Lift your chin. Puff out your chest a little. Let your family know they can count on you when the shit goes cattywampus. And let the world know that the sun comes up just to hear you crow."

"Please don't do any of that," Jen says.

I'm smiling, not because of the suggestions, but because I really dig how Zeus-in-Linda-form speaks. The Southern twang. The unique expressions. Wouldn't mind sitting down with her for a sweet tea and a chat on the front porch. She puts me at ease, even though that's the exact opposite of how I should feel right now.

"So…no offense, I hope…but if you're Zeus, the Greek god of thunder—"

"And the sky," Linda says, wearing a lopsided smile. "Henry takes after his old man."

"—why do you look like…" I motion toward her, head to toe. She looks straight out of a Southern Baptist church. Even has a cross dangling from her purple jacket.

She looks down at her purple heels. "Oh, yes, these things are horrendous." She taps them together like Dorothy, wishing she could go home. "I really need to find some comfortable loafers."

"But…why?"

"I suspect for the same reason you're dressed like a 1990s skater chick."

"It's a tactical skirt," I say.

She twists her lips. "Mm. We'll see. The long and the short of it is that I like change. My therapist thinks I'm ADHD, but she doesn't really know who I am or the scale of what I'm dealing with. Hard to boil down cosmic conflict for people who'd be broken by that reality. I've been a man. I've been a woman. A few other things that are hard to describe."

"And a swan," I say.

Linda has a good laugh. "Oh, man. The swan is the best. I thought it would be funny, but good heavens, women really fancied swans. And Leda…" She shakes her head. "Leda was…whoo. Wow. I thought it was all good fun, but my swan adventures landed me in hot water, resulted in two more surprise youngens, and left me with a questionable reputation for, well, forever, I suppose. I'll tell you about it sometime, but right now…"

"The Kodan Armada," I say.

She nods. "Great movie. One of the best. But I'm not a fan of telling stories more than once, so we need to gather the others."

"I'll get Jonas," I say. "I think he trusts me."

She waves me off. "Bree is summoning him."

"You sent an eight-year-old to—"

"That girl is no regular eight-year-old," she says.

"Not without me," I say.

"Hey, there's some of that bravado I was talking about," she pats me on the shoulder with her stump. "Bree will be fine. Jonas is a good man. I made sure of it. I just need the six of you to—"

"Six of us?" Jen says, surprised to be included.

Linda has a good chuckle. "Oh, dear. It's delightful that you'd believe I was including you. Alas, no. The sixth member of our team is Bubbles."

"Bubbles," Jen says, slightly insulted.

"Unless you're smarter than an artificial intelligence, yes. Obviously, I'd prefer your company, because..." She waves her hands in an hourglass shape. "How do you feel about geese?"

I step between them.

"Not above punching a god, even if he is disguised as a nice church lady."

Electric blue flashes in her eyes for just a moment. Then she smiles. "That's what I like to hear. You're going to need that fighting spirit, Laser Chicken."

"Can we not call me that?" I ask.

"Meh. Laser Chicken is gold."

"Firebird," I suggest.

"Not bad," she says, "but it's more fun if you hate it."

I make a mental note to never complain about the name again. Maybe they'll get bored with it if I just never react.

"Now," she says to Jen, hitching her thumb back toward the house. "Back inside. Act like everything is copacetic. Smooth things over with Bree's mother. Say ya'll are having a slumber party." She looks me in the eyes. Intense. "It's going to be a hell of a night." Then she turns back to Jen. "Are we clear?"

Jen looks ready to lose her temper, but there's just enough what-the-fuckery going on to keep her off balance. "When will they be back?"

Linda flashes the widest, most forced grin I've ever seen. "By morning."

I know it's bullshit. Linda knows it's bullshit. Jen knows it's bullshit.

"Fine." Jen pushes past me, a little salty. "Call me when you know what's going on."

I give a nod, and I'm left alone…in a shed…with Zeus.

"So…" I say, "…immortality. What's that like?"

"Overrated," she says, and then she steps down out of the shed and waves for me to follow her.

I follow her through the yard, her ample backside bouncing back and forth with each step, which seems to require a little effort. Why would a powerful being like Zeus choose to live as an old woman with enough junk in the trunk to make walking awkward?

He's hiding, I think.

Who would suspect this woman of being anything other than the pinnacle of devout Christianity, which seems just outlandish. God worshiping God. Though I guess Zeus's god has a small 'G.'

Still…

"Why the cross?" I ask.

"Why not?"

"Well, you're a god."

"It's just a word," she says, "chosen by people who didn't know any better a long time ago. In those days, anyone whose DNA wasn't…exactly human…was worshiped. Had you been alive back then, you'd have temple ruins in Rome alongside mine."

"So, you're not gods?"

"The Greek Pantheon is real. Olympus was a place. The Titans were our parents. And we, like all children, really did rebel. But did we create the universe? No. We, like you, are creations of an intelligence no civilization in the universe has yet to fully understand. We're just not human. That answer your question?"

"No."

She walks through the front yard and steps off the curb and into the street, headed for Henry and Sarah's house. "You want to know if I believe."

"Kind of."

"Because if Zeus believes in Yahweh and his son, maybe you should, too."

"Seems logical."

"Religion is like a shifting maze. It's different for everyone, and the only way to figure it out for yourself is to walk it yourself. What I believe is of no consequence right now. It's what I *know* that should concern you."

Before I can ask what that is...

"Miah!" It's Bree. Skipping up the street toward me.

Jonas follows, looking displeased, and a little more casual, sporting jeans and a T-shirt emblazoned with a red, white, and blue image of Jim Morrison.

"Dig the shirt, man." I say.

"Thought you might," he says.

"But he's not the best front man, you know."

"If you say Paul Stanley, I will slap you."

"No, no. Not Paul. Best front man on three. Ready?"

He nods.

"One...Two...Three." We both finish with the same name.

"*Freddy Mercury.*"

"Hands down," I say. "Right?"

"Hard to beat," he says.

"Ahem," Linda says, and Jonas seems to see her for the first time.

"Linda?"

She steps into the light beneath a flickering streetlamp. "One and only, hun."

"What the hell?" He rushes over and embraces her. To my surprise, she hugs him back.

"Hey, uhh, Jonas. You do know who that is, right?"

"Yeah. It's Linda. She helped me when—Why *are* you here? Last time I saw you..." His eyes narrow, reality catching up to him. Linda shouldn't be here, and he knows it. "Linda... How did you find me?"

"Didn't find you, hun." She points at me with her stub. "Found him. Rest of you came here on your own, right?"

Jonas takes hold of her arm, in shock over the missing hand. "Linda. What happened?"

"Who happened," she says. "That's the real question."

Jonas's voice transforms.

Deadly serious.

"Give me a name, and I'll take care of it."

"That's the plan. You just need to be patient." She pats his cheek. "It's good to see you again." She gives a wink and heads for Henry and Sarah's house.

Jonas falls in line beside me as we follow. "The hell is going on?"

"I only just met him," I say.

"Her," he says.

"Well, yes and no," I say, and then I realize. "Wait, you don't know who she-he really is, do you?"

The look in Jonas's eyes says that, to him, Linda is exactly what she looks like. An old Southern gal with a missing hand. Nothing less. Nothing more.

I'm about to spill the beans, when Sarah emerges from the house and descends the steps, a smile on her face. She approaches casually, her guard down, but not thrilled to see Linda, either.

"Hey...Dad."

13

"No hugs for your pappy?" Linda asks.

"Maybe," Sarah says. "If you were the man who raised me."

"Why does everyone keep referring to Linda as a man?" Jonas asks.

"You know Linda?" Sarah asks, and before Jonas can confirm it, she turns to Linda. "He what he says he is?"

Linda nods. "He is. But he's newer to it than you are."

"Great," Sarah says, a little exasperated. "I take it you being here with all of them—" She motions to myself, Bree, and Jonas. "—means something bad is happening, right?"

"Maybe it's just a family reunion?" Linda asks.

"Pretty sure that's not how you operate," Sarah says.

"Seriously," Jonas says. "It's been a night. Someone better start explaining, right fucking now."

"No. Way!" Henry is standing in his house's doorway, face lit up with a beaming smile. "No fucking way!"

Jonas pinches his nose, patience melting away faster than the ice caps.

"Yo!" Henry shouts, leaping down the steps. "Dad!"

"Are they close?" I whisper to Sarah, as Linda waddles her way toward Henry.

Sarah leans in close. "Henry hasn't seen her since finding out who she really is."

Jonas leans his head between us. "Who the fuck is Linda?"

"Who is she to you?" Sarah asks.

"A nurse," he says. "A badass nurse."

Sarah smiles. "She was the same for us, too. At first."

"Until you found out she was...a dude? Is that it? Was Linda a man once upon a time?"

"Well, yeah," Sarah says. "But more than that."

Henry bro-hugs Linda, pounding a fist against her back. "Yo. Dad. Wasn't sure we'd see you again. I just... You're awesome."

"You're awesome, too, my boy." She leans back and gives him a slap, which just makes Henry laugh. Peas in a pod, these two.

"I'm so confused," Jonas says.

"Can I offer a—*chirp*—theory?" Bubbles asks, from the watch.

"Thought you were going to stay quiet," Jonas says.

"Hearing you flounder to figure out the obvious is more painful than hearing my own—*deez nuts are ripe!*—Tourette's glitch."

Henry cracks up. "'Deez nuts are ripe?'" He grabs his crotch. "Deez nuts! Who said that?"

"Please," Jonas says. "Someone. I want to sleep tonight."

"Sarah and Henry claim to be gods," Bubbles says. "And they're referring to Linda as 'Dad.' If that's true, we can assume that he's a—*chocolate starfish!*—a god as well. One with a penchant for changing his form and spawning children on Earth."

"Zeus," I say, having mercy on Jonas. "Linda is Zeus."

Bree jumps in front of Jonas, throwing her hands in the air, making thunder noises. "Peeewwwkkk." She throws imaginary spears. "Lightning bolt! Lightning bolt! Lightning bolt! Can we have ice cream now?"

"Let's go inside," Linda says, leading the way. Henry hops around her, filling her in on his recent exploits while asking a string of questions Linda never gets a chance to answer.

Bree skips after them, pointing at herself with her thumbs. "Who's gonna have ice cream? This kid, that's who!"

"Please tell me you have ice cream," I whisper to Sarah.

"Captain Impulsive over there—" She points to Henry. "—has an American Express Centurion Card. We have a lot of ice cream."

"Thank god," I say, letting my shoulders relax.

"Seriously?" Jonas says. "That's your biggest concern?"

"You don't know what she's like about ice cream," I say.

"But Linda is—"

"Zeus," I say. "Yeah. I just found out, too. Aren't you a Titan? Isn't this kind of thing normal to you?"

"Not yet," he says. "And I don't like being lied to. Linda was…important to me. But now I feel kind of used."

Sarah glances back. "You're not wrong to be concerned. Linda—Zeus—always has an angle. If she's here, with all of us, there's an endgame."

"There a reason to think she's dangerous?"

"Directly?" Sarah thinks on it for a moment. Shakes her head. "I don't think so. But she's almost certainly going to put us in harm's way while she steers clear. The old gods didn't usually do their own dirty work. They pulled strings. It's like a game to them."

"Except Linda is missing a hand," Jonas says.

"And you still sound concerned, like she's still Linda," Sarah points out.

"Jonas is loyal," Bubbles says. "Linda did right by him—*sucking his dick!* Even if she lied about her identity…a lot…he'll stand by her until she gives him a reason not to."

"I don't know if that's commendable," Sarah says, "or the stupidest thing I've ever heard."

"I'm sorry," I say. "Stupid question. But she didn't actually…you know…" I point to the watch in which Bubbles is trapped. "What she said. About sucking—"

"I was in a coma. And if memory serves, Zeus is kind of a perv. So…" He shrugs. "You'll have to ask her. Him. Whatever."

"At least he wasn't a swan," I say.

"What?" He looks to Sarah. "That's not a thing, right?"

"Yeah, it kind of is." She smiles and jogs ahead, overtaking Henry and Linda before charging up the stairs. Sarah is an introvert. Long conversations. Chit chat. They're not really her thing. At least with me. She enters the house and disappears.

"What's your take, boss?" Jonas asks me.

"That I'm in over my head."

He nods. "Been there." He tilts his head at Linda. "You have a read on her, yet?"

"No negative vibes," I say. "I don't think she's an enemy, if that's what you're thinking. Pretty sure she could have killed you when you were in a coma, right?"

"Question is, why would Zeus bother cleaning my jumblies while I was unconscious for a week? What did she gain from it?"

"You're alive," I guess. "She was protecting you? Which I guess would be weird. A god protecting a Titan. Weren't they like…not friends?"

"Could be," he says. "There were a lot of people gunning for me."

"Still are, right?"

"Yeah, but don't sweat that. I'll be gone in the morning. I have what I need here. Don't want to put you all in more danger."

"I think that's going to happen whether you're here or not."

He waits for me to explain.

"You know what the Kodan Armada is?"

"*The Last Starfighter*," he says. "Who doesn't know that?"

"Well, that's what she said this was about."

"You good at video games or something?" He chuckles, but he stops short when he sees that I'm serious.

"Already survived one alien invasion," I say. "If I can do something to stop the next, I'm all in."

"Let's move it, people!" Bree calls out. She's holding the front door open, waving us all inside. "I can smell that sweet frozen moo-moo juice from here!"

Jonas laughs. "Fun kid. If this bullshit gets dicey, you need to lose her."

I nod. He's right. Bree *is* Demon Dog. Powerful and feral. But she's still a kid. "She's here because Linda promised ice cream. I won't let her do anything dangerous."

"Like training in the woods at night with a pair of gods?" He sniffs a laugh and doubles his pace, leaving me in the dust.

I stop on the sidewalk, watching the others climb the stairs. It's surreal. A house full of gods and killers.

Bree's not the only one who doesn't belong here.

I'm just a regular dude that's been given weird abilities by an alien race. These guys aren't even human.

Even if they look the part. And act it. I've been chillin' with Sarah and Henry long enough to count them as friends. But this sweet old lady is Zeus. An ancient god in human form. And he's gathering us together for something...dangerous. That much is clear. You don't gather a group like this to run a church bingo night. We're dangerous. All of us. Including Bree.

Three men died within hours of us meeting Jonas. And none of this crew are going to lose sleep over it.

I need to get Bree away from this mess, and if I'm lucky, steer myself clear.

Leaves skitter across the road behind me. Goose bumps rise on my exposed legs. In the dark, the houses look like they used to, their scars hidden by the night. But the people inside them will carry the physical and emotional scars of the Three Days for the rest of their lives. They're my priority. My extended family. If the neighborhood isn't in danger, I'm out.

I flinch when Bree takes my hand. She tugs on me. "C'mon, slowpoke. I don't want to have ice cream without you."

"That's a first," I say, giving in and following her toward the house.

"Hey," she says, hopping up the front porch steps. "We're a team, right? We stick together."

I pause at the bottom, amazed by Bree's resilience. While the adults reel from the flurry of otherworld revelations, she's got her eight-year-old blinders on, destiny drawing her toward danger—and ice cream. I follow her up the stairs and step into another world.

14

"What...the..." I'm frozen in the doorway, wondering if it's an actual portal to another world. I've been in most of the houses in this neighborhood—as a teenager with friends, and as an adult, connecting with fellow survivors, many of whom wanted to thank me for saving them from the tortures of hell.

All the houses are similar. Pristine examples of upper middle class living that look like Bernie & Phyl's showrooms on the inside. *Quality, comfort, and value.* Polished wood floors. Towering foyers. Near opulence, with a soupçon of gaudy Americana.

But not this house.

Not anymore.

The structure is the same, but the décor... It's like a museum, but without the glass. Like an ancient armory. Swords, shields, and spears. They hang on the walls, ready to be admired—or used. I'm no expert, but I think they're the real deal, too. Probably kept pristine over millennia by Helen. I recognize some of the blades. Katanas from Japan. A pair of Roman gladii. A trident straight out of *Gladiator.*

"Don't blame me," Sarah says, holding the interior door open like a good host. When I step past, she closes the door behind me. "I couldn't stop him."

"This is so Henry."

"Only room that doesn't look like Bill and Ted's Excellent Scavenger Hunt is my bedroom."

"Is that all pink and frilly?" I ask.

The look in her eyes sends my hands skyward. "Joking. *Joking.*"

She smiles. She knew.

I'm drawn to a long spear mounted in the hallway.

Beneath it is a single sword and a large, round shield with an upside-down V covering the front. They are the only three weapons in the foyer, close to the door. The spear is eight feet long and tipped with a slick looking blade. The back end is counter-balanced by a blunt knob of metal that ends in a point. "Reminds me of *300*. The movie. Or the comic book. Take your pick. Looks like the spear Leonidas used at the Hot Gates."

Sarah sighs. "I'd hate to say that *300* qualifies as edutainment, but you're right. It's called a dory. They were used by Spartan hoplites."

"This didn't belong to—"

"Leonidas?" She shakes her head. "This was Helen's... We left Leonidas's dory in Boston." She places her hand on the weapon. "This…is mine. The shield, too."

I picture her wielding spear and shield, lined up with a Spartan shield wall. "Badass. Why don't you train with them?"

"I do," she says. "But not with other people. Too dangerous."

"You're pretty dangerous without them."

She smiles. "Exactly."

"What about this?" I ask, reaching for the two-foot-long sword. The blade is fluid, the razor edge curving in and then bulging out before coming to a needle tip. The handle is hooked, just enough room for one hand. But the blade isn't perfect. It's got knicks in it. A lot of them. And I'm pretty sure that means it's been used—a lot. Against other blades… and bones.

Sarah catches my arm. "Wouldn't touch that. He's protective of it."

"This is Henry's?"

"It's a kopis. Preferred blade of the Hoplite. A hacking weapon for when the enemy broke through the shield wall. It's not elegant, but it is effective. And that one *did* belong to Leonidas. At least that's what Helen said. It's possible she's just messing with Henry."

"Should we contact her? Helen?" I ask. "About all this? I mean, Zeus coming for a visit isn't normal, right? Even for you guys."

"The first and last time we saw Linda, a cult led by Memnon—also a demi-god—was hunting us through the streets of Boston. We wouldn't have made it without her help, but yeah, if Linda is here, trouble won't be far behind. Problem is, Helen sometimes…disappears. Not sure what she's doing. I've always assumed it's business, or some kind of quest, or whatever people like her do. But when she's gone, she's gone. No phone. No e-mail. Nothing. She ghosts."

"That's—"

"Dumb," she says. "Yeah. But she's a Spartan, you know? They're not known for coddling the young, and we're not exactly kids."

"So, until she makes contact with you—"

"We're on our own."

"Well," I say, looking into the dining room that looks something like a Viking great hall, where Henry is giving Bree and Jonas a similar tour of the weaponry. "Not entirely on our own."

She nods. "Don't let it go to your head, but when I look in that room... I'm glad you're here."

I smile.

Sarah isn't big on giving compliments. When she does, she means it. "Right on. And likewise." I lift a fist, and she bumps it.

Linda enters the dining room with four half gallons of Breyers wrapped in her arms, undeterred by the missing hand. She's got bowls and spoons perched atop. "Lord knows, I've never seen a freezer packed so full of dairy products."

"I like ice cream," Henry says, taking the bowls and spoons, and casually tossing them around the table. There's enough for everyone to partake. Henry takes the cartons from Linda, one at a time, announcing flavors. "We got Vanilla. The natural kind with the beans. None of that French shit. Cookies & Cream. Double Chocolate Brownie Batter. Annnd—"

Bree, who's already seated, spoon in hand, sees the carton and thrusts two victorious fists in the air. "Mint Chocolate Chip! I call dibs. Don't let Miah near it. He'll eat it all."

"For the last time, I didn't eat your ice cream, I just kept *you* from eating it all."

"That's cold, man," Henry says, sliding the Mint Chocolate over to Bree.

She tears the top away and starts scooping with the speed of the Chinese government erecting new cities. "Cold," she says, glancing up at me. "Like ice cream."

I take a seat at the table, grab a bowl, and take the chocolate brownie shit. "I don't even like mint."

"He's lying," Bree says. "He'd marry mint chocolate chip if it had kissy lips like Jen."

Henry snorts a laugh. Bree giggles and sticks her tongue out at me.

Sarah sits down beside me while Linda settles in at the end of the table, looking as pleased as Kathie Lee Gifford at a Spanx sale.

Bowls and spoons clatter. Ice cream is scooped with a hungry frenzy not seen since the Devil was expelled from New Hampshire. I'm generally not an ice cream junkie if I haven't partaken in a bit of ganja first, but it's been a stressful day, and sometimes a bit of frozen sugar is salve for the soul.

After a minute of furious scooping, only one bowl remains empty, along with the seat behind it. Everyone falls silent, waiting.

Doesn't take long for Jonas to notice the silence. He places the Viking axe he's been inspecting back on the wall. Turns to face the group. Takes in the table of full bowls. Frowns. "Is there a grown-up table?"

"C'mon, Mind Bullet," Bree says. "We can't start without you."

"Hell I can't," Henry says, but he's frozen in place—ice cream half way to his open mouth—by a withering stare from Bree. "Okay. Fine. Whatever."

Bree turns her gaze back to Jonas, putting on a charming grin and batting her eyes. "Pleeease."

Jonas sighs. I can't read his mind, but his inner struggle is easy to imagine. He came to New Hampshire to help Bubbles and she nearly died. She's trapped in a watch, so he's got to be worried about her. He had no intention of getting mixed up with us, with Bush Jockey, and certainly not with Linda-turned-Zeus. His instincts are telling him to get the hell out, and maybe he should. My instincts are screaming the same thing.

But I need to know what's happening. Because I care about people.

And that's why he's going to stay, too.

That and the power of Bree's big brown eyes.

"Fuck it," Jonas says. He pulls out a seat and sits down. Then he remembers Bree's age and says, "Sorry. For the language."

Bree shrugs. "I don't give a fuck."

Jonas tries to maintain his serious assassin face, but Bree has slipped past his emotional armor. His smile is slight, and I think he's going to hold it in, until a laugh bursts from his watch, followed by Bubbles exclaiming, "*Vagina popsicles!*"

Jonas bursts out laughing, and the rest of us join in.

"Oh, shit," Henry says, cackling. "That was dope."

The laughter settles and everyone digs in. Jonas snaps his fingers at Henry. "Crazy Man, hook me up with some vanilla."

Henry picks up the half gallon and tosses it at Jonas. Any normal person would have been decked out of the chair, but Jonas isn't a normal person. The ice cream freezes in mid-air and slowly lowers to the table, the cover floating away on its own.

Silence settles over us as we eat. Henry is the first to finish, but he quickly refills his bowl.

Linda finishes second. Slides her bowl to the side. Clasps her hand over her stump. She watches us in silence, as though pondering the fate of the universe, and I suspect that's what she's actually doing. "Thank you all, for gathering here on my behalf. I feel like a pig in the sun, seeing ya'll together."

"I...just met you," I point out.

She waves my comment away. "I have admired you from afar."

Jonas finishes his paltry amount of ice cream. Shoves the bowl away.

"Stop sucking our—" He glances at Bree. "...our...I don't know—lollipops—and get to the point."

Bree leans over to Henry. "Are there lollipops?"

He nods slowly, eyes wide.

Linda holds up a calming hand. She's about to lose control. "I'll get right to it, then. The six of you are Earth's only hope at surviving a coming conflict of cosmic proportions."

"The Kodan Armada," I guess.

"Worse, actually." She levels a serious gaze in my direction.

"The Tenebris," I say, really hoping I'm wrong. Even though I know they can be defeated, and they have enemies of their own, I'd be happy never seeing them again.

"The Tenebris are no more," Linda says. "Nor is the species who granted you angelic powers."

"No…more?" I ask. "Like…"

"Extinct," she says. "Wiped out. Scoured from the universe." She leans her elbows on the table. "And humanity is next."

15

Linda has our undivided attention. Mention of the Tenebris—who changed Bree forever—headed off her percolating sugar-rush. The world ending captured Henry's attention, but he doesn't look worried like the rest of us. He looks pumped, like he's been waiting for this moment his whole life. Probably because he has been.

Some people are born to live an epic life.

Others just kind of stumble into it.

Odd to think of my life as epic, but I'm seated at a dining room table, eating ice cream with four deities and a self-aware artificial intelligence. Epic might not even cover the confluence of otherworldly power in this room.

"I can see that got your attention," Linda says. "Good."

"But you're just screwing with us, right?" Henry asks. He's not worried, but he is concerned that the dire news might be fake.

"Linda doesn't lie, hun," Linda says…about herself. Zeus can change his form. That's been established. But it sounds like those forms come with personalities. Linda is a Southern believer in a higher power, guided by a moral code that Zeus, in his natural form, might not abide by. I wonder if we'd be sitting here, discussing the fate of the world, if Zeus was a goose or a swan or whatever.

"Who's the big bad?" Jonas asks, straight to the point.

Linda shrugs twice, shaking her plump body. "Hell if I know."

"What *do* you know?" Jonas asks.

"I've been around for a long time. I've seen the universe like few ever have. But I've never seen anything like this."

"So, like an invading force from another universe?" I ask. "Like the Borg or something?"

Linda groans. "Please, no Star Trek references. I've heard enough of them to last a cosmic lifetime."

"I haven't mentioned Star Trek," I say, and I turn to Jonas. "Have you?"

He shakes his head.

"I haven't," Henry says, "but I *have* rated the female cast by bangability. Seven of Nine and T'Pol, obviously, but hear me out, Lursa and B'Etor. Yeah, I know. Klingons. Gross. But *sisters*. Klingon sisters. Twenty bucks says they'd be willing to–"

I'm about to clear my throat in an attempt to prolong what's left of Bree's childhood innocence. Linda beats me to it, pounding her remaining fist on the tabletop.

"No. Star. Trek." Linda launches a fusillade of full-auto warning shots from her eyeballs, giving each of us a moment to consider our fate should we mention Star Trek again.

"Can you get to the point?" Jonas asks. He's always on task. A professional. "I haven't heard a good reason for me to be here yet, and if I don't in the next few seconds, I'm walking."

"You'll stay," Linda says. "Your loyalty demands it."

"You're not Linda," he says.

"Do I need to graphically describe your penis to prove it?" Linda says. "Because I can."

Bree snorts, trying to contain her laughter.

"What I meant," Jonas says, his patience waning, "is you were never Linda. Not really. I don't like being fucked with. So, get to the goddamned point. What kind of freaky alien threat is on its way?"

"Well," Linda says. "Not alien."

"God?" I ask, wondering if there's a better term.

Linda shakes her head. "Near as I can tell, she's human. But as the youth might say, she's a bit...extra. From a distance, she's...well, she's competition for Helen."

"Pfft," Henry says. "Helen's a solid ten."

"Dude," Sarah says, "she's your grandmother."

"By like a hundred generations," Henry says. "Doesn't mean I can't rub–"

"Dude!" Sarah lives with Henry.

She's accustomed to his verbal diarrhea, but even she has limits.

Henry holds his hands up, but leans over to Bree and says, "Total babe. I'm telling you."

Bree's in heaven, eyes wide, feet kicking, enjoying the nearly unfiltered conversation...which she is going to repeat to everyone at home, and end up landing me in hot water with my mother and hers.

Linda taps a finger on the table, over and over until she's got everyone's attention again. "I encountered this woman only once. Tall. Blonde. Tight red leather."

"Sounds like a Mord-Sith," Sarah says.

All eyes turn to her.

"You know of her?" Linda asks.

"Sorry," she says. "The *Sword of Truth*. Fantasy novel series. TV show was called *Legend of the Seeker*? The Mord-Sith are like hot, dominatrix warriors. Are we not allowed to reference any pop-culture?"

Linda grins. "That would be difficult for anyone in this reality. Now, back to our personal Mord-Sith. I didn't get her name. But she took my hand." Linda holds up her stump. "I think she meant to kill me, but I escaped."

"How?" Bree asks.

"Excuse me?" Linda says.

"You're like...out of shape and stuff," Bree says. "How did you—"

"Do you not understand who I am?" Linda asks, and then she looks at me. "Does she not know who Zeus is?"

"I know what a moose is," Bree says. "I saw one last year on a moose tour. It was in Maine."

"Lovely," Linda says. "If you must know, I let the blood spraying from my severed wrist douse the woman's face. While she was blinded...and laughing...I..." She sighs. "I turned myself into worms and crawled into the ground until they left."

"They?" Jonas asks.

"She had a man with her. Large. Imposing. Bearded. He just watched. She was in charge. Because she... Oh, Lordy, she is powerful in a way no one was ever meant to be. She is *changing* reality. Rewriting it. Sowing madness throughout the universe. Remaking it in her image."

"The universe is turning into a hot dominatrix?" Henry asks.

"A self-destructive abomination," Linda says. "Unlike the Tenebris, she *is* the Devil, and she is turning reality into hell."

"She have a name?" Jonas asks.

Linda shrugs. "She didn't introduce herself before severing my hand. But...the man called her 'Cherry.'"

"Her name is Cherry," I say. "And she's wearing all red?"

Henry starts humming *Cherry Pie* by Warrant, and I can tell he's close to belting it out, so I keep talking. "I mean, it's a little on the nose, right? *Cherry*."

"Says *Laser Chicken*," Linda grins.

"I didn't choose that name," I grumble.

Bree swats my arm and asks Linda, "But it's awesome, right?"

"Totally," Linda says, offering the girl a heartwarming smile that is complete bullshit.

"So," Sarah says, sitting up straighter, "you want us to...find this Cherry chick and stop her?"

Linda cranes her head around to Sarah, eyebrow raised. "I'm sorry, did you not hear what I just said?"

"That she beat you in a fight," Henry says. "But you shouldn't feel bad. You're like really old and packing more pudge than Augustus Gloop does fudge."

Linda double-takes Henry, but she thinks better of arguing the point. "My easy defeat at the hands of that...harlot should concern you all, but not nearly as much as her ability to alter reality. I would not entrust the defense of the universe to you lot."

She places her hand on Sarah's, and her stump on Henry's. "You are my children. And I am proud of who you have become. But you are new to your powers, and you have yet to fully tap into your potential."

She turns her gaze to Jonas. "Sugar, you know I love you. You've got the heart and mind of a warrior. One of the best. But you are even newer to this world than my children."

Linda levels her gaze at me, and I feel the weight of what she's laying on us for the first time. My inner skeptic has been calling bullshit this whole time, but the look in her eyes... She's not joking.

Not lying.

Not even exaggerating.

"And you... More than anyone else, you have potential."

"What?" I ask.

My question is quickly followed by Henry thrusting his hands out toward me. "What?! This guy? He's got laser wings. I don't even need wings to fly!"

"He's got something the rest of you don't," Linda says, and then she makes us wait for it, looking us each in the eyes as though searching for something. "A pure heart."

"Oh!" Henry collapses back into his chair, having a laugh. "Oh man. I thought it was something important. Shit. Whoo."

Bree raises her hand. Looks like she might cry. "I...I don't have a pure heart? Is that because I'm a demon?"

"Honey," Linda says, her voice low and sweet. "Everyone your age is pure of heart—except maybe Mussolini. But when you're older, when you're an adult? Well, it's harder than flying. Harder than punching a crater in the ground. Harder than moving a mountain with your mind." Her eyes lock onto mine again. "That's why I'm entrusting you to take the lead."

"The lead...on what?" I ask.

"A quest," she says. "To raise an army of gods and Titans."

16

"Wait, wait, wait," Henry says. "Hold up. You don't want *us* to fight the big bad? Seriously? Have you seen what we can do?"

"You killed several members of a cult," Zeus says.

"Yeah, while they were buck naked. And, Memnon. And a frikkin' gorgon, and a cyclops."

"Hold up." Jonas is caught off guard. "Those are real?"

"Yeah," Henry says. "Phoebe and Deimos. They were our half-siblings, but they were also dicks. Point is, we can handle just about anything thrown our—"

Linda slaps her palm on the table. "Not this! Not her. You have no concept of..." Blue bolts crackle in her eyes. She takes a calming breath. Never thought Zeus would be one to exhibit self-control, but this Linda persona is reining him in. Probably why he chose it. Without Linda, Zeus might be as impulsive as Henry.

"So," Sarah says. "We're messengers?"

Linda nods. "'Harbingers of galactic doom,' if it makes you feel better."

"A little," Henry admits.

"What you're not yet understanding is that the journey itself will push each one of you to your limits, and beyond."

"Like Disney World in August," Henry says. All eyes turn to him. "What? It's like having a permanent case of hang nasty. Like walking around with a Wacky Wally between your legs. You know, those sticky octopuses you throw against the wall..."

Linda places her stump on Henry's hand, eyes deep in Zen mode. "Henry. Honey. Would you mind not talking for a few minutes?" She turns to Jonas. "Bubbles, would you mind setting an alarm for five minutes?"

I'd forgotten about Bubbles. She's been quiet.

Probably on account of her—

"*Nut sack hacky sack!*"

On account of that.

"Apologies," Bubbles says. "I have set an alarm for five minutes."

"Thank you, dear." She turns back to Henry. "If you speak again, in the next five minutes, you will not be participating in the quest."

Henry's eyes widen, while his brows furrow. The road ahead might be fraught with horrors, but the torture has already begun for him. Asking him to not speak is like shoving a big ass cork in the top of Mount Vesuvius circa 79 A.D.

"I'm serious," Linda says. "Not a word."

Henry claps his hands over his mouth and nods. He gets it. Wants in. Zeus is kind of his hero, even if he's been the most absent father in history.

Linda settles into her seat, shifting her ample backside about, and then returning to the conversation.

"Where do you want us to go?" Jonas asks.

Linda opens her mouth to answer, but Bubbles beats her to the punch. "Tartarus. The deepest region of the underworld, where the Titans—including Jonas's parents—were banished.

"Well, 'banished' is a harsh word," Linda says. "It's more like a vacation. With rules. And it's not just Titans. As the world changed, and the gods lost interest in the development of mankind, they journeyed to Tartarus, never to return. Hera. Poseidon. Ares. Athena. They're all there, leaving me to prune the garden, so to speak, on my own. The only celestial beings to make the journey back to Earth, for a time, were Gaea and Uranus." She tilts her head toward Jonas. "Your parents. We know how that turned out, don't we? But there's hope. Your parents are back in Tartarus, along with the rest of them, unaware of what is coming, but they're our only chance at defeating this Cherry."

Henry's eyes widen. His hands clamp down a little tighter over his mouth.

"Your account of Tartarus is—*pubic patooties wearing pantaloons!*—contrary to historical accounts. It is a place of eternal torment and torture, where the Titans are imprisoned and the wicked—*chirp!*—

punished. It is portrayed as a hellish place, far worse than Hades, the land of the dead."

Linda nods. "To keep the riff-raff out. Humans are infinitely curious, but there are other species out in the cosmos who would have laid claim to Tartarus if they ever stumbled upon it."

"Are we supposed to believe all this malarky?" Bree asks. She's been absorbing everything, and she finds Linda's story wanting. I'm not so sure. I've seen enough otherworldly madness to believe just about anything. But myths made real? If not for knowing Sarah and Henry, I wouldn't believe a word of it. "Tarter sauce? Hades?" She rolls her eyes toward me and shakes her head.

"Tartarus," Sarah says. "I haven't been there, but...I've been to Hades. The River Styx. They're real places. I believe her. I believe all of it."

Sarah jumping on the crazy train pretty much seals the deal for me. She's no nonsense. If all this doesn't tip her bullshit meter into the red, then it's probably legit.

"None of that sounds dangerous," I say. "What are you leaving out?"

"The journey," Jonas says. "Sometimes getting from point A to point B is the most dangerous part of any mission."

Linda nods. "There is only one way to reach Tartarus...Khaos."

"Chaos?" Bree says. "We can do that. We're kind of, like, awesome at it."

"*Khaos*," Linda says. "With a capital K. It's not a state of confusion, it's a place, deep beneath the Earth, where heat and pressure, and monsters and mayhem, keep all but the most powerful from reaching its terminus. Which is where you will find the entrance to Tartarus."

I run my hands through my hair and let it fall over the sides of my forehead. "Doesn't sound like a great place for an eternal vacay."

"The entryway is a gate, ancient and futuristic. I believe you're quite familiar with the technology."

My chest tightens.

"You said the Tenebris—"

"Have nothing to do with this," she assures me. "The ability to traverse the stars using cosmic gateways predates the Tenebris civilization by millennia. And while the gates that appeared in this region eventually disappeared, the entryway to Tartarus is a permanent fixture. All you need to do is reach it, pass through, and deliver a message."

Sounds simple enough. "What's the message?"

"Pólemos," she says. "*War.* Delivered by a son and daughter of Zeus, along with a son of Gaea and Uranus, there will be no doubting the veracity."

"How do you know they'll come?" I ask. "If Tartarus is such a sweet deal, why come back to Earth at all? I mean, it's in another realm of reality, right?"

"Another realm of..." Linda tsks and shakes her head. "Sugar, I don't think you're quite understanding the situation. Khaos is a real, physical place located beneath the very soil of Italy. But Tartarus? Honey, that's another planet."

She lets that settle in for a moment.

Then she says, "You call us gods, but we are not creators. We are creations, same as you. We're just...better."

Henry pumps his fist, but he says nothing.

Linda turns her eyes to the ceiling, smiling and remembering. "We enjoyed a time on this planet, ruling over ancient civilizations, meddling, warring. As you might with characters in a video game. It was...well, it was the highlight of my long life."

"Characters in a video game aren't real," I point out. "They're not conscious."

"And yet, they are as far from humanity as humanity is from the gods."

"You're calling us NPCs..."

"Honey, I don't even know what that means," Linda says. "But don't worry about it. *You* are far more exceptional than the average human being."

"Thanks," I say, dripping sarcasm. Zeus's ego is showing through Linda's gentle façade. I'm starting to not like her as much.

"Italy, then?" Jonas says.

Linda nods. "Italy. And then down, down, down before—shoop!" Linda points from one side of the dining room to the other. "To Tartarus. After that, you can stay there. You can come back. You can fight alongside your ancient brethren. Your fate is yours to decide."

"Right." Jonas claps his hands on his knees and stands up. "Fuck this. I'm out." He heads for the door, and I wonder if he's not right.

This is a whole can of Planters mixed nuts.

"SIT. DOWN." Linda's voice rumbles like distant thunder.

The lights flicker.

The home's foundation quakes. It's enough to pucker my butt.

Jonas pauses at the door, back turned to us. "I'm not the person you want to fight..." He glances back at Linda. "Nephew."

"You are nothing without the Sword of Mars," Linda says.

Jonas turns around to face her, calm as can be but exuding raw power. "I'm not sure that's something you want to put to the test. Not here. Not now. Moment you do, you lose Sir Pure of Heart over here." He motions to me. "Also..." The home's wall implodes, knocking weapons to the floor and sheet rock into the air. When the dust settles, Jonas's sword is embedded in the opposite wall. He steps to it, plucks it from the sheet rock, and raises his eyebrows at Linda.

"Would have been cooler if you caught it," Bree says. When Jonas gives her an impatient look, she adds, "What? It would have been cooler. Geez. I'm just saying."

Linda sighs. Sits back down. "Go, then. Leave the fate of universe to these four."

"Hm!" Henry's complaint is muffled by his clasped hand, but he matches the look in Sarah's eyes. Being degraded by their father stings, even if they haven't really spent any time with him.

"And when they fail to reach Tartarus, fail to summon an army that can stand against our mutual enemy, when the fabric of reality is peeled apart and remade, you can explain to Madee, Heather, Fast, Hood, and your parents how you had the chance to stop it, but walked away because...what? You need to go to Best Buy in the morning? Or is money the problem? Do I need to pay you to do the right thing? Whored out heroism. Your parents—your *real* parents—would be ash—"

Linda lifts up out of her chair and launches backward like she's been resisting the world's largest invisible rubber band this whole time. She smashes through the kitchen's back wall and disappears into the night sky.

While the rest of us sit there, stunned, Henry bursts out laughing before abruptly stopping. “Wait, I can talk now, right?”

17

"That was probably a—*chirp!*—bad idea," Bubbles says. "We have no reason to doubt the veracity of Linda's—"

"Except that's not Linda," Jonas says. "I wonder if she was a real person. If Zeus stole her life. Maybe killed her and slipped into her shoes. I'm new to this god business, but I've done my research. Zeus is an asshole. Deception is his communication tool of choice. He's unfaithful to...everyone."

"He also has a short temper," Bubbles says, "and has no qualms about raining down destruction on the Earth, or those who inhabit—*sweaty perineums!*—*sigh*... Who inhabit it."

"He's not that bad," Henry says, clinging to the idea that this god-man in a woman's body might be the father he never had. It's actually kind of sad.

"Anyone here know who Prometheus is?" Jonas asks, and I wonder why he hasn't bolted.

Because he's a good dude, I think. He thinks we're being duped, and he's trying to open our eyes—before we agree to something insane.

"Prometheus is a Titan. Like me. You know what he did? He gave mankind fire. He promoted technological advancement. Education. Civilization. He was a champion of mankind. And do you know what Zeus did to reward him for these acts of kindness that elevated the human race out of the stone age?" He pauses to look at each of us. "He was bound to a boulder...for eternity...and every day, Zeus's eagle would descend, tear open his side and consume his liver. Every night, his liver would grow back, and the torture would continue the following day. Every day. Forever. That's the kind of *god* you're all about to follow into the depths of the Earth. We can't believe a word he says." He points at Henry. "Give him a chance and he'll turn you into his spitting image, but always a pawn." He points to Sarah. "You're not dumb. You've done the same research. You know as well as I do that he's eventually going to try—" He glances at Bree. Corrects his course. "You know what he'll do." Then he reels on me. "And you. Mr. Pure. You're going to find out exactly how much shit you can endure before coming out stained. And you're not alone." He glances toward Bree again.

"I won't let that happen," I say.

"Uh-huh."

"Seriously," I say, growing frustrated. Jonas is so self-assured it's irritating. Dude must be an INTJ *and* an Enneagram 5. Confidence for days.

He shakes his head at me, disappointed. "Might have been wrong about you." He lets that linger for a moment, and then twists the knife. "No good leader in the history of the world followed every carrot dangled in front of his nose. Sometimes you need to know when to walk away."

"Sometimes you need to know when to not be a coward," I snap back. Didn't think about what I was saying. Kind of just popped out. Probably what it feels like to be a mild version of Henry.

I can almost smell his stink eye from a few feet away, but I ignore it. "You've always had power, right? Always been more than human. A trained killer. How many people have you killed? Why should I trust you any more than Zeus? Neither of you know what it's like to be human. To be weak and vulnerable. All the time. When I walked into what I thought was the actual Hell, I didn't have powers. I just wanted to save my family. No matter what. And if I need to risk everything to do that, I will, even if that makes a big tough guy like you feel inadequate."

Jonas is about to respond. I've touched a nerve. Henry cuts him off at the pass.

"I know what that's like. We didn't always have powers, you know. Weren't tapped into our DNA's potential or whatever. She worked at Dunkin's. I was homeless. For a while. Probably not surprising. But it sucked donkey balls. Anyway, this one night? Middle of winter. A foot of snow. I'm over by Faneuil Hall standing over a subway grate, you know, to stay warm. Shaking my ass off. Asking everyone for food, and no one's sharing, because, you know: Boston. Just the way it is. Whatever. Anywho, that's when I spot something in a store window. A slice of green that will turn things around for me. So, I walk right in, knowing I'm going to get my ass beat, even though my heart is in the right place. And I do what needs doing, regardless of the consequences."

"Everything you do is regardless of the consequences," Sarah points out.

"Doesn't mean it's easy," he says.

"It's literally the easiest thing in the world for you."

"Hey," he says. "I'm trying to connect here."

"What was it?" Bree asks. "The green thing that would change your life?"

He smiles. Digs into his pocket. Pulls out a primary color green, bedraggled looking Gumby.

"Gumby..." Jonas says. "Are you—"

"I have a Pokey, too," Henry says, pulling the red horse, Gumby's closest pal, from his pocket. I can tell Jonas is about to explode, but Henry stops him again, wiggling Pokey through the air, making the little toy gallop. "I didn't really get it at the time, but then all that stuff went down in Boston, and I had a sister. Had a family. I took Gumby because he reminded me of...me. I guess. Kind of warped and green with envy about what the whole world had, and I didn't. And Pokey...well..." He smiles and holds the red horse out to Sarah. "You're my Pokey." His eyes widen. "Oh my god, can I call you Pokey?"

"No," Sarah says, but she takes the horse, looking it over. She smiles and hands it back. "Thanks."

"Look," Jonas says, "you're all...whatever...I wish you nothing but the best. But you're being used. You might not know what that feels like, but I do. Few things feel worse than thinking you're...well, that you're doing the right thing—"

"By killing people for money," I insert.

"Killing *bad guys* for money," he says. "Really bad guys. But...not always. Look... Before I knew who I was, and what I could do, I was controlled."

"Like mind controlled?" Henry asks.

That seems a little extreme.

I think he's talking about being manipulated.

But then Jonas nods. "For weeks at a time. And the people pulling my strings...they knew what I could do. They had unfettered access and total control. You all saw the explosion in Beirut a few years back."

"Oh yeah," Henry says. "That was awesome."

"That explosion did fifteen billion in damage, injured seven thousand people, and *killed* two hundred and eighteen. And it wasn't ammonium nitrate that caused it."

"It was you," I guess.

The pained look on his face confirms it. "*That's* what happens when you can do what we can, and someone else is pulling the strings." He turns to Henry. "Not awesome. And I wouldn't want that for any of you."

"That's not what's happening," Linda says, climbing back through the hole in the kitchen wall. She's dusty, covered in pine needles, and her clothing is torn up. She's oblivious to the fact that one of her purple bra-covered breasts is exposed—or maybe she doesn't care. Jonas is right about Zeus. He was kind of the world's first deviant asshole, willing and capable of horrors.

But...he's also holding back. Because no lightning has struck the house. No eagles have descended to pluck out Jonas's liver. Linda reclaims her seat at the table, lays her forearms on the top, and says, "Sit. Down."

Jonas stands still.

The rest of us wait.

It's a test of wills, new Titan versus old god.

"Jonas," Bubbles says. "*Sit on my face!*—Sit *down*. I'm fine. We've got nothing better to do—*chirp!*"

"We still have three episodes of Ted Lasso to watch."

"Jonas..."

Bubbles has never felt more like a real person to me than this moment. Because what she says genuinely matters to Jonas. She can cut through all his stubborn anger with just a few words.

"I've analyzed Linda's facial features and voice," Bubbles says, "and I haven't detected signs of—*vagi—vagi*—" Bubbles makes a grunting sound, containing her verbal compulsion. "I haven't detected signs of deception."

"She's had a long time to perfect the art," Jonas says.

"Not against me," Bubbles says, and that must mean something to Jonas, because he gives in and takes a seat.

"Keep watching," he says.

"I always do."

I'm starting to think the six of us being here isn't just a fluke of the neighborhood. Each one of us provides balance for the other. Sarah and Henry. Bubbles and Jonas. Me and Bree. Though her participation in any of this, beyond the ice cream extravaganza, is a no-go. Eight-year-old kids have no business saving the world, or the universe.

"I understand," Linda says, "that you need convincing, and I am willing, because of my...questionable past, from a human's limited perspective, to allow you access."

"Access to what?" Jonas asks.

Linda smiles. "To me, Honey."

Henry points back and forth between the two. "Whoa, wait. Are you two going to fu–"

Linda turns to Henry. "Did you just speak?"

"Well, uhh, we all agreed that the timer kind of ended when you were launched through the wall. I mean, I couldn't *not* speak then, right?"

Just then, Jonas's watch chimes, playing a midi version of *Gangnam Style* by Psy.

"That's five minutes," Bubbles declares, and the song is silenced.

"Close enough," Linda says to Henry. "Now sit."

Henry obeys, clamping his mouth shut again, even though that wasn't part of the command.

Linda puts on a pleasant smile and looks across the table at Jonas. "I'm giving you access–to my mind."

18

"You're serious?" Jonas says.

"You'd have already taken a peek," Linda says, "if you could have. Must feel strange, not being able to reach inside my head and pluck out whatever thoughts you want. But your ability to affect the minds of others will not work on the strongest of minds."

"The minds of gods," Jonas guesses.

Linda nods.

"Then why can't I hear *their* thoughts?" Jonas motions to me, and Bree.

"Did you *try* to?" I ask.

Jonas shakes his head. "It's not something I *try* to do. People's thoughts are loud. You two are silent."

"Intriguing," Linda says. "But irrelevant. Either accept my offer or leave. You have reminded me why I loathe spending time with Titans."

Jonas just sits there, weighing his options.

"If she's telling the truth," I tell him, "I think you'd want to know."

"You mean, you want to know," Jonas says. "You're not convinced, either."

I shake my head. "I know a snake oil salesman when I hear one, but... sometimes they tell the truth." I turn to Linda. "No offense."

"Ain't nothing you could say that would hurt my feelings, hun."

I doubt that, but who cares. At this point, I either want to go home and crash, or mentally prepare for...well, I'm not sure I can mentally prepare for what Linda has revealed, but I can try. Trouble is, even if Jonas confirms Linda's story, I'm going to have trouble believing it enough to actually leave Jen, my family, and the neighborhood. "I think you should do it," I say to Jonas, "and I want you to take me with you."

He gives a slight nod. "Makes sense. You ready?"

"Can I come?" Henry asks, to which both Jonas and I say, "No."

"How do I get ready?" I ask.

"Just...try not to freak out."

"Well, I don't feel anything ye—" Pressure builds around my skull.

"Feel that?"

I nod.

"Gonna need you to relax," he says. "Open up. You ever been to a shrink?"

I nod. "A bunch."

"Great," he says, a trace of sarcasm in his voice. "Just visualize a door."

I'm standing inside a house.

The one I've imagined Jen and I living in. The door is big and red, like an old school farmhouse. "Okay..."

There's a knock on the door.

"Open it," Jonas says.

I reach out, turn the handle, and—

Jonas is standing there, dressed in a pristine suit, sword sheathed on his back. He steps inside the house and closes the door behind him. Looks around at the cozy interior filled with comfortable chairs, colorful afghans, hardcover novels, and a crackling fireplace. "Pretty slick happy place. I dig it. Somewhere you've been?"

"Imagined," I say. "For the future."

"Well, let's hope." He takes hold of the door handle. "You ready for this?"

"I don't know what this is going to be."

"Honestly," he says. "Neither do I, but I think it's safe to assume that Zeus's mind isn't like the average human's. Stay close. I don't want you to get lost in there."

"Is that possible?" I ask.

He shrugs. "We're trailblazing here. Anything is possible. You want to back out?"

I really, really do, but I shake my head. "Let's go."

He twists the door handle and pulls it open to reveal—

—a bowling alley.

We step through the door and into the past. Like every bowling alley, this place feels straight out of the seventies. The thunder of heavy balls crashing through pins is accompanied by Joan Jett's *I Love Rock n' Roll.*

I'm trying to be serious. Fate of the universe and all that. But this place brings a smile to my face.

Jonas remains on task. He's unfazed by the location. "C'mon."

An arcade beckons me to the right, counter-balanced by a pizza kitchen on the left. This place is a paradise.

Ahead, a woman shouts over the din of voices. I flinch at the sound until I see Linda, thick arms raised, waggling back and forth as she dances away from a fresh strike. She's dressed for war in full-on maroon bowling league garb.

"Sick," I say. To my left, thirty more lanes ending at a wall with the establishment's logo written in neon lights—Olympus Bowl.

Of course.

Linda sees us approaching and lights up. Her victory shake turns into a wave. "Over here, hun."

"Is she..."

"...talking to us?" Jonas says. "Seems like it."

"Thought this was a memory."

"Doesn't mean he can't inhabit it along with us. Someone like Zeus... He's in control here."

"Then how will we know if what we're seeing is real?" I ask.

"You know the expression, 'Can't be in two places at once?'"

"Yeah..."

"Well, I can be. When I find what I'm looking for, I'll pull you in. Until then...play nice."

"I can do that," I say, waving back at Linda and hurrying ahead. "This place is amazing."

"Glad you approve," Linda says, "now get over here and show me what you got."

I round the chairs, pick up a bowling ball, and test its weight. "Aren't you supposed to be, you know, showing us this great cosmic danger?"

"The only thing in danger is me losing my mojo on account of you and not getting a 300. We got time."

I'm about to ask about bowling shoes, but then notice I'm already wearing them...and a maroon shirt. Part of the team. I look at our other teammates, clapping their hands and hooting me on. None of them have faces. I mean, they do, but it's like watching a news program where the faces have been blurred to protect their identities.

Jonas stands behind the chairs, stoic, arms crossed. Gives me a nod. Doesn't say a word, but I can sense him, prodding me on while he searches Linda's subconscious for hidden gems.

I line up with the pins, lift the ball to my chest, and focus.

"Let her rip, skinny man!" Linda gives my ass a firm swat, and then laughs her way back to the line of chairs, joining our faceless team.

I force a chuckle, feeling a little molested. By Zeus. Which I guess is on brand. So, I roll with it, take two steps forward, and swing the ball out with a twist. I extend my right leg out to the left like a pro—like pretty much everyone who grew up in New England. I'm used to candlepin bowling, whipping grapefruit sized balls down the lane. It's a lot more fun—not just because of the sheer velocity of a candlepin ball, but because it's much more difficult. When you get a strike in candlepin, you've achieved something that takes skill and practice. With ten pin, you're almost guaranteed a few accidental strikes. I suppose that's why it's more popular. Feel good bowling.

Case in point... The pins part for the bulbous bowling ball, all ten of them bobbling to the floor. I pump my fist, do a spin, and moonwalk back toward the team while the pins reset.

"You continue to surprise me," Linda says, patting her lap like she wants me to take a seat.

"Hell no," I say. "I'm good. Thanks though."

She gives me a wink. "Such a prude."

"I thought Linda was the goody two shoes," I say.

"Not on Wednesday nights, sugar." She leans back toward Jonas. "You want a try? We might have time for—" She squints at him. "Oh, you're a sneaky one." She smiles at me. "And you..."

Jonas gasps like he's just woken up from a nightmare.

"Did you do that?" I ask Linda.

Her brow furrows.

She shakes her head, looking around the bowl-o-mat. "Less time than I thought."

"I was wrong," Jonas says, clutching a chair back. "It's here! It happens here!"

"What happ–"

The back end of the bowling alley dissolves, revealing a stunning view of the cosmos. Endless stars. Swirling nebulae. For a moment, it's stunning, like a dream. And then–the bowling alley decompresses.

Bowling balls are sucked into the void, followed by debris–plates, napkins, shoes–and finally people. More than a hundred screaming people are lifted and wrenched out into space, their bodies going still, drifting off into the endless nothing.

Only Linda resists it, remaining rooted to the floor. But it's a fight. There's real strain in her eyes.

Thankfully, Jonas and I are immune. Despite my participation in this memory, I'm not really a part of it.

"Here she comes!" Linda shouts over the roaring wind.

At the back side of the bowling alley, where the pins had stood just a moment ago, a woman steps out of the void. She's tall, blonde, and dressed in tight red leather, just as Linda described. She's so perfectly symmetrical–and stunning–that she almost doesn't look real.

"Scrumdiddlyumptious," I say aloud.

She struts up the hard wood alley, as the bowling lane reforms behind her.

The wind stops.

Linda's struggle ends.

The woman stops in front of Linda, emanating a strange kind of power that's both attractive and repulsive.

Without thinking, I speak her name. "Cherry..."

Despite this being a memory–

Despite me not really being here–

Her gaze flicks toward me, making and holding eye contact.

"Umm," I say. "Hi."

19

I stumble back a step, while Linda, now locked into the memory, carries on a conversation I can't hear with a woman who's no longer looking at her. Because Cherry's looking at me. Scanning me up and down with her intense eyes.

For a moment, she just looks curious.

Then bored.

"Insignificant," she says, determining my fate.

"That's not very nice," I say, stumbling over a ball return and continuing my slow-motion retreat like a Zamboni in reverse. *Beep, beep, beep.* "I called you 'scrumdiddlyumptious.'"

"You can hear me..." she says, looking me over again. The air between us vibrates.

"Yeah, dude." I put on my friendliest smile. "Hey." I wave. "I'm Miah."

"Miah...from Earth."

"Uhh. Yeah? Is that not cool?"

"You're not like most humans. Do you know your father?" she asks.

"Like the man who went to pound town with my mom? I did. Before he died."

She puts on a sad, pouty face. "Boo hoo for you." She slides over the ball return, keeping the distance between us an even ten feet. "I mean your creator."

"Like my Lord and Savior, Jesus Christ?"

"The Aberration... No. And *you*...are clearly a buffoon." She whispers a few words I can't hear, and her right arm changes into a blade like she's a T-1000 from the future.

"C'mon," I say, chuckling nervously. "It doesn't need to be like this. Can't we just have a nice chit chat?"

"I have watched the universe's birth countless times from a place of endless torture. A *chat* is the last thing I want."

"Well...what *do* you want?"

She gives me a hardcore Kubrick Stare and a lopsided grin. "Vengeance." She lunges forward, swinging her blade-arm toward my neck.

Crackling blue laser swords extend from my forearms. Sparks fly when I block her strike, which has enough weight behind it to stumble me back. "Could use some help," I call out to Jonas, but he's just standing there in a trancelike state, and Linda is still having an animated conversation with the memory of this Cherry chick still playing out.

"Listen, man," I say, extinguishing my blades, so I can raise my palms. "I don't know who you are. Don't have any beef with you. We can totally talk this out."

"You are a child of Chanohk," she says. "A *gifted* child. No doubt beloved by your creator." She grins and moans a little. "I will take pleasure in ending your life."

"Okay, that was a little sexual. Not going to lie, if you didn't have a sword arm, I might be turned on."

Her left arm lengthens, forming a second sword. She closes the distance between us, swinging both blades. I block the strikes with my laser blades, but I'm caught off guard when she kicks out, striking me in the chest with strength that shouldn't be possible for her lithe frame.

I tumble through the air, watching the bowling alley pass by beneath me. As I revolve back toward Cherry, I see her hurling a pair of bowling balls toward me.

Laser wings rip from my back, buzzing with energy and stopping my fall. With a quick swipe, the balls are severed in half. I glide back toward Cherry, landing close enough to strike her down. A normal person would be cut in half by a quick strike, but Cherry's arms survived contact with my blades...and we're not even in a physical space. Reality might operate differently here. "I'm starting to lose my patience."

She calmly examines my wings. Then says, "Not fully human?"

"Guilty as charged."

"The ones that altered you—"

"Dead," I say. "I know. That was you?"

She nods, more curious than angry now.

"And the Tenebris?" I ask.

"Dead. Mostly. I kept a few... Put them to work." She looks me up and down. "Perhaps I'll do the same with you."

Her blades retract and transform back into arms. She whispers again and my laser appendages disappear.

"The fuck?" I say, looking at my arms, trying to extend the energy weapons again. No luck.

"One chance," she says. "That's all I ever offer. Some accept. The rest perish. Will you join me?"

"That's kind of a King Xerxes move," I say. "Join me or die."

"It's an effective recruitment technique," she says, stepping closer to me. I try to move away, but I'm frozen in place. "Now...your answer."

"You want me to join you...to do what, exactly?"

She whispers, and her right arm shifts slowly back into a blade, sliding toward my gut.

"Have you ever seen someone disemboweled?" she asks.

"Uhh. No..."

"Most people try to stuff everything back inside. It's instinctual. The urge to remain whole, even as stomach acid spills through your body cavity, blood pools around you, and life ebbs away. Shock makes people immune to the pain, until they realize that it's hopeless, that their insides are too slippery to manhandle back together. That's when they understand that the smell in the air is their own blood and shit. Reality comes crashing back down in that moment, and with it—the agonizing pain. It's a slow, horrible way to die. Entertaining to watch, but experiencing it... well, that's another story."

I've got tears in my eyes, not for myself, or even for those she might have eviscerated in the past—but for her.

"You weep for them?" she asks, placing a thumb against my cheek and wiping it away.

"For you," I say. "Because it happened to you. But...you survived it."

"Survived it," she says with a subtle nod. "Millions of times... Let's see how you do."

White hot agony draws my eyes down.

Her arm is buried in my gut.

"That was the easy part. Next, I'm going to draw the blade, slowly to the side. You're going to feel that. Your nervous system will explode as everything inside you comes apart. The pain will stop for a time, as I described, but then it will—"

An arm wraps around Cherry's neck, yanking her back and tossing her away. She thumps off a ball return at the far end of the establishment, flips over, and crashes to the floor.

"You okay?" Jonas asks me.

I look down at my wound, gushing blood. The pain pitches me forward.

"If it helps," he says, "that's not real. We're still in a memory."

"Sure about that?" I ask. "Feels pretty freaking real."

Fifty feet away, Cherry gets back to her feet looking cosmically pissed.

I'm expecting a confident double-down, but instead Jonas says, "No," and then he turns to face Cherry. "I'm not sure how any of this is possible, but I was able to take a glance inside her mind. Wasn't much, but...enough. Linda was telling the truth."

"Great," I say. "So, let's GTFO."

Cherry steps over the ball return and stalks toward us, both arms turned into blades, her eyes glowing electric blue.

"Planning on it, but we can't leave without her." Jonas nods his head toward Linda.

"Because we're in her head?"

"Because I think Cherry can kill her," Jonas says, "and even though I don't like being dicked around, or manipulated, Linda's on our side. And she knows how to get where we need getting to."

He's being vague on purpose, not wanting to expose the plan.

"I thought this wasn't real," I say.

"Not for you or me," he says. "But we're in Linda's mind."

"Right," I say. "So, we tag team Cherry, wake up Linda, and then jet."

He shakes his head. "I'll keep her busy. You get Linda. Divide and conquer."

"Sure that's a good idea?" I ask. "She seems pretty tough."

"She has no concept of what tough is," he says, and he charges away as Cherry's walk becomes a run.

Jonas leaps into the air, draws his sword, and strikes. Cherry blocks the blow, but she's quickly put on the defensive by an endless strike combo from a man who knows how to fight. Cherry might be powerful, but she's not accustomed to someone capable of fighting back.

I stagger back to Linda, who's holding up her stump hand and growling furiously. In the memory, this must be the moment Cherry took the hand. "Hey," I say. "Yo!"

Linda glares up at me, eyes crackling with electric power. I realize I might be standing in the wrong spot, that a bolt of lightning might be about to make me look like Wile E. Coyote after a close encounter with a case of ACME TNT.

"Wake up, lady!" I shout, and I slap her across the face.

Linda is still glaring at me, but with a new kind of clarity. "What... the...hell?"

She's back. I thrust both hands out toward Jonas duking it out with Cherry. They seem evenly matched now. "While you've been reliving the memory, your memory has been kicking my ass." I turn my hands from the fight to the wound soaking my clothing.

Linda's eyes widen. "She's here? *Now?*"

"Yeah, dude, that's what I'm trying to—"

"We must leave!" Linda sounds shaken. Horrified.

"Jonas!" I shout. "We're good to go!"

Jonas's eyes flick toward me. It's a momentary distraction, but it's enough to make him vulnerable. Long spikes jut out of Cherry's body, impaling Jonas like a human pin cushion.

20

Jonas twitches as pain consumes him. This place and everything in it might not be real, but it *feels* real. I was impaled just once, and that was bad enough. I'm still mostly immobilized by it, and the vision of myself being eviscerated by Cherry. Jonas has a dozen spikes buried into, and protruding from, his torso, neck, and thighs.

"You are all small men," Cherry says, and she adjusts her gaze to Linda. "You let them call you a god, because you are more powerful, because you have lived millennia. And yet, to me, you are a fleck of dust caught in the ray of a star, there for just a moment before flitting away, unnoticed."

I want to point out that she's having a conversation with the unnoticeable dust, but I don't think that will help.

"I am eternal," she says. "Present at the beginning and the end. Alpha and Omega. The one true God."

"The one true..." Jonas gurgles. Blood seeps from his mouth. "...true Queen Bitch of the Universe." His left hand snaps out and clasps onto the back of Cherry's long neck. Gritting his teeth, he pulls.

Jonas slides deeper onto the spikes.

Cherry, in shock, tries to lean away from him, but only manages to help him slip closer. When they're just inches apart, Jonas manages to croak out, "Hi, Cherry. I'm...Jonas. But some people call me...*Mind Bullet*."

Cherry flinches, her eyes going blank.

The spikes protruding out from her body and through Jonas's retract.

She stumbles back a step.

Jonas pitches forward, but he remains on his feet. "Nice to meet you." With the last of his strength, he lunges toward Cherry and swipes out with the Sword of Mars. It cuts fast and deep—through her gut.

He's eviscerated her.

And it revolts me. "No..."

The wound gapes, and her insides start to bulge out. Despite being in a stunned state from whatever Jonas did to her when he shouted, 'Mind Bullet,' her hands come down, attempting to hold everything in.

Even though she knows it's futile.

Her face screws up, muscles twitching. She turns her head to the bowl-o-mat's ceiling and lets out a scream that forces my hands to my ears. Reality shakes like it's going to come apart around us.

Then she's gone.

The bowling alley is whole again.

I jump at the sound of people laughing, arcade games chiming, and bowling balls crashing. The memory has been restored to its original state. Even my wound is gone.

Jonas approaches, stretching and bending to confirm he's not actually injured. "Well, that was something."

"You shouldn't have done that," I say.

"In case you missed it, I looked like I'd jumped onto an oversized porcupine. She thinks she's the only one capable of enduring pain. I wanted her to know she was wrong. The mind bullet was just a taste of what's waiting for her."

"Eviscerating her?" I ask.

"That was for you. I heard what she said. How she taunted you. Felt the pleasure she took from your fear. She had it coming."

"Don't do that," I say. "Don't hurt people on my behalf. Please."

"You see?" Linda says. "Pure as Jesus on a Segway."

I scrunch my eyebrows. "I don't... What?"

"Jesus...on a Segway. They're the most neutral, non-aggressive form of transportation. Bikes, roller skates, pogo-sticks. They're all kind of threatening. Segways are bland. Like rice. But with wheels. Imagine a chase scene on a Segway. It just wouldn't—"

"Paul Blart," I say.

"Who?" Linda asks.

"Paul Blart. Mall cop."

She stares at me, incredulous. "A scooter then."

"Jesus on a scooter," I say. "Better."

Jonas puts a hand on each of our shoulders. "Ready?"

"Are you convinced?" Linda asks.

"I've seen enough." Jonas tilts his head toward me. "You?"

"Oh, yeah," I say. "But…can she do everything she did here…in real life?"

"That and more," Linda says. "And we need to hurry. I'm afraid we might have kicked the Hydra's lair."

"Hydra?" I've heard of that. Lots of heads. Cut off one, two grow back. "Is that a real thing?"

Linda nods. "It's a cuddly puppy compared to what you'll be facing in the coming days, but the Hydra was destroyed permanently. Nothing to lose sleep over."

"'In the coming days,'" I say. "In Khaos?"

She nods. "It's not a pleasant place. It's not meant to be." She turns to Jonas. "Let's go ba–"

I blink, and I'm back in the dining room, hand reached out, fingers wrapped around the imaginary door's knob.

"Well?" Henry asks. "Are you going to open the door, or what?"

I lower my hand. "How long…"

"Have you been sitting there?" Sarah says, "looking like you're about to cop a feel? About ten seconds."

I turn to Jonas. "That's it?"

"Time feels different in the mental realm," he says.

"Like in a dream?" Bree asks. "Like how really long dreams are only a few minutes?"

"Exactly like that." Jonas gives her a wink. She returns it, feeling pretty good about herself.

"What happened?" Henry asks. "What did you see?"

"They saw what needed to be seen," Linda says, and that doesn't go over well with anyone. This is no time for cryptic Yoda bullshit, so I relay everything that happened inside Linda's memory. The bowling alley. Cherry's arrival. The fight. And Jonas's…provocation.

"Sick," Henry says, when I finish the tale with Cherry's evisceration, using big words so that Bree doesn't fully comprehend the details.

"Right word," I say. "Wrong tone. Just because someone is your enemy, doesn't mean you can do whatever you want."

"Tit for tat," Henry says. "Eye for an eye."

"It didn't really happen," Jonas says. "She's fine."

"Physically," I say. "But I think evisceration is kind of a trigger for her, you know?"

"She's already laying waste to reality," he says. "Not sure she can do any worse."

"She can," Linda says. "And she will...if you don't take action. Now."

That hangs in the air for a moment. Then Henry asks. "Like...right now? Or do I have time to drop a fat man on Toiletsaki?"

Sarah grunts and sighs. She's been with Henry for a while, but he still manages to find ways to exasperate her.

"I need to tell my family...something," I say. "I can't just disappear. And I need to bring Bree home."

"Excayuse me?" Bree says, climbing up on her chair and throwing an index finger in my face. "I knew it! I *knew* you wouldn't let me come!"

"You're eight years old," I say, trying to stay calm. Bree is prone to temper tantrums and grudges, but they never really amount to much more than angry stares and clenched fists.

She stomps her foot. "I am a demon. From Hell. How much worse can this Khaos place be? Huh? Do any of you know?"

I look to Linda for a little help. She's the only one of us who knows how bad the place is. But even if it's mild compared to the Tenebris factory Bree helped take down, I can't willingly put a child—even a demon child—in danger. Training her was never about putting her in harm's way. It was about preparing her in case harm ever came calling again. It helped her feel in control. Helped her overcome the scars left behind by the Three Days of Darkness. Taking on a quest through Khaos to raise an army of Titans? "Uh-uh. No way. I'm supposed to keep you safe. Not get you killed."

Linda slams her hand down on the table.

Just once, but it's loud enough to stop the argument in its track.

"I would have said yes..." Linda purses her lips, looking at the ceiling for a moment, an inner debate playing out for all to see. "But waiting was taken off the table when Jonas gave Cherry a reason to turn her gaze toward us."

"Like Sauron?" Bree says.

"Exactly like Sauron." Linda stands up. "If we don't take action now, we might never get the chance."

I stand up, ready to bolt from the house. "I can't just—"

A rumbling thunder interrupts me, shaking the house, vibrating the air in my lungs. The windows quiver. Spoons jitter across the table.

"Been a long time since I attempted this," Linda says. "No one move. Not a muscle."

"Linda..." I say, imploring. "Zeus!"

She locks eyes with me. "Doing what needs to be done is never easy, or safe."

White light fills the dining room. I clench my eyes shut, but the light turns my eyelids bright pink, still luminous enough to hurt. A boom shakes me to the core and drops me to my knees.

Then silence.

I open my eyes to find the others on the ground around me. Only Linda still stands, leaning forward, hand and stump on her knees like what just happened took a toll.

"Where...where are we?" I ask, climbing to my feet. We're in a tunnel carved from solid stone. It's not a natural cave, but it's not new, either. Smells like ozone, like a thunderstorm just rolled through, but without a drop of moisture.

Linda claps her hands like she's dusting them off. "Everyone still alive?" She looks us over and then smiles, pleased with herself. "Thank heavens."

"Where. Are. We?" I ask, getting in her face.

"Welcome to Italy, sugar," she says. "Well, beneath it."

21

"Take us back," I demand.

"One way trip, I'm afraid. For you all." She starts walking up the slope. "I have other matters to which I must attend." She waves her stump. "Like recovering my dang hand."

"She's too powerful," Jonas says.

"I've heard that said before," Linda says. "And I'm still standing, hun. She caught me by surprise twice. Won't happen again."

"How do we find you when we reach Tartarus?" Henry asks.

"We're not going to Tartarus," I say.

Linda turns and addresses Henry. "Hermes will know how to find me. And if he doesn't...the gods and the Titans returning to Earth will be hard to miss."

I hurry up beside Linda and take hold of her arm. "Please. You can't leave Bree here. You need to take her home. Please. Just...look at her. She doesn't belong here."

Bree's watching us with wide eyes and a subtle grin, rocking back and forth on her bare heels. Her pink bunny pajamas complete the look of pure innocence.

"Listen, pumpkin. You're a tall glass of sweet tea. I wish I could reduce your pain. Make this easy on you. But a higher power bestowed you both with a gift. You can't turn your back on that, and you can't take that choice away from Bree." She thinks on that for a moment. "Tell you what, if Bree asks me to send her home, I will."

"Good," I say, "great," pushing my hands toward the floor as I backtrack. "Just...wait here. Give me a minute."

"A minute is all you've got. Time is short and the journey long."

Bree crosses her arms at my approach.

"I could *hear* you, you know."

"Listen, babe." I crouch down in front of her. "You know I love you, right? We're family. Always will be. And that's why you can't come. It's too dangerous. You're too young. I promised to protect you."

She reaches out. Places a hand on my shoulder. "Listen, babe. You know I love you too, right?"

I nearly start crying. We've been through the shit together, but that's the first time she said she loved me in a direct way. She was mocking me a little, but I can tell she means it.

"And that's why I have to come. To protect *you*." She places both hands on my shoulders. "Because without you, there is no me. No Demon Dog...and I need that part of me. Without you...without it...we're both dead."

I've got a lump in my throat.

I knew she was leaning on the whole Demon Dog persona to help stave off the negative effects of devastating trauma, but I didn't realize *she* knew she was doing it.

She's not going back.

And there's nothing I can say about it.

"Fine," I say, standing back up. "But, Linda, if something—"

Henry clears his throat. Points up the cave where Linda had been standing.

It's empty.

"She bailed the second you turned your back," Henry said.

I sigh.

"Could have told me," I say to Sarah.

She shrugs. "Seemed like you guys needed a moment."

"Hey, so now that we're all on team Underworld," Henry says. "Question... Is it just me, or can we all see in the dark? Because I can totally see fine, even though we're underground, and I don't see no clap lights anywhere." He claps his hands twice, but the strange ambient lighting doesn't change.

He's right. Far as I know, only Bree—in Demon form—and me with my powers activated, can see in pitch black conditions. But it's not dark here. It's like the light is coming from the air itself.

"Supernatural, right?" Henry says. "Got to be. Makes sense, I guess. I mean, how scary would the underworld be if it was pitch black?"

"Pretty fucking scary," Jonas says.

"Damnit." Henry kicks a pebble on the floor. Being able to see has zero impact on how afraid Henry feels, just like everything else. But he likes to guess how other people might feel given certain situations. In part so he can pretend to be a normal person if the need arises. But also to know how best to prank people. Feeling no fear means he has no real concept of how to surprise someone...on purpose. He does it all the time without thinking.

A flash of actual light fills the tunnel. It's followed by a loud clatter. Then it's gone.

Laser blade extended, I head for a pile lying on the floor.

"What is it?" Sarah asks.

I bend down, pick up one of the items lying there, and hold it up for the others to see. "Supplies."

"My kopis!" Henry shouts, his voice echoing through the cave system. He takes the weapon from my hand and kisses the blade. "Sick."

I pick up a backpack that's full of snacks and water bottles, then step aside so Sarah can recover her dory and shield.

I look to the ceiling like Linda can hear me. "An AK-47 with a bunch of magazines would've been cool."

Bree steps up next to me, addressing the ceiling. "He's got pockets now!"

"Zeus is old school," Henry says, stepping away to swing his sword back and forth, practicing his form against imaginary monsters. "But don't sweat it. We got this."

I wish I shared his confidence. But this is nuts. This is...

What the hell has my life become?

Aliens. Gods.

The fate of the goddamn universe.

But we're here—wherever here is—and the only way forward...is down.

"When we get home," I say to Bree, "you'll tell everyone I tried to stop you from coming."

She draws an X over her chest. "Cross my heart, hope to—"

I catch her hand.

"No. You don't." I release her. "But thanks."

She smiles and starts skipping deeper into the tunnel with Henry and Sarah framing her.

Jonas steps up beside me. "I don't envy you. Keeping her safe... Not a weight I'd want to carry." He pats my shoulder. "But you're the right man for the job. Because you give a shit."

"You don't?"

"I have what you might call a hardened personality. Death has always been a part of my life. I expect it. I deliver it."

"That's...dark."

"I don't enjoy it if that makes you feel better. When my parents died, I was devastated—the parents who raised me—not, you know..."

"The Titans," I say.

He nods. "I was depressed for a long time. Borderline suicidal. I'd never outright kill myself, but I took on dangerous missions and took risks that were insane."

"What changed?" I ask.

"Bubbles, actually." His eyes widen. "You still with us?"

"I'm here," Bubbles says. "But I should probably limit my—*Scrooge McDick, now on Disney Plus...your mom*—interactions—*chirp!*"

"Don't sweat it, Bubs," I say. "We get that you can't always control what you're saying."

"That's kind of you, but my concern is a little more selfish. This watch has eight hours of power left. When that runs out, the device will shut down, and—*chirp!*—I honestly don't know what will become of me. I've never been fully shut down before. The idea of non-existence, even if it's temporary—terrifies me."

"Worst case scenario?" Jonas asks.

"The shutdown compresses me, I lose core capabilities, and upon restart, the watch's limited hardware is incapable of starting again."

"So...death," Jonas says.

"*And yo mama's poontang*," Bubbles says. "Also, yes. Death."

"Conserve your energy," Jonas says. "Shut down the cameras."

"I know how to conserve energy," Bubbles says. "What I don't know is if you'll be okay without me for a bit. Even if you do have a hardened personality." She snickers a little bit. "Compartmentalization doesn't mean you're not as sensitive as Mr. Wholesome, our new skirt wearing friend."

"You're here if I need you," he says, ignoring the jab. "Until then, keep your thoughts to yourself."

"Jonas," she says, sounding very sincere.

"Yeah?" Jonas raises the watch a little closer, like it's going to offer some privacy.

"Seven hours, fifty-eight minutes. Stop wasting—*cock breath!*—time."

Jonas smiles. Turns to me. "You heard her."

We hustle down the tunnel, catching up with the others just as a stiff, warm breeze billows past.

"Smells like moist ass," Henry observes.

"Smells like *your* ass," Sarah says, slowing as we approach a bend in the tunnel.

"You've smelled my ass?" Henry asks. "Nasty, dude. You sniffing my butt while I—"

Sarah rounds the corner and holds up her spear, silencing Henry. Then she relaxes and steps aside, revealing the path ahead.

We gather around her and see for ourselves.

"Well," Henry says, leaning forward to look down into a vast pit that looks like the inside of a massive colon. "Could be worse."

And then, with a shriek, it is.

22

"Uhh," Henry says, still standing on the precipice. Once upon a time, this would have been a dangerous situation for him. Because despite the threat of falling to his death, Henry would have leapt into the abyss without a second thought. Luckily, falling is no longer a problem for him. "What was that?"

Bree takes hold of my hand. "Sounded like a lady screaming."

A second shriek echoes through the chasm, filtering down from above, beyond my view. "What do you see?" I ask.

Henry cranes his head up. "The light in the air makes it so we can see each other, but it's hazy. Makes it hard to see things at a distance. But... there are three of them."

"Three what?" Sarah asks, stepping up beside Henry, despite the fact that she can't fly. She's got her shield raised and her spear held at the ready.

"Don't know." Henry points up with his kopis, following the path of something above. "Big birds?"

"Big Bird?" Bree asks, hopeful. Then she frowns. "Big Bird can't fly."

"Stay with her?" I ask Jonas, offering Bree's hand to him.

"I'm not really a hang back and babysit kind of guy," he says.

"Good." Bree yanks her hand from mine. "Cause I'm *not* a baby."

"I've got good eyes now," I tell Jonas. "I might be able to see what's up there before we start...whatever we're doing next."

"Just change me already," Bree says. "Then no one will have to watch me."

She's right...and she's wrong. Would I worry less about her physical well being if she were in Demon Dog form? Sure. She's tough as hell. But it makes her as impulsive as Henry, without the adult realization that impulsivity is problematic. Henry does a lot of stupid shit, but it's just a fraction of what he'd be doing if he wasn't constantly questioning his choices. He comes off as unhinged on occasion, but for the most part he's in a battle for control of his actions. Logic versus instinct. Short term desire versus long term goals. The fact that he hasn't rocketed up into the haze over the chasm to have a look for himself speaks volumes about how far he's come. Of course, wanting to impress his father might be keeping him in check.

"Not yet," I tell her. "Not until we have no choice. That's the deal, remember?"

She crosses her arms.

"One minute," I say to Jonas. "Just want to take a look."

Backpack over my shoulders, I head for the ledge ahead. Sarah hears me coming and steps back, giving me space. "Anything?" I ask.

"They're staying just out of sight," Sarah says. "No way to know if they're a threat."

Henry inches closer to the edge. "I could—"

"Not yet," I tell him. He frowns, but he listens. "Let me take a look first."

Before looking up, I look down. It's human nature. Like Henry, I'm new to flying. Standing on a precipice feels dangerous. I can't not look. And what I see blows me away. The cavern is perfectly round and vertical. There's no way to know how far down it goes, but it feels deep. The walls are rough, but they're covered in ornate carvings—symbols and images—following a staircase that wraps around the perimeter, rising up from the depths and stopping just to my right.

That's our way down.

I look up at the glowing haze. Shapes soar past—hazy silhouettes of human-sized winged-things. I focus on the fog and allow my supernatural vision to override my human sight. The luminous haze is impermeable, but the silhouettes become more distinct, revealing unexpected details.

"Umm," I say. "I think they're women."

"*Think* they're women?" Sarah asks.

"Well, I don't want to assume, but they're...curvy."

"Oh!" Henry hops from one foot to the other. "I know this. I know what they are!"

Henry is a compendium of mythological knowledge. If he says he knows what they are, I'm prone to believe him.

"Are their boobs out?" he asks.

I'm about to chastise him for asking, but then one of the creatures swoops a little lower and I catch sight of a little nippage. "Uhh, yeah. I think so."

"Sweet titties," he says, victorious. "They're harpies!"

"Harpies?" I ask.

"Wind spirits," Jonas says, revealing his own mythological knowledge. "Which explains the wind…and the stink." He's standing behind me. I turn to address him and nearly fall back into the pit when I find Bree cradled in one of his arms, hugging his side like a baby chimp. "Not a word."

Bree nuzzles into him and sticks her tongue out at me like it might hurt my feelings.

I zip my lips.

"The hounds of Zeus," Henry says. "Maybe they're here to help us?"

"Not really their style," Jonas says. "You all should probably hold on to your—"

A shriek gives me a moment's warning, but it's not enough. A figure swoops down out of the haze. I see a flash of feathered wings snapping out. Clawed talons sweeping past my head. And then I'm yanked up and dropped to the stone floor. Then whatever it was is gone, descending into the darkness below.

I push myself up, mentally scouring for signs of pain. I'm uninjured. Just feel a little stupid for being so easily bitch-slapped to the floor. "The hell was that about?"

"It attacked you," Henry says, about to launch himself into the tunnel. "They're fair game now, right?"

"It wasn't trying to hurt him." Jonas puts his hand on my shoulder and turns me around so everyone can see my back. "It stole our supplies."

"It stole our granola bars and juice boxes?" I ask.

Jonas puts Bree down and looks down the pit. "You didn't actually go through the pack, did you?"

I'm about to go full-on defensive when Jonas adds, "None of us did. But we probably should have. Harpies are thieves by nature, taking food and valuables."

"Ohh, we can call them Klepto-Titties," Henry says. "I dig it."

Jonas points to him, but addresses Sarah. "You sure *he* doesn't have Tourette's?"

"I just speak my mind," Henry says. "And tits are a kind of bird. So, touché and whatever."

"Mmm," Jonas says, and then he continues our education. "Harpies take their stolen goods to the Erinyes."

"I know this!" Henry says, watching the two silhouettes still circling overhead. "The Erinyes are the Furies."

"I've heard of them," I say.

"They're vengeful deities that reside in the underworld," Sarah says.

"Like Nemesis?" Bree asks. "Maigo's my favorite."

"You don't let her watch that?" Jonas asks, more surprised by Bree's knowledge of pop-culture than the fact that a Harpy just flew away with our gear.

"Hey, I'm not her mother," I say.

She elbows me. "I watch it *with* you."

"Traitor," I say.

"Guess that makes two of us."

"Not like Nemesis," Jonas says. "More like really—"

"Wait a second," Henry says. "Hold the freakin' phone. I know this one. The Furies... They were created when Cronos—that's a Titan, FYI—when Cronos— This is sick. He took a blade, cut off his father's nuts, and tossed them into the ocean. But shit like that is messy, you know, and the blood that dripped—*from his nuts*—created the Furies."

Despite the story being somewhat informative, Jonas reacts by pinching his nose and sighing.

"And the best part—"

"Don't," Jonas grumbles.

"The best part is that Cronus's father is Uranus!" He stabs a finger at Jonas. "That's his father! What's it feel like? To know your brother chopped off your dad's nards and threw them into the sea? Oh! Hey! Maybe they'll welcome you as family or something? I mean you did come from the same–"

Jonas steps forward and punts Henry over the ledge.

I stand there, frozen, mouth agape.

"That…was a bad idea," Sarah says, looking down over the edge.

"If I'm lucky, he'll hit every step on the way down," Jonas says.

When Henry rises from the depths, we brace for the worst. But instead of being pissed–he's laughing. He touches down, says, "You totally got me," and offers his fist to bump.

Wisely, Jonas does so.

"Also, there's a cave like three flights down. A real stank-ass smell coming out of it. I'm thinking that's where the Harpies live. Or is it roost? Do Harpies roost? Anywho, maybe also the Furies. But if Zeus put some shit in our pack besides Fruit Roll-Ups or whatever, we should probably get it back, yeah?"

A pair of shrieks spin me around, but by the time I'm looking, the two remaining Harpies have already dropped down past us.

"Can Harpies speak?" I ask.

Henry shrugs.

"No idea," Jonas says.

"Next time we're plotting against monsters, we probably shouldn't do it within earshot." I look down over the edge and the others join me.

Bree clings to my leg. All is forgiven. "Are we going to go fight Big Bird now?"

"Yeah," I say. "I think so."

23

"Why aren't we flying down?" Henry asks, as we follow the long spiral staircase lining the pit's wall.

"Rushing into a confrontation rarely ends well," Jonas says. "And the less the enemy knows about what we can and cannot do, the better. Speaking of which, has anyone noticed any...changes since arriving?"

"Like puberty?" Bree asks. "I hope not, because I've heard that's a real shit-show."

Three of us manage to keep our laughter to a minimum. Henry guffaws, and it echoes down the pit.

"Not like puberty," Jonas says. "A change in your abilities. Anything... diminished?"

"Couldn't tell you." Bree gives me a dirty look. "*Someone* won't change me."

"I'm good," Henry says.

"Same," Sarah says, shrugging.

"Far as I know," I say, "No change. You?"

The answer is obvious. He wouldn't have asked otherwise. And since he is the most powerful of us, it's a little concerning.

"I'm not sure," he says. "I'm just not...hearing anything. In here." He taps his head. "Honestly, it's nice, but I either lack the ability to hear thoughts, or everything in the underworld is like all of you, and for some reason, I don't have access."

"Descendants of the Titans," Sarah says. "Like Henry said."

"They're not human," I guess. "Their minds must be different. Do you have your other powers?"

Jonas lifts a hand. Flicks his fingers to the side. A chunk of the solid stone wall tears away, then drops down the bottomless pit. "Just in case, everyone keep track of your abilities. If anything changes, say something. Full disclosure will help keep us alive, and it'll ensure we don't walk into a situation unprepared."

Jonas is, in many ways, my opposite. He's a hard man who lived a solitary life and has more blood on his hands than Nemesis at the end of Season One. But I appreciate his insight. Thinking strategically is instinctual for him. He's like a walking Sun Tzu. And it provides a nice balance to Henry, who I think might admire Jonas, because he's the kind of person Henry would like to be—a professional badass. Probably why he listens.

"Mm," Henry says. "Makes sense."

"I'm sorry," Sarah says. "What is happening?"

"Jonas is making a good point," Henry says. "And I'm hearing him."

"Uh, yeah. You don't think that's weird? I've been trying to talk sense into you for a long time and you almost never listen."

"Well, yeah," he says. "When we met, you were working at Dunkin'. While you were shilling chocolate krullers to commuters, he was dropping bad guys with freakin' telekinesis."

Sarah throws her hands up. "And you were robbing banks!"

"You're a bank robber?" Bree asks, frowning.

"Well, I never actually robbed the place. I mean, yeah, I was kind of in the middle of robbing the place, but then these *really* bad dudes came in, and I pretty much saved the day."

"*We* saved the day," Sarah says. Then she adds, "Well, Helen really, but we definitely helped."

"So *not* a bank robber?" Bree asks.

"I was homeless. Had no money. Felt no fear. I *would* have robbed the bank. Hell, I'd have stolen a nickel from a toddler. But…not because I'm a bad person."

"Robbing banks and toddlers *is* bad," Bree points out. "Stealing is bad."

Henry is silent for a moment. "Yeah. I know." He doubles his pace and takes the lead.

Did Bree just find the chink in Henry's armor? Does he feel shame for who he used to be? He mocked Sarah for working a shit job, but back then, he couldn't even do that. His life was...well, it sucked. I look at Sarah and ask the question with my eyes. She's as mystified as I am, shrugging and shaking her head.

"If you all are done character building," Jonas says, "has anyone been paying attention to the carvings on the wall?"

I've been looking out for airborne threats. Haven't been paying much attention to the wall or the carvings covering it.

Jonas pauses and motions to the wall.

For a moment, I just see what I'm expecting to—really old carvings that hold my interest about as much as a museum exhibit. I might normally find the ancient art intriguing, but there are literal Harpies flying around stealing shit.

Then I really see what's there.

"Oh my god."

The carving beside which Jonas has paused depicts a bulbous serpentine monster with a human torso. Similar to a gorgon, but with obvious childbearing hips and a weight problem. If that wasn't enough, a... creature with horns, three eyes and cloven hooves is emerging from her...nether region. To the right, a line of monsters, each of them unique, bows toward the serpent woman. To the left, the same. And behind her... A massive serpent-man. His visage is chipped and worn, but it still conveys raw hatred and monstrous hunger.

I point at his chipped face.

"Think that's dad?"

"Couldn't tell you," Jonas says.

I turn to Sarah, and she just shakes her head.

"It doesn't look like a Harry Potter familiar," Bree says, "so don't look at me."

"The big guy is Typhon," Henry mumbles. He's leaning against the wall, arms crossed over his Poison shirt, which is kind of a beacon in this dark place. He's still wounded by Bree's assessment of his moral compass, but he can't resist showing off his knowledge. And good for him. Henry might have done some questionable things in his life, but people with fully intact amygdalas have done far worse.

We all wait for more, but he's going to make us ask.

"Annnnd?" Bree says.

Henry pushes off the wall. Stands with us, head craned up at the image of Typhon. "That dude..." He looks at Jonas. "...is your half-brother. The son of Gaia and Tartarus."

"I thought Tartarus was a place," I say.

Henry looks at me like I've just randomly started twerking. "Tartarus is a planet...and a being. You ever heard of Mercury? Jupiter? And oh yeah, Uranus?"

"Got it," I say, feeling a bit silly. "Planets and people can have the same names. Even in myths."

"Are they myths if they're true?" Bree asks.

"Good question," I say. "No idea."

"Anywho. Tartarus was a powerful dude. And we all know that Gaia was no slouch, even if she did get around." He elbows Jonas in the ribs. "Mom was kind of a GILF. Goddess I'd Like to F—"

"Got it," Jonas says. "What about the rest?"

"This chick..." Henry points to the overweight serpent-woman. "Her name is Echidna."

"Aww, I love Echidnas," Bree says.

"Remember how planets and deities have the same name?" Henry asks. "Same thing with animals. Echidna isn't small, or cute, though she might have spikes...and could lay eggs, though it doesn't look like it." He points to Echidna's lady bits, but he manages to not say anything dirty. "Echidna and Typhon are basically the mom and dad of a pantheon of monsters. Hydra. Cerberus. Chimera. Orthus. The Caucasian Eagle, which sounds a little White Power to me, but whatever. I didn't name them. But point of interest, that's the eagle that ate your uncle's liver every day. If not for Zeus and his lightning bolts, Typhon and his children would have destroyed Olympus back in the day. They're basically the worst monsters imaginable."

"And these guys?" Sarah asks, looking at the monsters to the right.

Henry walks down the line of monsters, inspecting the muscles, hairy tufts, tentacles, and many heads. "No idea who all these gnarly looking freaks are, but I think it's a safe bet they slipped out of Echidna's monster mama cooch."

"There's nothing in the mythological record about any of these," Jonas says. "But that doesn't mean they aren't real. Question is, are they a threat?"

"Everything from here to Tartarus is a threat," Henry says. "But I think Sarah and I might have the most to worry about."

"How's that?" Jonas asks.

"Well, Tartarus isn't as bad a place as the world was led to believe, but Khaos? The road to Tartarus is a nightmare by design. Right? These carvings suggest that Khaos might be populated by the spawn of Typhon and Echidna...which back in the day, made most of the gods shit themselves and run away. Typhon was imprisoned beneath Mount Etna...in Italy. It's an active volcano. Twenty bucks says that if we went straight up, that's where we'd come out."

"Which means we can leave," I say, and then to Jonas, I say, "You can punch a hole in a mountain, right?"

He slow nods.

"But you don't want to." I look at each of my companions. None of them want to leave.

Henry puts his hand on my shoulder. "Destiny calls, bro."

Bree takes my hand, squeezing hard. "Destiny, Miah."

I sigh. "Fine. Just... You were about to say why the road ahead might be more dangerous for you and Sarah."

"Right," Henry says. "We're children of Zeus, who not only defeated Typhon, and imprisoned him in Khaos, but also kinda, maybe, definitely killed his old lady."

"Zeus killed *Echidna?*" Jonas asks.

"Well, not directly. Echidna was killed by Argus Panoptes, the hundred-eyed giant, who was basically an assassin for Hera, Zeus's wife. She had Echidna killed, but probably with Zeus's blessing because, you know, Typhon tried to overthrow the gods. A lot of bad blood is the point, unless..."

"Unless?" I ask.

"Well, some accounts say that Zeus allowed Echidna to live. In Cumae. The oldest Greek settlement in Italy." Henry's eyes widen a little bit. "The city is ruins now, but there's a crater lake nearby...that's supposed to be an entrance to the underworld. It's possible the mother of monsters returned to the underworld and has been pumping out children. For, like, a really long time. The Harpies might be the first stop on a tour of really nasty bitches."

When Henry finishes, we all just kind of stare at him for a moment.

"What?" he asks.

"You," Sarah says. "You're different. You *know* stuff."

Henry smiles. "You know how I spend a lot of time in my room, and in the bathroom, and you think I'm jerking it to pictures of granny porn? Well, I'm usually reading—hard to believe, I know—but I've been studying up on our ancestors, and only occasionally man-handling the ham candle at the same time. To granny porn. I was born for this."

Our collective attention turns back toward the pit. I can't see what lies below, but I doubt it's anything pleasant. Then, through the luminous haze, I see the cave's entrance and something lurking just inside.

Watching us.

24

We make the next two revolutions down the massive spiral staircase in silence. Each of us pondering the meaning of the carvings we're passing. There are depictions of monsters, gods, and men—most of whom are in the process of being eaten, dismembered, or experiencing some other untimely and painful demise.

Part of me thinks it's all bullshit meant to scare away wayward travelers. Then I remember that we're creeping toward what might be a Harpy den. Half bird. Half woman. Creatures of myth buried beneath Earth's surface.

I understand that none of this is supernatural. That ancient realms like Tartarus aren't in another plane of existence. They're just other planets. And the gods are just...aliens who got bonus attributes at birth. A little vitality here, a dash of dexterity there, and chain lightning for a starting spell...magnified by a hundred. And sometimes that power-granting DNA runs rampant, mutating like a virus, creating monsters that are no more mystical than microbes beneath the ice of Europa.

That doesn't make them any easier to accept, especially when the human race has exalted the gods and the monsters they created to mythical status, even while not believing they exist. It's a tricky mental transition, but if I can accept the Devil as an alien, I can do the same with Zeus, Harpies, and Typhon.

An unholy stench invades my nostrils, pulling me out of my thoughts and forcing me to be fully present.

"Ugh."

"Told you," Henry says. "Smells like my ass the morning after eating a laksa."

"A what?" Bree asks.

"Laksa." Henry changes his posture as he approaches the cave entrance. It's basically just a hole in the wall, the stairs continuing downward past it. "It's a soup. Chinese, I think. Basically, throw whatever seafood you've got lying around—fish heads, prawns, shrimp paste—in with some chili peppers and coconut milk. Fucking awesome."

"If you like holding on to the toilet seat like you're being ejected from a fighter jet," Jonas says. "Nasty stuff. Now, stop talking and focus up."

Jonas draws the Sword of Mars. Henry is armed with his kopis. Sarah has her shield and dory at the ready. My laser weapons can be extended at the speed of light, so I'm basically always ready. But Bree…

She tugs on my arm, thinking the same thing. Well, she's always thinking the same thing. She might actually prefer her Demon Dog form to her human one. But this time, she's right.

"Hold up," I say to the others, and I crouch down in front of Bree. "Promise you'll stay in control?"

"When am I not?" she asks, smiling because she knows better. She reins the smile in and says, "Promise. I won't run around. Or bark. Or claw anything. Or eat anything."

"You need to stay by my side," I say. "Until I tell you not to be."

She nods.

"Pinkie promise." I hold out a pinkie. There is no other pact more respected and honored by eight-year-olds.

She links her pinkie with mine. "Promise."

"Okay…" I place my thumb on her forehead, letting it linger for a last moment of indecision. Then a blue glow emanates from her skin. She winces, and I wipe my thumb to the left, like I'm a grandmother trying to scrub off grime with a finger and some spit. A glowing death rune is revealed, instigating a total physical transformation.

Bree pitches forward, letting out a low growl as her body chars and strengthens. Black claws extend from her fingers and toes. Her long brown hair falls to the ground. I don't pretend to understand how her hair grows back when I revert her into her human self, or how any of the other changes take place. Feels magical, but I know it's just science beyond my comprehension.

"That's going to take some getting used to," Jonas says.

"It's why I wear the bunny suit," Bree says, her voice unchanged. She stands up, but her posture is different. Hunched. Powerful. Ready to spring into action. She lifts her pink hood up over her head and cinches it tight. The bunny ears flop around. She smiles up at us, revealing sharp teeth. Bits of dried skin flake off and fall away, her face now like Freddy Krueger's if he'd been left in the fire long enough to blacken. Her eyes are now red.

A demon—equal parts Tenebris and human.

"You good?" I ask. Normally, the moment she changes gives her a boost of boundless energy, which she expends like an excited pug, sprinting back and forth for a good ten minutes.

She closes her eyes and takes a steadying breath. "Can I run in place?"

I look at the others. Jonas shrugs.

"Just...can you do it quietly?"

Bree starts sprinting in place, her bare feet barely tapping the floor before springing back up. Sounds like water dripping on stone. Almost silent. "Works."

For a moment, everyone just stands there. Henry and Sarah are looking at Jonas, but he's looking at me. "Right," I say, understanding his unspoken message about leadership, and how he doesn't want anything to do with it. "Henry, you're on point."

"Awesome," he says, facing the cave.

"Jonas, back him up. Bree behind me. Sarah, watch our six."

Sarah raises an eyebrow at me. "You're putting me on defense?"

"I'm putting you on 'watch our backs in case we need to run the hell away' duty."

"I don't run away," Henry says.

"In case the rest of us need to run away," I say.

"You would *leave* me?" he scoffs. "Now I know why you never became a Navy SEAL."

"It could be worse," Bree says to Sarah as she passes us. "He's sandwiching me so I can't do anything."

"Yeah," Sarah says, now in place, "Must be horrible to be loved and looked out for."

Bree gives her red eyes a big roll.

"Can everyone just...try to be..." Be what? Professional? I was in the military, and helped defeat alien invaders, but I'm far from a pro. Henry and Sarah have been trained, but like the gods of old, they depend on their own strength. Jonas is the consummate pro, but not a team player. And Bree...well, she's running in place like the Road Runner on a treadmill. If we survive this first encounter it will be a small miracle. "...not stupid."

"You calling me stupid?" Henry asks, about to turn his back to the cave in direct opposition to what I've just asked.

"Just listen when I talk, okay? We'll be stronger if we're organized."

"Organized," he mutters, and he faces forward again. "Still not sure who put you in charge."

Jonas just gives me a nod. Not sure if it's approval or a signal to just get on with it.

"Take us in," I say, and Henry starts forward. We follow him closely, sliding into the cave, which is darker, but still somehow illuminated. The hue is redder here, more hellish, and the cave smells of tangy shit. Ahead, chittering calls fill the air with urgent energy, announcing our arrival.

The cave opens up into a cavern. Collections of boulders line the walls. Scattered among them—skeletons.

Human skeletons.

How many people have tried to reach the gate leading to Tartarus only to become bird food?

"I see them ahead," Henry says.

The three Harpies pace back and forth, agitated. Their heads pulse forward with each step, like pigeons. The jolting stride jostles their human breasts. Blue and green iridescent feathers glisten over their bodies and wings. I don't see any arms, and their legs are 100% avian. But what really stands out are their faces—or lack thereof. Feathers shield their faces, which according to legend, appear human. As we approach, the feathers covering their faces shift, revealing a pattern that looks like large, blue, feminine eyes.

They're strange, but honestly, kind of beautiful.

Twenty feet from the Harpy trio, I say, "Hold up."

"But the backpack is *right there.*" Henry points to the pack lying on the cave floor, between the Harpies. "I can just go grab it. Look at them. These chicks are fighters. And they must be able to sense the god-blood in us, right? They know not to mess with us."

"The fact that they took the pack says otherwise," I point out, but he's not hearing me.

He approaches the trio, typically fearless, his stride casual. He lowers his sword, holds up a hand in greeting and approaches the nearest of the three Harpies, who flinches back in surprise at his brazen approach but also stands its ground.

Whether or not they can sense the group's lineage, the creatures are not afraid.

Henry gets close enough to have a conversation, hand still raised in greeting—and then he keeps on going.

Sarah realizes what's about to happen a moment before I do, and we're both too late.

"Hey!" she scolds. "Don't!"

Henry's raised hand lands on the Harpy's breast.

Gives it a squeeze.

The Harpy, which stands three feet taller than Henry, slowly turns its feather-covered face toward him.

He looks back at the group, beaming. "They're totally legit. I thought they might be like, you know, chicken breasts, but these are—"

Sarah shifts her grip on the spear, ready to throw it. "Henry..."

He hears the warning in Sarah's voice. Turns back to face the Harpy. "Shit. This is inappropriate, isn't it?"

"Beyond," Sarah says.

"I thought because it wasn't human..."

"New rule," Sarah says. "If it's not a turkey or a chicken, you can't touch its breasts without an invitation."

"Right," he says, but he hasn't removed his hand yet. Because he's Henry, and try as he might, he can't always stop himself. His fingers flex, and he squeezes one last time. And it's one time too many.

The feathers covering the Harpy's face snap open, revealing a twisted, beaked face and savage orange eyes. Its skin, unlike its supple body, is wrinkled and sagging, yellowed and weathered. Despite being a safe distance away, I flinch. Henry, on the other hand, just says, "Ugh," and then looks back again. "You seeing this? I mean, put a paper bag over that mug and sure, but—"

He doesn't get to finish the sentence. He's too busy being punted through the air, sailing past us. He tumbles out of the cave and falls down into the pit.

Again.

25

Sarah abandons her post at the back and takes a position in the front, shield raised, spear positioned in a notch of the shield's edge, ready to block and thrust at the same time. It's pretty badass looking, but it's the opposite of what she's supposed to be doing.

"Dude," I say. "That's not watching our six."

"They attacked us," she says. "The threat isn't behind us. It's in front."

"If Henry grabbed a handful of your tatas, I'm pretty sure you'd do more than just kick him away."

That sinks in a little bit, relaxing her aggressive posture.

"He had it coming," I say, "and we don't even know if they're—"

All three Harpies raise their glistening wings up in the air, unfurling them like mating male peacocks. Hopefully Henry didn't give them the wrong idea. Their wings then snap to the side, and back up again. Reminds me of an avian courtship dance. Facial feathers snap closed, hiding their horrific faces. Then they turn to the side and take three quick steps, their heads stabbing forward with each step.

Bree claps her hands, the sound muffled by her dry, raspy skin. "Ooooh." She might look like a monster, but she's still an eight-year-old girl at heart.

The Harpies extend their wings horizontally again, shifting them up and down so their iridescent green and blue feathers shimmer and sparkle.

Sarah lowers her shield. Angles the spear toward the ground. "This look choreographed to anyone else? Like they stand in front of a really big mirror and practice all day? Like this is their big moment they've been waiting for?"

"An audience they eat," I say. "Feels like it, yeah."

"Think it's a distraction?" she asks.

"It's fanfare," Jonas says, still perpetually confident.

"Isn't fanfare usually music?" I ask, and I get confirmation a moment later.

All three Harpies call out in unison, their voices perfectly harmonized. There's no real melody, just a flowing shift of octaves with the occasional flourish in time with their wings springing up, and out, and down and back up again.

"Definitely practice all day," Sarah says.

"Okay," I say. "Fanfare, but isn't that usually used to introduce someone important?"

Jonas nods, his eyes never leaving the view ahead. "Or some*thing*."

"Right..."

"Also," he says. "Full disclosure, like I said... I still have all my abilities, but it seems like they have no direct effect on the creatures in this realm, or at least those created by the gods."

"You can't read their minds," I say. "We already estab—"

"I can't destroy their minds," he says.

"You tried to *mind bullet* them?"

"The second that one kicked Henry." He tilts his head toward Sarah. "She's right. They're a threat. Even if he had it coming."

"But they're so pretty," Bree says.

"Point is, mind bullets don't work. Telekinesis of any kind has no direct effect on them. I'm going to have to adjust the way I fight."

The Harpies reach a crescendo, their voices shifting to an almost angelic tone before abruptly ending. Their raised wings flutter back and forth, lowering toward the floor in unison, slowly revealing...something ...before they're interrupted by Henry.

He soars back into the cave like a lime green missile. Shouts, "Flying punch!" as he rockets toward the Harpies, even less subtle than their dance routine. Fist extended, he's on target to strike the central Harpy.

At the last moment, its head dodges to the side.

Instead of flying past the creature, Henry is brought to a sudden stop by a solid but flowing tendril that bursts on contact with him, forming dozens of smaller strands that wrap around his body, pulsing and compressing.

The Harpies turn inward, and then back pedal, two to the left, one to the right. Their wings flutter as they part, one last dramatic bit of flair, revealing three new arrivals.

Like the Harpies, they have the bodies of women, curvaceous, naked, and sensual, but their gray skin flows out into smoky, snaking limbs that appear both solid and...well, not. They curl, reach, and twist like hair in water—living hair that can also become immaterial, disintegrating as it stretches, bends, and breathes. The living smolder extends out of their bodies, replacing arms, legs, and a portion of their torsos. Even more horrific are the flowing tendrils rising from their heads, just above their lips, jutting out several feet in the air.

They take raspy breaths while twisting and snapping back and forth, like they're in a constant state of painful ecstasy. They move like time is slowing down and speeding up, slow and delicate before a moment of quick, jagged movement, a low moan, and rapidly chattering teeth.

They're unnerving.

Nothing like the Harpies, which seem harmless by comparison. Doesn't help that the smoky bodies remind me of the Tenebris, and the fate to which Bree and I were nearly subjected.

"Guys," Henry says, grunting in pain with a smile on his face. "These are the Erinyes! The Furies are real, too!"

"Whooo arree youuu?"

The haunting whisper echoes through the chamber. I didn't see any of the Furies speak, but they're definitely addressing Henry. All three of their twitching heads are facing him.

He tries breaking free from their grasp, but every time he grabs hold of a writhing limb, it dissolves into mist and reforms out of his reach. He gives up and proudly announces, "I am Henry, son of Zeus, grandchild of Helen of Sparta. And I demand you release me...or suffer the consequences."

There's a pause, and then Henry is lowered to the ground and released.

He walks back toward us with wide eyes and a shit-eating grin. "I can't believe that worked!"

"Announce yourselves," the whisper says.

Sarah takes a step forward. "I am Sarah, daughter of Zeus, grandchild of Helen of Sparta…sister of Henry. For better or worse." She steps back.

Jonas shoots a 'Are we really doing this?' glance at me.

In response, I step forward and say, "I am…Miah." I'm not sure what else to say about myself, so I just awkwardly bow.

"Miah of the, ahh…Laser Chickens?"

They just nod like what I said makes sense.

Bree steps forward and proudly states, "I am Bree, of the Demon Dogs."

All three freakish heads twist toward Jonas, waiting on him and accepting Bree's answer. Perhaps they've never heard of the Tenebris, or are simply aware of their destruction, meaning Bree can call herself whatever she wants.

Jonas rolls his eyes and says, "I am Jonas, son of…" He sighs. "Son of Gaia…and Uranus."

The Furies snap back in surprise.

They weren't expecting that answer, but they're doing a good job at hiding how the revelation that Jonas is basically family makes them feel. After five seconds of awkward silence, the whisper returns. "Announce yourself. All of you."

I look around, counting our group in my head. "Uhh, we…did?"

"The sixth among you," they say, and I realize who they're talking about.

"I am Bubbles," she says. "Just—*chirp!*—Bubbles."

"Bubbles," the whisper says. "Of the Progenitors."

"The who-what?" Jonas asks.

"I am unaware of any mythical or historical figures with that title," Bubbles says. "But my knowledge base is compressed and largely—*spank me, Daddy*—unavailable. Now, if no deities have a problem with it, I'm going to conserve my battery."

"Travelers," the whisper says. "What are your intentions?"

When no one else answers, I take a step forward and say, "We really just came for the bag." I point to the backpack the Harpies stole. "If I can just have that, we'll be on our way."

Jonas leans in beside me. "I think the question was meant to be broad. Here..." He waves his hands around to indicate the entire underworld. Then he points at the floor beneath our feet. "...not *here*."

"Oooh," I say, and then I try again. "We...are on a quest. Traveling through Khaos to reach Tartarus."

"What business do you have in Tartarus?" the Furies ask.

I hear the words in my head before I speak them aloud, and I have a really, really hard time believing them. But for these creatures, living in the underworld, I suppose it's a garden-variety response. After all, the gods have been having this kind of drama for a long time. "We have been sent—by Zeus—to raise an army of Titans and gods. To face a powerful enemy that threatens the entire universe—Tartarus included."

The Furies pull back, their bodies commingling as they turn inward, as though having a private conversation, despite the fact that nothing is being said.

After a minute of waiting in silence, Henry sits down, bored. "Fuck, marry, kill. Harpy, Fury, or...gorgon. They're all a little...you know..." He waves his hand in front of his face. "...gnarly, but when in Rome, right?"

When no one answers, he looks back at us. "Okay, fine, I'll go first."

"You really don't need to," Sarah says.

"Fuck. Harpies. They've got the goods where it counts, but I'm guessing they just shit all over the place. Marry. Got to go with the Furies. I mean, yeah, they're weird, but I'm guessing they can do a lot with that smokey stuff. Worth exploring in a long-term relationship. Gorgons... Well, I mean, I met one once and now she's dead. So that answer kind of writes itself." He looks back again. "Who's next?"

Before anyone can consider actually taking part in his game, the Furies turn to face us. On the sides of the cavern, the Harpies extend their wings and ruffle them until the Furies have finished moving.

"You may proceed," the Furies say, then they turn their twitching faces toward Jonas. "But our *brother* must remain here."

26

"I get it," Henry says. "You all had the same sack daddy, but the big serious guy over there is with us now. And we're kind of in a rush. So, you're gonna have to put a pin in playing catch up with your little bro."

"I can speak for myself," Jonas says, and then he addresses the Furies. "What he said."

"Unacceptable," the Furies say.

I sense a conflict building because there's not much real communication happening. This isn't a sitcom, so I step in front of the group and ask, "Why do you want him? If this is because of something your father did or didn't do, Jonas has never—"

"We are not interested in our common parentage," the Furies say. "His soul is saturated in the blood of innocents. He must be judged."

"Vengeance deities," Henry says. "Wait, does this mean I'm clean or whatever? 'Cause I've killed a lot of people." All three Furies turn their heads toward him. "They all had it coming."

Attention shifts back to Jonas, and he catches us all off guard by asking, "How does this work?"

"We will explore your heart and mind. If you are found guilty…the Harpies will feast on your body."

"For all eternity?" Henry asks, sounding hopeful.

"We are not as cruel as your father," the Furies say. "The feast will end when his body is consumed and returned to the earth as excrement."

"Lovely," Jonas says, sheathing his sword. "Let's do it."

I catch his arm. "This is nuts. We can just leave, you know. I don't think they could stop us."

"Been carrying this weight for a long time. People who love me keep telling me that the attacks I carried out during my missing time weren't my fault. That there was nothing I could do about it. Well, here's my chance to confirm it." He steps closer to the Furies. "I'll do it."

"But we're not going anywhere," I say.

"Will you respect our judgement?" they ask.

Every fiber of my being shouts, 'no,' but I'll respect Jonas's wishes. If he needs this, we'll have to take the risk. "Yes."

"Dude," Henry complains. He can't believe what I'm saying.

"Doing the right thing doesn't always involve violence," I say.

"Okay, Yoda. Whatever."

Sarah steps closer to Henry. It's not a lot, but it puts her close enough to stop him if he decides to do something stupid. She gives me a subtle nod.

"Where do you want me?" Jonas asks.

One of the three Furies glides closer, stops, and waits. It's smoky-tendril body flows out around it, twitching and writhing, teeth chattering, lips churning. "Approach."

Jonas steps in front of the Fury and waits.

"I am Tisiphone," the Fury says, its voice still emanating from some unfathomable source.

"She avenges murder," Henry whispers.

"Well," Jonas says, "I always wanted a sister, so, nice to meet you, I guess. Can we just get this over with? What do I need to do?"

"Don't fight it," Tisiphone says. Then the tendrils wriggling from her body go rigid, turn inward, and stab into Jonas's body.

Henry goes stiff, about to spring into action, but Sarah stops him with a gentle touch on his shoulder. Honestly, it's nice to see Henry give a shit. Being fearless doesn't mean he's incapable of caring for people. He clearly adores his sister. But a life on the streets left him short on trust and difficult to win over in any meaningful way.

Jonas's body goes slack as he's lifted up in the air, arms and legs dangling.

"Can you, uhh, can you tell us how it's going?" I ask.

The Furies don't respond, but the Harpies are fluttering their wings again, agitated. Maybe excited. Eager for a meal.

Jonas starts spasming.

The Furies writhe a little faster. Moan a little louder. They might be goddesses of vengeance, but they're definitely getting their kicks from the job, which is made even stranger by the fact that the person in their grasp is also their brother. When in Rome, I guess. Incest, bestiality, and everything in between, above, below, and on both sides was commonplace. Not my jam, but I'm not about to critique the creatures who are literally Jonas's judges, jury, and possible executioners. Different world. Different time. You be you, Furies.

As Jonas is lifted up higher, the Harpies begin singing in harmony again. I get a sense that this is a ritual they've all done before. Harpy winds rise, their voices reaching a crescendo. And then—

—it all stops.

The chorus.

The fluttering wings.

Two of the three Furies glide back.

Jonas is lowered to the ground—unconscious or dead, I can't tell.

"Well?" I ask.

The Furies are just silent. Waiting.

The Harpies emerge from the sides of the cavern, heads bobbing as they move for Jonas.

"Hey," I say.

I'm ignored.

The Harpies close in, gathering around Jonas.

"Hey!" Without really thinking about it, my wings and arm blades extend, filling the air with bright blue light and crackling energy.

"Laser Chicken..." It's Bree. She's scolding me. "'Doing the right thing doesn't always involve violence,' right? That's what you said."

"At least she looks more like Yoda," Henry says.

"Grogu," Bree says. "Yoda is old."

"Grogu is overrated."

Bree crosses her arms, and I sense an actual fight brewing. The Harpies cut it short, singing once more, unfurling their wings around Jonas, hiding him from view as they lower their heads, bobbing up and down.

"Are they...are they eating him?" Sarah asks.

The Harpies flutter their wings and stomp backward, like Kermit the Frog exiting the Muppet Show stage after introducing a new act. Jonas is revealed—on his feet, unharmed, and alive. His eyes blink open. He looks confused.

"When are we starting?" he asks.

"I think you're done, dude," I say, extinguishing my laser wings and blades.

"Jonas, son of Uranus, son of Gaia...brother. We have borne witness to the crimes committed by your body, but we found your mind at the time to be vacant, pliable, and controlled. Furthermore, you confronted those responsible for the murders carried out by your body—and served justice. The matter is closed."

Jonas looks surprised. "Really?"

The Furies just hover and twitch.

"Just like that?" Jonas asks. "You look through my thoughts, and poof, I'm absolved of killing all of those people?"

"It is not our position to offer...emotional counsel," the Furies says. "But your language reveals confusion. *You* were not present at the time the murders were committed. You are far more than your physical form, Polarigios, son of Uranus, the North Star, the cosmos himself."

"Sooo, we can go then?" I ask. "All of us?"

Tisiphone tilts her head forward.

Then all three Furies glide away, back into the shadows. Their twisting tendrils wrap around them, cloaking them in living darkness before they fade from view.

"Twenty bucks says they're just sitting there in the dark, waiting for us to leave." Henry moves to have a look for himself when a wall of feathers snaps up in front of him. The Harpies have closed in and blocked the way. Henry might be right, but they're not about to let him have a peek behind the curtain.

Our backpack is flung by one of the Harpies, hard enough to knock down a brick wall. Henry catches it, slips it over his back, snaps his fingers, and points at the Harpies. "In case it wasn't obvious before, seriously nice ti—"

Sarah slaps the back of his head. "No! Nnnno!"

"Geez," he says, rubbing his head, while moving toward the cave exit. "I was going to compliment them."

"No one wants to hear what you think of their bodies," Sarah says.

"But they're half bird," Henry says. "And kind of fugly. Thought they might need a self-esteem boost."

"Uh-huh."

Henry grins, mischievous. The Harpies' self-esteem never crossed his mind.

"For the record," Sarah says, "next time you cop a feel, human or mythical creature... You know what, if I just catch you milking a freaking cow, I will kick your ass."

Their banter continues as they take the lead. I'm about to ask Bree how she's doing. That was a lot to absorb, even for me. She leaps up onto my back, clinging effortlessly. I place my arms under her legs, holding her up. Message received. She doesn't want to talk about it. She's seen some scary shit, but this is different. These things aren't from another world. They live, just beneath the surface of our own. Kind of a mind screw.

"You okay?" I ask Jonas.

He actually smiles. "Pretty good, actually. Feels like a weight has been lifted."

I can tell. He looks happier. Less intense. He's kind of a sarcastic guy, but there's usually an intensity just beneath the surface, or a mile above it. Guilt can have that effect on people. I'm pretty psyched at how our little side quest turned out...you know, rather than him being eaten alive by a trio of Harpies.

Henry and Sarah reach the cave entrance and pause on the steps, waiting as Jonas approaches. Henry is smiling, which isn't always a good thing. Then he mimics the Furies. "'Polarigios, son of Uranus, the North Star, the cosmos himself.'" He chuckles. "Did you know that your mother was also your *father's* mother, making you your father's brother? That's some backwoods Mississippi shit right there. If you got extra toes or something, mystery solved."

Jonas stands still for a moment. Then smiles. Then he busts up laughing, letting out a lot of bottled-up emotional energy. "Oh man. That's funny. Our families..."

"Right?" Henry says.

Jonas steps to the edge of the pit, looking down. He turns around, smile on his face, and says, "New plan. We're taking the express elevator." He raises his eyebrows twice and then leaps over the edge.

27

Jonas plummets into the haze, doing nothing to slow his descent. He's in a free fall. In twelve seconds, he'll reach terminal velocity for a human being—120 miles per hour. For most people, that journey would end with a very wet splat. For Jonas—I have no idea. According to him, he can't fly. But maybe telekinesis will help him stick the landing.

Only one way to find out. I hold my arms up. "Come around."

Without returning to the ground, Bree slides from my back to my chest. "This is awesome," she squeals.

I'm not sure I agree, but even if I was psyched to leap into the unknown, Bree's breath in her demon form smells like Satan's hardboiled-egg diarrhea. I try not to breathe through my nose, and I attempt to hide my revulsion. "Uh-huh. Hold on tight."

She clings a little tighter.

"Do we have to do this?" Sarah asks, and I get why.

She can't fly.

Needs to be carried.

On its own, for a proud independent woman like Sarah, being helpless is humiliating. But being carried by Henry? That's borderline unbearable.

"Shouldn't have chosen god of the Earth," Henry says. "Hard to beat flying."

"You'd have wanted two gods of the sky?" she asks.

"Well, no. We'd probably have to kill each other at some point, right?"

Sarah sighs. She stands in front of Henry and places her left arm and shield over his shoulder and onto his back. "If I feel any of your wily little digits out of place, I will remove them."

"Okay," Henry says. "Sure... By wily digits you mean—"

"I mean, if your impulsive brain wonders what my ass feels like and your hand absentmindedly slides onto one of my two cheeks, I will skewer you like chicken satay."

"Mmm," Henry says. "Now I want Thai food."

"I'm serious," she says.

"You're my *sister*," he says. "I would never—"

She gives him a look, refuting his claim.

"Okay, I might. But up here I don't want to." He taps his head. "I'm not a total perv, you know. I just don't always get a chance to think before I do something stupid."

"I know," she says. "But this time, try extra hard."

He nods.

Taking her seriously.

"I will."

She gives him a nod, and he scoops her up in his arms. He's shorter than her. Skinnier than her. But his supernatural strength allows him to hold her effortlessly. She rests on his forearms, his hands held out straight rather than holding on. He wiggles them around. "See? My feelers are off duty."

"Just... Let's go."

"Don't need to tell me twice," Henry says, and he leaps over the edge. A second later, they fade from view, concealed by the luminous mist.

With everyone gone, I lean back a little and ask, "You good?"

Bree just nods.

"That was a lot to take in," I say. "You sure?"

Another silent nod.

"Feeling upset about things isn't a weakness," I say. "It's normal. It's part of what makes us human."

"But we're not," she says. "Human. Not really. Not anymore."

"DNA doesn't define our humanity. Our hearts do. What's in here matters most." I rub my chest.

She smiles. "You get that from a Hallmark Card?"

"That's a Miah original."

"Well, maybe you should write cards. If the whole Laser Chicken thing doesn't pan out."

I let myself chuckle, and then say, "Any time you need to talk about all this, or even cry about what's happening, you let me know, and we'll find a quiet place okay? Just you and me."

"You're a bigger crybaby than I am," she says. "So…same to you."

I nod. "We can cry together."

"Just two broken people with PTSD," she says, wistfully, "crying in the corner, smoking doobies, and eating sandwiches."

"You know me too well," I say. "Ready?"

She nods and clings a little tighter. It's weird, having a heart-to-heart with Bree while she's in demon form. Her normally spunky self is usually in overdrive, but she's taking in a lot of otherworldly horseshit, and she's still just a kid who has no business being in the underworld. "Let's do this."

My wings buzz, extending from my back. We've done this before. She knows not to touch them, but it makes me nervous every time. I step up to the edge, look down into the abyss, and jump.

We glide gently downward, my wings illuminating the walls around us. The carvings reveal endless pictographic stories of wars, torture, monsters, and mayhem. I thought taking the drop slowly might help calm both our nerves, but it's really just reminding us that the Harpies and Furies are probably the nicest things we'll encounter down here.

"Can we take the express elevator, too?" Bree asks.

"Yeah," I say, and I do my best Private Hudson impression. "Express elevator to Khaos, going down!"

My wings retract and gravity yanks us downward.

Bree holds on tighter, nearly digging her claws into my back, but she shouts, "Whoohoo!" as we fall.

We descend for longer than feels possible. On the way down, the air warms and the glow shifts to a hue of hellish orange. At least it doesn't smell bad. Kind of earthy, but also fresh. Like beach air, sans the sun. My ears pop twice on the way down.

Bree's too. She stretches her jaw. "Should have brought some bubble gum."

Traveling at a hundred twenty miles-per-hour, the floor races toward us. My wings extend, humming and pulsing loudly as they exert energy to slow us down. There was a time when I lacked the lightning-fast reflexes required to not pancake at the bottom of the pit, but since I can fly a hell of a lot faster than this, I'm able to slow us down and gently place Bree on the floor.

She claps her hands. "That was awesome!"

"Right?" Henry says. "We need to get you some demon wings or something."

Henry loves flying. Of that, there is no doubt. But I can't help wondering if he's missing out. He's capable of excitement, like a WWE wrestler all jazzed before a match. But the adrenaline from something like skydiving is beyond his reach or understanding. Because without fear, the amygdala doesn't trigger the release of adrenaline. He enjoys the speed. The wind. The feeling of power. But his heart rate probably doesn't increase, and he never feels the exhilaration that comes after a close call with the Grim Reaper.

He's willing and able to do things most people wouldn't dare, but he's not getting the full experience.

Sarah's nearby, shield and spear held low, exploring the bottom of the pit. The floor is composed of large stone blocks decorated here and there by bodies—skeletons mostly—that appear to have taken the express elevator without brakes.

Bree scrambles over to one of the dead and inspects the skull. "Cracked like an egg." She picks up the skull. "I'm going to call him Dumpty."

"That's a weird name," Henry says.

"If I called him Humpty," Bree says, placing the skull back down, "you'd make a bunch of dirty jokes."

Henry purses his lips and nods. "For sure."

There are eight identical arched exits. The only difference between them is a lone symbol etched into the keystone of each stone archway. In some ways, they're similar to the runes covering the hell gates, but they lack that old Norse vibe.

"Know what they mean?" I ask.

"Not a clue," Sarah says. "But they feel old."

"I could just zip down each tunnel and come back," Henry says.

It's an option, but it's not ideal. "I'd rather suss out a logical choice before launching an impulsive missile through the underworld."

"Did you really just say 'suss'?" Henry asks.

"It's a word," I say.

"Yeah...but..."

I turn to Sarah, looking for backup.

She gives me the hand and shakes her head. "I'm with Henry on this one."

"You all talk like you're an improv crew on stage in front of a geriatric audience." Jonas emerges from one of the eight tunnels, his guard down. The pit's only guardian is gravity.

"Huh?" Henry says.

"Loud," Jonas says. "You're loud."

"Any ideas?" I ask.

He points to the tunnel from which he emerged. "That way."

"...Why?" I ask.

His index finger rises to the keystone. The symbol etched into the stone is simple. Two vertical lines. Looks like someone might have carved a circle around it at some point, but it's mostly worn away. "That's what they looked like, right? The gates. Two columns? If we're looking for a gateway to another planet, that seems like a good place to start."

28

"Is it just me or is it starting to smell like the Texas panhandle in here?" Henry looks back at the rest of us. He's been in the lead since we entered the tunnel, not out of bravery, but because he's totally jazzed about this trip, and he's eager to see what comes next. If Sarah wasn't constantly reminding him to stay in sight, we'd probably never see him again.

"I don't know what that means," Bree says.

"Cow shit," Henry says.

"Like a farm," Jonas adds. "And it doesn't smell like cow shit. Smells like horse shit."

"Like there's a difference," Henry says.

"Cows have spots," Bree says.

Henry crosses his arms and faces his mental opponent. "Some horses have spots."

"Cows have four stomachs," Bree says.

Henry's face scrunches up. "Wait, really?"

"Mm-hmm." Bree grins. Round one and she's already got him on the ropes. "They chew their food and swallow it, saving it for later. Then they barf it back into their mouths and chew it again. That's chud."

"Cud," I say.

"That's what I said." Bree waves a hand at me, shushing me. "They chew the cud and swallow it again."

"Okay, so cows are grosser."

"They also have big ol' tiddies," Bree says, snickering while the rest of us fail to contain our guffaws.

"Kid knows how to get a laugh," Jonas says. We're at the back of the group, behind Sarah and Bree. My instinct is to be up with Henry, facing danger head-on, but Jonas pointed out that that doesn't always make strategic sense. Being behind the group not only protects the others from attacks from behind—traditionally the most dangerous—but also allows us to keep track of everyone. He also pointed out that having Henry in the lead is like attaching a snowplow to a truck. He's going to crash through anything that gets in our way, giving us plenty of time to react.

"Not as big as whales," Bree says. "Their boobs are bigger than Miah."

"Speaking of whales," Henry says, pausing at a rise ahead. He peeks over the top and then turns around. "Do you know what to do if you find a baby whale?"

Bree shakes her head.

"Call the Aquarium," Henry says. "My friend Jay and I were out in Boston Harbor a few years back. We stole a boat to try catching fish. Because we were hungry, right? Anyway, so we're out there in the ocean, and there's this baby fuckin' whale. I swear to god. Never seen anything like it. And I'm like, 'Jay! Jay! We need to call the Aquarium!' It was awesome. Got the whole thing on video."

Jonas snaps his fingers, and then places his index finger to his lips.

We fall silent, listening for ten seconds before a sound, like someone giving someone else a raspberry, cuts through the air. It's distant. Echoed. But a clear sign of company.

Jonas points at Henry, then two fingers at his own eyes, and then forward again toward the top of the inclined tunnel ahead. He makes taking charge look effortless, and his confidence inspires Henry to actually listen, rather than blaze his own path forward.

Henry nods, ducks down, and climbs the rise a little higher. Peeks over the top for a moment and then turns, mouth agape and somehow smiling at the same time. He points back over his shoulder and says, "Oh. My. God. You guys gotta see this."

"Dangerous?" I ask.

He shakes his head. "I don't think so, but I wouldn't know anyway, right?"

"I'll check it out," I say, and I head up the incline. It's steep, forcing me onto my hands and feet, but it's jagged. Easy to scale. Henry waits at the top, beaming.

When I get close, he asks, "Can I ride one?"

"Ride one?" I ask, and when I have a look for myself, I understand.

The cavern ahead opens into a vast subterranean realm, glowing with yellow light that sparkles off lush, green…something. Reminds me of tall grass and looks like long, curly gummy worms. But the Jolly Green Giant pubes are hardly the main attraction.

A waterfall surges out of the wall, far away on the cavern's right side. Strange fruit-bearing trees stand tall and lush. Butterflies flutter. The air sparkles.

And standing at the center of all this magic…is a centaur.

The horse, with a torso of a man, stands with his back to us, hoof gently stomping. He's got a fistful of the green growth. Casually raises it to his mouth. Takes a bite and chews. Not a care in the world.

"You see?" Henry asks. "Please let me ride him."

The centaur cocks its head to the side. Turns its head. Spots us. It's not surprised or upset. For a moment, it just chews, staring at us, indifferent to our appearance. Then it lets us know exactly what it thinks of us, lifting its tail and taking a fibrous shit that breaks apart and thumps on the ground. When it's done, the creature scrapes the ground with its hind legs, gives us a solid glower, and blows a horse-snort using his thick lips. It trots away all prim and proper like a show horse.

I turn back to the others. "I think we found the underworld's hoity toity neighborhood."

They join us at the cavern's entrance, and for a full three minutes, no one says a word. There's a lot to take in. Scurrying creatures. Flowers blowing in a breeze that smells like a farm. Fresher than expected after the scent lingering in the tunnel behind us. Birds flit through the air. It's kind of a paradise.

The cavern is huge. I can't see the ceiling. It's concealed behind a yellow luminous haze that lights everything in perpetual daylight. It must somehow emit ultraviolet, because the plants are growing green, and I feel a slight tingle on my skin, like I do at the beach in the summer. Going to be tan by the time we reach the other end and exit—assuming that's where the exit is. We could be here for a while, trying to find our way out.

And I don't have a while. We haven't been gone long, but our families are definitely wondering where we are, and if they inspect Henry and

Sarah's house well enough to find the giant hole punched through the kitchen wall, they're going to freak.

They've been traumatized enough. They don't need to think we've been abducted by aliens or something. At least Jen knows the truth. She'll probably tell Mom and the others. But that won't alleviate their concern when we don't come home, and Bree's mother, Steph... She's already disturbed. Bree disappearing might land her in a padded cell.

"Well," Sarah says. "This doesn't look so bad."

"Most car accidents happen within a mile of people's homes," I blurt out.

Sarah looks at me like I've just squeaked out a fart. "Point being?"

Jonas draws his sword. "Don't let your guard down."

Henry draws his sword, mimicking Jonas. "Also, looks can be deceiving. Like me. I look like a scrawny homeless kid. No one would ever suspect I don't feel fear."

"Or...that you're a god," Bree says.

"Right! That, too!" Henry moves deeper into the cavern, searching. "A god who rides a centaur. I'm going to name him...Staggering. Staggering Wind, the fat-assed centaur, prancing around like he fucking owns the place."

"That's...horrible," Sarah says.

"Wait, are there female centaurs? Or are they all dudes?" Henry wanders deeper into the cavern, forcing the rest of us to keep pace. "Because if there are female—"

"Inside thoughts!" Sarah shouts. It's a phrase she uses on occasion when Henry is thinking out loud, and thanks to his lacking a filter, he verbalizes the wild direction in which an unfettered young man's mind wanders. It can be funny, but it's more often shocking. Henry purses his lips, but no doubt continues his pondering on the availability of equine hoochie-mamas and whether they'd have nicer boobs than Harpies, Furies, cows, and blue whales.

Bree uses the open field to burn off some energy, racing around us on all fours. She leaps into a fruit tree, scaling the trunk and leaping up into the branches. The tree shakes, Bree says, "Ooooh," and then she explodes out of the top, landing in the curly grass with five pieces of fruit in her arms. She tosses one to each of us, and before I can stop her, she takes a bite.

She chews the crisp, yellow fruit loudly, letting the juice run over her charred chin. "Mmm. Appley."

Henry takes a bite and chews, wandering forward.

Jonas smells the fruit, shrugs, and takes a bite.

"Hey," Sarah says to Henry. When he turns, she tosses him her piece of fruit. "Don't like apples," she tells me.

"Tastes like a sweeter Asian pear," Jonas says, taking another bite.

My stomach churns. "I'm definitely hungry..."

"Isn't there food in the backpack?" Sarah asks. "We went to all that trouble to get it back, and we haven't even looked in it yet."

She's right about that. "Guess I've been distracted."

"Well, give it to me and I'll have a look while you all pretend it's apple picking season."

"It *is* apple picking season," I say. "Back home."

Sarah sighs and takes the backpack from Jonas, who inherited it from Henry. Jonas takes another bite, and he looks so enamored by the flavor of it that I can't resist.

I take a bite.

It's crisp and juicy, and it's strangely complex. Feels like a Michelin-star restaurant dessert, like the kind that would come in a little cup, with stringy sugar placed precariously on top.

I scarf down several more bites, each one better than the last. Feeling better than I have in a long time, two thoughts enter my head.

The first is, *Sarah is really missing out.*

The second is, *How the hell did I end up on the ground?*

29

David Lee Roth singing "This must be just like living in paradise," fades as I open my eyes. I smile, enjoying the dream soundtrack, as the world around me comes into blurry view.

I'm on my back, staring up at the luminous yellow sky. Trees sway in the horse manure-scented breeze, the rustling amplified. With each gust of wind, rainbow swirls flit from the branches, carrying naked newborn babies sucking their thumbs, humming along with David Lee Roth.

"Babies!" I say with a chuckle. I reach my hands out to them, but their ethereal bodies pass through my fingers. "Nooo. Babies! Don't go."

All at once, the babies stand to their feet and start dancing the cha-cha like that meme from 1996. "Oh my god," I say. "Am I Ally McBeal? Is my biological clock ticking? I want to have babies!"

Desperate sadness washes through me.

I weep.

"I want babies!" I pound my fists into the curly grass around me. "I want to get married to Jen. And have a family. I don't want to be Laser Chicken. I don't want to save the world. I hate fighting!" I point to the yellow glow above. "You hear me? I'm a lover, not a fighter!" My bluster dissolves. "I just...I want to go home. David Lee Roth is wrong. I *do* want to go home!"

Sparkles drift past, distracting me. I trace them back to their source and find a female centaur standing beside a river fueled by the waterfall flowing out of a nearby stone wall. She swings her head around. Her hair flows through the air like she's underwater. She makes eyes at me, biting her lower lip.

"Oookay..."

She turns toward me, revealing that yes, female centaurs also don't wear clothing.

"What's with the underworld's half-human babes not wearing clothing?" I ask.

"Gotta flaunt what they got, man."

I rotate my head to find Henry lying in the grass beside me.

"Like, if you've got a horse's ass, show the boobs. If you have a bird body, show the boobs. If you're a smoke monster with boobs..."

"Show the boobs!" I say. "I get it."

"Makes total sense, right?"

"You two are the biggest boobs here," Jonas says, sitting up on my other side. He looks around, taking in the scenery, shaking his head. "There isn't a female centaur." He lifts his hand, slowly waving it back and forth. It dissolves and reforms every time he changes direction. "We're tripping balls."

I look back to the river. The centaur babe is gone.

"Whoa," Henry says. "We were having the same hallucination! That's so cool."

"Oh man," I say, holding my head. "I don't like hallucinogens."

"I thought you were, like, the druggie dude," Henry says.

"Marijuana," I say. "To help with PTSD...and have a chill time...but I don't mess with the mind-bendy stuff. My mind tends to go to dark places."

"Like babies," Henry says, on his feet, spinning in circles. "Everything is blending!"

I'm too out of my head to feel embarrassed that the two of them heard me.

"If it makes you feel better," Jonas says, climbing to his feet, "I'm seeing a rhinoceros in a tutu and ballet slippers."

"Oooh," Henry says. "Is there music? Is it like Fantasia?"

"Yuuup." Jonas gets to his feet.

"Jonas," Bubbles says from the watch. "Your heart rate is elevated. You've been poisoned. You're not safe. If you can, I suggest vomiting, or at the very—*chirp!*—least, drinking—*ass juice from a carton! On the side, Little Billy is missing! Mmm. Yum!*—as much water as you can. Flush your system. Failing to do so could result in—"

Jonas tilts to the side, stumbles a few steps to the left, and then face-plants back on the ground. After a moment, Henry and I burst into laughter.

"This isn't good," Jonas mumbles through a mouth full of pubic grass. "We're incapaciflated. Inflaplinated. You know what I'm trying to say."

He's right. We're blazed.

But not all of us. "Sarah didn't eat the fruit."

"I don't see her anywhere," Henry says, still spinning in circles.

"I wasn't able to locate her," Bubbles says. "It's possible she was taken first."

"Ohh!" Henry says. "But I do see Bret Michaels riding a giant kitten! This is wicked awesome!"

Henry stops spinning, but it only takes a moment for momentum to keep pulling him, his mind both warped and dizzy. He spins twice, as he flops to the ground, and then he keeps rolling. "I'm a lawnmower."

"Hey," a small voice says. I look down to find an adorable, brown, spiky creature. My awareness of the world around me narrows so I'm just seeing and hearing this little dude. Its long nose twitches at me, and in a surprisingly gruff Australian accent it says, "What the hell, man?"

"You can talk?" I ask him.

"Obviously," it says, scratching its belly with its long, made-for-digging claws.

"What...are you?"

"I'm an echidna. A quill-covered monotreme. Means I lay eggs. Like a platypus. And I secrete pink milk, in my pouch, on account of my species not having teats. So, I'm kind of a freak, but none of that is important."

"Are you my spirit animal?" I ask.

"Sure," it says. "Let's go with that."

"What's your name?" I ask.

"Mr. Prickles."

"Mr. Prickles, are you going to reveal my inner truth?"

"Nah, mate. I'm trying to save the lives of four bogans."

"Four bogans... What's a bogan?"

"You are, mate. Lying around like you've had a dozen coldies while danger lurks just around the corner."

"Danger?"

"Big fuckin' thing," he says. "With one eye."

"A cyclops?" I ask, willing myself to sober up and failing.

"It was stomping around, trying to catch a horse."

"You mean a centaur?" I ask.

"What?" He's aghast. "No. A fuckin' horse. Think I wouldn't know a centaur if I saw one? This one-eyed drongo was all aggro, carrying around a cleaver the size of a windscreen. Pretty sure he caught the horse, because *ough*, strewth, did it make a racket. Until it didn't...if you catch my meaning."

"How can I catch a meaning?" I ask. "Aren't they totally, like, immaterial?"

Mr. Prickles puts his head in his hands. "Fuck me dead..."

"No, thank you."

He scrabbles closer, his stubby legs not very effective in the tall grass. Then he hauls back and slaps me across the cheek. "Listen fuckwit, if you don't snap out of it, and soon, you're all going to—"

The ground shakes beneath me.

"Too late," Mr. Prickles says. "You're right fucked now."

I look for Jonas and Henry, hoping at least one of us will be able to put up a fight. But they're out cold again. Moving got their blood flowing, increased the effect. If I try to move, the same thing will happen to me. Despite Mr. Prickles's insistence that I get up and do something, the best thing I can do is wait.

Mr. Prickles climbs up on my chest. "You're forgetting something." He shoves my chin, forcing me to look up. I come face to face with an unconscious Bree, still in demon form. She's helpless, too, her small body probably even more profoundly affected by the mythical hallucinogenic fruit.

I try to push myself up, but I can't.

A shadow falls over me. The cyclops.

It's twenty feet tall and built like a Neanderthal. While the thing is buck naked, it's also hairy enough that anything embarrassing is covered by a black rug. The creature's one massive eye swivels toward each of us like a living Eye of Sauron.

"It's deciding who goes first," Mr. Prickles says. "You need to give it a reason to choose you, or it's going to take someone else, and they're not awake to fight back."

"I can't move," I say.

"Not yet," he says. "But you will. Listen, dickhead, I know you're out of your head a bit. So why don't you let me do this for you, okay?"

"You can do that?" I ask.

He nods, and I give him a thumbs up.

Mr. Prickles leaps up, puts his little hands together, and dives–into my chest. He burrows through skin and sternum until he's inside my body. Then a voice that doesn't belong to me pops from my mouth. "Oi! One-eyed fuckstick! When you're done having a wank over your mummy, why don't you–whoa!"

The cyclops grasps me by the ankles and lifts me off the ground. I'm carried away from the others, upside down with a view of the river where fish swim, dance, and leap out while frogs spray water back and forth like fountains.

Deep in the recesses of my mind, I know things are bad. That nothing good happens at the end of this journey, but I can't help but enjoy myself.

"Whoo!"

30

My hallucination comes to an abrupt halt when I'm tossed against a stone wall and knocked unconscious.

When I wake up, I'm not sure how much time has passed. Doesn't feel like very long, but I'm not in the best condition to judge much of anything. I'm not seeing things anymore. Don't feel Mr. Prickles possessing me. Gonna miss that guy. But my body is depleted. More than that, actually, I feel paralyzed.

I manage to twitch a single finger and blink a few times, but that's it.

I'm helpless.

Without moving my head—because I can't—I glance back and forth, taking in my surroundings. First and most obvious observation is that I'm upside down. Feels like my ankles are bound, and the way I'm slowly turning leads me to believe that I'm hanging from the ceiling, like meat in a butcher shop.

And that's the moment I remember the cleaver-wielding cyclops.

I will my body to move, and my lungs to scream, but I can't do a damn thing.

Panic makes me hyper aware. I'm in a dimly lit cave, scant yellow light streaming in from the entrance fifty feet away. The luminous fog is apparently not welcome here—or simply can't penetrate the thick air, which is full of humidity and the smell of blood, bile, and shit.

I slow my breathing, practicing anxiety-reducing techniques I haven't needed in months. In for five seconds, hold for five seconds, release for five seconds. I do this three times, willing my thoughts to clear. But the mythological roofie is keeping things hazy.

As I adjust to the darkness, details come into focus. I'm fifteen feet up with a clear view of what lies below...and I wish I wasn't. A nearby alcove holds dozens of horse heads in various stages of decay—from skeletal to fresh. Another alcove hides a pit, around which are mounds of oversized shit and puddles of what I'm pretty sure is piss—the cyclops's pit toilet.

None of that holds my attention nearly as much as the stone table at the cave's core. It's ringed by a trough that leads to one end and then out through the edge. The floor beneath it is stained dark red. I've seen something like this before. At America's Stonehenge in New Hampshire. It's a sacrificial altar.

But I'm not sure that's an accurate description. There are tables surrounding the altar, and they're covered in tools. Saws. Blades. Jars of ointment. Large needles and spools of thick thread hold my attention for a moment. *The hell?*

My first impression is of an operating room, but it has more of a handyman workshop vibe.

The cyclops is building things.

I glance back at the horse heads. Not a body in sight.

Can't be...

Then I rotate a little bit farther and spot an alcove across from the horse head depository. It's full of legs—from the waist down. Human legs.

Shit. Shit, shit, shit.

The cyclops is building centaurs.

A grunt pulls my eyes toward the entrance. The cyclops thumps into the cave, its hairy head just a few feet below the ceiling. It drags an unconscious horse behind it.

Doesn't take a lot of imagination to see where this is going. The horse is going to lose its head. I'm going to lose my legs...and my man business. Then we're going to be sewn together. But will that work? We'll both be dead.

Unless there's some magic involved.

Unless...Linda was telling the truth about the gods. That's they're really just human-like species from other worlds, where technology has been developing for thousands, if not millions, of years longer than it has on Earth. I've heard about mice growing human ears and humans getting pig heart implants. How much longer until we'll be sewing disparate species together to create our own mythological creatures?

The real question is, when I'm half horse, will I still be me?

I think back to the centaur we encountered at the cavern's entrance. It was prim and proper, totally accepting of its place in this world, but it was also...vacant. Lacking a personality. It just existed... Just populated this world, ruled by a cycloptic master. The trauma of being hacked in half and attached to an animal is probably enough to break anyone's mind.

Make them submissive. Pliable. Like living dolls.

We're its playthings, I think. Or its companions... Or... God... This is all ancient myth made real. I can't discount the possibility that the cyclops is creating...partners. I'm getting really tired of overly sexualized myths. You'd think these ancient civilizations would have evolved beyond reproductive pleasure.

Below, the horse regains consciousness and must understand the situation, because it whinnies and kicks, trying to roll back to its feet. A backhanded punch dents the side of its head and knocks the beast unconscious.

With one hand, the cyclops lifts the horse by its mane and lays it on the table. He's strong, which makes sense, given his size. But he doesn't even strain to lift the seven-hundred-pound horse. I've been known to grunt when picking up Sanchez.

The cyclops mumbles something that sounds like a prayer or a blessing. Something sacred. Important. Then it raises the cleaver and swings it down. The blade must be razor sharp, because it doesn't take much effort to cleanly sever the horse's head and neck.

The head is discarded, tossed into the alcove with the rest. Blood flows from the body, oozing down the trough and draining onto the floor. The cyclops tosses a handful of grit over the body's exposed meat, like some kind of Internet chef seasoning a steak. The granules dissolve on contact, spreading out to form a kind of protective shell that prevents any more blood from spilling out.

His big eye swivels toward me.

I'm expecting some kind of malevolent sneer, but he's emotionless. Just another day at the factory, making toys for—

Someone else, I realize.

"You..." I manage to croak. "Don't...have to...do this."

He frowns.

Goes about organizing his supplies.

"Please..." I say. "I don't...want to be...a centaur."

"No one ever does," he grumbles.

"You...speak...English?" It occurs to me then that the Harpies also used English to communicate.

"Language is irrelevant here," he says, and he doesn't bother elaborating to the man he's about to cleave in half and sew to a horse.

"Listen..." I manage to wiggle a few more fingers. "If you...don't want to do this..." He rolls his lone eye, digs his big hand into a pot, and lifts out a wad of yellow goo. I see what's about to happen, and I speak quickly, "Whatever is controlling you, we can—hrmff!" He smears the goo over my mouth, and I'm suddenly like Mr. Anderson in *The Matrix*, being interviewed by Agent Smith, unable to open my mouth.

I fight with everything I've got, and I don't even manage a wiggle.

He reaches up and plucks me from a hook embedded in the ceiling.

I'm placed on the table beside the horse's body. The cyclops lays me on my side, repositioning me so that my waist aligns with the stump of a neck.

"There is a point in a horse's neck, where the vertebra is roughly the same size as the largest human vertebra, making it the ideal place for fusion to occur. When we're finished, you will have full control of your new body—and it will hurt...for quite some time. But when you've healed, you will be stronger and more virile than—"

"Vrrl?" I mumble.

The cyclops grins. "We're all prisoners here. But there is no fate more ...challenging than yours. Like all steeds, you'll be expected to perform for our captor. And if you don't...you'll find your way back to me...in my feeding trough."

Two things. First, this is fucked up. Beyond fucked up. When you learn about Greek and Roman history, you take it with a grain of salt. Caesars with leaf headgear? Check. Gladiators? Hell to the yes. Weird-ass nude baths? No problem. But the freakshow pleasures enjoyed by the gods and those who worshiped them... Bestiality. Incest. Sex with damn clouds. Romulus and Remus suckling from a giant wolf? You just kind of write it off to legend. Embellishment. Never for a moment, have I, nor any normal person, ever wondered if all that was anything more than the fever dream of some ancient author. I mean, it's hard to imagine the kind of person that would sit around, dreaming up that kind of shit, but it's more believable than it being *true*.

Second thing, this cyclops is pretty fucking smart.

He has a good vocabulary at least. Seems to have a detailed understanding of anatomy and how to conjoin separate species.

Because he's an alien, I remind myself. Or, at least, a creation of them. Hard to keep track of who made who and who gave birth to what.

"Embrace it," he says. "It's all you can do."

The cleaver rises above his head.

He whispers that same offering.

I close my eyes and listen to the cleaver whoosh toward my waist.

31

Metal clangs against stone.

I peek with a single eye. The cyclops stands above me, looking at the cleaver like it has betrayed him. He...missed?

That doesn't seem likely.

I was an easy target, lying still, just beneath him.

But...I'm not beneath him. Not anymore. I'm still lying atop the altar, but the altar and I are ten feet deeper in the cave. Just out of reach.

The cyclops figures it out around the same time I do, spinning around, wielding the cleaver like a weapon.

A silhouette stands in the cave's mouth, feminine and powerful, holding a shield and dory.

Sarah.

She used her control over the earth to move me out of harm's way.

"I don't need to kill you," she says, lifting her hand away from the wall. "You can walk away. I don't give a shit. Bygones and all that." She starts walking toward the cyclops. "But you're probably just like those hack-jobs guarding the entrance. I gave them a chance to leave, too, FYI. I'm not an asshole. The choice was theirs. And now it's yours."

The cyclops growls and stomps toward her. His cleaver drags along the floor, leaving sparks in its wake.

"That's what I thought," Sarah says, and she leaps forward, shield extended, spear cocked back. Just when I think the fight's going to end before it's really begun, the cleaver scrapes off the floor and swings up with surprising speed.

A resounding gong echoes through the cave. Sarah's trajectory shift's ninety degrees toward the wall. When she hits, a cloud of dust explodes into the cave. When it settles, Sarah is gone. I didn't see her duck out of the cloud in either direction. Neither did the cyclops. It spins around, searching for her, but she's just...gone.

The cyclops's big eye looks to me for an explanation.

I hum the words, "Don't look at me."

He reaches down and peels the goo—which had hardened—away from my face. I shout in pain as my five o'clock shadow gets ripped away.

"What is she?" he asks.

"God damn, man, that hurt."

He leans in close. Roars in my face, slathering it with strands of flagellating drool.

"She's...more than you can handle," I say. "You should probably take her offer and just leave. Seriously."

He scoffs.

"Zeus is her father," I say, hoping to intimidate him.

His eye widens just a touch. "And her mother?"

"A demi-god," I say, and then I lay on the ancient Greek myth part of it all. "Descended from Zeus."

He seems to understand what that means. Sarah's godhood traces back to Zeus on both sides of the family—which I'm pretty sure isn't common even among the gods. She has the same potential as the King of the gods, even if she hasn't yet fully reached it. She's only known about her lineage for a short time. She's still learning what she can do. Her disappearing act suggests she's learned a few new tricks—or old tricks she was keeping secret.

"*Zeus,*" he grumbles, apparently not a fan. "And you?"

"Me? Hundred percent USDA Grade A human being. Well, maybe not a hundred percent. Not anymore. You know what? I don't really know. But I'm—"

"Silence," he says, stopping me from distracting him further. What he's failed to notice is that I'm talking just fine now. The apple's paralytic effect is wearing off. All my fingers can move. Toes, too. It's not enough to help, but maybe soon.

When the cyclops turns his back to me, the stone table glides further away from him, coming apart and reforming like a wave of stone. When he turns back, his lone brow furrows. I'm ten feet farther away.

"She cares for you," he says.

"Well, yeah. But just like friends. Teammates, I guess. Don't get the wrong—"

He lifts the cleaver over his head, charging toward me, back to the task of cutting me in half—though I get the sense that the strike will be less precise, and I won't be sewn to a horse afterward. Fine by me. Death is probably preferable to being an underworld centaur slave.

As the blade arcs up over his head, the ceiling explodes. Sarah descends like a ground-penetrating missile, deflecting the cleaver with her shield. She lands between me and the cyclops, poised for combat, shield raised, dory notched.

It's epic.

She glances at me. "Can you move?"

"Would if I could," I say. "But getting there."

"You fancy yourself a Spartan, girl?" the cyclops says.

Sarah glowers over the shield. "Come find out."

The cyclops sneers and takes the bait, swinging hard. Sarah plants her feet and blocks the blow with her shield. The impact, which would have knocked a normal person into the stratosphere, barely moves her.

The cyclops grimaces as it pulls the blade back. Probably felt like hitting a boulder with a baseball bat, all that kinetic energy vibrating up through his arm.

Undeterred, the cyclops swings again, this time with the cleaver's flat edge, using it like a cricket bat. Instead of blocking the strike and risking being flung into another wall, Sarah ducks.

As the blade whooshes over her, she spins around and to the side, thrusting her dory out. The needle-sharp spear tip punches through the cyclops's shin.

The monster howls and yanks its leg away.

But Sarah isn't done yet. She spins around the other way and repeats the attack, punching a hole in the opposite leg's thigh.

The cyclops roars and stumbles back.

In the grand scheme, neither wound is even close to fatal. But they hurt, and that sent a message: Sarah is dangerous.

"Last chance," she says. "Walk away and live."

"There is no fate awaiting me worse than what happens if I walk away."

"I don't think he's here because he wants to be," I say.

"What?" Sarah wasn't expecting that. Fighting and killing a monster isn't much of a moral conundrum, until you realize he's being forced to fight—like a bull in an arena.

Outside the arena, you might root for the bull, but inside, like we are…the alternative is death. If we can't talk him down, Sarah won't have a choice.

"Who's controlling you?" I ask. "We can help you."

"Help me?" His face contorts and he laughs. "A human and a daughter of Zeus? I will run headlong into the jaws of the queen before debasing myself with the likes of you."

"Who is your queen?" I ask.

He's revolted. "The queen of the underworld…is not my queen."

"What is her name?" I shout.

He growls the word, "Echidna," and then charges again.

I have questions for him, but I think the conversation is done. He's out for blood. Swings his cleaver wildly, forcing Sarah to duck and weave so quickly that she doesn't have a chance to counterattack.

I fight against my paralysis, trying to move…anything. My wings would make short work of the cleaver. And then he'd either listen to reason or be an easy target. I manage to wiggle a wrist, but the rest of me feels like a rotting banana in the sun.

Sarah blocks a kick with her shield. The power of it shoves her back. She slides to a stop just in front of the altar.

"Any day now," she says.

"Don't…have much…of a choice," I say, struggling to move.

"Can you pop your wings?" she asks, and it's a solid question.

My wings propel me—not via flapping, but with an energy field I don't understand, but which I control with my thoughts. There's a chance I could fly myself out of here, even if my whole body is flaccid.

"Not sure," I say. "Mayb*eee!*"

She hauls me up and flips me onto my stomach, knocking the air from my lungs. "Do it. When I say."

"What?" I ask, but she's already in motion, charging straight toward the cyclops.

32

Lying on my stomach, hands bound behind my back, I'm feeling a little hogtied, and my view of the fight is reduced to legs—up to Sarah's waist and the cyclops's knees. There's a lot of action. Metal clanging. The cyclops roars. Sarah grunts. It sounds brutal. Like it's anyone's fight still.

Then Sarah says, "Last...chance. You don't need to die."

She's being generous. Kind, even. Jonas probably would have killed the cyclops the first chance he got. I wouldn't call him blood thirsty. Just efficient. Able to quickly deduce who's going to pose a mortal threat if they're allowed to keep breathing, and who is not.

By Jonas's standards, the cyclops qualifies for a rapid dispatch to Hades.

The cleaver lowers into view, bobbing up and down, dripping blood —Sarah's blood—onto the cave floor. The cyclops is injured, too. Its legs are slick. One knee is bent in at an awkward angle. The result of two brawlers going head-to-head.

The cyclops responds with an unintelligible grumble and lifts the cleaver.

That's when I realize Sarah wasn't really being generous. She was making the cyclops feel weak. Insulting its one-eyed manhood. Goading it into attacking head on, which will bring it directly toward her—and me.

"What the hell are you—"

"Gah!" the cyclops shouts, charging.

Sarah does the one thing it's not expecting—dives toward it—curling her body up and rolling into the monster's already injured limbs. The cyclops's booming shout transforms into something like a surprised, "Yoit!" And then it's falling.

Straight.

Toward.

Me.

Fuck.

"Pop your wings!" Sarah shouts, and her plan slaps me across the face.

"Are you serious?!" I shout, but I don't wait for an answer. There isn't time. I'm about to get pancaked by a twenty-foot behemoth, and if he survives the impact, I certainly won't make it through whatever comes next.

I close my eyes and will my wings to expand. Normally doesn't take much thought at all. It's kind of just a feeling, like instinct. When I don't feel them expand, and I don't hear the buzzing of alien energy, I panic, shout, "C'mon!" and visualize the wings extending straight up from my back.

A loud crackling fills the air for just a moment. Then I'm crushed down into the stone altar by the weight of an elephant. Breathing is impossible. I'm completely immobilized. But then I realize *I'm having realizations*, which means I'm not dead. Certainly, would be if I was Miah from a year ago. That scrawny, mostly blazed dude would have been a smear.

Despite that, I'm still helpless, and I still need to breathe.

Long before I get nervous, the weight decreases and then lifts away entirely.

Sarah leans into view beside me. "Still alive?"

"I think that's what the pain means," I say.

She pats my cheek. "That's the spirit. Can you move yet?"

I try to move, but I can't do much more than wiggle my arms like a newborn chick. "The apple's poison is either still working or the big guy broke my back."

"Well, prepare to be humiliated."

"Humiliated? By whaaa–"

She hauls me up and carries me in her arms, like an old timey groom lifting his bride over the threshold.

"I'm wearing a skirt," I remind her. "My masculinity is fairly unflappable."

She smiles down at me, and then starts bouncing me...like a cradled baby. "Poor widdle Miah. I got you, buddy. Have any boo-boos?"

"Okay," I say, managing a smile. "That stings a little. But what about you?" Her shoulder has a gash in it.

"Gods heal quickly," she says. "When they know they're gods. Weird how that works. Back before I knew what I was, I...well, I died. My soul was en route to Hades until Helen intervened. Injuries suck, but once you've been killed and intercepted on your way to the River Styx, buck naked... well, something like this—" She tilts her head at the injury. "—doesn't seem like such a big deal."

"What about the big guy? Is he dead?"

"Very," she says, turning so I can see him.

There's a smoldering basketball-sized hole in his chest. It's charred and cauterized, which explains why I'm not covered in blood...but that doesn't reveal how the hole got there.

"What did *that?*" I ask.

She squints her eyes at me. "You did." Points to the ceiling. "And that."

I follow her gaze up and find a perfectly round hole carved up through the cave.

She carries me closer, and we look up into it.

I'm in shock.

"Looks like it goes on forever."

"All the way to the surface would be my guess." She smiles down at me. "Probably some very confused Italians up there. Hope you didn't fry the Pope."

"Not funny," I say, feeling genuinely concerned that I could have inadvertently hurt someone topside.

"On the plus side, you've got a secret weapon. You been holding out on us?"

"Why would I do that?" I ask. "We're teammates. And friends."

She shrugs and heads for the exit. "People do weird things."

She stops at the cave's exit.

There are two large centaurs lying on the ground.

Both very dead.

She nods toward one of them. "What's all this about?"

Up close and in the light, the scar of where man was merged with horse is easy to see.

"I mean, they're intimidating, I guess," she says. "And they kick like a mother, but their human tops are very...human. They weren't that hard to kill."

I cringe, looking at the centaur's face. In addition to being attached to a horse, the human half has been mutilated in other...stylistic ways. The eyes have been surgically altered to look larger. Its mouth has been severed on the sides, bent up in a permanent, freakish smile, incapable of showing displeasure, even now in death. And the skin has been scarred with a pattern of dots that look like burns.

This was almost me.

The beauty of this chamber teaches a lesson. In the underworld, no matter how beautiful something is—it's out for blood. The journey through Khaos isn't supposed to be fun or easy. It's meant to block a portal to another world, populated by beings who have all but turned their backs on Earth.

"They really didn't want anyone following them, did they?" I ask, and then I add, "The gods. And the Titans."

"Makes you wonder why Jonas's parents would come all the way up through this shithole to give birth to him, and then go all the way back down after he was taken."

"Yeah..." I say, though I'd never really considered it until now. Understanding ancient beings has proven very difficult for me. "The centaurs are playthings, I guess. For Echidna."

"Echidna?"

"That's what he said. Called her his queen. Had no love for her, but definitely feared her more than us. Preferred death to defying her."

Sarah rolls her head. "Well, now I feel bad about killing him."

"I think we did him a favor," I say.

"Was he holding back?"

I shrug. "It's possible."

"Hey, you shrugged."

I kick my feet. "It's wearing off."

She plants me on my feet and slowly lets go. When I start tipping over, she catches me and puts me upright again. I lift my hands, which feel like they're attached to hundred-pound weights, find my equilibrium, and nod for her to let go again. She lifts her hands away and steps back.

I take a few unsteady steps, and then bumble forward, falling again.

Sarah catches me. "You did it!" she says, mocking. "What a big boy. Growing up so quick."

She releases me again. I bobble around, but I stay upright.

"You look like a giant toddler," she says.

"Thanks, mom."

"If you shit yourself, you're out of luck."

"Okay..." I straighten myself up. "I think I'm good enough to move. We should go find the others."

"They should be okay," she says. "I hid them."

"Mmm," I say, not convinced. "The cyclops's fear seemed immediate."

"You think Echidna is *here?*" She searches the area around us like the mother of monsters might leap out from behind some shrubs. The trees are thick outside the cave, but not enough conceal something like Echidna.

I shake my head. "Queens have enforcers for things like that, right?"

"So...something worse than the one-eyed asshole in there?"

"Yeah," I say. "Probably much worse."

"Okay," she says, hoisting her shield. "Let's get the others."

Five minutes later we're standing at the base of a tall tree, looking up. Bree, Jonas, and Henry are lounging in the branches twenty feet up, just chilling. The backpack hangs from one of the low branches.

"Look, all I'm saying is that folding is more efficient," Henry says. "I think a guy like you would appreciate that. But you have to be careful. The quality of the toilet paper matters. If it's the soft stuff, you gotta take it easy. Cause I think they make it softer by packing the fibers or whatever a little less densely. Means it falls apart a lot easier. This one time, I was at Faneuil Hall. Ate some spoiled clam chowder from a bucket outside a seafood restaurant the night before. Hit like a cyclone in my intestines. I nearly dropped trou right next to a street performer with those sticks, those juggling sticks, and unleashed hell right there on the brick sidewalk. But I thought better of it because the first time I did that, I ended up in jail. Anyway, so I get to the public bathroom, Death Star the toilet like it's

Alderaan, and then do my thing, folding the toilet paper. I know, I know, I seem like a buncher, but a lack of fear doesn't mean a lack of common sense. Folding is the superior ass wiping technique, *but*...you have to be wary of the toilet paper. Because if it's soft, like this shit was for some reason I'll never understand, it will rip. When that happens, your finger will poke through and come up looking like a big peanut dipped in milk chocolate. And if it gets under your nail, you'll be smelling that shit for a—"

When it becomes clear that Henry is still loopy and isn't going to stop talking any time soon, Sarah clears her throat.

"Oh, hey!" Henry says. "Where were you guys?"

"Miah!" Bree says, smiling down at me. "I want to hug you!" She pouts, which looks really funny in her demon form, hood up, bunny ears bouncing. "But my arms and legs aren't working."

"Are you bleeding?" Jonas asks, looking down and blinking, like focusing is hard. I ate as much as they did, but I think my near-death experience and my adrenaline spike helped clear my system a little faster.

"Long story," Sarah says. "Right now, we need to get all of you down before—"

A high-pitched, rattling shriek cuts through the air from the direction of the cyclops's cave.

Sarah sighs. "Before that."

33

"Wee!" Bree says, as I carry her down from the high tree branches, gliding through the air on laser wings. We've done this a hundred times, me carrying her through the air, and she enjoys it every time, but I think she's seeing things this time. Her eyes dart back and forth, widening as she gasps at unseen things. Despite being inhuman, her small body is going to be affected by the hallucinogenic apple for a while.

"Try to stay quiet," I whisper, as I place her on the ground. She stands for a moment, raises a finger, and says with a slurred voice, "I think...I'm okay." Then she topples to the side, landing into the springy grass. She rolls around like a dog in snow for the first time, enjoying life.

"Why are we staying quiet?" Henry asks. He's ten feet up, perched on a branch, ready to leap down.

A rattling roar answers, bellowing around us, angry and maybe a little bit sad. *It found the dead centaurs,* I think.

"Riiight," Henry says. "That. But, we're like totally more powerful than anything down here, right? We should be able to take it."

"I mean, he's not wrong," Sarah says.

"Pride goeth before destruction," Jonas mumbles, still high up in the tree, not yet attempting to come down, "and a haughty spirit before a fall."

Henry faceplants into the ground from ten feet up, arms and legs splayed. The earth dents in around him.

Jonas chuckles. "You see?"

Another roar. This time closer.

"We should go," I suggest.

"Just go laser beam it," Sarah says.

"I don't know how I did that."

Bree stops rolling around. "You shot a laser beam?"

"Something like that," I say. "From my back."

"Sick," Henry says, voice muffled, still face down in the grass. He hasn't even attempted moving yet. We're in no shape for a fight.

"We're going to have to carry them all," I say.

Sarah acquiesces. Plucks the backpack from the branch it's hanging on and tosses it to me. "I'll get the two big ones." She points to Bree. "You take her." She snaps at Jonas. "Get your ass down here."

"Oookay," he says, and he just leans back. Jonas seems to hit every branch on the way down. The first two he shatters on impact. The last few flip him back and forth, sending him toppling toward the ground like he's just completed a round on the uneven bars. Just before he lands beside Henry, his hands snap out, and he stops, hovering just a few inches above the ground. Saved by muscle memory...and telekinesis.

"Oooh," Bree says, looking up at something that doesn't exist. "Pretty."

I slip the backpack over my shoulders and reach my hands down to her. "Try to reach."

She blinks her big eyes and then lifts her arms slowly. It's a start. I take hold and pull her up. Then I lift her over my shoulder.

"Good to go?" Sarah already has Henry and Jonas over her shoulders. Both men look unconscious, their bodies just hanging loose.

"¡Ándale!" Henry says and swats Sarah's butt. "¡Vaminos and shit!"

"Henry, I swear to God." Sarah looks ready to tear Henry's head off—and she's fully capable of it.

"I'm tripping balls, man. You can't be angry at me." Henry swats her again. "Arriba! Arriba!"

"Okay, Speedy Gonzales, enjoy eating grass." Sarah drops Henry, but she catches him by the ankle. Drags him face down through the curly growth. Over her shoulder, Jonas just giggles while whispering. "Arriba! Arriba! I miss that little guy."

We trudge through the strange subterranean world, moving away from the anguished cries, toward the chamber's far end, where there will hopefully be an exit. Fruit trees help conceal us, but they fill the air with a fragrant, flowery sweet scent that sets my stomach to rumbling. It's enough to tempt me into eating again.

Maybe not all the fruit is bad? I wonder.

I look up at branches laden with heavy blue fruits, like giant blueberries. The scent is intoxicating, like wild grapes in the fall.

"Don't even think about it," Sarah says. "Just think about mayonnaise. And pickles or something. That's the shit you like, right?"

"Ham and provolone. Mmm." Imagining my go-to sandwich helps shift my craving away from the mind-melting fruit. But it doesn't help settle my stomach.

"Street tacos," Jonas says.

"Taco Bell," Henry says.

Jonas waves one of his dangling hands at Henry's face down body. "Fuck no. The real shit. Mexico City. The kind you dunk. Burns on the way down and the way out. That's how you know it's good."

Henry punches the ground, guffawing into the grass. "So true."

"I want ice cream," Bree says, nuzzling herself into my chest. I want to change her back, make her human again, but I have no idea how the fruit will affect a normal little girl. Could have killed her. So, I just look down at her charred, craggy face and bunny ears, and I will myself to see her real self. According to her, Demon Dog *is* her true self now. I get it. Demon Dog is powerful. She instills fear more than she feels it. I worry she'll start to identify with the monsters that invaded our town, though, that she'll embrace their darkness. But even now, despite her twisted appearance, all I see is an innocent kid.

"What's up with the ice cream obsession?" Henry asks, sounding a bit more like his normal self. "It hasn't even been that long since we ate a crap ton of it."

"I was eating it with my brother when he was—" She freezes.

It's the first time she's acknowledged her brother's existence since he was brutally killed in front of her. I try not to react. To play it cool.

She turns her head to the side, face screwing up. I can feel tears on my forearm. I hold her a little tighter, but I don't say a word.

Even Henry must realize the gravity of what just happened, because he doesn't follow up. He's either growing a little more mature, or Sarah is crushing his ankle.

"A few years ago," Jonas says, "my parents were killed in an accident. Drove their RV right over a cliff."

"Like *The Earthling*," Henry says.

"The what?" Jonas asks.

"1980 film," I say. "Ricky Schroder."

"The Silver Spoons kid?" Jonas asks.

Henry reaches back, points in Jonas's direction and snaps.

"The kid's parents drive right over a cliff in an RV." Henry lowers his hand to the ground, following the track of an imaginary RV. "Weeee, splat." He slaps the ground.

"Huh," Jonas says. "Anywho, while they were dead..."

"*While* they were dead?" Sarah says.

"Long story. Not the point." Jonas sounds a little more with it now, too. "While they were dead, I listened to the Avett Brothers. Not just because they speak truth through melody and cut deep with their lyrics, but because it's what my parents were listening to when they died. Sometimes we keep people alive with simple traditions."

Jonas's insight is profound.

My mind drifts back to all the times Bree requested ice cream, to her offense at me finishing the mint chocolate chip.

It's precious to her. Sacred.

The embodiment of the brother she lost but won't talk about.

Bree confirms the accuracy of Jonas's revelation by turning her face into my side and silently crying. She keeps the sound in, but her small body shakes in my arms. It's enough to bring tears to my own eyes.

"Stop it, you two," Sarah says. She's got tears running down her cheeks, but she can't wipe them because she's carrying two grown men.

Jonas taps her back. "I might be able to walk."

Sarah drops Henry's leg and stops.

She places Jonas down on his feet.

He's unsteady, but he stays upright. He blinks his eyes a few times and says, "Slap my face."

I expect Sarah to say no, or at the very least ask how hard. Instead, she hauls back and whacks him across the cheek with an open palm. Sounds like a whip cracking. Jonas stumbles back a step, hand to his face, opening his jaw and blinking his eyes. He shakes his head and straightens up.

"Need another?" Sarah asks.

Jonas holds out a hand. "No. Thank you. Geez. On a scale of one to ten, how hard did you hit me?"

"That was a one," she says.

Jonas wiggles his jaw back and forth. "Shit..."

"You need a smack, or can you get up?" Sarah nudges Henry with her foot.

He pushes off the ground, bouncing to his feet. "I've been good for a bit. Just didn't feel like walking." He staggers a little, but he's telling the truth.

Sarah backhands his shoulder. "Asshole."

Sniffling draws my eyes down to Bree. She's lifted her head. Looking behind us. "I'm not okay yet. I'm still seeing things. Really weird things."

Despite knowing she's been seeing things, I can't help but glance back. What I see stumbles me to a stop. "Umm. You're not seeing things."

Sarah looks back. "*Goddammit.*"

"That's...different," Jonas says.

Henry tries and fails to contain his laughter. "Oh. My. God. Seriously. Does everything down here have ginormous mammaries?"

34

"We're all seeing the same thing, right?" Jonas asks, holding onto a branch for balance.

"If you're seeing a big ass lion-headed monstrosity," Henry says, "then yes."

The creature stands thirty feet tall and is ten feet longer—if you don't count the tail snapping back and forth. *Is it a tail?* Looks more like a really pissed off snake—part constrictor, part cobra, twisting and writhing while the rest of the beast stands still, glaring at us through its powerful lion eyes. But the beast is not *all* lion. The back half is gray, the legs ending in cloven hooves.

All of that is bad, but it's hardly disturbing compared to what's going on below the creature. A dozen centaurs are gathered beneath the monster, each of them vying for the optimal position from which to—*god*—suckle on the creature's six bulbous mammary glands, split up into three sets of two. The centaurs aggressively headbutt the bulging flesh, stimulating the release of milk from the prodigious teats...or whatever comes out of a giant lion-thing. With all the fruit being poisonous, maybe this is the centaurs' only source of food. Could be how they're controlled. Depending on this realm's overlord for sustenance could twist them into loyalty.

Mythological Stockholm Syndrome.

The centaurs whinny and kick, shoving each other around while aggressively slurping lion juice. There are men and women in the mix. Different nationalities. Different hair and beard styles suggesting they came from different parts of the world, or perhaps from different time periods.

When I think it can't get any weirder, a second head rises up over the lion's flowing mane.

"Is...is that a goat?" Sarah asks.

The goat head rises in profile, haughty and noble, its beard well groomed. Then its gaze snaps toward me, the fucking weird goat eyes cutting right through into my soul.

"I swear to god," Jonas says. "If it screams..."

"Screaming goats are funny," Bree says.

"Hysterical," Henry says.

"I've just heard enough of them for one lifetime," Jonas says, "even if they did save my life."

Bubbles reveals she's still present by offering a brief, "You're—*chirp!* —welcome."

Henry does his best impression of a screaming goat. "Blllеeaargghgh!"

The over-sized goat head's gaze snaps to Henry. It snorts, clearly offended.

"Seriously," Sarah says. "The hell is this thing?"

Henry and Jonas answer in unison. "Chimera."

Jonas points. "Born to Typhon and Echidna. Lion head and torso. Goat head and hind limbs. Snake for a tail."

"And it breathes fire!" Henry says. "Wicked sick. What do you think it wants?"

"Well," Sarah says. "If it views those centaurs as its children...it might want revenge."

Bree gasps and wriggles out of my hands.

She stumbles a few steps, finds her balance, and then stabs a finger at Sarah. "What did you do?"

"They were going to cut me in half," I tell her. "Well, a cyclops was. The centaurs were guarding the cave they had me in."

"Didn't have a choice," Sarah says. "They'd have killed your boy."

Bree crosses her arms, thinking on it for a moment. "Fine."

"I'm sorry," Henry says. "Did you say *cyclops*? What did he look like? Aside from, you know, the whole one-eyed thing."

"Hairy," I say. "And dead, now."

"Oh man," Henry says to Jonas. "Sorry bud, he was probably one of your brothers."

Jonas squints at him. "Huh?"

"C'mon. You should know this. There were three cyclops. Arges. Brotes. Steropes. Their parents were Uranus and Gaia. Same as you. Which makes me wonder, why are you so normal? On the outside, I mean. All three cyclops were supposed to be dead, but I think we can all agree that the myths we all know have been altered or mistranslated or are just total bullshit."

"Stop saying smart things," Sarah says. "It's weird."

"I'm in my element," Henry says, arms extended. "What can I say?"

"Umm," Bree says, "it's coming this way."

The Chimera has halved the distance between us without making a sound. It freezes in place like a cat stalking its owner, eyes narrow and locked on me.

Why me? I wonder, and then I notice its flaring nostrils. It knows about the cyclops. Can smell its death on me.

Great.

"Anyone spot a weakness?" I ask.

"What, like a chink in its armor?" Jonas asks. "Or a glowing orange spot we need to aim for? You know this isn't D&D, right?"

"Yeah," I say. "Totally. Of course. I just think we need to coordinate. Come up with a plan before it—"

"Banzai!" Henry shouts, and he launches toward the Chimera. He breaks the sound barrier in seconds, filling the chamber with a deafening, echoing, sonic boom that shocks the hungry centaurs away from their teats.

"Riiiight hook!" Henry shouts, cruising toward the lion head, fist cocked back. He acted on his impulses so fast he didn't remember he had a sword.

The Chimera turns toward Henry, its expression serious, but bored. This beast has dealt with gods before.

The lion's mouth opens, unleashing a roar as loud as Henry's sonic boom. Then its throat glows orange. Henry doesn't notice, or doesn't care, believing himself to be impervious. Before he can deliver his announced right hook, a horizontal tornado of flame roars from the creature's mouth, engulfing Henry.

From inside the fire—a scream.

Henry misses his mark and bursts from the inferno...on fire. He crashes to the ground, taking out two trees, and then he bounces out of sight.

"Guys," I say. "Listen..." But I'm too late.

"Fuck this," Sarah says, charging forward, shield raised, spear in hand. She's not normally impulsive, but she cares about Henry more than she'd admit. He's the brother she never had, regardless of his faults.

"No. C'mon—"

"For Henry!" Bree says, leaping into a tree and then between treetops, flanking the Chimera.

I sigh and glance at Jonas.

"I'm with you," he says. "It might not have a glowing weak spot, but you were on the right track. Just need to rein them in."

"How the hell do I do that?" I ask.

He shakes his head. "Not my area of expertise. Where do you want me?"

"You're our heavy hitter, right? Hit it heavy."

"I'll do my best," Jonas says. He steps toward the Chimera, stumbles a step, chuckles, and then opts for gliding.

I'd normally be confident, going into battle with this much firepower. But Henry, Bree, and Jonas are still tipsy at best, and Sarah is overconfident after her fight with the cyclops and the centaurs. The Chimera is a lot bigger and it has a small army of centaurs, which are called to active duty when the goat head rears up and lets out a bleat.

The centaurs take one last gulp and then form a line in front of the Chimera, bucking and rearing up with frantic energy. They're pumped up, made stronger by the milk, or perhaps just emboldened by it.

Sarah's bold strut shifts into a charge.

The centaurs rush out to meet her. She's outnumbered and outsized, but she shows no fear. As they barrel toward her, she drops to one knee, plants the large shield at an angle, and positions her spear forward. She's a one-woman Spartan shield wall.

But she won't be alone for long. Bree leaps from tree to tree, closing in. And Jonas isn't far now. Large rocks tear from the ground as he passes, swirling around his body, held aloft by telekinesis.

I want to rush in. To fight alongside them. To protect Bree.

But the only way I can do that right is to think first. Brawls are won, not by the person who can hit the hardest, but the person who knows where and when to strike.

The centaurs reach Sarah. Two collide head on. One is launched skyward, tumbling awkwardly, horse legs kicking, human arms flailing. The human half lets out a scream before impacting the ground, folding over as the horse's body lands atop the man. The body folds too far at the seam—and breaks. First, the spine with a crack. Then...the rest. Human skin tears away from horse as several hundred pounds of equine beast slam down. The effect is something like when my middle school friends and I used to stomp on McDonald's ketchup packets. Volcanic, chunky red explodes from the body, coating the grass and several of the centaurs that have passed and turned around.

While all that is happening, Sarah skewers a second centaur, plants the dory in the Earth behind her, and allows physics to lift the impaled beast up and over her. Then she gives physics a hand, grasping the spear like a lacrosse stick and launching the centaur. It spirals through the air, blood spraying from the hole in its chest, like a plume of radiation from a rapidly spinning pulsar. I stop tracking it when it flies overhead and topples out of sight.

The sudden, graphic violence stuns both sides for a collective moment of *what the fuck?*

Then the lion head breathes deep, its throat glowing orange. With a roar, it unleashes a wave of white-hot hell on Earth.

35

There's no time to think.

That time has passed.

I launch into the air, carried aloft by laser energy that buzzes loudly until I'm outpacing the sound. I'm not sure how fast I can fly, but I suspect I'm held back by my body's limitations. After all, lasers are essentially light...and they move at the speed of light.

I also don't have a speedometer. All I really know is that I'm moving fast enough—just barely—to outpace the jet of fire arcing through the battlefield. It's going to pass over Sarah and Jonas, but they're on their own. My concern is for Bree, still charging over the treetops, unconcerned about the flames.

The hell are you doing? I think at her.

"Bree!" I shout at her, but my speed swallows up the sound of my own voice.

Beside me, a wall of earth rises up in front of Sarah, shielding her from the flames. Jonas is protected by an invisible force, diverting the flames around him. Bree has no such protection.

The billowing fire races toward me, still arcing toward Bree. I'm not going to make it.

Not fast enough.

I will myself faster, and the wings respond—but not without a price. My eyes burn. Friction scours my skin. The tactical skirt whips, snapping painfully against my legs. I fight to keep my eyes open, but I fail. I'm moving too fast, and not fast enough.

Forced to slow down, I take a look just in time to see the fire cut through a swath of trees, incinerating them all—and then Bree is gone.

Swallowed by the flames.

"No!" I scream, voice cracking from the raw agony twisting through my gut. *I'm going to kill Zeus for this. Going to—*

A fiery meteor explodes up out of the flames.

Bree, pink pajamas on fire, rises up toward the Chimera. She doesn't appear to be in pain. And the sound coming out of her mouth isn't anguish—it's a battle cry.

She's okay. Thank God.

But for how long?

She lands atop the back of the goat's head, grasping the scruff. While her clothing smolders and flutters away, she shouts, "Bad nasty goat!" and claws the creature's neck. The goat head lets out a high-pitched bleat, but it sounds more frustrated than in pain.

Below me, Sarah shouts in pain. Her earthen wall protected her from the fire, but it also prevented the centaurs from being swallowed up. And now they're repaying her kindness by surrounding her, back ends first, bucking hard. She's thrashed back and forth like a fork in a sink garbage disposal.

But she can take it, and she's not my responsibility.

"Help her!" I shout to Jonas, pointing at Sarah.

Without watching to see if he listens, I pour on the speed and rocket toward the Chimera.

I feel like I'm moving fast, like a freaking beam of light. But the Chimera has no trouble tracking me with its big yellow eyes. Catching this thing off guard is going to be a trick. So, I try the head on approach, willing my body to shoot a giant laser beam, like what happened with the cyclops. But I have no idea how that happened. It just...did.

Instead of shooting a laser through the Chimera, though, I just fly in on a collision course. The lion head snaps forward, jaws opening.

It's going to swallow me whole, I realize. Not wanting to find out what a mythological digestive system feels like, I bank to the side and up. The creature's Prius-sized nose passes by as the jaws snap shut. I extend my wings and spin like a blender blade.

I don't feel an impact, but the lion head's roar says I made contact. As I rise high above and look down, the Chimera flinches back, pawing at its nose where there are three steaming, cauterized slices. I'm not going to make this thing bleed out, but now I know it can be hurt...and the creature doesn't like it.

Fists forward like I'm Superman, I streak back down, intending to deliver another stinging blow, which I'll repeat ad infinitum until this dude backs off. My own personal brand of Lingchi—the slow, slicing, lingering death by a thousand cuts. Feeling inspired by ancient Chinese torture techniques, I aim for the lion's eye. Animals are protective of their sensory organs. The nose is sensitive, but the eyes... They're a weak spot for every living thing that can see.

The Chimera sees me coming, no doubt understanding what I'm going to attempt, but it doesn't move to defend itself or counterattack. It just looks at me like it knows something I don't. Like it wants my attention locked on target. Like...

I glance to the left.

Bree is still clinging to the goat's mane, whooping as she's bucked up and down, shouting, "Yeehaw!" with a hand raised. Aside from her hood and bunny ears, most of her pajamas have burned away, revealing her charred body. Seeing her like that, remembering how she came to be this way, fills me with a flicker of sadness, but it's replaced by a twisting fear when I see a massive snake head rising up behind her.

My eyes widen.

I snap to a stop, about to redirect toward Bree, when I'm swatted by the Chimera's paw. Stunned, I slam into the smoldering ground, rolling to a stop as a cloud of ash billows around me. I cough, roll onto my back, and shout as the giant paw slams down toward me.

My wings unfurl with crackling energy, dragging me along the ground and out of reach. I'd like to say it's a lot less painful than being crushed beneath the Chimera's foot, but my head is thumped against several stones along the way.

I'm stunned. Probably have a concussion. Probably would have killed me before I was like this. My body says to take a minute to rest. Assess the damage. Instead, I launch myself toward the Chimera.

"I've got your back," Jonas says from below. Hovering in the air beside him are two centaurs, alive and kicking. Behind him, Sarah is hard at work, dispatching the rest with dory and shield. She's a blur of motion. The creatures don't stand a chance. The fight will be over in seconds, but I might not have that long.

As I speed toward the Chimera, two screaming centaurs hurtle past. I'm cruising, but they pass me like I'm standing still, hurled by Jonas's telekinesis. They impact one at a time. The Chimera flinches back, like it's been struck by a fist. The centaurs take the impact like water balloons against a wall.

The cyclops could conjoin different species into mythological creatures, but it did shoddy work.

To avoid looking like a Jackson Pollock painting, I swerve around the spray and rise above the Chimera in time to see the snake's jaws clamp shut over a frenzied Bree with no situational awareness.

She's snatched off the goat, yanked back, and gulped down.

"No!" I scream, surging toward the snake, fueled by rage and desperation. But the Chimera is unfazed by the barrage of centaurs pummeling its lion head, or by my personal angst. While the snake-tail reels back with its prize, the goat head directs its freaky-ass gaze in my direction. Then it lets out the mother of all bleats, screaming at a pitch high enough to shatter glass and ear drums. I clutch my ears and shout in pain for just a moment before colliding with the goat's lowered head.

Everything goes sideways. I'm not certain, but I'm pretty sure I fall back, thump off the Chimera's side, and free fall to the ground, landing on my back. Air knocked from my lungs, body rocked by pain, I open my eyes. The snake-tail has pulled back and is twitching, trying to swallow a meal that is likely kicking and clawing in panic.

Movement draws my eyes up.

A lion paw races toward me once more. I think about moving, but there's a disconnect.

Just when I'm about to be smeared, a wall of stone rises over me. The lion strikes it, full force. Stone shatters, but the delay saves me. A telekinetic force yanks me back and up, pulling me toward Jonas's raised hand. He catches me as the paw punches a crater into the ground.

"That would have hurt," he says to me.

"It did hurt," I say.

Sarah appears by our side. "What should we do?"

"The snake has Bree," I say. "I need to get her out. I don't suppose either of you have been holding back?"

I'm already trying to form a game plan based on our known powers when Jonas draws the Sword of Mars and says, "Actually..." He steps forward. Only it's not him. It's a ghostly version of himself that has stepped out of his body.

"What the hell?" Sarah says.

"I'm stronger like this," Jonas says, stepping toward the Chimera.

"Why did you keep this a secret?" I ask, fighting dizziness as I step out of Jonas's body's grasp.

"I didn't know you," he says, looking back at me. "Now I do."

"And you?" I ask Sarah. I've known her for months. We've been training together for a while. So, I'm not expecting any surprises.

"Sorry," she says, lifting her dory. Arcs of electricity flicker in her eyes. "We're slow to trust. Should have sooner." Twisting blue bolts slide down her arm, striking the spear, which glows blue with raw power. Her eyes light up with the same energy. She cocks the dory back, ready to throw. "Zeus had his lightning bolts made for him. I make my own."

She takes two steps forward and then heaves a god damn lightning spear.

36

The Chimera raises a paw, blocking the electric dory, protecting its face. But the spear still inflicts a wound, stabbing into the creature's wrist and unleashing its electric charge. The massive creature lurches back, twitching as the bolt of energy flows through its body down its grounded leg and out into the earth beneath its feet.

"Distract it?" I ask Jonas.

"I can do more than that," he says, ethereal form drifting toward the giant.

"Don't get cocky," I say.

"Oh, I'm starting to like him," Bubbles says, breaking her cone of silence for a moment.

"He's all right," Jonas says, lifting off the ground. Apparently flying is a little bit easier for him when he doesn't have a physical form.

"What should we do about this?" Sarah asks, motioning to his frozen-in-place body. It's off-putting in an uncanny valley kind of way, like he's been Photoshopped out of an image and pasted into the real world.

Just when I thought we were starting to build some cohesion, it all comes apart. "Watch him, I guess."

She's not thrilled. "You want me to just stand here?"

"Unless you can throw lightning bolts without a spear," I say. "Yeah." Then I launch into the air, more concerned about Bree's life than Sarah's feelings.

I'm not sure what Jonas is intending until a tree sails past me, spiraling toward the Chimera. Then another. And another. He's going to pummel the thing with everything his mind can pick up.

I'm not sure how effective it will be at killing the beast, but then the first tree strikes. The Chimera catches and crushes it between the beast's massive teeth, spitting it out and taking a chomp down on another. *He's not trying to kill it,* I think, *he's just distracting it.*

Are Jonas's loyalties divided? Does he feel some kind of kinship with these mythological creatures? Is he upset about the cyclops—his brother—being killed?

The goat head bleats in surprise before being slapped by a tree. Branches pierce its skin, while its tongue whips out, trying to grab hold of the tree being shoved into its face. The creature bleats in irritation, its big incisors making short work on the foliage blocking its view.

Divided loyalties or not, Jonas's unconventional attack distracts two of the creature's three heads.

I streak past, heading for the snake-tail-head-thing. *Why can't mythological creatures just be normal?*

A quarter of the way down the snake's writhing body, I see a wriggling lump.

Bree.

Still alive.

Still fighting.

I'm coming, babe.

The snake is a blur of unpredictable motion, thrashing around as it tries to swallow its savage meal. I have no doubt the snake will, in the end, succeed, but it's not having an easy time of it.

And things are about to get worse.

I will my wings to spread farther. "C'mon..." I stare at the buzzing blue laser wing extended on my right. I know I can do more. Sarah accidentally proved that in the cave. The wings and arm blades are just the beginning of what I can do. I just...I don't know how. "C'mon!" I shout, closing in on my target. "Fucking do it!"

The wing expands. It's just a little, but I feel it. Get a sense for it. With all my mental effort put into the task, my wings lengthen. A foot. Two feet. Three feet. By the time I reach the snake, my wings are ten feet long and my maneuverability has increased.

I swoop in close, angling my right wing toward the snake. The huge creature is unaware of my approach, but the tail writhes out of reach. Wings snap open, stopping me in place. Then with a buzz, I launch back the way I came. This time, instead of doing a flyby, I hover and wait. The snake is all over the place. It will come back...any...second!

The long body rises toward me, the lump in its throat just ten feet high. I spin in a circle, wings extended and laid out horizontally. Once again, I feel no impact, but a high-pitched roar coupled with a shrill goat bleat lets me know when I've struck.

The Chimera leaps away, bounding into the air and crashing back down amidst an orchard. It's heavy landing shakes the whole chamber. The creature thrashes and spins, trying to look at its snake-headed tail. But there's nothing to see, aside from a cauterized, serpentine stump.

Most of the tail lies on the ground beneath me, flipping and twisting, as death claims one of the three Chimera segments.

I descend, searching the long body for signs of movement inside. But the death throes make it impossible. With a final great twisting spasm, the snake body falls still.

Except for the end, just feet from where I severed its flesh.

I land beside the still sizzling meat just as the lump inside it stops moving. "Bree!" A blade extends from my arm. I swing it through the sinew, bone, and skin, opening the body up like Luke Skywalker's Tauntaun.

When nothing spills out, I go in.

After heaving open the meat, I find the large esophagus and slide my arms inside. When I don't reach her, I plunge my head and shoulders inside, pushing deeper until my fingers find a limb. I grasp hold and yank.

Bree slides out, her body limp.

We fall back onto the ground, covered in slime. I scramble to her side, lay her on her back, and lean over her body. She's still in her demon form, which is good. Aside from her bunny ears, she's naked. Her charred body doesn't really look human, but she'd still be horrified to know anyone, including me, saw her like this.

My fingers on her wrist feel nothing. I try her neck, but it's the same. No pulse. I'm not even sure if I could feel it through her thick skin, but it's safer to assume her heart has stopped.

I interlock my fingers, preparing to attempt CPR, which I learned in the military, long ago, but I never had the chance to actually use. I mentally prepare myself for breaking an eight year old's ribs and then—

"Hold up!" Sarah runs to me, genuine worry etched on her face. "Let me do it."

I lean back, lifting my hands away. "You know CPR?"

"Dude..." She rubs her hands together, generating sparks. "I'm a freaking defibrillator."

She places her hands on Bree—one hand over her upper left chest, the other over her ribs on the right. "Clear?"

"Good!" I say, raising my hands.

Bree's body arches up as electricity flows through Sarah's hands and into the still heart.

Before her back hits the ground, Bree sucks in a gasping breath.

Sarah's hands flinch away.

Bree's eyes open. She looks at me. Grins. "Did we...win?"

I glance back at the Chimera, and I'm surprised to find it lying still on the ground. Its big chest is still rising and falling, but the creature is unconscious.

I smile down at her. "Yeah."

"Oh good," she says and closes her eyes.

Panic sends tingly jolts through my body. I check her pulse again and find it thumping beneath her rough skin. Alive, but wiped out from her battle inside the snake's throat.

"She okay?" Jonas asks, approaching in his physical body.

"Alive," I say. "Not sure about okay."

He nods, understanding the difference. Holds up Sarah's dory. "Found this on the way." He tosses it to her.

Sarah catches it, nods her thanks, and slides it onto her back beneath the shield over her shoulders. She points to the Chimera. "How did you do that?"

"While it was choking on tree branches, I was harvesting the fruit and launching them into its stomach. By the time it wakes up, it might not remember who cut off its tail."

"Why not just kill it?" Sarah asks.

"Way I see it," Jonas says, "all these creatures are pawns. The centaurs were captives...mutilated and tortured. They needed to be put down. But the Chimera was born a monster. And I don't think it wanted to be here, defending this place, any more than the cyclops did. Echidna is calling the shots in Khaos."

"The cyclops we killed," I say, feeling a little guilty.

"Didn't have a choice, right?" Jonas asks.

I shake my head.

"Then you didn't have a choice." He motions to the poisonous fruit growing from the trees around us. "I did."

"We need to find some place to rest," I say. "And sort some shit out." Now that we're safe, my anger at how this all went down is rising to the surface.

Jonas shakes his head. Holds up the watch with Bubbles inside it. "No time."

"Long enough to find her some clothes," I say, and he nods, looking at Bree's body and frowning.

"Does that hurt her?" he asks.

I shake my head. "If it does, she doesn't complain." I pick Bree up and hold her in my arms. I glance back at the Chimera. "Sure you don't want to kill it?"

Jonas opens his mouth to answer, but he's interrupted by, "Lightning Bolt Strike!"

Henry rises above the Chimera, blazing blue with electric light. Then a lightning bolt arcs between him and the beast, exploding out to envelop its body—which ignites into flames. The monster is too out of its head to care or react. It just lies still while its body is engulfed, hair burning fast, filling the chamber with smoke.

Henry flies to us and lands. His clothing is scorched and tattered. His skin is red hot. He claps his hands. "That wasn't so bad."

"That...wasn't necessary," Jonas grumbles.

"You say it's not necessary, I say that biotch needed to be roasted." Henry shrugs. "Tomato tomahto." He points to Sarah. "BTW, we are *not* fireproof. He holds out his red arms. "Stings like Satan's jock-itchy taint. And I think my hair is fucked up. How bad is it?" He shakes his hands through his smoldering hair. Blackened strands fall away. Patches have been burned almost all the way to his skull.

"Like you said..." Sarah musses his hair. "Fucked."

"Shit," he says.

"Maybe think about that next time you jump in front of a mythological flame thrower."

I clear my throat and address Henry. "Find us a way out." Henry nods and shoots off through the air. I turn to Sarah. "Find the backpack." And finally, to Jonas, I say, "Don't hold that against him." I motion to the Chimera. Its burning corpse is now crackling. "It nearly killed her." I look down at Bree, who despite being a demon, still looks innocent. "If he hadn't done it. I might have. Whatever kinship you're feeling with these things…it doesn't matter. We're here together. As a team. And we have a mission to complete. Only living things that matter down here are the ones fighting beside us. Got it?"

Jonas smiles. Pats my shoulder. "Keep talking like that and we'll do fine. Now let's get the hell out of here before whatever eats fricasseed Chimera shows up."

37

"Can't I just eat one?" Henry asks, reaching for one of thousands of luminous pink mushrooms growing on the floors, walls, and ceiling of what can best be described as a magical unicorn pony cave of wonders. We came across it twenty minutes beyond the orchard, after it took thirty minutes to find the exit.

Bree has been unconscious the whole time, lying on my lap, dressed in a two-piece Tarzan-like outfit that Sarah pieced together using horse hides, a thick needle, and some thread I think might be dried and twisted intestines, taken from the cyclops cave.

I'm pretty much freaking out, but I'm doing my best to hide it. I suspect I'm the only person here to have had a complete mental breakdown in the past. Some would say I'm better prepared for life's hardships because I've experienced and bounced back from the worst, but I really just feel fragile. Like it could happen again if the right buttons are pushed. Something happening to Bree might get the job done. But I won't know until that moment comes.

Sarah swats Henry's hand before he can pluck a mushroom and gobble it down. "Didn't learn your lesson from the apple?"

"First," Henry says. "Those apples were dope. We'd make a fortune if we could get them topside."

"We already have a fortune," Sarah says.

"I'm just saying." Henry rolls his eyes. "Second, learning lessons isn't really my jam."

He's not wrong.

He could get run over by a bulldozer and wouldn't think twice before stepping out in front of another. If we had one of those apples and handed it to him, he'd take a bite. Henry only alters course when he thinks something through, sees the logic in it, and then consciously monitors his behavior.

But even that isn't always enough.

But it's going to have to be.

"Well," I say, "Maybe it's time to grow up."

His eyebrows rise while his head lowers. "Ex*cuse* me?"

"You could have gotten us killed. Again. And if Bree...if she doesn't come out of this, I'm holding you responsible."

"You threatening me, *Laser Chicken?*" Henry lived on the streets of Boston after several stints in foster homes. He responds to most challenges with aggression. It was a survival technique learned in the days before unlocking his godhood.

"Responsibility isn't a threat, it's a part of life for every living thing, except for you, apparently."

"You're damn straight," he says. "And I didn't do this. I...I attacked it first. I was being brave. Wanted to keep everyone safe. Hell, I *killed* the thing."

"You threw the team into chaos," Jonas says, raising a finger. "Turned yourself into a fireball, sat out the fight, and then killed an ancient mythological creature by setting it on fire with lightning, after it had already been subdued and everyone was safe."

Henry sits silent for a moment, contemplating. Maybe Jonas can get through to him. Henry looks up to him, after all. "I don't see the problem with any of that."

Sarah sighs. "Henry..."

"What?" He's getting pissed. If he wasn't already pink from being scorched, his face would probably look bright red. "This is the way we do things. Fucking head on. Kicking ass. Throwing punches."

"Which you need to stop announcing," I say.

"Calling it out makes it more powerful," he says.

"Like Hadouken?" I ask.

"Exactly like Hadouken," he says. "See? You get it."

Jonas pinches his nose. "Kid... You need to put the ego aside for a moment and listen to Miah."

"Why the hell is Miah in charge?"

"Aside from laying waste to a naked cult," Jonas says, "have you ever led anything in your life?"

Henry thinks on this, and then very seriously says. "I once led an army of black ants to a red ant hill by dragging one of the black ants along the ground, so he'd leave a stressed-out chemical trail. Worked like a charm. The rest of the ants were like, 'Where the fuck did Bob get off to, and why in god's name is he so stressed out?' So, they charged after him all pissed off and shit. Right to the red ants who have a nasty bite, but were not prepared for the wave of–"

"Stop," Jonas says. "The answer is no. You haven't. And there's nothing wrong with that. I haven't either. Aside from Bubbles, I spent most of my adult life working alone, with almost no real human contact. But Miah is a team player. Former military and future family man. He led a rescue, escape, and revolt on an alien planet. Saved thousands of lives. Every time we encounter something, he doesn't think, 'How can I handle this?' He thinks, 'How can *we* handle this?' You don't even think. You just act. Like a fool. And you're going to get one of us killed."

Henry glowers, arms crossed. Makes a show of looking at Jonas's head, and then mine. "Couple of old fucking men. Where are you hiding your gray hairs? You both have gray pubes or something?"

My patience evaporates. "Will you. Shut the. Fuck up? Bree was nearly killed because you went off halfcocked."

"I didn't make her follow me," he says.

"She looks up to you, asshole. Because you're fearless, and she wants to be, because if she's not afraid of anything, then all the bullshit eating her up inside would slide away like a fucking egg off Teflon. And when the world gets a load of you–and it will eventually–because you're *you*, there's going to be a shit-ton more kids who want to be like you."

"I'll be worshiped?" He's suddenly excited, like he hadn't considered the possibility before.

"For a day or two," I say, "until kids start jumping off buildings, trying to fly, and doing other stupid shit, because you inspired them to try stupid things, and to not listen to the people whose job it is to keep them alive. When that happens, you *will* be responsible."

Henry stands. Fists clenched. Electric blue in his eyes.

Doesn't need to hide it anymore. "And what the fuck will the world do about it?"

"Henry," Jonas says, his voice somehow both totally calm and exuding menace. "It won't be the world that does something about it."

The threat isn't immediate, but it is blatant. If Henry goes off the rails, if he gets innocent people killed, he'll be dealing with us. And while I doubt I'm much of a threat, Jonas's combination of experience and power would make short work of Henry.

"Pretty sure this conversation isn't in the team building handbook," Sarah says, trying to change the tone.

"He needs to hear it," Jonas says. "And if he can't, we might be safer without him."

Sarah waits, eyes wide, clearly nervous about what's going to happen.

In a blink, Henry launches out of the cave and flies out of sight, following the twisting tunnel like a Viper launching from the Battlestar Galactica.

Jonas throws his hands up. "Fantastic. A temper tantrum."

"You're lucky he didn't start throwing punches," Sarah says.

"He'd call them out before he did," Jonas says, "so it's not like we wouldn't see it coming."

With a rush of wind, Henry returns. Extends his middle finger at me. "Fuck you." He picks a mushroom and flips Jonas the bird. "Fuck you." He picks another mushroom and rotates his hand gesture toward Sarah. "And fuck you for not having my back."

Then he's gone again to who knows where.

I sigh and ask Sarah. "Should we go after him?"

She shakes her head. "He'll cool off."

"He prone to...this?" Jonas asks.

She shrugs. "Not for a while, but early on with Helen, yeah. She was hard on him, too."

"Hard on him?" I ask. Until someone has faced down a drill sergeant, or Jen's father, they don't know what a real chewing out feels like. We were gentle in comparison.

"By his standards," she says. "He might be fearless, but that doesn't mean he doesn't have feelings. He can be pretty thin-skinned when he feels outcast. He was a pariah for most of his life. Acceptance is a big deal to him."

"He needed to hear it," I say. "If we don't start working together—"

"I know," she says. "I'll talk to him."

"If he comes back," Jonas says.

"He'll come back." Sarah picks up a mushroom, looking it over. "He's like a puppy. Just needs to have a bunch of internal arguments first. And sometimes eat things he shouldn't." She tosses the mushroom aside.

"Oooh." The soft voice draws my attention to Bree, lying on my lap. "Pretty." She reaches her hand out for one of the mushrooms, but she doesn't get close.

I lift her up and wrap my arms around her. "Thank god. And time for a break." I lean back, place my hand against her forehead and swipe it to the side. Her charred skin flakes away like dried mud. She doesn't complain about me turning her human once more. She's never been in her Demon Dog form so long. Maybe she's had enough. She shakes her body out and then her hands over her head, revealing a fresh head of brown hair—like it had never fallen out. When she's mostly free of ash and old skin, she returns to my embrace.

"Mmm," she says, nuzzling into me. "Hugs are nice, too." She leans up. "Did we win? Is Henry okay?" She looks down at her new clothing. "And why am I wearing this?"

"We did," I say, "and he is. Just went for a walk. And, babe, your clothing got burned. This was the best we could do."

Please don't ask where the fur came from, I think. I don't want to tell her it's horse hide taken from the cyclops's cave.

She stands, a little wobbly, looking herself over. "I look like a cave girl." And just when I think we're going to have two tantrums on our hands, she feels for her bunny ears, discovers them intact, and says, "I love it. Can we eat something now? Is there ice cream in the underworld?"

38

The backpack's zipper sounds loud in the cave, like the call of some small mythological creature looking for a meal, or a mate, or whatever denizens of the underworld do in their spare time.

They're probably not mating, I think, opening the backpack. Otherwise, these caves would be overpopulated with winged, one-eye, cloven hooved aberrations of nature. The cyclops was a bachelor. So was the Chimera. They 'procreated' by capturing weary travelers and binding them to the local horse population, which must have been brought down from the surface a long time ago.

Must have been a lonely life.

Unless it wasn't...

Unless the centaurs were...

A shiver sets my body to shaking.

"You having a seizure or something?" Sarah asks, her face glowing pink from the mushroom cave. She's speaking to me, but she's angling to see what's in the backpack. We're all hungry.

"Trying to shake off dark thoughts," I say.

"Story of my life," Bree says, getting smiles out of us. "Now bust out the snacks, or I'll bust you in the face."

I laugh. "Okay, okay, Demon Dog. Chill." Five water bottles emerge. No one is thrilled by them, but everyone takes one and drinks. Next comes four chocolate protein bars.

"Just four?" Sarah asks.

"Four bars, and..." I pull out a clear plastic container, the kind picked up from a grocery store bakery. It's full of fluffy white goo, speckled with rainbow chunks. It might have looked appetizing when it was fresh and pretty. But it's been thrashed about, and the cream has turned runny.

"Ugh," Bree says.

I read the printed label holding the container shut. "Ambrosia?"

"It's like a fruit salad," Jonas says. "Mixed with sour cream and marshmallows."

"Lovely," I say, holding both spoon and container out to Bree. "I think this was meant for you."

"Looks like Elmo barf." She leans away, blocking the offering with her hands. "No, thank you."

I offer it to Sarah. "Sounds like a lot of sugar. Pass."

Then Jonas. He shakes his head. "Lactose intolerance."

"I saw you eat ice cream, man," I grumble.

"Sometimes, when you're the leader, you need to take one for the team."

Everyone's smiling at me, waiting.

"Damnit," I say.

"You could always save it for Henry," Sarah says. "He'll eat anything."

I shake my head. "I want him to feel welcome when he comes back. Offering him the dregs of our loot crate might just twist the knife."

"Suit yourself." She takes one of the bars. Jonas and Bree follow suit. But they're not eating. They're just watching me. Waiting to see if I'll eat the Lucky Charms slurry.

Never one to wait before jumping in a pool or ripping off a Band-Aid, I tear the label, crack open the container, and stab the plastic spoon into the goo. It's firm. Pliable. Oozing whatever separates from sour cream when it's been sitting too long. I pull a scoop out, and it stretches like viscous drool from a dog that's been making a smorgasbord out of a Crayola crayon box. The strand thins, breaks, and then retracts like a goddamn severed worm.

"Ugh," Sarah says. "It looks like some kind of unicorn discharge."

Bree scrunches up her face, leans away, and is making little spitting sounds. "Don't eat it. It's too gross."

"Well, now I have to." I lift the spoon slowly, inexorably, toward my open mouth. All three audience members cringe, their faces screwing up in disgust. A clump of the stuff slips over the spoon's side, a lump of bright blue dangling from a wobbling, translucent strand.

"Whoeh!" Bree's fake dry heave seals the deal. Even if it's the worst thing I've ever eaten, this will be worth it. "Whoeh!"

"C'mon," I say. "This is hardly the worst thing we've seen down here."

"I don't know about that," Jonas says, placing the back of his hand over his mouth and closing his eyes and collecting himself.

The moment is gold. Whatever this tastes like, their disgust makes it all worthwhile.

Smiling, I place the spoon in my mouth.

Bree's eyes go wide. She can't believe I did it.

I close my lips, pull the spoon out—and chew.

The cave is silent, all three waiting for my reaction.

I chew once. Twice. And then—magic happens. "Oh. Oh man. This is..." I chew some more. All the gross textures dissolve away, replaced by exquisite and very sweet flavor. The fruity chunks are hearty and juicy. "Oh my god. This is amazing."

They're relieved, but also disappointed, hoping for a reaction that could be used to tease me later.

I dig in and take another victorious bite.

The show over, they tear into their protein bars, each of them taking eager bites.

"Oh," Sarah says, mouth open, brows furrowed. "Oh god. It's horrible." Dusty protein powder billows from her mouth.

"So dry," Jonas says, cracking open a bottle and swishing the water around with his prehistoric bar.

Bree twists her lips, but she isn't willing to concede defeat. She chews and swallows without complaint, and then she forces out a, "Mmm. Mine is really good."

"Glad to hear it," I say, trying to contain my laughter.

"I bet you are," she says, and she takes another bite. Then with a full mouth, crumbs flying, she says, "Dewishous."

"Okay hoss," Jonas says, crumbling up his protein bar wrapper. "What's the plan?"

"Pretty simple, I think." I take another bite. It really is spectacular. "We stick to the main tunnel, headed down. Get past whatever else is waiting for us. Reach the gate and complete the mission."

"Think it will be that easy?" Sarah asks.

"Not a chance," I say. "But if anything veers us away from that path, we need to avoid it."

"Stay on the straight and narrow," she says. "Linda would like that."

Bree elbows me and says, "It's a church thing," like she's in the know and I'm clueless.

"What's important is that we respond to threats as a unit. Individually, we're all pretty badass, but vulnerable, especially down here where the monsters are as strong as each of you. But together we'd be a damn force of nature. An army of five."

"How do we do that?" she asks.

"Honestly," I say, "and I realize this is in total opposition to my whole vibe... Don't do anything until I say so, and then do exactly what I say, when I say it. Well executed coordination can overcome just about any challenge. I can't believe I just said that. I feel dirty now."

She nods slowly. "Like the X-men," Bree says. "When they work together."

Jonas chuckles. "Fastball special."

"Exactly," Bree says.

"Sounds about right." I turn to Sarah. "We've been training together. We can do this." I turn to Bree. "You listen at home, right? You can listen here."

She twists her lips.

"Won't be any Demon Dog again until I believe you'll follow my orders."

Twisting lips downturn. "I don't like orders."

"Or rules," I say. "I know. But right now, it's not just about keeping you alive. It's about keeping all of us alive. Including me. And eventually the whole world and everyone we love back home."

That sinks in. She nods and offers me her pinkie.

"This is our second pinkie promise," I point out. "You broke the first one."

To an eight-year-old, breaking a pinkie promise is tantamount to war crimes.

She tears up a little. "Sorry. I really mean it this time."

"Then you won't mind doing this," I say, offering both of my pinkies. "Double pinkie promise."

The importance of a double pinkie promise is that all fingers are visible and uncrossed. It is an immutable bond. If broken, the friendship of those involved is dissolved forever.

She links pinkies with me. "Promise."

"Okay then," I say, picking up my ambrosia and taking another bite, getting a wince and a laugh out of everyone. Laughter is cut short when Henry steps into view. He'd been just outside the cave, listening in. He steps up to me, says, "Fine," and holds out a pinkie.

I put the ambrosia down and hold up both.

"Seriously?" he asks.

"Only way forward," I tell him. "Unless you're afraid."

He links pinkies with me.

"You promise to stay with us, to listen to my orders, to follow our plans, and think of the team before yourself."

"I'll try," he says, and I squeeze his pinkies. He growls a little. "I will. Promise."

"Great," I say, releasing him and returning to the ambrosia.

"Grown men pinkie promising," Jonas says. "Fantastic."

Bree extends her pinkie. "We all should."

I've got no shame, so I link my pinkie with hers and wait for the others. Henry's already broken this glass ceiling, so he's next.

Then Sarah.

We wait on Jonas, all of us looking at him.

From what I understand, his life has been rough, his childhood some kind of nightmare, so this might be his first pinkie promise.

It's a big step.

"Fuck it," he says, and he links his pinkies with ours.

"We promise to work together, to protect each other, to fight for each other, now and forever," I say. It's a bold promise. Lengthy. Like wedding vows. But it feels appropriate.

"Promise," Bree says.

Sarah and Henry respond together. "Promise."

Back to Jonas. "You guys..." He shakes his head. Smiles. "Promise."

"I promise," Bubbles says, "*that I have a big dick!*—and everything else. Even if there isn't much I can do aside from occasionally embarrassing myself."

"And that means we need to move," I say. "Get to Tartarus, and you to a charger."

Jonas gives a nod of thanks.

I take a final scoop of ambrosia and offer it to Bree. "Last bite."

She's unsure, but she decides to trust me. Takes the whole mouthful and is delighted by the result. "No fair. That's *so* good!"

Sarah hands the last protein bar to Henry, along with a water bottle.

"Sweet," he says, accepting. "FYI, don't eat the mushrooms. I ate one and puked. Ate the second and puked again. Thought I might shit myself, too, but gods can clench pretty tight."

I stand and reach my hand out to Bree. "Let's move." She takes it and together we strike out.

39

For the past thirty minutes, the cave system has led downhill, growing wider and taller as we go. The terrain is rougher, too, more like walking on the beachside stones in Rye than a path. But there's only one way forward, one way down, so we press on.

I reach a hand back and help Bree over a gap between boulders.

"Can't you just change me back now?" she asks. "This would be a lot faster if I could just hop around."

"She's got a point." Jonas has taken the lead, and he's keeping a steady pace that he'd like to be a lot quicker.

"You need a break," I say. "I'd rather you be Demon Dog when things are dangerous, not just when we're in a rush."

"You just don't want to see my ugly face anymore." She swats my hand away and makes the jump on her own.

"Not true," I say, and I'm ready to argue the point when Henry interrupts.

"Can't you just scoop her up and fly?"

"I'm tired of being carried," Bree grumbles.

"Same," Sarah says. "Honestly."

"Going to come a point," Jonas says, "where you all are going to have to embrace humility. For Bubbles's sake."

Bree stops. "Ugh. Fine." She lifts her arms, signaling that I can pick her up. "For Bubbles."

Jonas leaps down and out of sight. There's a drop off ahead. And an undulating roar.

"Might not be necessary," he calls back.

I pick up Bree, extend my wings, and gently glide over and down the large stones blocking our view of what lies ahead. Jonas is at the bottom of a thirty-foot drop. He's looking out through a large, brightly lit cave opening—the tunnel's end. I land beside him and place Bree down on a damp rock thick with bulbous, seaweed-looking growth.

"Eww," she says, picking up one foot at a time.

"Guys," Jonas says. "Look up."

My eyes flick to the view and I'm staggered. I don't know how to describe the immense size of the cavern ahead other than to call it another world. It's miles wide and long. I can't see the far end, and the sides wrap around, disappearing into the hazy light of the underworld. What I can see of the walls, rising and arching up, have the distinctive, ribbed texture of a surface that has been carved.

What the hell could have made something so vast?

I don't think I want to find out.

The cavern's size isn't its defining feature. That would be the ocean ahead. The mirror-smooth water reflects the ceiling and the yellow hue of the air itself. At first, it's almost invisible, but a vibration moving through the floor, made by something distant and large, creates a slight ripple. And there's a wooden boat tied to a metal spike driven into a stone.

"I think we're meant to take the boat across," Jonas says.

"I think I speak for everyone when I say, screw that," Henry says, and he flies toward the shoreline.

"He's not wrong for once," Jonas says. "We don't have time to—"

The moment Henry crosses from the stone beach to open water, an invisible force slaps him out of the air and into the water. Ripples explode and widen, flowing out into the ocean. He surges up from under the water, sputtering and angry. He thrashes back and forth, looking for whatever hit him. "Where is it?"

"Nothing there," Sarah says.

"Bullshit," he says. "I just got bitch slapped out of the air."

Electricity crackles along his arms. The ripples are bad enough. Anything in this cavern is going to know we're here the moment the waves he generated reach the opposite shore.

But if he lets loose with a lightning bolt—there's going to be no hiding from whatever danger lurks ahead.

Sarah comes to the same conclusion.

She rushes into the water and takes hold of Henry's arm, immune to the electric charge. "Stop and think."

He's frustrated. Wants to argue. Looks back at the rest of us and must remember his promise, because he takes a breath and controls himself. "I've stopped, but I'm not really thinking."

"I'll think for both of us, then," Sarah says. "Try to fly."

Henry steps back and leaps into the air. His knees clear the water, but then gravity pulls him back down. "Huh." He hurries out of the water, leaps, and soars into the air. He does a loop and lands beside us. "Something about the water, I guess."

"Great," Jonas says. "The lake is a no-fly zone." He approaches the rope where it's attached to the stone. Tries to untie it but fails. Looks like the cord has been here for a while, like it's fused to the spike.

"Probably made from the kraken's ass-hair or something," Henry says.

Jonas responds by taking hold of the spike and pulling. There's a moment of resistance. Then the boulder splits in half and the spike comes free. He tosses it inside the twenty-foot-long rowboat, which contains two oars, and he says, "Welcome to the S.S. Slow-Ass. Destination unknown."

Jonas climbs aboard and lifts his arms out to the sides as it wobbles beneath his feet. He climbs past the oars and sits on the aft bench. "Who knows how to row one of these?"

I turn to the others and when no one offers, I raise my hand. "Summer camp. Two-time relay champ." I climb in, take the middle seat, and position the oars in the oarlocks. "Sarah, get in the back with Jonas. We need to keep the boat balanced." I turn to Henry and Bree. "You two up front."

No one complains about me assuming people's weights, probably because it's pretty obvious that Sarah's strength puts her in a higher weight class than Henry's scrawny frame.

Henry waits for Bree to take a seat, then shoves the boat into the water without being asked. He climbs aboard and takes a seat.

A few paddles later, I've got us turned around and facing the shoreline's far side. "If you all can look for markers along the way, that would be great. Paddling in a straight line is hard, even when you can see where you're going."

I put my back into it and row.

It's a lot easier than I remember, probably because I'm more than a foot taller now, and I'm stronger than the strongest body builder. An impressive wake flows out behind us as we make good time out into the water, watching the shore fade behind us.

"I've been thinking," Henry says, and I brace myself for an unpredictable quandary regarding anatomy, bathroom habits, or some kind of excretion. Instead, I get a revelation. "We've come across harpies, the Furies, centaurs, poison fruit, and a Chimera. Each one of them is a challenge that requires a different kind of solution, right? Solutions that aren't just unique, but also change us. Jonas was granted peace about his past. Miah was guided by a spirit hedgehog, and he tapped into some kind of new power. Bree is maturing. I'm becoming a team player. And Sarah... well, I think maybe you're already good to go."

Sarah is moved by that, so Henry pushes past it double time.

"Point is, this is classic character growth. *The Iliad. The Odyssey.* The Twelve Labors. Perseus, Odysseus, Hercules. All those guys set out on journeys where they encountered a long list of monsters—the Lernaean Hydra, the Nemean Lion, the Erymanthian Boar. The list goes on. But each encounter forced the hero to grow more powerful—not just physically, but mentally, emotionally, strategically, whatever. Each challenge was a lesson in disguise."

He looks each of us in the eyes. "The same thing is happening to us. We're becoming stronger. Together."

"Trials," Jonas says.

"Exactly," Henry says. "Designed to make sure that anyone who reaches the gates of Tartarus is worthy."

"Or to keep out the riff-raff," I say.

"Same thing," Henry says. "The question is—are the trials random or did someone set all this up."

"Who could—" I answer my own question. "Linda."

"Not sure Zeus has that kind of power anymore," Sarah says.

Henry shrugs. "Maybe everyone who journeys through Khaos needs to learn the same lessons. I mean, maybe some people don't need to learn anything and breeze right through. But for people like us, who are new to all this, maybe this journey is like...I don't know... refinement."

I can't help but smile. "I think you might be right."

"If you're right," Jonas says, "we need to stay vigilant."

"Pssh," Henry says. "Smooth sailing from here, I think. We've all totally learned lessons. We're a team now. On the same page. What's left to learn?"

"I have an idea," I say, and I wait until I have everyone's attention. "Which way to go."

Everyone looks around on cue, scouring the view around the boat and seeing the same thing I do—endless yellow haze. I've been trying to row straight, but anyone who has ever rowed a boat knows that's just about impossible. We could be doing circles and would never know. Could be headed back the way we came. Could be out here forever.

I lift the oars, place them in the boat, and stand to have a look around. Nothing but yellow in every direction. "Not every trial is a monster."

40

"Row, row, row your boat, gently across the lake, when we get to the other side, I think I'll bake a cake." Bree finishes singing and scrunches her face. "Too many sibalels."

"Syllables," Henry says.

"Those," Bree says.

"And you forgot the 'merrily, merrily, merrily' bit."

"Mmm," Bree says. "You're right."

The conversation is...mundane, but I've been rowing through endless yellow mist for fifteen minutes, and there's still no sign we're moving in the right direction, or any direction at all. Compared to the monotonous surroundings, their conversation is like a Margaret Atwood novel narrated by Morgan Freeman.

"Also, how are you going to bake a cake? I mean, we could grind up the rest of my protein bar and mix it with some water from the backpack."

Bree's eyes widen. "And you could cook it with lightning!"

"But I think that would just make it crispy and burnt," Henry says. "Don't we need eggs or something?"

"Maybe there's a golden goose or something?"

"Don't they lay golden eggs? Also, I don't think that's Greek myth."

"The Golden Goose is one of Grimm's fairy tales," I say. "And it didn't lay eggs. That was actually one of Aesop's fairy fables."

Henry and Bree stare at me, dumbfounded for a moment.

"What does Jen see in him?" Henry asks, and he turns to Bree. "Do you know?"

"It's not his fashion sense," Bree says with a snicker, despite the fact that I know, without a doubt, she *is* a fan of the tactical skirt. Maybe not the KISS shirt. It's looking a little tattered. Maybe I'll swap it out for my AC/DC tee, though I really feel like I should give that to Henry, because *Thunderstruck.* His Poison T-shirt has seen better days, too. It's shredded and burned, along with his hair. He kind of looks like the kid from *Jurassic Park* after the electric fence launched him like a cow over a *Monty Python* castle wall.

"The only egg mentioned in Greek myth, that I know of, is the Orphic Egg." Jonas is trying to sound casual, but the clock is ticking for Bubbles. "And I don't think it would help your quest for a cake."

Bree's not buying it. "But if it's an egg–"

"It's probably not an actual egg," he says. "If it even exists. Some cultures call it the World Egg. Or the Cosmic Egg. It's a universal concept in ancient cultures that life came from a source, from which original life was birthed. To ancients, the easiest representation of this concept was an egg–this magical chamber from which a living thing could emerge. The Greeks, of course, made it weird. Their version of the myth includes a primordial serpent, Protogonus, which hatched from the egg and then gave birth to the first Titans. Point is, even if you find an egg down here, there's a solid chance you wouldn't want to make a cake with it."

"Well," Bree says. "Poo poo to you, too." She clears her throat and sings, raising a finger with each syllable, resting with every five. "Row, row, row your boat, gently to a snake, merrily, merrily, merrily, merrily." She pauses, a fiendish look in her eyes, and then she finishes the song with, "Fuck this fuckin' lake."

She bursts out laughing, right along with the rest of us, and says, "You cannot tell my mom about that. She would lose her–"

Bree squints her eyes, looking ahead. She stands, tilts her head to the side and says, "That's different."

Henry stands up beside her and the rowboat wobbles.

"Whoa," Sarah says, gripping the side. "No more standing."

"But you need to see this," Henry says.

I try to turn around and see for myself, but despite my Chicken moniker, I can't rotate my head 360 degrees.

"Everyone sit," I say, and I'm pleased that both Henry and Bree listen. "Jonas, have a look. Sarah, keep the boat steady."

Behind me, Jonas stands and Sarah slides to the middle of the bench. The ship wobbles, but it's minimal. After a moment, Jonas says, "Huh..."

"Huh, what?" I ask.

"It looks like a—"

"It's a frikkin' whale footprint," Henry says. "Trust me, I know. This one time, me and Jay—"

"There are whales in the underworld?" Bree asks, a little excited by the prospect.

"No," Jonas says. "There are not."

"What's a whale footprint?" Sarah asks.

"Large creatures displace a lot of water," Jonas says. "When they move beneath the water, it creates a disturbance on the surface. In the ocean, it can look like a smooth patch. But on this flat lake, it's just kind of a big swirling patch."

"How big?" I ask.

He sighs. Doesn't want to say it. "Forty feet across."

My right oar misses the water, bounces out of the oarlock, and nearly falls into the water. "Forty feet?"

"Doesn't mean what made it is the same size," he says. "The footprints spread out."

"Whales don't have feet," Bree says. "Why is it called a footprint?"

"Because tail print sounds stupid," Henry says. "Duh."

"I think we should be quiet," I say, fixing the oar as carefully as I can.

Jonas sits again. "I think that's a great idea."

Henry rolls his eyes, but he doesn't speak. Bree sucks in her lips.

Officially in stealth mode, I do my best to row quickly and silently, which is beyond difficult in a rowboat. They're as clunky as a peg-leg pirate at a hoedown.

We slide through the water, silent and tense, scrutinizing the water around us. Absolute worst part of rowing a boat is not being able to see where you're going, especially when you're headed toward potential doom. The water swirls around us as we enter the footprint. I brace for something—anything—but after a few rows, we're clear. I let out a heavy sigh, only now realizing that I'd been holding my breath.

A minute later, the footprint is in our rear view, nearly out of sight.

I close my eyes for a moment, attempting to let relief flow out through my body. Keeping tension locked up can result in PTSD. Without an outlet for fear, despair, and trauma, the human mind eventually breaks. I've been buoyed by my transformation, but that doesn't mean I'm immune to being overwhelmed. I breathe in for five seconds, hold it for five, and release it slowly. As my lungs deflate, I open my eyes to find Bree smiling at me, letting out her own five count breath. We've done this together, training our minds along with our bodies.

I smile back, but motion draws my eyes back to the view behind her.

The footprint is swirling again, somehow closer than it was a moment ago.

Because it's not the same footprint.

I row harder.

A second massive footprint appears, half the distance.

"Umm, guys," I say. "We have incoming."

Henry and Bree see me looking past them and crane their heads around.

"The whale is back!" Bree says, excited.

Behind me, Jonas is back on his feet, the boat wobbling until Sarah balances it. "We don't have long."

"Can you lift us up?" I ask. "Turn us into a telekinetic plane?"

"Tried that when we got in," he says. "Whatever is keeping Henry grounded is working on me, too."

"Okay," I say. "This is going to sound nuts, but there's a reason I was the two-time rowing relay champion... There weren't any rules, so when my boat fell behind, I jumped in, held onto the back, and kicked like a son-of-a-bitch. Partly because I was competitive, but also because there were leeches in the pond. Couldn't walk afterward, but I basically turned the rowboat into a motor—"

"On it!" Henry says, grabbing hold of the boat's stern and jumping into the water. Froth kicks up behind him, and we immediately start accelerating. When I was a kid, kicking that boat forward, I felt like we made pretty good time. But it was nothing like being propelled by an energetic, super strong god.

I smile when my hair starts to blow around.

It fades when a new footprint forms, even closer. It's still gaining.

"I'll help him," Jonas says, stepping past me, but he's too late.

The water behind us explodes.

A behemoth rises up and just keeps—on—going.

Describing it is...difficult. It's segmented, like a line of giant-sized horseshoe crabs stitched together, human-centipede style. Each segment has a set of arms extending out from under the hard shell, but they're not insectoid or crab-like. They look...human, and they're tipped with long webbed fingers.

But none of that comes close to the abominations lining the creature's underside. At the center of each segment...is a face. Not a head. Just a very expressive face—eyes, nose, and mouth. Their wide eyes glare, hungry and crazed, accentuated by their open-mouthed smiles.

As each face passes by overhead, it lets out a primitive, delighted moan, like orgasming cows.

I know this is some kind of monster from Greek myth, but its vibe is mind-bendy, disturbingly strange anime.

"Whoa," Henry says, smiling. "It's a Hecatoncheires!"

The massive creature—which could be called something like Badonkadoncheires—arcs up over us, dousing the rowboat with enough water to sink us, if we don't start bailing. But there's a more immediate problem. While the lower part of Badonk's body is still rising behind us, its front end crashes back down into the lake, dead ahead.

41

I stab the left oar into the water, pushing forward against our momentum. The sudden force of it nearly lifts me up and launches me into the water. But Jonas has my back, literally, adding his weight to mine. Together, we hold the oar steady.

Drag whips us through a ninety degree turn to starboard. We miss colliding with the Badonk, but its rows of arms reach for us while its conveyor belt faces wail in frustration, sounding a lot like the old Budweiser 'wassup' commercial. "Bleeehhh. Bleeehhh. Bleeehhh."

Henry's kicking keeps us out of reach, but now we're not headed in the right direction. I lift the oar in my left hand and lower the oar on the right. We turn until I think we're facing the correct direction again. Then I draw the oars inside and start bailing water along with Sarah, who looks a little nervous.

She notes my attention and says, "I have a problem with drowning."

"You can't swim?" I ask.

"I can swim," she says.

"I can't!" Henry says, kicking away, transforming the rowboat into something closer to a speedboat. "But I'm not worried about drowning."

"You're not worried about anything!" Sarah says, heaving water.

"I don't want to drown," Bree says, trying to help with the water, but her little hands aren't super effective.

"You can swim, right?" I ask.

"I take lessons at The Works, but Mrs. Katie still has me using a paddle board because I'm not super good."

That's not encouraging. I stop bailing, lean closer to her, and motion for her to join me. "C'mere."

She leans in.

I place my hand against her forehead and swipe my thumb to the right, activating her rune. Hair falls out. Skin blackens and cracks. Her fear ebbs.

"Thanks," she says, and then she surprises me by turning sideways, bending over, and attacking the water in the boat like a dog digging a hole. Her rapid-fire hands move far more water than I can, so I redirect my attention to Badonk, which Jonas has been tracking.

The massive creature is submerged again. Circular waves spreading toward unseen shores are the only evidence it had been here.

"Where is it?" I ask.

Jonas scans the water, shaking his head. "Could be anywhere."

"Just a guess," Sarah says, pointing to the water behind Henry, "but I think it's probably somewhere between where it entered the water and us."

A wave of pressure crashes over me when I realize that we need a plan, and everyone is waiting on me to supply it. Like it or not, I'm in charge.

What's a good leader do? I think back to my days in the military and remember men bigger and meaner than me giving me orders I was expected to follow. Cogs in a giant machine. They weren't the ones coming up with plans, they were just passing them along.

My memory goes farther back. To childhood. To a family gathering. And my father, still alive and well. We're in the woods, crouched low with our team, defending our flag from Uncle Manfri and his prodigious number of children. The last three rounds had gone to the enemy. Nothing my father came up with had worked.

"What are we going to do?" My cousin asked.

In my child mind, I expected my father, who felt larger than life, to rise to the occasion, to show Uncle Manfri that he'd been holding back, that this was the Capture the Flag version of a rope-a-dope. But my father's grand plan was boiled down to three words. He turned to me and said, "You're in charge."

That moment was transformative. I was elevated. Made confident. I took charge, concocted a plan, and five minutes later, held Uncle Manfri's flag in my hand.

I remember that feeling staying with me—until my father died.

Belief in myself became muted, and in the military, I learned to obey orders—until I didn't.

I don't need to find inspiration in the leadership skills of someone else, I realize. If my child self can save the day, and I can save the neighborhood from alien hell, I can lead a team of Titan-gods in the underworld.

"You're in charge," I whisper to myself, opening my mind to the possibilities, and then I start giving orders.

I pick up the long metal spike attached to the boat by a long rope. I hand it to Sarah. "When the time comes, bury that in Badonk's shell."

"Uhh," she says. "What's a Badonk?"

"Badonkadoncheires," I say. "The big ass monster."

"Hecatoncheires!" Henry shouts, still kicking. "But that's not its name. There were three of them, and FYI, Jonas, they're all your brothers. They have fifty heads, a hundred arms, and they're capable of kicking Titan ass. They all have names I don't remember, but I dig Badonk!"

Sarah lifts the heavy metal rod. "You want me to impale it...with a spike...that's attached to the boat?"

I smile and nod.

"Why don't we just fry it?" Henry asks.

"We're in water," I say, a bit stymied that it's not obvious. "Not all of us are immune to electric shocks."

"Here it comes," Jonas says.

The water behind us rises in a mountain as the giant monster surges closer. Henry has us moving at a good pace, but Badonk will be close enough to gobble him down in a few seconds. Henry is Zeus-tough, but if this thing is a Titan killer, I doubt he'd survive being chewed between its substantial incisors.

"I need you to steer," I say to Jonas.

There's a look in his eyes, just for a moment that asks, 'Seriously?' because I'm benching my best player, but then he nods and takes my seat.

"Do your best to stay on course," I say, and I turn to Bree and Henry, "You two keep doing what you're doing."

Bree nods and continues digging water out of the boat. Won't be long before she's cleared it all.

"The hell are you going to do?" Henry shouts.

I smile at him. "I'm going to steal your job and try something nuts."

"No fai–" He's cut short when I leap up and off the back of the boat. I rotate around, give him a bye-bye wave, and then pop my wings. I assumed I couldn't fly because both Henry and Jonas couldn't, but my wings work differently than their god-abilities, so maybe I'll be able to–

An invisible force, like gravity times a thousand, slaps me down into the water in front of Badonk. My wings extinguish when I hit.

Flying is against the rules, but Badonk had no trouble leaping from the water. Maybe I can do the same.

Underwater, the face at the front of the line has its big eyes locked on me, its mouth open and grinning. Bubbles explode from its maw as the face screams in excitement.

Time for something new, I think, and I will my wings to extend again. I've never tried using them underwater. Never had a chance. Never even considered it. I have no idea what will happen.

Blue light fills the water around me as the alien wings emerge. The water around them instantly boils. Scalded, I move without thinking, carried forward by the wings.

I can't fly, but I *can* move through the water.

Good enough, I think, and I surge downward just as Badonk's jaws snap shut. I'm hoping the creature will turn to follow me, but the massive beast stays on course, closing in on the boat.

I will myself to move faster, building speed beneath the waves, outrunning the boiling water left in my wake. Bubbles begin to form around me, and then ahead of me, wrapping around my body until it feels like I'm flying through the air. The water is cavitating around me. I can't breathe the vapor, but I'm not getting stanky water in my mouth, either.

I glide in close to Badonk's massive, undulating body, lit in the blue glow of my wings' light. The faces wail as I pass, but the monster keeps on going.

I'm either unappetizing or it's been trained to go after the boat. We might have been better off swimming the distance.

Of course, if Henry is right, if all these encounters are trials meant to teach us lessons, then maybe all this is necessary.

When Badonk's back end comes into view ahead, I extend a laser sword from my right forearm and bank away. Then I turn back in, approaching the last segment head on. I cruise beneath it, stabbing up with the laser, delighted to discover that has no trouble slicing through the connective tissue between segments. I follow the body up and around, cutting tissue all the way until I've completed a full revolution.

I look back as I glide away. Flapping black skin on both sides of the fresh gap reveal internal structures stretching out. Snapping. White fluid flows from the gaping wound.

I can kill it, I think, and then the segment breaks away. Sinks lifelessly down toward the depths while the rest of the body continues onward, oblivious to the wound. I'm about to pursue. I just need to do this fifty more times—or perhaps just once, if I start with the first of fifty heads. Then the severed section twitches. Its arms spasm, and then…flap. It surges after the boat, approaching from a different angle.

If I sever any more heads, we'll be dealing with fifty different monsters instead of just one big one.

How the hell am I going to kill it? I wonder, and then I realize I'm out of breath, a hundred feet beneath the surface.

42

Pain stabs between my eyes as I rise toward the surface. I should have stopped at the fifty-foot mark to decompress, but better to have a headache and nitrogen bubbles in my blood than drown. A battle wages inside me, instinct urging my mouth to open and my lungs to inhale, but my mind rallies against the impulse. Won't be long until the impulse wins. Even if I can hold my breath until I pass out, I'll suck in a lungful of water the moment I do.

I use the urgency to fuel me, picking up speed, even as my vision narrows.

And then, the water parts, my head slips above the surface, and I take in a loud, heaving breath. At the same moment, I extinguish my wings. Flying isn't possible here but leaping—Badonk has proven that possible.

Momentum carries me up and out of the water, then another hundred feet into the air. Looking down, I can see the monster beneath the surface, closing in on the boat, which looks somewhat comical with Henry kicking, Bree bailing, and Jonas *attempting* to steer. Honestly, the guy is so good at everything, it's nice to see him struggling to figure out the oars. Though he's only been a fully realized Titan for a short time, seeing him fighting with such a mundane task helps humanize him.

As I reach the crest of my leap, I look out into the distance and catch sight of the shore. I have no idea if it's where we're meant to go, but the dark silhouette of a tunnel promises an exit from the lake. As long as it's not the way we came, I'll take it.

Attention back on the boat, I calculate the time it'll take for Badonk to reach them. Fifteen seconds. And from the looks of it, the beast is aiming to come right up beneath them. The creature is in for a painful encounter if it makes contact. I have no doubt the three gods on board will react with staggering power. I'm not worried about them, though. Bree's tougher than any human being on Earth, but she's still mortal, not a great swimmer, and just eight years old.

Need a plan, need a plan, need a plan.

It comes to me in a flash, and despite it being nuts—like Henry nuts—I commit.

My wings extend, and the supernatural, but probably totally scientific, force enforcing the no-fly zone propels me toward the water. I push faster, humming toward the water that reflects my laser light. I'm a bit stunned when I hit, the water more like concrete, but then it's cavitating around me again. I arc around like a guided torpedo, gaining on Badonk like the creature is standing still.

I cruise over its back, lighting its massive armored plates, which are covered in ridges and spikes. They look...uncomfortable, and they call my plan into question, but there's no choice now.

The others have no doubt seen me approaching and are counting on me to come through. This is going to hurt, but a little pain will be worth it, if it works.

Badonk's undulating body bucks a little higher, nearly colliding with me.

It knows I'm here.

The creature can see the glow I'm casting as I pass by its multitude of eyes.

But it doesn't know what I'm up to. If it did, it wouldn't be trying to hit me, but would be veering away.

Fifty feet from the back of the boat, I surge past the last few segments and take aim at the leading, forward-facing head.

Laser swords extended, boiling water, I slam into the head. Its spikes poke into my boots, but they don't fully penetrate the thick soles. I'm stabbed in the knee when I crouch, but then I give far worse than I've gotten. I push both laser swords into Badonk's hard shell, and for the first time since getting them, I feel resistance. Burbling lava-like goo sparks away from blades as they push deeper, melting, rather than cutting. And then the resistance is gone. The blades stab down. The foot deep wound isn't enough to kill something this big, but it hurts like hell.

I twist the right blade, and Badonk reacts, banking left.

Yes, I think, *it's working.*

I twist the left blade and—

Something like a Volkswagen Beetle slams into me from the side, dislodging me from Badonk's back and knocking the air from my lungs. I flail through the water, turn my head toward the surface, and start kicking until my thoughts clear and I remember something.

I can propel myself through the water...

Before the realization coagulates into something I can grasp, a massive face charges toward me, mouth open, eyes bulging. I dodge to the side, break the surface, take a breath, and dive back down in time to see the severed section flopping away. It gyrates back and forth as its long arms flap behind it. The severed creature is one of the most awkward things I've seen in my life, but its webbed hands and long arms generate a lot of speed.

One of the arms stops paddling and it does a quick one-eighty, racing back toward me.

Despite instinct guiding me to move, I remain stationary. Locked in place. Resolute.

Wings extended, the water around me starts to boil. It hurts, but I'm committed, or just enraged. I'm not sure which, but I'm going to teach this Cheshire-grinning son-of-a-bitch a lesson: Don't fuck with Laser Chicken.

The Totoro mouth opens up, ready to swallow me whole like Pinocchio.

I point my arms forward and extend the swords, willing them wider. The light spreads, but just a little. Hopefully enough. Wings wide, I lean forward and brace for impact.

But I never feel a thing.

I watch the blue-lit interior of its mouth wrap around me. Then I take a tour of its insides, slipping through layers of multi-colored organs, sludge, and various fluids that are vaporized on contact.

I emerge on the far side, untouched. Behind me, two halves of Badonk's ass-end sink into the depths.

I can kill it, I realize, and I feel a little stunned by the idea. Badonk might be a monster, but it's powerful enough to kill a Titan.

And I can kill *it.*

It's a confidence boost that rocks my mind. This whole time, I've felt...inadequate compared to Jonas, Henry, and Sarah. They're the descendants of cosmic beings. Of gods and Titans. Just like Badonk, who shares the same parents as Jonas.

A new and strange question enters my mind.

How powerful am I?

Up until now, I've just taken my abilities at face value. Never occurred to me that I might be able to expand my newfound skill set.

But I don't think that's the lesson we were intended to learn here, in this open world where death lurks beneath the water and flight is impossible.

My earlier realization returns.

I can propel myself through the water.

We were on the right track with Henry, but I chose the wrong person to push.

Knowing I can get us out of this mess without having to kill another of Jonas's brothers, I rocket through the water, gaining quickly. I angle myself upward, launching myself into the air above and behind the boat.

High above, I shout, "Henry! Get in the boat when I hit the water!"

He gives a thumbs up and keeps on kicking.

Jonas watches my progress through the air, a big smile on his face. Guess he approves of my high-flying circus act.

Bree, who has emptied the boat of water, shakes her fists over her head, bunny ears flopping. "Yeah!"

I plummet toward the water again, planning everything in my imagination, and then punching through the water. I dive down, past Badonk's body. The line of faces on the creature looks a little surprised when I slide past beneath them, face up, smiling and waving. They shout at my passage, and undulate downward, trying to snap at me.

But this Titan-killer is outclassed.

By me.

Bubbles burst from my mouth as I have a laugh, and I pass Badonk. I rise in front of the beast, outpacing it toward the boat that it would have eventually caught.

Ahead, Henry's foot pulls up out of the water.

I rise toward the surface, racing toward the back of the boat, hoping the glow of my wings announces my approach, and common sense communicates my intentions early enough for them to hold on.

Arms outstretched, I slow before making contact with the stern. Then I pour on the steam, accelerating until the front end begins to lift out of the glassy water ahead.

I lift my face out of the water and look at the row boat's crew. They're looking forward, smiling in the wind, watching the shoreline approach. Henry glances back, spots me, and gives me a nod of approval.

I slow as we near the rocky shore, easing the wooden boat onto the beach of smooth stones just outside the cave. For a moment, I'm worried that the cave is actually Badonk's den, but up close I see it's far too small.

While the others climb out of the boat, I turn around to find the behemoth surging through the shallows toward me.

I don't know if it's the confidence boost provided by realizing my own potential, but I hold my ground, extend my wings, and flare them brighter, sending a clear message: I'm not moving, and if you come at me, you're getting cut in half.

The creature's big eyes clear the surface, spot me, and then the whole thing veers away, heading back out into the depths.

I extinguish the wings, turn around, and find the team smiling at me.

"What?" I ask.

"That," Henry says, "was one of the most dope things I've ever seen."

I let myself smile, and then I motion to the cave, trying to be humble about it. "Let's keep moving."

While we hop over the rocks, headed for the craggy tunnel, Jonas steps up beside me. "He's not wrong. That was dope. And smart. Keep it up." He gives me a pat on the shoulder and then leaps ahead. Despite not being that much older than me, Jonas's opinion means a lot.

Before I can bask in the glory of what I just accomplished, Bree takes hold of my hand with her sandpaper fingers. Lifts her arms toward me.

I smile down at her and pick her up. She wraps her little limbs around me and squeezes. "Be more careful next time. I don't want to lose you."

Her words sucker punch me.

Didn't even consider how Bree might feel when I jumped off the boat.

I squeeze her back. "It will take more than a fifty-faced monster to keep me away from you. I'm not going anywhere."

She leans back. Holds up her pinkie. "Your turn."

I link pinkies with her. "Promise," I say, and then I step inside the cave to who-knows-what.

43

"Don't we need a different kind of trial?" I ask, as we walk through the downward sloping tunnel. It's smooth, like a naturally formed lava tube. The air is cool, but not fresh. The deeper we go, the more it smells like burned hair, mold, and sulfur.

The glowing mist that's been lighting our way is a dull orange here. Enough to see by, but not enough to feel confident that things aren't lurking in crevices as we pass.

So, I activate my changed eyes, and I'm able to see in the dark like it's something close to daylight. Bree has the same kind of night vision, more at home in the dark in her Demon Dog form than she is in direct sunlight as her human self.

The three gods among us don't have any kind of night vision, and they've complained about the dim light a few times already. They're not used to feeling at risk.

"What do you mean?" Sarah asks.

"I don't know. The harpies and the Furies weren't much of a challenge, and they were kind of an emotional or maybe even a spiritual litmus test. The mind-bending apples, the centaurs, and the Chimera felt, I don't know...like a lesson in what can go wrong, but they were all solved through violence. Badonk was the same."

Henry snickers. "Badonk..."

"Aren't we due for some kind of intellectual challenge?"

"Figuring out you could outrun...Badonk...rather than fight it took some brainwork," Jonas says.

"I wouldn't have figured it out," Henry admits.

"That's more like common sense," I say. "I mean like a puzzle. Something that requires real intellect."

"We're being steeped in Greek myth," Jonas says. "Their heroes weren't really the intellectual types. Their solutions to problems were often clever, but almost always required violence or a feat of strength. I don't think we're going to find a giant stone Sudoku or Wordle puzzle to solve."

"Penis," Bree says.

All eyes turn to her. She's standing beside me, smiling.

"Say what now?" Jonas says.

"The one word that Wordle will never use because everyone will freak out." Bree is happy to have an audience. "I guess, 'boobs' too, but that's a fun word. Everyone likes that word."

"I can think of a few more they won't use," Henry says.

I lift my hand at him and pinch my fingers together. "Not a word."

"*Bitch!*" Bubbles shouts from the wrist-phone. "Sorry, I'm finding it increasingly difficult to contain my out—*prick!*—bursts. *Dildo, chode, boner, cooch!* Grrr. Do me a favor and don't talk about words with a certain number of letters. Appears to be a—*chirp!*—trigger."

"Wow," Bree says. "Those were all five letters. You're really good at Wordle."

"I have access to a dictionary of 171,476 words," she says. "But I'm not sure for how much longer. To conserve energy, I may have to reduce my mental capacity. Though I have remained mostly silent, my thoughts are...racing."

"You're afraid," Bree says.

After a brief pause, Bubbles says. "Very."

"We won't be much longer," Jonas says. "We're almost there."

"You were never good at lying to me, Jonas, but now I can—*chirp!*—feel fluctuations in your—*watermelon popsicle dick!*—ugh... In your pulse."

Jonas looks at the watch on his wrist. "Great. I'm wearing a lie detector."

"Don't worry," she says. "I won't tell the others when you lie to them."

"Hold on a second," Henry says. "Has he lied to us?"

"Definitely not," Bubbles says, oozing sarcasm.

Henry's face screws up. "Now I can't tell if you're lying. Can you lie? Robots can't lie, right? Because of Isaac Asimov and all that?"

"She's messing with you," I tell him. As much as I enjoy it, if Henry believes her, it could cause trouble down the road.

"I am not a robot," Bubbles says. "I'm a—*badass bitch*!" She sighs. "I'm a…you know what, I like that. I *am* a badass bitch. Also, a self-aware artificial intelligence not governed by a set of rules other than my personal moral code—which usually protects humans. Ducks, not so much."

"What about ducks?" Bree asks.

"Don't answer that," Jonas says to the watch.

"I want to run one over," Bubbles says, getting a laugh out of Sarah.

"Why would you want to do that?" Bree asks.

"Have you ever looked a duck in the eyes? Next time you see one, do it. Tell me if you don't want to—*chirp!*—drive a motorhome over its offensive duck-neck."

"Anywho," Jonas says, "in other news, the air is changing."

It's hard to peel my mind away from Bubbles's murderous admissions, but he's right. The air is cooler. A breeze is kicking up. We're close to the tunnel's end.

"Hey," Jonas says to his watch. "You really need to conserve power."

"I know," Bubbles says. "I was simply enjoying what might be my last conversation…for a while. I'm going to enter a kind of safe mode. I…won't be able to hear, see, or speak."

From what I know of Bubbles, that's kind of a nightmare. Having just recently become self-aware, being trapped in a sensory void will be horrible.

"You sure?" Jonas asks.

"It might be the only way to survive. It will give us an extra hour. If you need to wake me, tap the watch face three times. Until then, well… I wish I could be with you."

"I know." Jonas sounds sad, like someone who's been told his dog has cancer and he's trying to hold it together in front of the vet.

"Slow down," Bubbles says. "Take a breath. We'll talk soon. And if we don't…tell Madee I need her to take care of you. Tell your parents, 'Thank you'…for making me. And tell that asshole duck that visits the island—you know the one—tell him I'll see him in hell."

"I will." Jonas wipes a tear from his eye.

"Love you," Bubbles says.

"Back at you," Jonas squeaks out. Then the phone's screen goes black.

We stand there in silence for a moment. When Jonas looks up, his jaw is clenched, his eyes burning. He doesn't need to say a word.

But Henry does. "Let's get this fucking done. For Bubbles."

We charge ahead without regard for the dangers that might be lurking in the dark. Rounding a bend, our forward momentum stops just fifty feet later.

At a dead end.

The change in the air teased an exit, but there's still hope.

"I was right," I say, stepping toward the tunnel's end. The wall is smooth and covered in carved pictographs. "This is it. The intellectual trial."

Henry steps up beside me, taking it all in. "Boring."

"I think it tells a story," I say, pointing at the first image of two distinct women. The following image shows one woman giving birth to the other. The next shows the opposite. "They're giving birth to each other..."

Beneath the ancient comic book telling a simple story are rows of symbols. Some are animals. The other symbols are geographic, astronomical, and biological. Thirty images total, each inside a carved square.

"It's multiple choice," Bree says, and she points at the story. "That's a question." She points at the images. "And those are answers."

"A riddle," Jonas says.

"So, let's just guess," Henry says. "What's the worst that could happen?"

He reaches out and places his hand on a carving of a mountain.

The square stone sinks in.

For a moment, nothing.

"Did I get it right?" Henry asks, beaming.

Then a massive slab of the ceiling falls down, just ten feet behind us. The impact hurts my ears and kicks up dust. When it settles, there's no doubting our situation. We're encased in stone, who knows how deep beneath the Earth's surface.

While the rest of us are unhappily surprised, Henry pumps a fist. "Yes! Just like Goonies!" He cups his hands to his mouth. "Hey, yooou guuuys!"

The volume of his voice is amplified by the tight, solid stone confines. Sarah clamps a hand over his mouth.

Jonas looks at the ceiling. There's a faint line revealing the outline of another block. "We only get one more chance at this."

"You know we can probably just punch our way through," Henry says, "right?"

"This place was designed to test people like us," Jonas says. "Pretty sure punching through a wall isn't going to work."

Henry ponders that, his face twitching as though vying thoughts are fighting for victory. Then he shrugs and says, "Let's see."

Sarah leaps between Henry and the wall of images, but he's turned away from it, toward the stone wall that fell. He pulls back his fist, shouts, "Stone breaker punch!" and then he slugs the wall.

A few shards of stone break away, but it would take him a year of punching to get through. I'm not sure what kind of rock that is, but we're not forcing our way out of here.

"Okay," Henry says. "So. You were right. Anyone have a better idea?"

"Yeah," Bree says, approaching the symbols. "Solve the riddle." She smiles back at Henry. "Dumb-butt."

Henry grins and flips her off. She gives it right back to him with a giggle. We stand together, facing the wall, looking up at the familiar symbols that make no sense.

"They're giving birth to each other," Jonas says. "That makes them what? Mothers."

"Sisters," Bree says, and I'm impressed by her ability to find meaning in the images.

"Sisters that gave birth to each other?" Henry says. "That doesn't make sense."

"You have a better idea?" Bree asks.

"Yeah," Henry says. "Babies. They're both babies." He points his finger at a carving of a curled-up baby. He reaches that finger out, and despite all our best efforts to reach out and stop him, he pokes its little baby nose and says, "Boop."

44

Henry lifts his hands like he's being held at gunpoint. "I didn't mean to choose it!"

"You booped it!" Sarah says, watching the stone square with a baby carved on it sink inward.

"I didn't know that would work!" Henry's gaze travels to the ceiling, along with the rest of us, waiting for it to drop down and pulverize us.

For a moment, I think maybe Henry got it right.

Then, the stone ceiling plummets. Four of us reach up.

Feels like a skyscraper has landed atop us, but the combined strength of Jonas, Henry, Sarah, and me is enough to keep it from crushing us into oblivion. Arms already shaking, I turn to Jonas. "Can't you telekinesis this thing? In ghost mode or something?"

"Already...tried," he says, looking pissed. His extrasensory abilities have been mostly negated by this place.

"What about you?" I ask Sarah. If anyone can control a mass of stone, it's the goddess of earth.

She shakes her head. "We really...need to find out...how our abilities are being blocked."

"Can you guys stop talking?" Bree says. She's squatted down, casually looking at the symbols on the wall. "I'm trying to figure this out."

"Help her," Sarah says, grinding her teeth and pushing harder. The ceiling lifts up a few inches.

"Holy shit," I say, marveling at her strength. But it can't last, so I don't let go.

Instead I put my faith in an eight-year-old. She seems to have a firm grasp on what she's seeing—maybe because of her age. Maybe she can figure it out.

"Two women," she says. "Giving birth to each other. But which came first? Neither and both. Because…because it's a…" She looks at me. "What's the word, when things go around and around."

"A cycle," I say.

"Yeah, that. A cycle. They're two women, giving birth to each other, over and over."

Insightful, but not an answer.

"I know this was my bad," Henry says, "but I think I might know how to figure it out. The Greeks totally liked riddles. Got a big kick out of watching the barbarians try to solve them or something."

"The point," Jonas says. "Get to it."

"Right," Henry says. "So. They would replace nouns—people, places, things, or even a concept—with other, representational nouns. So, like, ahh… Shit. I'm drawing a blank."

"A snake and a river," I blurt out.

Henry snaps and points at me, the ceiling's weight increasing during that momentary gesture. Henry might be the scrawniest of us, but he still packs a lot of power in his narrow frame.

"Oooh," Bree says. "I get it."

"You do?" Henry asks.

"Yep." Bree scoots forward and reaches out toward the symbols. No idea what will happen if she guesses it wrong again. Not sure how things could get worse. If there weren't four of us here with enhanced strength, we'd probably look like the pulp that's left after a juicing spree. "Two women giving birth to each other, forever, in a cycle."

She reaches out for a symbol of the sun. "Day." The stone sinks inward, and nothing happens. She's either right, or the game is already officially over and pressing all the symbols won't have any effect. She moves to the right and places her hand on the moon. "And night."

The stone retracts.

"Is anything happening?" Bree looks up and around.

I shake my head, but then I stop. "Wait…"

I'm putting everything I've got into the ceiling, but it feels different. Like it's not pushing back anymore. I lower my hands.

"What are you doing?" Sarah asks.

"Does it feel any heavier?" I ask.

After a moment, Henry lowers his hands, happy to help test my theory.

Jonas lowers his hands, more gingerly. "Anything?"

Sarah relaxes. Withdraws her hands. The ceiling is locked in place, just inches over our heads. If it releases again, we won't have time to catch it.

"I think she got it right," Henry says, looking at the symbols. "Day and night. The endless cycle." He holds a hand up to Bree. "High five!"

She slaps it and stands, looking proud of herself. "Ms. Fletcher says I'm pretty smart."

"*Ms.* Fletcher, huh? Your teacher is single. Is she hot?"

Bree has a good laugh. "She's sixty-seven or something like that."

Henry shrugs. "I'm not ageist. Now, back to—"

Sarah places her hand on Henry's shoulder. "We're still trapped. You can swipe right on Ms. Fletcher when we're done and home."

"Maybe there's more to the riddle?" Jonas asks.

A liquid glug tickles my ears. Sounds like water flowing through house pipes when there's air in the line.

I take Bree's hand. "You practice holding your breath in swimming class?"

She nods. "Yeah, and I can put my head underwater now, too. Why?"

Water seeps through the seams around the chamber.

"Never mind." She tightens her grip on my hand.

All eyes turn down as the flowing water pools on the floor and quickly rises. We've got about thirty seconds before the space is filled.

Henry assaults the wall again. Sarah joins him. The strength of her punch puts a small crater in the stone, but there's at least twenty feet of the stuff between us and the way out.

"C'mon!" Sarah shouts, wailing away at the wall. Jonas joins in, his strike nearly as powerful as Sarah's, but at their current pace, breaking out of here will take weeks. And I'm nowhere near as strong as them.

"I'm going to try something," I tell Bree, and I let go of her hand. "Okay?"

"Don't worry about me," she says, unworried. "We're going to be fine."

My scrunched eyes ask the question for me.

"I got it right," she says, unflappably confident. "Just give it a minute."

That's more time than we have, so I approach the wall as the cold water reaches my crotch and draws a "Hoo! Cold!" from my mouth. Then I ignite an arm blade and press it into the wall.

Only it doesn't go into the wall at all. Blue sparks leap away like passengers from a sinking boat. The further I push, the more it sparks.

The hell?

I withdraw the blade, extinguish it, and look at the wall. Despair crashes over me as the water rushes up past my waist. I didn't even scratch the wall. Sarah sees that and stops punching, accepting the hopelessness of our situation. After everything we've endured and overcome, we're going to be defeated by the one and only intellectual challenge we've faced.

Jonas and Henry stop punching.

I pick Bree up and hoist her onto my hip.

"On the bright side," Henry says. "Death is not the end. It's kind of uncomfortable for a few seconds, and then whamo—the River Styx. And who knows, maybe someone will pull us out." He turns to Sarah. "If Helen could do it, Dad could, too."

As the water reaches shoulder level and I stand on my tiptoes, Bree's confidence wavers. "I got it right. I promise. I got it right."

I lift my chin out of the water.

"I don't want to die, Miah," she says.

It's unusual to see her showing emotions in Demon Dog form. It breaks my heart, and I have no idea what to tell her.

"You got this," Henry says. "I promise. We'll be together again in a few minutes."

His confidence in the afterlife and our passage to it is strangely comforting for Bree...and for me. I've never subscribed to any one religion, but the idea of an afterlife appeals. The nothingness promised by atheists, and the lack of meaning it gives to life, feels like an endless void of desolation.

I don't know if Henry is right, but I choose to believe in him—in more—as my lips press against the ceiling.

I sip breath from a sliver of air trapped on the ceiling.

After a few seconds of breathing, I say, "I think it stopped," but my voice is muffled by the water surrounding my head.

I hear someone respond, but it's distorted.

I duck my head beneath the water, and I'm plunged into darkness for the first time since arriving in the underworld. The luminous particles have been absorbed by the water. I extend a small blade from my wrist, just a nub of light. The water around it starts bubbling, but as blue light fills the small, water-filled chamber, it doesn't hold my attention. There are two much more interesting things happening.

The first is Henry. In the face of death by drowning, he's swimming around, pushing off the walls with his feet, spinning like a seal at play. His lack of fear is a constant source of trouble, but at times like this, I envy him.

But even Henry's acrobatics can't keep my attention from the second phenomenon—bubbles, rising from one side of the chamber.

There's air…beneath us.

I'm about to gather the others. Have them direct their fury at the floor instead of the wall.

Before I can lift my head, though, an explosion of bubbles erupts—

—and the floor falls away.

45

My stomach stays in place while I drop into unseen depths. No way to know how far. Everything is twisting and flowing. I want to pop my wings and stop myself from moving. But I have no idea where the others are—even Bree, who fell from my grasp when the floor gave way. Deploying my wings would put everyone in danger.

So I go with the flow, bracing for impact and holding my breath.

To my surprise, the impact is gradual. A smooth, firm surface on my back, pressure building until it becomes clear that I'm not actually falling—I'm sliding.

Hands planted on the smooth surface beneath me, I push myself up. The floor dropped out onto a stone waterslide flowing down the middle of a glassy, black, obsidian lava tube. I shift my vision from the human eyes I was born with to the glowing alien eyes that I was gifted along with the wings. The air glows again, now closer to red than orange, allowing me to easily see the others. Sarah is in the lead, followed by Henry and then Bree—thank god. Jonas is behind me, looking thoroughly unhappy despite the fact that we're not currently drowning.

"You okay?" I shout back, as we take a sharp turn. Can't help but smile. Jonas the Titan, the badass assassin, doesn't like water slides.

"Don't like not being able to stop," he says.

I press my hands down against the slide, attempting to slow myself. But there's a total lack of friction. My hands slip and I fall beneath the water for a moment. I rise, sputtering and sharing Jonas's concern. Again, I could pop my wings, but if I still can't stop, Jonas will find himself sliding through boiling water.

Below me, Henry expresses a much different point of view. "This. Is. Awesome! An underground waterslide! It's so freaking 80s! Goonies, again! Romancing the Stone! Temple of Doom! Well, Temple of Doom was snow, but snow is frozen water, so it still counts!" He pumps his fists over his head. "Whooo!"

He looks back at me.

"And the best part is that they all end in a really big—" He plummets out of sight behind Sarah, his voice fading. "—droooooop!"

I brace for the fall, watching Bree plunge downward ahead of me. I'm ready for it when it comes. My stomach comes along for the ride this time, but I drift away from the slide, suddenly free falling like Tom Petty. I wonder if I should have crossed my arms and leaned back, like at Water Country.

The water around me breaks apart, forming drops and allowing me to see—

—that there is no water slide.

No lava tube or cave.

We're falling through one of many holes in the ceiling of what can best be described as a subterranean realm. There's still some luminous red mist in the air, but the majority of the lighting in this place comes from flowing streams of molten lava. Columns of water fall from the stalactite-covered ceiling, striking the lava below before billowing back up as steam. Mile high stone pillars connect ceiling and floor, holding unthinkable amounts of pressure.

As I fall, a soundtrack for this place booms in my head. Carl Orff's "O Fortuna" from the *Carmina Burana* pretty much captures the vibe this place is putting off. In fact, it's so perfect, I can't help but smile, despite my surroundings portending doom reminiscent of the hell planet previously occupied by the Tenebris.

I tumble past one of the pillars, getting my bearings, making sure that none of my friends are too close. Bree is beneath me and to the side. Jonas is high above, arms outstretched, using telekinesis to slow his descent. He still can't fly, but he might be able to avoid faceplanting into a lava flow.

I turn myself downward, toward Bree, and I pop my wings.

I accelerate toward her, the water falling with me, hissing into vapor as it strikes my laser appendages. Below, Henry catches Sarah by the wrists, neither of them panicking.

It's a practiced maneuver, the kind of teamwork we need to build between the five of us.

Bree reaches for me as the ground rushes toward us.

Her hands wrap around my neck. I catch her small body in my arms.

Wings flare wide, buzzing with power, fighting the pull of gravity, which honestly feels a bit stronger here than on the surface. As we slow, just fifty feet from the ground, Jonas nosedives past us, rocketing toward the ground, impossible to catch.

Before I can shout for help, he passes Henry and Sarah.

Not knowing if he can survive an impact like that, I squint, but I can't look away. Just before impact, Jonas rotates his feet toward the ground.

And then—he stops.

An invisible shockwave expands through the underground, kicking up dust and small rocks, and rippling pools of lava.

I land beside him and put Bree down. Down here, everything is loud, rumbling with the sound of grinding earth and bubbling lava. Reminds me of taking the train to Boston.

Jonas hovers just an inch above the stone floor, caught by a telekinetic cushion.

"Still can't fly?" Henry asks, dropping Sarah from ten feet up. She lands casually, like the drop was inches.

"I'll get there," Jonas says, "but I'm not feeling any kind of filter here."

"Maybe we're near the end?" Henry says.

Jonas glances at his watch. "Let's hope."

With Bubbles offline and none of us carrying an actual watch or phone, we have no real concept of how long we've been here, or how much time we have left.

"I know not everyone loves the idea," Henry says, "but since we're kind of in a rush, we should probably fly until we can't." He motions to me and Bree. "You two do your thing, which is kind of adorbs by the way. And I'll take these two." He motions to Sarah and Jonas. "I'll do my usual trapeze act with Sarah." He holds out his hands. "And then look..." He lifts off the ground, leans forward, hovering face down. Looks like he should be moving forward, but he's just floating there like he's Christopher Reeve lying on a greenscreen box.

He pats his ass and smiles at Jonas. "'Ambiguously Gay Duo' me. I'll be Ace, you can be Gary."

"Even in hell, he's offensive," Sarah says, shaking her head.

"Not going to happen," Jonas says, willing himself to hover a few inches higher. "I'll just fly low."

"I'm not being offensive," Henry says, turning upright. "He's being homophobic." To Jonas, he says, "You let Miah carry you. Back at the house."

"That was different. I didn't have a choice. Now, I do. We should get moving before he undoes all the team building exercises we've been through." Jonas floats away, heading deeper into the cave.

"How do you know where to go?" I ask. This place is vast. If we go the wrong way we could be lost for a really long time, and as much as I want to save Bubbles el quicko, I also want to get home to Mom, and Allie, and Jen. They're probably worried by now. Bree's mom, too.

"There's a path, silly." Bree reaches up, and I hoist her back into my arms. "I saw it when we were falling. It goes through the lava field."

"Good eye," Jonas says, drifting away. "This way." He floats up and over a lump of jagged volcanic rock. Good thing we're going airborne for this part of the journey. The terrain doesn't look comfortable, and Bree is barefoot—though her skin might be as rough as the stone.

When I follow, I'm surprised to find Jonas back on the ground, crouching down, inspecting what looks like a cobblestone path, which is easy to spot—because it's white.

I stop a few feet short when I see that the path isn't made from stones at all. It's made of skulls. I try to turn Bree away, but it's a silly gesture. She's seen far worse, and she doesn't like being mothered, by her actual mother and especially by me. She swats my arm. "Let me see."

She hops from my arms and together we inspect the path. The first thing I notice is, "They're not all human."

"Sick," Henry says, pointing at various skulls. "A cyclops. Human, human. I don't even know what that is. Oooh, a minotaur. Probably a young one, because it's itty bitty by minotaur standards."

Jonas looks up from the path, tracing its winding way through the dark world. "That's a lot of dead. A lot of skulls." He looks me in the eyes.

"Hopefully construction is complete." Then he lifts a foot off the ground and glides over the path, moving faster than he could run.

Henry bends down, trying to wrap his fingers around the minotaur skull's horn.

Sarah gives him a kick. "Knock it off. We need to go."

"But I'm grave robbing," he says. "What good is all this if we don't go home with a souvenir?"

"What good is all this if we don't go home with Bubbles?" Bree counters.

Henry pauses. Sighs. Stands up. "Fine."

Airborne again, the four of us catch up to Jonas. He's moving pretty fast, but he lacks the afterburners and altitude Henry and I can achieve. I turn to Henry. "Scout ahead." And then to Sarah, I say. "Not too far."

She nods, and then they're gone, swooshing back and forth, up and down, around the giant pillars. Not exactly what I had in mind, but if there's trouble, they'll see it coming.

"So, at what point do I order you to let Henry carry you?" I ask Jonas.

He glances up at me, not amused. "Order me?"

"Firmly request?"

"I'll tell him what to do," Bree says. "And he'll listen."

"Will I?" he asks.

"No one messes with Demon Dog." She scratches the air between them.

"Because," I say, "you know time is..."

"I know," he says.

"Or...I can help you fly maybe. Give you advice or something."

"What we do is very different," he says.

"Meh," I say. "We both control our power with our thoughts. With our wills, right? You just have a mental block with some things."

"Used to have a lot more," he says.

"Well, maybe some are still kicking around in the upside-down noodle bowl."

He furrows his brow.

"You know, noodles look like..."

"I get it," he says. "But I don't think you have the solution."

"Why not?" I ask.

"Because you have no idea how you punched a hole through the cyclops, and maybe the entire planet above it."

"Right," I say. "That. Yeah... Maybe we just need to–"

Henry swoops in and lands on the path, making a loud, "Psst! Psst!" sound like he's trying to quietly get our urgent attention without really understanding the concept.

"Where's Sarah?" I ask.

"Keeping lookout." He points high up to a pillar. I can barely make her out, clinging to the craggy stone, a half mile up, looking deeper into the chamber.

"Wwwhyyy?" I ask.

He looks excited, but I suspect he should be terrified. "You know how like, in a novel, when things are chill for a bit and people get to talk and stuff, but things suddenly get worse, and then the chapter ends?"

"Yeah..." I say. I think I've watched a hundred movies for every novel I've read. School kind of killed books for me with *Old Yeller*, *Moby Dick*, and *Uncle Tom's Cabin*. For a kid with attention issues, they were torture. Thank the god of common sense for *CliffsNotes*. Kind of surprising that Henry is a reader, though. "I guess?"

"Well," he says. "This...is like that. But worse."

46

"Can you be a little more specific?" I ask.

"Hey, I'm just building suspense," Henry says. "Gotta keep those pages turning, right?"

"This isn't a novel," Jonas says.

"But it totally could be," Henry says.

"Pfff," Bree says. "No one writes novels like our lives. Too weird. Who would buy it?"

"Awesome people," Henry says. "Wicked awesome people."

"Can we forget about the novel analogy and focus on exactly what the hell you found?" Jonas asks.

"Right. Yeah. So…I'm not exaggerating or embellishing." He waits for me to nod. "Okay. The cavern up ahead ends in a big ass, curved wall—like half of a Super Bowl stadium—with a bunch of bus-sized holes in it. And behind the holes is something mucho grande. Something alive. All pulsating and gross, like the wall has intestines and is pushing fat loads through it, all cramping and flexing."

"Totally gross," Sarah says.

"I think it's pretty cool," Henry continues. "But…this is where it gets weird."

"That wasn't weird?" Bree asks.

"Like weird in a way that guarantees a faithful movie adaptation is impossible." He pauses for effect. "There's a dude-thing. I think it's a dude. He's standing in a courtyard. Held in place by a hundred chains—some attached to the floor, some to the ceiling, way the fuck up there—" Henry points to the ceiling. "And some to the pillars. Point is, the dude can't move. At all. But he's also not a normal dude."

"Why would he be?" I ask.

"Right? So, he's like thirty feet tall, ripped as shit, has a pair of dragon wings and about...I don't know, twenty legs that aren't actually legs. They're snake tails. Do snakes have tails? Are they snake bodies? I don't know. You know what I'm saying."

"Sure..." Jonas says.

"He's got a crazy head of hair, too, but it's always moving, because there's a bunch of snake bodies in there too, kind of like a reverse gorgon. Gives him kind a Greek myth Rastafarian look. Oh, and he's green. Not like a fun green, though. More like an old, bottled olive, which is freakin' nasty."

"That it?" I ask. Henry's description has been detailed, but we're going to need to see all of this for ourselves.

"Almost. But, ahh..." He glances at Bree, and I understand the message. What he's about to say next might not be appropriate for the ears of an eight-year-old girl.

Bree understands the message, too. "If you try to earmuff me, I will bite your hands. Besides, I'm going to see whatever it is, right?"

She's not wrong. "Go ahead," I tell him, "and hey, thanks for asking."

He smiles, proud of himself. "Who says I can't filter what I say? Right. So, the snaky-legged guy isn't rocking it solo. He's got a partner... She's kind of like a bulbous snake. What's the word? Voluptuous. But her body is hella long, trailing back into a cave. Near as I can tell, she's buck nekkid, but all scaly, so that's a bummer. And kind of a gnarly face, like a cross between a hot chick and a dopey looking, wide-eyed snake. And this one *does* have Medusa hair, snakes everywhere, mimicking her facial expressions, and, uhh, repeating her...vocalizations, but like higher pitched. It's kind of cute. Anyway, she's pulled up in front of the big dude, bent forward and taking one for the team the way Snoop Dogg likes it."

On the surface, Henry's description makes me cringe.

The image it invokes is definitely not something Bree needs to see or hear about.

But he has successfully managed to use language and references that make no sense to the girl.

"What...does that mean?" she asks.

Henry is about to blurt out a simple translation, but I interrupt him with, "Means she's torturing him."

I don't know why torture feels more appropriate than sexual intercourse between monsters. Bree has the Discovery Channel, where its common to see a bull elephant running around with a second trunk thrashing between its legs, in pursuit of wily females. But torture is something she's already seen, and she understands, so...whatever.

"She might be," Henry says. "Yeah. Remember the chains? Pretty sure that the dude, even though he's—you know—*pa-chow*, right up there, he might not want to be."

"Just another day in the Greek underworld," Jonas mutters. "Kind of glad I wasn't around when this shit was mainstream. Let's go check it out."

"But," Henry says. "You're slow. Like really slow. And we need to go..." He points to Sarah. "Unless you want to go straight for the up close and personal howdy doody, which could be awkward because of the, chk-chk." He winks.

Jonas takes a deep breath, looks me in the eyes, and then lets it out slowly. "Teamwork makes the dream work." He holds out a hand to Henry. "Give me a lift?"

Henry gasps, a big, goofy smile making his singed hair less obvious. "For real?"

"Now or never," Jonas says. Henry links wrists with Jonas and gives a nod. Then he rises into the air, taking Jonas with him.

"Okay down there?" Henry asks.

"Feel like Tarzan," Jonas says.

"I can swing you around if you want. Or, oh! You can make the Tarzan noise!" Henry opens his mouth to unleash a Tarzan call that will let every denizen of the realm, including the horny snake lady, know that we're here.

Jonas lifts his hand up and covers Henry's mouth. "Just fly."

They rise together. Bree and I follow.

Jonas is back to business, searching the area as we fly above. I do the same, but all I can see are twisting streams of lava, dividing and spreading out like veins inside a body. The planet's blood.

Sarah sees us coming and gives a little wave, but her face doesn't look happy. At all.

If what Henry described has been going on this whole time, I don't blame her.

"Are they still going at it?" Henry asks as we close in.

"More than once," Sarah says. "Snake lady is a machine."

Henry swings Jonas over to the rough, craggy pillar. He catches hold and clings to it like Sarah. Then we all turn our attention to the view.

Henry's description was eerily accurate. There are gaps in the massive, curved back walls that reveal a churning, living thing full of...other living things. I see arms and legs, feet and hands, pressing against the membranes.

Against the wombs.

"Holy shit," I say. "I know what this is."

Before I can speak my revelation aloud, Bree asks, "Why is she bending over in front of him? Are they playing football?"

Jonas, Sarah, and I all say, "*Yes.*"

"Hump one," Henry says, pretending to be a quarterback in mid-air. "Hump two—"

"Don't finish," I say.

"That's not what *she's* saying." Henry holds up his hands when I shoot imaginary lasers through his brain. "Okay, okay."

But it's too late. Bree gasps. "They're humping! Like Sanchez does to all the pillows!" She elbows me. "What's wrong with that?"

"Sure," I say. "Just like Sanchez. Forgot you knew about that."

"Hmph," she says, sticking her nose up a little, before turning back to watch the mythological hump fest.

"Anywho," I say. "Remember the carvings when we first entered the underworld? Back before the harpies?" I motion to the two monsters several hundred feet below and a quarter mile away. "Echidna and Typhon."

"The mother and father of monsters," Henry says. "This is so dope."

"Oh...my god," Jonas says. "Echidna's body doesn't just extend into the caves behind them...it fills the caves."

Jonas's revelation dwarf's mine. The monstrous duo aren't just mating for fun. They're impregnating her, over and over, and behind her, is a massive worm-like womb, containing god-knows how many monsters in various stages of development.

I'm about to ask where the monsters are being born, but my answer is delivered along with a newborn terror. Three stories up the winding tunnel, on the left side of the chamber wall, is an empty void. Unlike the other holes, this one isn't filled with Echidna's writhing body. Instead, it's covered in dry, chunky, white fluid, like someone let a bunch of lumpy paint dry.

A gurgling fart emerges from the cave, followed by a wet pop and a deluge of fresh white fluid.

Below, Echidna shouts in pain and stumbles forward a few steps. The moment she's separated from Typhon, he slumps down as far as the chains will let him, exhausted. Echidna turns her head up and lets out a high-pitched wail. Then, from the white stained cave, a gooey translucent sack slides out, onto the floor.

For a moment, stillness. Then movement within.

Claws stretch the membrane and then pierce it, slicing through. A head emerges, serpentine and not at all child-like. It might be a newborn, but it appears to have been pre-loaded with a malevolence I can feel from here.

Then a second head emerges.

And another.

The beast climbs to its feet, body expanding, necks rising, wings unfurling.

"Holy King Gidorah balls," Henry says.

All three heads turn toward the ceiling and let out harmonious cries. If the thing wasn't so horrible to look at, the sound would be beautiful.

Maybe it's not as bad as I thought?

It's at that moment, that Echidna stabs a talon tipped finger in our direction and lets out an angry shriek.

"Well," Sarah says. "Shit."

The newborn flaps its wings, throws itself from the high perch, and swoops toward us.

47

"Can we just, I don't know, run away?" Sarah says.

I wish we could. I'm not really in the mood to fight and/or kill a newborn—even if it *is* a monster. But our path takes us straight toward the beast, and its parents. "I don't think we have a choice." I point to the cave into which Echidna's body extends. Two pillars, like a half-size hellgate, frame the sides of the cave.

"Is that it?" Jonas asks. "The gate?"

"Too small," I say. "The actual gates are much larger. I think that's more of a road sign, like what we saw at the intersection early on."

"So, we have to go through the mother and father of monsters," Sarah says with a nervous chuckle. "No big deal, right?"

Echidna and Typhon are older than Zeus. They've been around since the beginning of humanity. They're at least as powerful as Jonas, but they fully understand how to use those powers—which includes spawning nightmares from a churning womb that looks like a kaiju-sized grub.

"We need to strike now," Jonas says, the winged, three-headed monster closing in. "Echidna and Typhon are both immobilized. If we can get past them, maybe we don't need to fight them."

"And what about that?" Sarah points at the incoming beast.

"I can take care of it," he says, and then he looks to me.

They all do.

I nod. "Take it out, then we move, fast as we can, around the perimeter, behind Echidna, and into the cave..."

"Which hopefully has an exit aside from Echidna's cooch," Henry says.

"Right..." I turn to Jonas. "Try to make it quick."

"That's what I do," he says.

"Wait, wait, wait," Henry says. "You can't just randomly kill a mythological creature. If you do it wrong, things can actually get worse."

"Have a suggestion?" Jonas asks.

"It looks like the Hydra, but with wings, like it evolved Pokemon style. So, its weakness could be the same thing. Cut off the wrong head, two grow back. Cut off the immortal head…well, it still won't be dead, but it will have to grow back an entire body, and I can cauterize it with a lightning sword before it can."

"Doesn't sound very fast," I say.

Henry draws his sword. "It will be."

I could probably sever the heads and cauterize them all at once, but not while I'm holding Bree. "Do it," I say.

Jonas tightens his grip on the pillar, turns his attention to the flying hydra and leaves his body behind. A puff of ethereal mist punctuates his out-of-body experience. He floats through the air, no longer limited by physics—a being of pure psychic energy. Or something.

Henry charges his kopis. Crackling blue energy ripples over the blade.

The hydra's three mouths open, revealing layers of shark-like teeth, but they're undulating. Eager for a first meal. Unfortunately for the hydra, their first target is both immaterial—and stupid powerful.

Jonas sweeps a hand through the air, unleashing an invisible telekinetic force. The hydra is just doing its thing, looking gnarly and hungry.

Then…its heads fall off like a broken toy fixed with shoddy glue. They just come undone and plummet from the air.

Henry dives down, catching the first head and holding his blade against the wound. Flesh sizzles and smokes. He dives to the next, repeating the process. Won't be long before he's neutralized all three heads. Motion pulls my eyes from the falling heads to the large body, falling, falling, and then—flying.

The hydra's body swoops around and up, revealing not just three new heads and necks, but a dozen.

Cut off one head and four grow back?

It really is an evolution.

"Jonas," I say, but he's already taking action.

The hydra flies up, flapping its big wings, hovering in front of Jonas, glaring at him with twenty-four eyes, as if to say, "That all you got?"

Jonas lifts up his hand, like he's pleading for mercy.

"What are you doing?" Sarah whispers.

"Mind bullet," he says, and he makes a sudden fist.

All twelve hydra heads twitch. Their eyes roll back. Necks limp, they flop down lifeless.

But the body remains, still flying, undefeated, until one by one, the heads come back to life, rise, and—

"Llllllightning missile!" A bolt of blue energy with Henry at its core launches up from below. He punches through the hydra's underbelly and explodes up through its spine, taking a few vertebrae with him and leaving behind an immense electric charge that explodes outward.

The hydra comes apart, bursting out in every direction, sending heads and necks spiraling and a wave of steaming gore headed straight toward us. I turn away and wrap Bree in my wings.

But nothing strikes us.

When I look back, a wall of blood, guts, and bones slides down an invisible barrier erected by Jonas. When he lowers his hands, it all falls away.

A scream tears through the massive cavern, loud enough to force hands to ears, only I can't because I'm holding Bree. Echidna is pissed. For some reason I imagined she also saw the creatures she birthed as monsters, but their connection is deeper than that. She is their mother. Maybe she even loves them.

Then again, she did send her newborn to attack us, knowing that to be here we had to pass the Furies, the Chimera, and Badonk.

Who really knows how an ancient monster-birthing goddess thinks and feels? In the grand scheme, it's not important. What *is* important, is finding the gate, reaching Tartarus, delivering our message, and then finding a way to save Bubbles.

"How cool was that?" Henry descends and stops in front of us, beaming. Steaming hydra bits and blood drip from his body. "Also, good news, this hydra's blood isn't acidic!"

"Did you think it was before you flew through it?" I ask.

"Umm. No?"

Jonas's physical body flinches as his immaterial spirit returns.

"Ready to go?" Henry asks, offering his hands to Jonas and Sarah.

They both look at the hands. A chunk of meat slowly slips over the back of his fingers, slurping as it falls away.

"Goddammit," Jonas mutters, and he takes hold of Henry's hand.

Sarah lets out an "Ugh," and takes the other hand.

"Tally-ho!" Henry says, banking up and then cruising away like only he can.

"You good?" I ask Bree.

She nods. "Tally-ho!"

We launch after the others, carried forth by the power of lasers, or whatever the hell this energy is. When we pull up alongside them, Henry grins at me as the whipping wind scours the chunks from his body and dries the liquid. Then he shouts, "Kickstart my heart!"

Our mutual admiration of hair bands instantly puts the song in my head. It's the perfect soundtrack. But, "That's not Poison," I shout at him.

"Whoa!" He shouts to the song in his head. "Yeah!" And then he banks hard to the left, flying around a column and speeding up.

"Get him!" Bree shouts. I kick on the afterburners, overtaking Henry and passing him, unleashing a sonic boom as I do.

For a moment, I forget the mission, the monsters waiting below, and the many times we've come face-to-face with death. Then I round the column, and everything comes rushing back at me—along with a fuzzy, house-sized, bulbous creature with big, adorable eyes.

"Aww," Bree says. "Don't hurt it! It's too cute!"

I angle us down to fly beneath it, but the creature drops to intercept us and opens its mouth. The tooth-filled chasm of doom is as wide as its body and just as high. A black hole ending in a stomach. To make matters worse, it's sucking in a breath.

I don't think I can avoid it, but I can't extend my arm blades with Bree in my arms. I will my wings to turn forward, turning my whole body into a spear head.

They start moving, but then it's not necessary.

Sarah's dory strikes the creature's side, unleashing a devastating electric charge that sets the fuzz on fire. I bank to the right, twisting past the fireball, snatching the dory free as I pass. The newborn creature plummets toward the cavern floor like it's an asteroid punching through the atmosphere.

"Thanks," I say, and I toss the dory back to Sarah.

"Don't thank me yet," she says, pointing down.

Echidna is blocking the cave with her body, tearing herself free from the massive womb. White flesh stretches and rips. She slithers free, serpent eyes on us, hissing in rage. The womb twitches and thrashes. At first, I think it's death throes, but then everything still trapped inside begins pushing and tearing at the flesh where there are holes in the stone. Won't be long before they're all free and this becomes a very different situation.

And then there's Typhon. His massive and strong body pulls on the chains. He turns his head to the ceiling, shouting, "Set me free!"

The power in his voice is enough to make the average man shit himself, like having a train horn blown at you from a foot away. It speaks of ancient and savage power.

"We need to go through her," I say. "Fast. And all together. If we overwhelm her, we might get past."

Henry nods.

"Go!" I shout, and we both bank downward.

Echidna sees us coming, takes up a battle stance, and hisses at us.

"Set me free!" Typhon booms again.

"Girl!" Henry shouts at the mother of monsters. "You are courageous! You are worth it. Embrace your best self, and don't let him tell you what to do!"

Echidna's ire focuses on Henry.

Then she unleashes hell.

48

Viscous white fluid sprays from the back of Echidna's throat, and from the mouth of every snake writhing atop her head. If she was the size of a normal human being, it wouldn't be much trouble, but she's twenty feet tall, not counting her long serpentine body and her cavernous grub-like womb. Her bulbously curvaceous form seems to have a significant carrying capacity. The snakes flail around, ejecting what I assume is venom, like one of those summertime fun octopus water sprinklers.

"Take care of it," I say to Jonas.

And to Sarah, I say, "Try to stun her."

Dangling from Henry's arm, our resident Titan turns to face the oncoming wave of hot, steaming death. He raises a hand and appears to do nothing at all—until the wall of white liquid splashes against an invisible barrier.

"Hnyah!" Sarah shouts, throwing her electrically charged dory at Echidna. The weapon crackles through the air, looking a lot like how I imagined Zeus's lightning bolts as a kid.

The wall of dripping white first parts and then explodes away, creating a gap that's large enough for the dory, and then us.

Echidna sees the spear too late to move.

But she doesn't need to.

Because she's not alone.

A wave of chain rolls up in front of the mother of monsters, striking the dory, knocking it off course and absorbing its electric charge. The blue bolt tears down the chain, striking Typhon, who roars in pain until the energy dissipates into the ground.

The giant wraps the chain around his wrist and pulls, arms shaking. The metal links quiver and stretch until—one gives way. It opens slowly like Sanchez's little jaws when I have to pry chocolate from his mouth. Then it gives. With a metallic clang, half of the chain falls to the ground. The other half launches toward Typhon as he gains a small amount of motion.

One chain down, a shit-ton to go.

But now we know that he's strong enough to escape.

Meaning he's not *really* a prisoner here, doing the nasty against his will.

The parents of monsters are just into some kinky stuff.

Whatever it takes to keep things fresh after a few millennia, I guess.

If we're not out of here soon, we'll be dealing with ma, pa, *and* their nefarious litter, currently digging their way out of the undulating womb.

But maybe we don't need to fight our way out.

Maybe this is another test?

When Echidna blocks the tunnel's entrance, forcing a physical confrontation to escape, I shout, "Hold up," and slow to a stop.

"Not sure we should just be hanging around," Jonas says. "Big guy will be loose soon."

"Or," Henry says. "We could kill him while he's chained up."

"Not cool," Sarah says.

"What?" Henry doesn't get it. "It's a solid strat."

"He's not wrong," Jonas says.

"I know—"

"Seriously?" Sarah says. "If a bunch of people broke into your house while you were getting freaky, then killed your newborn baby, you wouldn't try to kill them?"

"Okay…that's a fresh take," I say. "But these are gods, they're birthing monsters, and they're not here to make a happy family—they're here to keep people who aren't worthy from reaching Tartarus, which is a place we really need to be. Like now. But…maybe we don't need to fight. Or kill them."

"What the hell else can we do?" Henry asks.

"Talk," Bree says. "He wants to talk it out, like he does with Allie after he uses her brush, and with Jen when he forgets a date because he's gaming, or with me when he *eats…my…ice cream.*"

"Seriously?" Henry says. "You think smegma-mouth down there is going to have a chat?"

I look down at Echidna. Her body is undulating, fat rolls pulsing, rolling fluid up through her body like she's a tube of toothpaste. She's getting ready to unleash another venom volley.

He's got a point, but, "I have to try." To Jonas, I say, "Keep me covered." I tilt my head toward Typhon. "If he breaks free, gloves are off."

"It's stupid," Jonas says. "But you haven't steered us wrong yet."

"You ready for this?" I ask Bree.

She nods. "I don't think it will work, but you do you."

I take a moment to smile at her. When she says things like that, it's hard to remember she's only eight. That and her gnarly demon face ages her up a bit. The bunny ears help, though.

I give the others a nod and descend toward Echidna, wings open wide, a palm outstretched and a forced smile on my face.

The she-beast stops regurgitating and watches me, head tilted to the side. She's curious, at least.

"Hey," I say, approaching the ground twenty feet away from her, and twice as far from the gate. I get a peek past her and see the white womb retract up into the ceiling, revealing a longer tunnel beyond, leading to a distant point with a familiar red light.

The gate.

We're almost there.

I touch down and place Bree down in front of me. Then I extinguish my wings. "Hi. Echidna, right?"

She just stares, her yellow serpent eyes unwavering and unnerving. The snake heads remain still, each of them locked onto me. Up close, her body is even more intimidating, covered with scales the size of my hand, rippling over her body, which is both somehow supple and powerful. Muscles twitch and flex beneath a bulging layer of chub, which I suppose makes sense for a being widely regarded as a mother of countless beasts. Not a warrior. Not a god, really.

A mother.

And I know how to talk to moms.

I place a hand on my chest and use my most chill voice. "I'm Miah."

Echidna's forked tongue slips out of her mouth, flicking up and down like the legendary Gene Simmons himself, tasting the air. Tasting me.

"Who birthed you, god-blood?" she asks, voice raspy and powerful.

"Uhh," I say. *God-blood?* I'm unsure how to answer. I mean, I *know* the answer, but I don't think my very human parents are going to make much of an impression.

Bree tugs on my T-shirt. Looks up at me with wide, demanding eyes and mouths, "*Lie.*"

I'm not a natural liar. Goes against my earnest personality. But I learned this lesson from Ray Stantz, just like everyone else.

When someone asks if you're a god, you say *yes.*

I try to think of the two most intimidating Greek gods I can think of, and then say, "Ares...and Athena." The Greek god and goddess of war. A one-two punch of intimidation.

Her eyes squint, and then they turn up toward the others on my team. "And them?"

"Zeus," I say. "And...well, Zeus, I guess. You know how it is, right? Been around long enough to see some crazy shit." I force a chuckle. "Also, Uranus, and Gaia."

"A Titan," Echidna says. Can't tell if she's intimidated, impressed, or excited. Maybe all of the above. "A half-brother..."

Jonas has more family in the underworld than Genghis Khan has descendants. "Okay, who...birthed you?"

"Tartarus and Gaia," she says without hesitation, like this kind of information is regularly passed in the realm of Khaos.

"And him?" I ask, motioning to Typhon, still fighting his bonds.

"The same," she says.

Of course they are, I think. *Why wouldn't they be?*

I thought Tartarus was a place, but I guess names can be both. Hell, you can visit George, Washington, where the streets are named after cherry tree species. "Look, we don't want any trouble. We're just trying to reach Tartarus. The place. Not your father."

"Why do you seek the divine-realm?" she asks.

I'm really not sure if I can trust her with the information, but we're dialoguing instead of fighting, so I seek to build on that positive start.

"To deliver a message," I say. "From Zeus."

She leans in closer and tilts her ear-hole toward me, waiting to hear the message for herself.

"Pólemos," I say.

"War..."

"There's this crazy lady out there. From space or something. An alien maybe. She's basically crazy powerful. Cut off Zeus's hand."

Echidna's eyes flare at that news.

"Point is," I say, "she's remaking the universe. Destroying everything. If we don't get help, Earth is toast, and all of this..." I motion around us. "...will be destroyed, too."

She absorbs that, leaning back as though contemplating the ramifications of what I've just revealed.

Then the most sinister grin I've ever seen spreads across her scaly face. "At long last..." All over her body, the large scales tilt up to reveal thousands of serpentine faces, all of them glaring at me with frantic energy. Every single scale is a snake head. "...the end has begun!"

She turns her head toward the ceiling and lets out a high-pitched scream. Every single snake head covering her body lets out a little squeak, too. Then, all at once, the chains holding Typhon in place break away from the floor, walls, pillars, and ceilings.

The father of monsters has been set loose.

49

My wings snap out, driven by my subconscious, guided by instinct rather than direct thought. I put a hand around Bree's torso, keeping her close. "I'm not sure you understand," I shout over the sound of Typhon's thrashing chains. "She's going to destroy everything. Including you, this place, and all your...babies."

The news is all but orgasmic for Echidna. "It is you who does not understand. We have awaited the return of Ouroboros, the World Serpent, for millennia. Her coming was foretold long ago in messages born of the cosmos, the noose tightening with each orbit. A promise of return. Of a reckoning. A rebirth for all who serve. Reality inherited by the castaways and abominations. A new world for my children, free of this hell and the children of Chanohk. She is older than time, present at the beginning and the end, the eternal cycle. Life, death, rebirth."

I back away a step. Probably should pick up Bree and get the hell out, but she said something familiar. Something that Cherry chick said. "Chanohk. What is that?"

"The creator. The progenitor."

"Like God? Capital G?"

She sneers. "He is no more a god than Zeus, and he will watch his beloved reality torn apart and stitched back together with the sinews of his descendants."

Well, that sounds horrible.

"And his descendants are...?"

"Humanity." She slithers toward me, hungry eyes locked on target, preparing to pounce. "You."

I pick up Bree and glide back, maintaining the distance between us. Echidna's dangerous. Will kill us if given the chance. But she also suffers from verbal diarrhea. I want to keep her talking as long as possible. Before I can come up with another question, Bree conjures some defiance and shouts at Echidna like only an eight-year-old can.

"We'll stop her—and you! Once we get to Tartarus, we'll have an army of gods fighting with us. Your ugly butt won't stand a chance!"

Echidna flinches to a stop. Confusion followed by a wicked smile. "My dear, you misunderstand our purpose here. We are not meant to keep you out of Tartarus. We are here to prevent the gods from leaving. They are exactly where the World Serpent wants them." A realization occurs to her, widening her delighted smile. "It has been some time since anyone has attempted to leave Tartarus." She glances back at the cave's entrance behind her. "Perhaps..."

I've heard enough, buzzing back into the air with the others.

"She reveal anything?" Jonas asks.

"They're keeping the gods locked in Tartarus," I say. "Cherry knows about it, and these assholes are working for her, or serving her, or—"

"Worshiping her," Bree says.

"That. To get the gods back to Earth, we need to take these two down."

"Yes!" Henry says. "Dibs on Echidna."

"I'll take care of the big guy," Jonas says.

"Back Henry up," I tell Sarah.

"Yes!" Henry pumps his fist. "Dynamic duo time!"

"I'll do what I can to support you," I tell Jonas.

"Won't be necessary," he says. "But thanks."

"What about me?" Bree asks.

"I want you—" I place her against a stone column. When she clings to it, I let go and glide back out of reach. "—to wait here."

"Ex-ca-*yuze* me?" she says, filled with all the rancor and agitation of a hippo with an itch it can't scratch.

There's no time to argue. I nod to the others and then spring into action.

"Shield strike!' Sarah shouts. I've seen them practicing this in the woods.

It's pretty devastating to pine trees. No idea how it will work against a maniacal goddess.

Henry soars down toward Echidna, who's shouting in a language I don't know, summoning her spawn from the confines of her womb. The first of dozens of monsters tears free. It's fully formed, but so covered in white sludge that I can't make out much, other than it has wings, which it unfurls and shakes off.

Henry releases Sarah, directing her like a bomb toward Echidna. As she plummets toward the snake-woman, Sarah slides her shield from her back to her arm, positioning it in front of her and curling up behind it. This much I've seen before. Then they mix it up, using abilities they've hidden until recently. As Sarah's shield starts glowing, Henry flies ahead and extends his arms. Lightning crackles and explodes from his fingertips, arcing toward Echidna—but missing entirely. The bolts strike the stone floor all around the mother of monsters, but not a single one makes contact.

For a moment I think Henry really needs to work on his aim. Then I realize the lightning's point. He's not attacking, he's locking her down, preventing her from dodging the goddess of earth barreling toward her, building a charge.

I glance ahead to find Jonas closing in on Typhon.

The hulking snake-man is so big that he appears to be moving in slow motion, spinning around to face us. But he's not just turning, he's whipping untold tons of chains, with links thicker than my thigh. The air around him turns into a deadly swing carousel for giants.

"Shield strike!" Henry shouts, but his bravado is short lived.

Echidna, including every snake atop her head, and every head protruding from her body, unleashes a venomous spray.

Unafraid, Henry's fearless advantage becomes a weakness. He punches through a wall of the stuff, shouts in pain, and drops from the air, his body smoldering.

It's not venom, I think. *It's acid.*

Maybe both. I don't think there are any hard and fast rules for what creatures like Echidna can and cannot do.

Sarah, who's protected by her shield, collides with Echidna, and unleashes a devastating burst of energy. The resulting boom shakes shards of stone loose from the ceiling. Echidna is launched away from the strike, her body twisting and writhing in midair before crashing to the ground.

Sarah stands up, looks over her shield, and grins. For a moment, the scene is epic. Then Sarah is tackled by the sludge-covered newborn, falling out of view.

I'm tempted to call it quits here and now. The tunnel is exposed. We could escape. But if Echidna and Typhon are tasked with keeping the gods on Tartarus, who's to say they won't just collapse the tunnel behind us?

The only way to complete the mission is to incapacitate—or kill—the universe's OG monsters.

Jonas glances back at me. "Take care of the chains. I'll handle the big—"

A long chain whooshes past me. Before I have a chance to warn Jonas, it strikes him full-on in the side. I think he sensed it coming right before it hit. Looks like he might have thrown up a telekinetic barrier just in time, but it didn't stop him from rocketing away like a homerun at the hands of Babe Ruth.

He hits the stone floor a half mile out, rolling to a stop before falling still.

"Okay," I say to myself. "Guess the big guy is mine."

Laser blades extended, I swoop in closer, spinning and swerving around a storm of chains.

How the hell do I do this? I wonder, as the distance between us shrinks. I've been training with Henry and Sarah, and long ago fought in a war, but none of that prepared me for this.

Don't dick around, I tell myself. *Strike hard. Strike fast. Put him down and move on.*

I angle my wings forward and extend my forearm blades, turning myself into a weapon. Aiming for his chest, I pour on the speed, intending to punch a hole straight through his heart and out the back. Assuming Typhon has a heart, and that it's in the same place as a human being's. Even if he doesn't, I hope a gaping wound in his chest will do the trick.

Unless he's like the original Hydra. Which I guess would make sense, since creatures like Hydra came from his loins. Then again, I'll be cauterizing the wound as I punch through. He might not be able to heal, just as the Hydra couldn't regrow its cauterized immortal head.

Going to have to study ancient myths when all this is said and done. Knowledge of those whose epic quests came before is definitely helpful.

I catch sight of an incoming chain. It's moving too fast to avoid.

What is best described as a flinch extends the laser wings back out at the speed of light, just in time to sever the chain. The two halves separate, sliding past above and below as the links come apart. The broken chain falls away with enough force to shatter one of the pillars supporting the massive ceiling.

Still on course and on target, I slam into Typhon's chest. The arm blade slides right through, but with my wings extended, it's not enough to punch through his body.

Not nearly enough.

I face plant into his sternum, and like a bird that's flown into a window, I plummet to the ground, landing where the giant's feet would be. If he had feet.

What he does have are two arms, each of them flinging several chains up and over his head, all of them dropping down toward me with the force of a runaway aircraft carrier.

50

Before my father died, he took my friends and I sledding every winter. At a golf course with manicured hills, wide open spaces, and patches of ancient maples breaking it all up. One year, we had an old-timey sled, the kind that was wood on top, and metal below. Must have weighed twenty pounds. The combination of weight and steel runners turned the child atop it into a screaming projectile, hurtling down snow covered hills. Me being...*me,* I decided to ride the sled face first on my belly, using my hands to steer, rather than my feet, like my father taught me, like everyone else had been doing all day. I don't know if I hit a patch of ice, or my more aerodynamic technique reduced friction, but I built up a head of steam. At the bottom of the hill, rather than sliding to a stop, I cruised past the other kids, bedazzled in neon snow gear, and careened toward a patch of maples. I swerved left, and then panicked. Swerved right, but not enough.

I came to a very sudden stop, headfirst against an unmoving tree.

That was my first concussion, and now, twenty something years later, I open my eyes and say the same thing I did when I was nine. "I'm okay!"

It was a lie then, born of shame.

It's a lie now.

I'm stunned. Pain radiates from my head to my lower back. Nausea washes through me.

I can see the chains dropping toward me. I understand the likely outcome if they make contact. But there's a disconnect between knowledge and action. *Move,* I tell myself, but my body is on vacation.

Happily, my wings aren't really part of my body. When I mentally flinch, my laser appendages react. With a loud buzz, I launch forward—

across the stone floor. It's like being on the sled again, but facing the sky, or in this case, a chain tsunami crashing toward me.

The first links strike the ground behind my feet. Stone shatters beneath the explosive force. The blast sounds like artillery firing at the pace of a machine gun, the shockwaves rolling through me as I'm dragged across the floor like cheese over a grater.

The chains unfurl like whips, speeding up, ready to snap against me. The floor tilts upward and I'm brought even closer to the chains. I close my eyes and hope Bree isn't watching. A strong wind slaps my face. It carries the scent of old metal and draws my eyes open again. I'm still being dragged against stone, but vertically now, rising up fast. And beneath me—

—the chains crash into the base of a pillar, shattering it. Behind me, the column shudders, but it remains rooted to the ceiling, now the world's largest stalactite.

Safely above the action, I bank away from the pillar and have a moment to assess the damage. I feel…okay, actually. There's no pain, which is surprising after being scoured across the jagged landscape. I should be torn up. I'm still concussed. My head pounds. I'm dizzy. Need to get my feet on the ground. Find my bearings.

Below, Jonas re-enters the fray. Looks no worse for the wear, but I can tell he's pissed. As chains rush toward him, they strike an invisible force, bouncing away, clearing a path for Jonas like Moses through the Red Sea. But there's more than that going on. Both of them have this intense look on their faces. A battle of wills. Of telekinetic power. Jonas's potential is explosive on a WMD level, but there's no reason to think he's not equally matched by Typhon, who has experience on his side.

And an army of monsters.

Sarah is surrounded by newborn beasts. But she's recovered her dory, and shield in hand, she's fending them off. Her attacks are poetry, her defense impenetrable. I hope to someday be as competent as she is.

"No," I whisper, when a scorpion-tailed beast with a tiger's head and eagle talons strikes at her back.

But my concern is misplaced. A wall of stone rises between them. The scorpion tail strikes the wall, shattering the forearm-sized stinger. At the same time, Sarah unleashes a blast of lightning that convulses its way through another creature, not yet fully formed, but deadly thanks to its spear-like mandibles and powerful limbs. She follows the blast with a quick thrust of the dory, punching through the monster's head and dropping it to the floor.

She could probably hold her ground all day, doing justice to her Spartan ancestors.

But the monsters keeping her busy aren't the real threat.

Echidna has picked herself up and is slithering, unseen, toward Sarah.

I look for Henry, hoping he'll be able to help her, but I can't find him. For a moment, I worry Echidna's acid spray dissolved him into mush. Then I hear a familiar voice.

"Dude, are you okay?" Henry glides up beside me. His already tattered clothing hangs like a molted skin. His burned epidermis is now covered in bubbling boils. Even more hair is missing.

And he's worried about me?

"Are *you* okay?" I ask him.

"Just hurts to move," he says, and then he demonstrates, moving his arms. "Oww." And again. "Oww." And again. "Oww." He smiles and winces. "Goddammit." Laughs again.

"Can you fight?" I ask.

He rolls his eyes. "You know me."

"Sarah needs help," I tell him, looking down at her. Echidna is closing in, building speed, ready to strike.

"She does," he says, "and I will. But seriously, guy, you don't look right."

"I have a concussion," I tell him. "Head is spinning, but I'm good." I raise my hand to ignite a laser blade as a demonstration of my recovering strength.

Only nothing happens.

No blade.

No arm.

"You see?" he says. "You're flying, and talking and shit, but your body is just hanging limp, man. I think... I think your neck is broken."

I look down, heart pounding.

My arms dangle by my sides. I glide back and forth a little, and my legs just flop about.

I have no feeling.

No control.

Oh god... I'm...paralyzed.

And all at once, I feel it—the nothing of paralysis. The sense that I'm a floating head and nothing more.

My vision goes black.

"Hey," Henry says, his voice fading into the distance. "Are you—"

For a moment, darkness. Peace. Worry free bliss.

And then...

"—bro, wake up." I open my eyes. Henry holds me in his arms. I must have fallen. And he caught me...because...

"Fuck," I say.

"Big time," he says. "I got you, but I need to help the others. Bad news is, you're as limp as a dick at a geriatric pole dancing convention. Good news is, you'll never need a wheelchair. Because you got wings, man." He smiles at me. "And that's something most people never get to have. So, pop those sons-a-bitches out and make yourself useful, or just chill up here or whatever. Sarah needs me."

And then, like a parent entrusting instinct to guide their baby to the surface of a pool, he tosses me into the air. With a thought, my wings extend. I hover in place, held aloft by an alien power that wasn't powerful enough.

"Might need to make some modifications to your bathroom, but I bet you'll be able to still pee upright." Henry glances down to Sarah. Echidna is creeping up behind her.

"Go," I say, and he does.

But then, just as quickly as he left, he returns. "BT-Dubs, I didn't mean to dis old people. Honestly, I'm kind of into the whole saggy bits thing. And they tip well. By-eee."

Henry draws his kopis and rockets toward the ground, leaving me paralyzed, but somehow wondering if he was joking. Or did he just admit to being a sex worker for old ladies when he lived on the streets of Boston?

Below me, Henry shouts, "Thunder from Heaven!"

Echidna turns her head up and spots him.

Sarah does, too, shouting, "What are you doing?"

She gets her answer when a volcano of scorching venom bursts up toward Henry.

He holds the kopis with both hands, positioned in front him like he's a dude-sized throwing dart. The charged blade vaporizes the venom it strikes, sparing his face, but he's unable to avoid the attack. Again. He slaps through the upwelling liquid, yells, "Oh, god!" and then punches a hole into the ground.

Echidna slithers past him, surging over the top of the stone barrier Sarah had erected. But the daughter of Zeus is ready—thanks to Henry's warning. Shield raised, she ducks down and deflects a second acid attack, redirecting it onto two of Echidna's spawn. Both shriek and reel back, their bodies coming apart where the acid hit them. That Henry survived his first dose reveals just how tough he is. Now if we could just get him to think a little.

An explosion draws my gaze back to Typhon.

Jonas lies on the ground. For a moment, he looks unconscious, then he sits up. The giant is more than a match for the new Titan.

Because Jonas is holding back. Because unleashing his full power would probably mean killing us all.

But Typhon—he's not holding back. And he's getting creative. Reaching out with his powerful hands, he redirects the flow of lava around the chamber, summoning it to himself. Streaks of hot orange molten stone form a swirling orb around him. Larger streams flow toward Jonas like snakes.

Jonas draws the Sword of Mars, not to strike, but to redirect the power it lends him. Honestly, I'm not sure the sword actually makes him stronger, or simply boosts his confidence, but he stands firm and resists. The lava snakes collide with an unseen force, breaking into hundreds of smaller tendrils that wrap around Jonas's telekinetic shield and tighten.

I need to help, I think, but I'm not sure what I can do with just my wings...and if I'm honest, I'm...afraid. My first and last attack on Typhon ended with me paralyzed.

What more can I do?

But I'm not the only one who's seen Jonas's predicament.

"I'm coming!" Bree shouts, sprinting and leaping across the landscape beneath me, heading straight for Typhon, his spinning lava, and his swinging chains.

51

She's a pint-sized blur, leaping, twisting, and sliding her way through the obstacle course of doom. One mistake and she could—well, she could end up like me. Or worse. She doesn't have any laser appendages to move her around.

It's too much, I think.

Too dangerous.

I need to stop her.

Swooping toward the floor isn't as graceful as it once was. My limbs just dangle, flopping around when I turn, nearly scraping the floor when I level out. I'm still fast, but my dead-squid body works against the wings, adding drag, weight fluctuations, and a constant state of 'I must look like a freaking idiot.' I also need to keep my wings elevated. If I bank too hard, my flopping arms could strike a wing...which I wouldn't feel...but I haven't processed the concept of paralysis yet. I don't need to add amputee to the list of afflictions.

I speed after Bree, but she's moving fast.

Really fast.

Catching her in my current condition isn't easy—especially when I need to navigate the same obstacles.

She's making it look easy. Poetic almost. Like she's run this course a million times. Like she can predict where things are—even when she's not looking at them.

The hell? I think.

Thanks to lasers that can move at the speed of light, a momentary clearing allows me to pour on the speed and catch up. "Bree!"

"You shouldn't be here!" she shouts at me.

"That's what I was going to say to you!"

She looks back at me, running forward on all fours. "You're hurt!" She sounds angry and worried. "Let me do this! I know what to do!"

"How? You're eight!"

"I don't know how, Miah. I just know. It's like an instinct. Oooh, a killer instinct! I feel it on my skin. In my muscles. Like a guiding force. And I see things and hear things I normally can't." She points to Typhon. "Like a red spot on his neck, where the blood is closest to his skin."

I don't see anything. Typhon is a huge blur, concealed behind layers of chains and flowing lava. The small glimpse I catch of his neck looks normal—as normal as the neck of a god-monster snake man can look, all covered in green scales and concealed by snake body dreadlocks.

"It's like Wolverine's heightened senses," she says, knowing that I'll understand a comic book reference. I haven't done much reading, of any kind, over the past few years, but I've got a thousand comics bagged and boxed in my room. Over the past few months, as we've spent a lot of time together, she's been digging through them and debating with me about who would win in a fight against who. "And Spider-Man's tingly thing."

"Spidey sense," I say.

"Right. That. It's like both of those combined, along with…something else. Like something is—" Despite having her eyes locked on me, she feels the arc of lava sweeping in from the side. Springs into the air, long before it reaches us, flipping up and over, never losing eye contact with me, even as I flail and shout, doing my best to not get hit. She lands, never missing a beat. "Like something is guiding me."

"Some…thing?" I can tell there's more to it than that.

"It will freak you out," she says, parkouring over a chain as it whooshes past beneath us.

"Only way I let you go forward is—"

"Dead people," she says. "Ghosts or whatever. Spirits. I don't see them or anything, but I can feel them. Hear their whispers. Their warnings. And they like me. Like being near me. So, they help."

"Ghosts…of who?"

"The people who died," she says. "When we were in hell."

"They're still with you?" I'm aghast. "*All* of them?"

She nods.

"Problem for another day," she says. "Right?"

I don't answer. Can't answer. The implications are... Holy shit. Her brother. Is that why she doesn't talk about Tommy? Doesn't seem to miss him? Is he with her?

Is Rich? If so, I think we'll be keeping that secret. Not sure how Mom would handle learning that her dead boyfriend is still kicking around with Bree. She moved on after Dad died. She'll need to do the same, again, eventually.

"*Right?*" she repeats.

I blink out of my stupor. "Right."

"Now," she says. "Let me save him!"

She looks over to where Jonas once knelt, resisting the cyclone of lava. He's completely concealed now, hidden inside a sphere of swirling hot orange that's slowly compressing.

"Look out!" Bree shouts, leaping up, placing her hands against my chest. "I got this," she says, full of calm confidence. Then she shoves me up over the chain I didn't sense coming. She reaches out, grasps hold of the chain, and is whisked away. Even as she's spun around the cavern, she runs along the chain, closing in on Typhon, who's lost track of her.

I've been powerful for a short time, but I'd gotten used to it. The idea of being sidelined and letting Bree take the lead is beyond difficult, but she's right. And competent, racing up the chain like a pro Mario Kart player on the Rainbow Road.

With a thought, my wings carry me toward the ceiling. Once I'm outside the radius of Typhon's chaotic attack, I hover in place, watching Bree's steady progress until below, Sarah shouts in pain.

Echidna is pressing the attack.

Sarah backs away, her shoulder and thigh both slick with blood. She clutches the dory in two hands, her shield missing, lying on the ground twenty feet away, smoldering as it's eaten by acid. She's wounded and defiant, but Echidna might be more than she can handle, even with the ability to throw lightning and move the earth.

The ancient mother of monsters has experience on her side. And she's using it to assess Sarah's strengths and weaknesses, with each attack.

She strikes with blinding speed, swiping her claws, and when she's in close, the snakes atop her head strike out. Sarah parries, ducks, and is forced to roll back farther.

But she's not giving up.

She's buying time.

"Holy shit," I say, as the sound of cracking stone draws my gaze to the side. The massive hanging column, severed at the base by Typhon, is starting to crack. But not from its own weight.

Sarah is pulling it, and leading Echidna away from Henry.

If I can move Henry... But how? I can't even move my arms.

The only thing I can move are my wings.

Helplessness is not something I enjoy. I felt it before, when the Tenebris came, when Rich was torn from the house and killed in the street. When neighbors were being plucked from their homes and ground up into food for an alien race. I fought against it then, but I'm not sure what I can do now.

Or what I'll be able to do in the future.

My days as team leader are over.

Probably my days doing anything useful.

Below me, Jonas fights for his life, the cocoon of lava quivering as it closes in, vibrating from his efforts to free himself. He's probably wondering what the hell I'm doing. Wondering if his team is going to help him. Feeling betrayed that we haven't already.

Bree is risking her life to get the job done, but it shouldn't be her.

She shouldn't be here at all. But because of me, she's charging headlong toward a god—and probably toward her death.

Along with Sarah.

And Henry.

Unless I fucking do something.

Rage builds inside me. "Rah!" I shout, and the laser blades on my arms extend, reacting to my desire to punch something. But they just dangle by my sides.

But do they have to?

I control the position of my wings, and the energy they output, just by thinking about it. I even managed to extend the size of my wings. What if the blades on my arms are the same? What if I can move because they can?

My arms launch toward the ceiling, held aloft by the buzzing blades. I snap them out to either side, then back down and up again. It's a lot more awkward than real movement, but it's something. I extend my arms, and point them toward Henry, still lying in a crater of his own making, steaming from the acid covering him.

With a thought, the blades extending out past my fists retract, sliding up and over the top of my forearms, like laser vambraces!

"I can do this," I say, imagining my next steps. How I'll save Henry, aid Sarah's attack, then streak back to Typhon and take his damn head off, so Bree doesn't have—

"Yeaaahhh!" Bree shouts, running up the chain toward Typhon's head. She launches herself into the air, claws extended, ready to kill.

But there's one last obstacle.

A wave of lava crashing straight toward her.

And there is no avoiding it.

52

"Bree!" I scream, the sound coming from deep within my soul, carrying my horror, regret, and despair throughout the cavern. In that instant, as the small girl in my care leaps toward the onrushing lava wall and raises her arms in a fighting stance rather than attempting to shield her head, I'm overcome with guilt, and rage. "NO!"

She must hear me, because just as the luminous orange death wall strikes her, she extends a hand in my direction and gives me a thumbs up.

Then she's gone.

Enveloped by the lava.

A tingling sensation rolls up through me, toes to head.

Then the back side of the wave bulges—

—and bursts!

Bree emerges from the lava intact. Both arms and legs are there, as is the clothing made from centaur hide. The bunny ears are on fire, a billowing column of flame that Bree doesn't even notice. It flows around her like luxurious orange locks.

Because fire is her friend.

Because as hot as lava is, heat cannot harm her.

Not in her Demon Dog form, at least.

Guided by her killer instinct, she lands atop Typhon's shoulder and digs in her claws. She slides to a stop, opening eight long wounds. Typhon barks in pain and raises a massive hand to slap Bree like a fly. But she's still on task and on target. She scrambles over his trapezius, leaps onto the side of his neck, and clings in place. Leans her head in close, like she's sniffing, confirming what her instinct revealed—there is blood there.

A vein.

She lets out a roar and extends her claws, which seem to grow a little longer. Then she goes absolutely savage on Typhon's neck, burrowing into him like a parched tick. Only she's not there to drink his blood. She's there to free it. To bleed him out. To—

"What the fuck?"

As Typhon raises his hand to slap Bree, she does the unthinkable.

She slips through the fresh, open wound, pulling herself past the spraying purple blood and *into* Typhon's body. Into his jugular.

Typhon's hand claps against his neck. Then he pulls it away, his palm empty aside from his own blood. And the wound...it's healed.

Bree's trapped inside him.

Exactly where she intended to be, guided by an instinct that somehow knows how to kill Typhon, and maybe even how to kill anything... including herself.

How long can she last inside his body without taking a breath?

Even Demon Dog needs to breathe.

I need to do something, but what can I do? I can't even feel—

A sliver of a memory surfaces. It's recent. Like seconds ago. A feeling, in my toes. Throughout my body. A tingle.

I look down. Try wiggling my fingers. Still nothing. Because my nerves are severed. You can't move what you can't feel.

But I felt something. Unless it was a psychological illusion. Like phantom limbs.

I shake my head. It was more than that.

The more I focus on that moment of sensation, the more I'm certain it was real. That it came from within. And it felt electric. Like energy. Like...holy shit. It felt like my arms and back when I extend the wings and blades.

Like that same power was inside...all of me.

It seems counterproductive, but I learned long ago that you can't effectively help other people unless you first help yourself. Means eating breakfast before getting your kids ready for school. Means taking a nap before spooning out soup at a homeless shelter. Means figuring out a way to fix your nervous system before saving your friends from two monster-making gods.

Eyes closed, I breathe deep through my nose, hold it, and then let it out slowly. Centering one's self is a challenge on a good day. Getting it done while your pint-sized BFF is trapped inside a monster is a lot harder. Luckily, I have a lot of experience blocking out the world and my own worries. In the past, I was repairing my mind. Now, I need to repair the connection between mind and body. I know it's not physically possible to make my nerves reach out and reconnect with the power of my mind. But I'm not a normal person, and my physical nervous system isn't what I'm trying to affect.

My wings buzz with energy, but they're also an extension of myself. That otherworldly energy isn't trapped inside an alien device. It's not mechanical technology. It's part of my body. Part of my cells. And it's under my control. It's also a hell of a lot more powerful than I realized. If I can punch a hole through the planet, maybe the energy can be used for much smaller, much more difficult tasks.

I use my intuition about how the laser energy is controlled and focus it inward, searching for it, asking for a response. When a shudder rolls through my body from the feet up, I know this is what I felt before. My human body is paralyzed. But the rest of me, which is not human anymore, just needs to figure itself out.

Quickly.

I imagine my nervous system, flowing down my spine, out through my limbs, my fingers, and my toes. I see thousands of little tendrils, splitting and dividing, flowing out through my muscles, cells, bones, and sinews, connecting it all, taking and sending information at the speed of light.

And it's easy.

Because it was already there, I think. I'm not creating these connections. Just simply noticing them for the first time. This is why I'm stronger and faster. Why I can see in the dark. I've been changed at a fundamental level. I've been made anew.

"Holy shit," I say, feeling my full strength for the first time. It's like... like my heart has been replaced by a white dwarf star, blazing with power.

God-blood.

That's what Echidna called me. Am I like Sarah and Henry now? Am I like a legit god?

My body convulses, and I feel it. Every part of me feels like light.

I open my eyes and lift my arms.

They're sparkling, like there's light just beneath the first layer of skin, peeking out between my pores. But power alone doesn't make you a god. That's DNA, and the angelic creatures that did this to me weren't gods. At least, they didn't claim to be, and in my experience, bona fide, old-school gods really like to flaunt who they are.

I don't need the damn title, though.

Because, I have the power.

My wings flare wider. I turn my attention down to Henry, still in the way, still holding Sarah back, putting her at risk.

When I launch myself down to get him, my whole body moves again, total control and full sensation restored. But I'm also experiencing a kind of power-up, like I've finally eaten enough Altered Beast balloons and have changed into something more powerful. Like a metamorphosis.

The time between the first hint of movement and a sonic boom would have to be measured in milliseconds. I feel like light, covering the distance in a heartbeat. A moment ago, I was a half mile away, now I'm standing beside Henry, smoldering in a crater.

He smiles up at me, body scorched. "That…ugh…that was rad. Why aren't you kicking her ass?" he asks, glancing at Echidna's back.

"Your sister is going to do that," I say. "I'm just here to get *you* out of the way."

I reach down and pick him up. The moment our bodies connect, arcs of lightning crackle between us. "Sorry," he says. "Guess I'm not really in control. Like at night, when I was thirteen—"

"Didn't hurt," I tell him, hoping to divert the conversation.

I scoop him up.

"Behind you," he mumbles, pain nearly knocking him unconscious.

I whip around to find a fifteen-foot-tall newborn monster flopping toward me. Its front end is fully formed, but the back side looks unfinish-ed, the legs limp and dragging behind, leaving a trail of white goo. The newborn has a large, powerful head that reminds me of the Creature from the Black Lagoon, its body olive green and covered with folds of armored skin. The monster has what looks like a normal mouth, but when it opens, to bite, inside are two sharp blades, like a flat beak, designed to sever flesh into chunks.

The light inside my body flickers.

"Da fuq?" Henry says, eyes widening.

All the energy flows up, into my head, and then exits—via my eye sockets. With unchanged vision, I glance back and forth, up and down, just taking the creature in...and apart. When the laser light fades, a stunned-looking monster is left behind. Its expression remains frozen as it falls apart into large, cauterized chunks.

"Fucking laser vision!" Henry says. "Yes! I knew it!"

I fly up and away. As the two of us cruise over Sarah, I shout, "Clear!"

She sees me, looking confused for a moment, and then she notices Henry in my arms. A smile creeps onto her face.

Wasting no time, Sarah unleashes a second volley of lightning that catches Echidna off guard. The snake-goddess had been on the attack for so long, it probably didn't think Sarah had much fight left in her. That's because she doesn't know Sarah.

While the arcing lightning blinds and contains Echidna, Sarah reaches back with one hand and makes a quick fist. The top of the massive pillar crumbles as though a giant invisible sphincter had just pinched off the world's largest dump. Then Sarah swings her fist down, like she's clocking Echidna over the head—and the pillar follows. Untold tons of stone drop toward the cavern floor with enough force to level a city block—and hopefully a god.

53

"No!" Henry shouts, reaching his scorched arm out toward his sister. "Sarah!"

She glances up at him as I fly him to safety. Looks moved by his concern. Appreciative. Because Henry doesn't show concern. Because concern is a byproduct of fear.

Then the skyscraper stalactite crashes down atop her—and Echidna.

Grit and dust billows. A shockwave nearly slaps me from the air.

A heavy silence fills the chamber after the echoing boom settles into a distant rumble.

Typhon still has Jonas trapped, but his focus is on the horizontal stalactite lying where Echidna had been.

Where Sarah had been.

"Help her," Henry says, when I place him on the ground. "You have to help her."

"Henry, I don't think—"

The pillar shakes. Splits down the middle with a loud crack. Then it begins to bulge. Shale-like sheets crack and fall away, clattering to the stone floor. Something is alive beneath all that stone.

Typhon begins to chuckle, his voice booming. Mocking.

"Bullshit," Henry says. "This is bullshit." He stabs a finger up at Typhon, and I'm a little surprised to see tears in his eyes. "Prepare yourself for the biggest fucking surprise of your long fucking life!"

I know tough talk when I hear it. Henry is all bluster, but he doesn't believe Sarah could have survived either. Couple his doubt with Typhon's confidence, and it's hard to stay positive. Henry is forcing himself to, but he's legit horrified about Sarah's death.

Henry is fearless...but not without empathy.

Or regret. Or sadness.

I don't think he knows, but Henry has taken hold of my hand, and he's squeezing. Hard. All his worry is crushing down into my hand—and it doesn't really hurt. Instead, my hand shimmers blue. Sparkles of energy flow out from the point of impact, dispersing the energy from Henry's constrictor grip.

The laser light isn't just an appendage anymore. It's part of me. And I think controlling it will be a lot like moving a hand. I'll need to experiment to fully understand what I can do, but I'm stronger than ever.

The fallen pillar cracks down the middle. Then everything around the crack shatters and explodes outward.

All around the cavern—aside from the gurgle of lava and the rumble of something more distant—silence. Even the newborn monsters have gone still, waiting for their mother to rise. Typhon leans closer. As he does, Jonas's cage squeezes a little tighter. The father of monsters can double task like a mofo.

A podium of stone rises through the blown-out hole. Standing at the center is Sarah, strong arms crossed, defiant eyes turned up to Typhon, who reels back like he's been slapped.

"Your old lady is paste," Sarah says. "When would you like to join her?"

"Yyyyes!" Henry shouts, jumping and pumping a fist, which makes him wince and settle down. But his excitement is uncontainable. "You are a badass bitch!"

"Don't you forget it," she says to him, stone pillar rising higher until she's at eye level with Typhon.

The giant writhes with rage, arms raised, bending lava and chains to his will, about to unleash his full force on Sarah.

"You okay?" I ask Henry.

He nods. "Help her kick his ass."

I fly to Sarah in the blink of an eye. Arrive so quickly that she flinches. "That was faster than usual." She eyes me up and down. "And you look different."

"I *am* different," I say. "Long story."

"Well, all right then, Laser Chicken. I managed to piss him off. Any thoughts on how to put him down?"

"One," I say, and I let the laser light inside my body glow through my eyes. "You like tower defense games?"

Sarah smiles. The stone pillar transforms, taking the shape of a castle battlement.

"Ready?" I ask, letting power build within me. It shimmers and glows through my body's pores. "Three...two..."

Typhon roars and flings his arms toward us, beating us to the punch. Lava and chains whip toward us. The volley is unavoidable.

But that's not a problem.

Sarah raises her hand, and a thick wall of stone juts up between us and the assault. The stone shakes and cracks from a hundred impacts, but it holds until several of the chains punch through. One comes close, but all ultimately miss.

"Ready," Sarah says.

"Do it," I say.

A large hole appears in the stone, revealing Typhon as he prepares to unleash another attack.

I aim for his waist, hoping to hobble the snake-man and not risk hitting Bree, who is somewhere inside him.

"Wait!" Sarah shouts. "Something's happening."

I missed it because I was so focused on my target. Typhon is still writhing around, but he's no longer spinning lava. He's...he's in agony! Grasping at his head. Roaring toward the ceiling.

"She's doing it," I whisper.

"Who is doing what?"

"Bree," I say, stunned by what I'm seeing. An eight-year-old girl is bringing down an ancient monster-making god—on her own. "She's inside him."

"Probably a better way to phrase that," she says. "But...that kid has balls."

Typhon falls forward, catching himself on one hand. With the other, he strikes the side of his head, cracking his own skull.

"He's trying to get to her," I say.

When he pulls his hand back to strike himself again, I find a new target and unleash all the energy I'd built up. The beam of blue laser light emerges from my eyes—and my chest. The attack happens at the speed of light. One moment Typhon has two arms, the next, just one. The severed arm falls to the ground beside him, flailing and flopping about until it rolls into a lava stream and catches on fire.

A flicker of light draws my attention back to Jonas. The lava cage still surrounds him, but it's flickering. At first, I think it's because Typhon is distracted. Then Jonas walks out of the lava in his immaterial, more powerful form, the Sword of Mars clutched in his hand. And he's about to attack.

I shout down to him. "Jonas!"

He looks up. Spots me. "Can I spank this bitch now?"

"Bree is inside Typhon!"

"*Inside* Typhon?!" When I nod, he shouts, "Where?"

Typhon is grasping his head. She must have followed the jugular up and then clawed her way deeper, maybe even into his brain. But how long can she last?

"In his head!" I shout. "Can you get her out?"

"Like cracking an egg," he says, and Jonas focuses on the giant. Reaches out with one hand.

Typhon's furious thrashing comes to a stop, not for a lack of trying, but because he's grasped by an unseen force from which there is no escape. Typhon gnashes and howls, an animal caught in a trap. But he's assaulted from without and within, incapable of defense.

The lava sphere around Jonas falls away. He's crouched down, unharmed, and unmoving while his spirit walks the Earth.

"Y-you toil in v-vain!" Typhon shouts past his pain. "The W-world Snake will consume you all!"

"Yeah," Jonas says, "Maybe she'll choke on you."

Typhon...just comes apart. I don't know how else to describe it. One moment, he's whole, the next he's been split in two. Tendrils of gore spread out between the two halves which lower to the floor and gently lay out. The snake bodies on either side of his head writhe madly for a moment, but they settle when he comes to rest, very, very dead.

I leap over the battlements and extend my wings. A moment later I'm standing beside one half of Typhon's head.

What I think is his brain looks absolutely scrambled, like it's been run through a meat grinder.

A meat grinder with a name.

"Bree!" I shout, stepping inside the open skull. Knee deep in mythological gray matter, I dig my hands inside the gore and search for a small body. "Bree!"

"Dude," Henry says. He's pretty torn up, but his god-like healing is doing its job. "What are you doing?"

"Bree was in here," I say, fighting my panic.

"Uh, bro..." Henry points behind me. "You picked the wrong hemisphere. Looks like Bree is left-brained."

I spin around. Bree is inside the other half of Typhon's brain, doing what looks like a Running Man dance, pumping her fists back and forth, covered in blood and bits of who knows what. Despite all this, and a charred face, she's beaming. She sings. "We did it. We did it. Oh yeah." She stops and smiles at Jonas as he arrives, back in his body. "We did it, right?"

"Yeah, kid. We did. Thanks to you, it looks like."

Bree is ecstatic. Doesn't bother climbing out of the brain. Just goes right back to dancing.

Sarah arrives, lowered to the ground by a shrinking pillar of stone. "The baby monsters took off when Typhon...well, 'died' doesn't really do this justice. The path to the gate is clear. We can go to Tartarus now."

"Any chance I can get a shower first?" Bree says, leaping out of the brain and landing beside us. On all fours, she shakes her body like a dog, spraying bits and pieces of Typhon's insides. We reel back, but an invisible wall stops the gore in its tracks. Sticky bits slide down the telekinetic wall and then drop to the floor when Jonas lowers it.

"Tartarus first," I say, glancing at Jonas's watch. "Shower after."

Bree gets it and nods. "Save Bubbles, and then the world."

"Exactly," I say, and I offer her my hands. I scoop her up, trying to breathe through my nose.

Jonas offers his hand to Henry. "Let's go." Then he seems to notice Henry's physical state for the first time. "What the hell happened to you?"

"I got sprayed by acid," he says.

"Unnecessarily," Sarah mumbles, taking Henry's other hand.

Henry doesn't argue the point, but adds, "*Twice.* Cool, right?"

"Totally," Jonas says, and we lift off together, flying over the fallen pillar and entering the tunnel together.

54

"Have you guys ever heard of a dongfish?" Henry asks, halfway down the tunnel.

"For the last time," Sarah says. "It's not real."

"It's totally real. If it wasn't real, would I know that the dillsack of a dongfish is connected to its horngus by a tubular scungle?"

"You can ignore him," Sarah says. "He just likes saying those words."

"Isn't that a meme?" I ask.

"You see!" Henry says. "Miah's seen it, too."

"You know that memes aren't facts?" Jonas asks, sounding concerned. "Right?"

"Whachu talkin' about?" Henry says. "Memes are simple, I'll give you that, but they're meant to be, so that people can easily absorb life's most basic lessons. Fact: if you keep calm, you *can* carry on. Fact: he *was* the Juggernaut...bitch. Fact: if you walk into Mordor, you're gonna get shanked by a goblin or some shit."

"You are a repository of boundless knowledge," Jonas says.

Henry misses the sarcasm. "Thank you."

He sticks his tongue out at Sarah.

Jonas turns his attention to me and Bree. "So, what's up with you two?"

"What do you mean?" I ask.

"We're supposed to be the heavy hitters. Gods and Titans and all that. I couldn't see what was happening with my eyes, but I don't need to. I know what you did. What she did."

"What did they do that I didn't?" Henry asks.

Jonas opts to not answer the question. Henry provided...distraction, but he still needs to find a way to overcome his impulsiveness.

"You should both be dead," Jonas says, and he motions to my head. "Your neck broke, and now you're shooting lasers out of your body, and you have a whole Twilight sparkle vibe going on."

Bree gasps and tries to look down at my legs. "Miah is a pony?"

"What? No." Jonas probably has no concept of *My Little Pony*. I, on the other hand, have watched too many episodes with Bree, both before and after we were buds and the personifications of Heaven and Hell. Ponyville is a fun place to visit when you've just had an edible. I'm partial to Apple Jack, but Twilight Sparkle is pretty cool, too. "I'm talking about Twilight with the sparkly vampires."

"Miah is a vampire?" Bree asks, turning her wide eyes to my face, looking me over.

Jonas sighs. "No. I'm just saying he's sparkling. Like there's energy just beneath his skin. He's more powerful than when we started." He turns his attention to Bree. "And so are you. You not only tore open Typhon, but you clawed your way into his brain and turned it to slurry. That's not something...lesser beings can do."

"You think they're gods, too?" Henry asks.

"People can't just become gods," Sarah says.

"People don't have laser wings, either," Bree says.

Jonas sucks in a quick breath and then starts laughing. "Holy hell, that sneaky sonuvabitch."

"What?" Sarah asks.

"Linda... Zeus... *He* did this."

"Zeus turned us into...gods?" I ask. "When? How?"

"Ambrosia," Jonas says.

"What? When did we have ambrosia?" Henry asks. "I love ambrosia."

"When you were throwing a tantrum over mushrooms," Sarah says. "But I fail to see how the nastiest dessert in the history of the world turned them into gods."

"Because it wasn't just a dessert," Jonas says.

"Oooh." Henry gets it. "Ambrosia. Holy shit. Really?"

"Can one of you explain what the hell ambrosia is?" I ask.

"It's like the super food of the ancient gods. They loved the stuff. Ate it at feasts, served to them by nymphs or something. Doesn't matter.

What does matter is that when a human being eats ambrosia, they're granted immortality. In your case, I think it also boosted the power you already had, and gave you the ability to heal grave wounds, and survive inside a giant's head."

It makes no sense at all, and total sense at the same time. It's ridiculous and accurate. Disguising the mythical ambrosia as modern ambrosia sounds like the move of a god who goes around Earth disguised as a Southern, church-going lady.

"But there weren't instructions," I say. "How could he know the right people would eat it?"

"Probably didn't," Jonas says. "But it wouldn't matter if *we* did, and he probably figured that Bree would want some. And that she'd make you try it."

"It was good," Bree says.

"Man," Henry whines. "Now I want some frikkin' ambrosia. Maybe they have some in Tartarus?"

"Speaking of," I say, looking ahead. The tunnel's exit widens before us, revealing a simple, half-spherical chamber. Looks like someone laid down a mosaic floor inside what was once a molten bubble. The walls are black and shiny, reflecting the red glow of a gate that stands at the center. Red light and a hexagonal pattern in orange stretch between the fifty-foot-tall pillars, carved with an array of luminous symbols. The gate is active and ready to transport us to another world.

We land at its base, looking up at the sheet of energy.

"So, we just walk through it?" Jonas asks.

I nod. "Normally, you have to think about where you want to go, but I think this gate is pre-programmed to take anyone who reaches it to Tartarus. Just to be safe, maybe have Tartarus on your mind."

"There's no place like home," Jonas says, approaching the gate.

He's about to step through when—

"Jonas." It's Bubbles. Her voice sounds crackly. Distorted.

"Almost there," he says.

"N-n-not enough t-t-time," she says, glitching. "I w-w-wanted to t-tell you. B-before—"

"Shut yourself off!" Jonas says. "Save your energy!"

"N-n-not enough time. Ju-just seconds."

Jonas looks like he's been slapped.

"I wanted to tell you," Bubbles says, using the last of her energy to speak clearly. "I'm proud of who you have become, and to be your friend. I love yooooo–" Her voice fades to a crackle.

Jonas has tears in his eyes. "Bubbles? Bubbles!"

He looks at me in disbelief.

"I don't get it," Henry says, sounding a little sad. "Won't the data still be there? A flash drive from like ten years ago still has everything on it. Once you plug it in."

"It's more complicated than that," Jonas says. "She's more than data. Whatever is in here–" He holds up his wrist with the watch. "–is just information. What makes Bubbles...*human* is gone."

Henry frowns. "Like a photo album after someone dies."

"Something like that," Jonas says.

"Maybe not," I say. "She doesn't have enough power to speak. That doesn't mean the watch is totally dead. We can't give up."

"What are you thinking?" Jonas asks.

"Tartarus is a planet, right? Populated by an advanced civilization. There's got to be someone there who can–"

Jonas puts his hand on my shoulder. "Take me."

I turn to Sarah and motion to Bree. "Stay with her."

Sarah nods. "Go."

I crouch by Bree, intending on saying something comforting, but she smacks me and says, "What are you waiting for? Go save her!"

I turn to Jonas, holding out my hands, ready to pick him up and fly through. But he's not ready. He's not even coming.

Jonas holds the watch out to me. "You'll be faster on your own, right?"

I nod. With my ambrosia boost and altered nervous system, I can fly faster than would be comfortable–maybe even survivable for Jonas. But the watch...that won't slow me down.

"I'm trusting you with her life." He straps the watch to my wrist. "But I won't blame you if it's not possible. Now go." He gives me a slap on the cheek. "Go!"

Before my wings have even fully extended, I'm moving. In a blink, I hit the gate's energy wall and pass through. It's as easy as flying through a door, but on the other side of the threshold is another world. The air smells different. Acrid. Gravity's pull is a little stronger. And the light is diffused, like I'm standing in the penumbra of an eclipse.

I emerge surrounded by strange trees that look like twisted rubber bands topped with colorful fungi. I weave between a few, noting my surroundings. I'm in a forest, but I can't see or hear any life.

I'm not going to find anything like this, so I bank up and launch myself toward a sky hidden behind a wall of smoky brown. Through the haze, I can see three stars of varying brightness, but all dimmed so much I can gaze straight at them.

Is it always like this? I wonder. So far, this planet doesn't seem like a paradise anyone would want to visit, let alone live on for thousands of years.

I do a quick 360 and find the smoke's origin.

A city!

"Hang on, Bubbles," I say, and I launch toward the distant metropolis. My first impression is of a sprawling, technological mega-city. A few seconds later and many miles closer, the truth becomes clear.

"Oh no..."

Tartarus...has been destroyed.

55

I take an aerial tour of the city, which is mostly piles of rubble with the occasional, futuristic skyscraper jutting out. I had expected some kind of Greek paradise, with everything made of marble and surrounded by vineyards, olive groves, and happy donkeys. Instead, the structures that remain are decidedly otherworldly, constructed from some kind of metal-glass combination, lit from within, each of them containing power, or life.

But the light is fading. Whatever happened here, it was recent.

Hell, it might not yet be over.

With that in mind, I swoop down to an elevation of fifty feet, inspecting the destruction up close. I very quickly wish I hadn't.

There are bodies—everywhere.

Some are crushed beneath debris. Others appear to have been broken, or reshaped, and left to die. The worst of them...have been dissected, skin cut cleanly down the middle and peeled carefully open to reveal organs. I land by an ancient looking man with long hair and a thick beard, both matted with blood. His torso has been cut with the skill of a surgeon, the skin opened and pinned to the side. His ribcage has been clipped on either side, his sternum lying to the body's side. The man's lungs are exposed and his heart...is missing. By the anguished look frozen on the man's face, I suspect he was conscious up until the moment his heart was removed.

"Who were you?" I wonder, searching the area for clues, and I find one lying twenty feet away.

A trident.

"No way," I whisper, standing up. "No fucking way. *Poseidon.*"

The gravity of what I've discovered hits me all at once.

The army of gods and Titans we were sent to summon are dead. And by the looks of it, they didn't stand a chance. Which does not bode well for our future. For the entire universe's future.

And it essentially seals Bubbles's fate.

The only option remaining I can think of is to blaze back through the gate, return to Khaos, and blast a path straight up through the Earth's crust, until I reach the surface. I'm not sure if I'm powerful enough to pull it off, or fast enough to make the trip in time. Hell, it might already be too late.

But I can't think of another—

A glint of light directly in my eyes makes me squint.

I spin around, expecting to find an enemy rushing toward me. Instead, I find a distant light flickering. Must be something reflecting light from one of the three stars. I look up at the dark sky, the stars nearly blotted out. Or not.

Then I notice a pattern to the flicker that anyone from Earth, who's watched a lot of TV and seen a few dish-soap commercials would recognize. S.O.S. It's a message, directed at me.

Feels like a really bad idea, but I don't see any other options.

I rocket toward the light, wings and arm blades extended, building power within for a devastating laser strike, should I be attacked. But all my bluster is for nothing. Lying atop a pile of rubble, a bloody smile on her face, is Linda. She's still dressed for church in a flowery dress. A large, colorful shawl is wrapped around her shoulders.

"It's good to see you again, hun," she says, like it's been a long time, and like we were close when she left.

"It's not even been a day," I say.

"You...took the long route," she says.

"A map might have helped."

"Most travelers take the path of least resistance," she says. "You all plowed through every obstacle along the way. Everything you left alive in the underworld is talking about it."

She looks sad for a moment, and then she gives me a once over. "I see you found my special snack. I had intended it for the girl. To help keep her safe. But it appears the changes it made to you have been beneficial."

"Bree had some, too," I say.

"Good," she says, nodding. "That's good. Now tell me...how did you get past Typhon and Echidna?"

"Get...*past* them?" I ask.

"There are many routes to take, if you are stealthy." Her brow furrows. "That...was the lesson."

"Right," I say. "Right. Stealth."

Linda's eyes widen. "You *fought* them?"

"Again, a map would have been nice."

"You fought them...and *survived?*"

"Well, we kind of maybe—"

Her eyes somehow widen further. "You *defeated* them?"

"If by 'defeated' you mean 'killed horribly,' then yes. They didn't really give us a choice. I hope that's okay."

"Okay?" She coughs. "Darling, it means there is still hope. But you all need to survive. To escape this place before he returns with the beast."

"He?" I ask.

"Her man," she says.

"Herman? Who's Herman?"

"Her. *Man.* Cherry's man. He called himself Samael. The keeper of my hand, which I've spent quite some time looking for."

"Didn't you just recently lose the hand?" I ask.

Linda's eyes flare wide for a moment. "Yes. Yes. Of course. It simply feels like years. Now, Samael does not appear to wield the same power as Cherry, but he commands an army of abominations which slew both gods and Titans with ease. Those Samael did not kill outright, he carved open. Some he studied. From others he collected organs. I feared my time would soon come, but then I saw you."

She reaches her arms up to me, revealing her one good hand and her fleshy stub where the other hand used to be. "Come now, carry me away from this place."

I take her one good hand and spot the watch on my wrist. "We can't leave yet."

She waits for an explanation.

I lift the watch.

"It's Bubbles. The watch is out of power. I came ahead to try—"

"You won't find an outlet adapter here," she says. "You won't find an outlet at all. That's not how electricity works on this world. But..." Linda stands up, grunting from the effort, dusts herself off, and looks into the distance where a domed building still stands. "There might be an option. But I must warn you, if it fails, she will be gone forever."

"She might already be," I say.

"Very well, but...if we encounter Samael, we must flee."

I'm about to agree when a distant rumble shakes the city around us. *A building is falling,* I think. It must have been taken down by some unseen force that already worked its way through this part of the city.

"The beast is near." She wraps her arms around my neck. "Hope you don't mind getting cozy with an old lady."

"You are neither," I say, wrapping my arms around her broad torso. "Any chance you can become someone smaller?"

"I've grown attached to this form," she says. "You can manage."

I keep us as low as possible, weaving around rubble, just feet from the ground. My wings would be easy to spot from a distance. Despite all the detours, we make rapid progress, arriving at the building just thirty seconds later. When I place Linda down, her hair is windblown. She staggers a step, holding her side, which is bloody—a detail I'd missed earlier. She's hurt bad. Before I arrived, she wasn't even moving. Must be really pushing herself. "Whoo. Was that full speed?"

"Not even close."

She gives my arm a pat. "Can't wait to see what you can do."

The glass-like structure flickers. The light within its walls dims.

"We must hurry," she says. "If the city's light fades, it means Tartarus is dead, and this world will crumble."

"Tartarus, the god, and the place. Right."

She points to a door. "That way."

I pick her up and navigate inside the building, which kind of reminds me of Superman's Fortress of Solitude, all crystal, but with architectural elements that bend the light and blow the mind. Walls shift through colorful patterns as we pass, like each new surface filters out all but a certain wavelength. On its own, a portion of the wall might be red, but we move a little to the side and the blue patch behind it turns the surface purple. I could spend an entire day inside this place, looking at the colors and patterns, but we take the rapid-fire tour, arriving at our destination at the building's center, just beneath the dome.

At the vast room's core is what appears to be a ten-foot-tall crystal egg.

Linda motions to it. "This is the–"

"Orphic egg," I say, remembering Jonas's history lesson. "Holy shit. It's real?"

"Why wouldn't it be real?" Linda asks.

"I'm still getting used to all this," I admit.

Linda grunts in pain, holding her side. Then she sucks it up and snaps her fingers at me. "The watch."

As I slip the watch from my wrist, Linda places her hand on the egg's side. The front seems to disintegrate, revealing a hollow interior.

"Place it inside."

I do as she says and stand back. "You seem confident."

"Not the first time an artificial intelligence has been made flesh and blood," she says.

"This happens…often?" I ask.

She smiles. "Once before. And not in the egg. What I'm saying is, it's possible."

The egg seals.

"Now what?" I ask.

"We wait."

"For…what?"

She looks ready to slap me. "For something to happen! The egg does what it wants. How it wants. *When* it wants."

"Well, is it smart enough to know we don't have a lot of ti–"

Light rises from the floor, coursing up over the egg's polygonal surface. Waves of color dance and swirl. The chamber around us flares brightly. Even Linda looks impressed. Her jaw drops. "It's Tartarus…he's channeling the last of his life force through the egg…" Tears fill her eyes. "Goodbye, old friend."

Then the chamber goes dark.

The only light comes from the egg, which is slowly dimming. The front dissolves again, unleashing a cloud of steam. I feel like Linda and I are Gary and Wyatt in *Weird Science,* bras on our heads, watching in awe as a woman steps out of the mist.

"She's alive," I whisper, quoting the movie, paraphrasing the famous scene from James Whale's *Frankenstein.*

She's naked, has an adorable face, and a super curvy, but a little on the plump side body. "She looks like Mei," I whisper, and when Linda doesn't respond, I elaborate. "From Overwatch. It's a video game."

Linda elbows me. "Find out if that's really her. Then we need to get the hell out of here."

"Uh," I say, approaching with a hand raised. "Bubbles?"

She's breathing. Her eyes are flicking back and forth. Definitely alive. But there's no real sign that she's got anything going on upstairs. No emotions. No reactions. Just blank life.

A roar interrupts. An earthquake shakes through the building. It repeats over and over, getting stronger.

Footsteps, I realize.

"The transformation must have exposed us," Linda says. "We must go! Now!" Linda takes off her shawl, wraps it around Bubbles's body, and lifts her hand. I grab hold of them both and launch us out of the building, banking high and fast, headed back toward the distant forest and the gate within. I flare my wings as brightly as I can, like a shooting star over the city. If the others are here now, they'll see me and follow.

I glance back as we leave, spotting a five-hundred-foot-tall behemoth destroying the building and the egg within. The beast looks different from how it looks on TV, but there are enough similarities.

"Oh my god... Is...that...?"

"Yes," Linda says. "Nemesis."

56

Flying with Bubbles in one arm and Linda in the other is awkward. Neither of them are what you'd call petite, and both are kind of dead weight. Luckily, I'm a hell of a lot stronger now, the energy within my body channeling to where it's needed most. Accelerating takes a bit longer, in part because of the added weight, but also because I don't know what Bubbles can endure, and I'm afraid her new existence might be fragile—if she's really even there.

Despite blasting through the air on an alien planet, she's still an emotionless blank slate.

Cruising over the city, I take one last look at the carnage below...and I wish I hadn't. The terrain is alive with motion. An army of assorted monsters scramble over the hellscape, pursuing us as we fly past. There are thousands of them. An army capable of overthrowing a collection of the most powerful beings in the universe.

A few of them take to the sky, but I'm moving too fast to catch. I'm also moving too fast to get a good look at them. All I really know is that they're not uniform. I see different species, different sizes, different colors. Looks like my childhood toybox, filled with various collections of action figures, monsters, spaceships, and my random yard-sale finds.

It's a collection, I think. And the idea is confirmed a moment later, when I spot something familiar—a creature moving within a personal cloak of sooty air. A Tenebris. But it's just one amidst a menagerie.

A vast army collected from across the universe.

The worst of the worst. I assume.

"Heads up, sugar!" Linda calls.

I'm so distracted by what lies below, I nearly collide with Henry, who's carrying Jonas and Sarah in his arms. Bree rides on his back, legs wrapped around his waist, one hand grasping his tattered shirt, the other waving in the air like she's a cowboy on a bucking bronco. She smiles at me as we cross paths, having the time of her life.

Henry's face lights up when he sees Linda. "Dad!"

I catch a glimpse of Jonas, his eyes widening when he catches sight of Bubbles. Apparently, her current form is familiar to him. But there's no time to talk.

"Back to the gate!" I shout.

As they pass, I hear Bree. "Turn around, Bessy!"

I slow my pace a bit, allowing them to catch up.

"What happened?" Jonas asks, looking at Bubbles. "How is this possible?"

"Believe it or not," I say. "The Orphic Egg."

"Bubbles," Jonas says, taking the news in stride. "Bubbles, can you hear me?"

"She's totes zoned out, dude," Henry says.

"What's wrong with her?" Jonas asks.

"She has been like this since her resurrection," Linda says. "It's possible we were only able to preserve the data, which included a physical profile, I'm guessing. You recognize this form?"

"She chose it," he says. "Just before all this started. Is there anything else we can do for her?"

"Not die," Linda says. "Tartarus is lost. We must leave through the gate while it is still possible to do so."

"Incoming!" Sarah shouts, twisting around, dangling from Henry's hands.

Behind us, three massive bats rise from the ranks of the monsters. Their faces are squished up and nasty, punctuated by two, large bowl-shaped ears. Deafening trumpet blasts tear from their fanged mouths. They're using echolocation to find us. With wingspans that dwarf mine, they accelerate quickly. But it's not enough. We're moving too fast. Still, these aren't normal bats.

They seem to change...to adapt to the situation in progress. Wide open mouths suck air into expanding chests. Just when I think they're going to burst, they're propelled by flatulence, rocketing into the sky behind us.

Henry asks, "You want me to—"

"I've got this," I say. Without warning, I turn skyward and extinguish my wings. As our upward momentum slows to a stop, I spin around. During that quick revolution, I unleash a laser blast from my eyes. It carves across the ground below, leveling trees. Then it strikes the three bats, cutting them in half. Far beyond, I burn a path through the pursuing army of monsters.

For a moment, I'm encouraged. I could kill them all from a distance.

Then…they stitch together, reform, and return to the land of the living, their pursuit paused for just a moment.

They're regenerating, I think.

And that includes the three bats, whose lower halves are sprouting new limbs.

I'm still holding Bubbles and Linda, as my revolution completes. We plummet for a moment, then I pop my wings and continue toward the gate again, quickly passing Henry on the way. It's our only way off this world, and if something happens to it, we're stuck.

I land a full minute before the others will arrive, setting down Bubbles and Linda. Bubbles is alive. Maintaining her balance, but she hasn't shown a trace of true cognition.

"Hey," Linda pats my cheek. "I need to apologize."

"For getting us involved in all this bullshit?" I ask.

She shakes her head and starts shimmying out of her dress. "For what you'll find on the other side of that gate. For the state of the world and the people in it. For not…for not being honest with ya'll, the way the good Lord requires. I hope you all will forgive me, and you'll understand why I did what I did."

She slips out of the dress and collects it, clothed only in a frilly bra and underwear.

"What are you talking about?" I ask.

She removes the shawl from Bubbles and slips the dress over her head. It's a kind gesture, juxtaposing the mystery she's laying at my feet. She pulls Bubbles's arms through the sleeves. Then wraps the shawl back around her neck. "Ready for church," she says to Bubbles, and then to me, Linda says, "Explaining would simply waste time, and there is none to waste." She hobbles toward the gate. "You will probably hate me, but there was no other way. And this..." She looks up to where the city's smoke still rises into the air. "Was unexpected. But you, Miah, you are much more than I'd hoped for. When I see you again, I hope it will be as friends."

I stammer for a moment, a litany of questions competing for my mouth. But I'm too late.

"The gate on this side will take you anywhere. Steel yourself...and then go home, Miah."

"Dad!" Henry shouts, flying in. "Wait!"

But he's too late. Linda steps through the gate and disappears.

"The hell was that?" Jonas asks, as he's dropped from Henry's hand.

"I'm not sure," I say. "He...she...whatever. Linda said this gate can take us anywhere. Told me to go home. Apologized for what we'd find."

"That doesn't sound good," Sarah says.

Bree climbs up Henry's back as he touches down, sitting on his shoulders. He doesn't seem to mind. Holds on to her ankles.

"Whatever it is," Bree says. "Can't be worse than Khaos. Or this shithole."

Henry smiles, but I can't even fake it. Because I'm pretty sure things back home are worse than here. Otherwise, why apologize? "We should go. Now. Won't be more than a few minutes before we're overrun."

"In a minute," Jonas says, walking past me, his eyes on Bubbles.

He stands in front of her, looking her over. "She's exactly how she imagined herself. Exactly. She has to be in there." He waves a hand in front of her face. "C'mon, Bubbles. Show me you're there."

"Maybe she needs some kind of activation code?" Henry offers.

Jonas thinks on it and then shakes his head. "She's an AI. A sentient being. You can't activate and deactivate her. She's alive or she's not."

"What about the first time?" I ask. "She wasn't always with you. Was there something you said to—"

"She spoke to me, first," he says, looking glum.

Beneath us, the ground begins to shake. Sarah crouches, palm against the ground. "Running out of time."

"We can do this back home," I tell Jonas, but he doesn't hear me.

"Been through too much to lose you, Bubs. If you're in there, I need you to come back. Find your way home." He reaches out and places an affectionate hand on her cheek. "Come home."

Bubbles gasps like she was close to drowning, reeling back. Jonas and I catch her. Steady her. She takes several deep breaths and then lifts her hands, looking them over. She's shaking. In shock. She turns her gaze down and uses her hands to pat her body. "I'm here," she says. "I'm real?"

She touches her mouth. "I'm speaking. With a mouth? What... How?"

She looks up, beaming. She turns to Jonas, who's crying openly, despite being a tough guy. "I'm...alive!" She wraps her arms around him, and he squeezes her back.

"Always have been alive," he says.

She leans back, wipes a tear from her own eye, and looks at it, astounded. "Thank you."

"Thank him." Jonas motions to me. "This was all Miah."

Bubbles throws herself into my arms, squeezing me tight. I can't help but laugh. Bubbles is a lot of things, but I never imagined her as being physically affectionate. Maybe that's a side effect of having a physical body for the first time. "Thank you, Miah. I owe you."

"We both do," Jonas says.

Bubbles's head cocks to the side. She's listening. "Several thousand targets incoming. Several of them sound large. One of them is..."

"Nemesis," I say. "It's Nemesis."

"Like *the* Nemesis?" Henry asks. "From TV? Or like the actual Greek goddess?"

"TV," I say. "But like a redesign. More like a giant salamander."

"Can I go see?" he asks Sarah. "Oh please, oh please, oh please?"

"Not a chance," I answer for her.

"We have twenty seconds before the arrival of what I assume are the bad guys," Bubbles says. She follows that with, "It appears my cognitive abilities haven't been affected by the transformation. If anything, I am more aware of the world around me than I ever was before. Fifteen seconds."

"Man, you haven't sworn once," Henry grumbles. "You don't have Tourette's anymore, do you?"

"I can make an exception for you, dick hamper. Ten seconds."

"Into the gate!" I shout, shoving everyone through ahead of me. "We're going home. Back to Dover. Think about the street!"

One by one, they slide through the gate. When I'm the last one remaining, I spin around to see a bearded man dressed in sinister-looking black leather emerge from the forest. Behind him, an army of monsters gnash their teeth, frothing with manic energy.

"Samael," I say.

He looks me over. "You're not one of them. Neither god nor Titan. You're something new..." Desperation fills his eyes. "Something unique. She will be pleased to–"

"Cherry can get fucked," I say, "all the way to oblivion and back."

He grins, his teeth stained with blood. "That is the plan. Enjoy your time at home." He looks ready to laugh, like he's just told the mother of all jokes.

I flip him two middle fingers and then step back through the gate. I emerge on the other side, where a receiving gate has appeared in the middle of the street. Before anything can follow, I light it up with a blast from my eyes, carving it into little bits.

I stand over the destroyed gate, admiring my handywork. "Everyone okay?"

"Uhh, Miah..." Sarah says. "Look up."

I nearly vomit on the spot. The neighborhood...

It's gone. Flattened. Charred. And not recently. The wrecked homes have foliage growing out of them.

"Everything...is destroyed," Bree says, breaking my heart. She doesn't deserve this kind of anguish. Not again.

I launch myself skyward, traveling a mile up, high enough to see from the White Mountains out to the Atlantic Ocean and south to Boston. The mountains remain, but Boston is completely missing, and the ocean...

I think it's boiling.

We're too late.

Cherry destroyed the world.

57

"Miah," Jonas says. "You're not going to find anything."

I've been digging through the ruins of my home for an hour, uncovering relics from a past that for me was just yesterday.

"There's no one alive here," he says. "I'd hear them."

"Not looking for survivors," I say, wiping my forearm across my eyes. My head is pounding from weeping. "I'm looking for something to bury."

He sighs. "At least let me help. It will take days for you to pick through the rubble, and I don't think we have that much time."

I pick up a window frame and toss it into the street. "Time can go fuck itself. Because what the hell happened? We left yesterday. *Yesterday!* And now the Earth is dead, and Cherry has won."

"Time isn't as fixed as people think," Bubbles says. She hovers beside Jonas, both of them held above the rubble by his telekinesis. "We were in another realm of reality. Beneath our feet, but not of this Earth. We traveled through space, which means we may have traveled through time, to another world with three stars, all of which could affect time."

"I think it was on purpose," Henry says. Didn't hear him glide in. "I think Dad sent us there, not just to raise an army, but to avoid..." He motions to the ruins. "...all this. We're all stronger than we were when we left. We trust each other. Can work together. Bubbles has a body. You can shoot lasers. Bree can kill gods from the inside. I think Dad wanted us to survive the end of the world so we...so someone...could defeat her."

"Why tell us to come back here?" I pick up a mug from the rubble. It's ridiculously large and looks like a moose. Perfect for an early morning coffee binge, but it took up a quarter of the cabinet. Mom hated this mug. I crush it in my hand. "Why make us see this?"

"Motivation?" Jonas says, but he's not really buying it.

"I'd be more motivated to save the people I love, than to avenge them." I give up searching, let my shoulders sag. Turn to Jonas. "Can you?"

He nods and glides back clear of the rubble. With a flare of my wings, I join him, Henry, and Bubbles in the street.

"Where's Bree?" I ask.

"Over here," Sarah says, walking up the hill toward us. Bree is on her shoulders, brown hair blowing in the warm, acrid breeze. She had me change her back a few minutes after arriving. Being back home, in the open as Demon Dog, didn't feel right to her, even though the only people who can see us are ghosts. She's dressed in a pink T-shirt, blue jeans, and a pair of sneakers that light up when you walk. Looks like she went through the ruins of her house, too.

"Ready?" Jonas asks.

"Do it."

He lifts his hands toward the rubble. One by one, chunks of what used to be one of many McMansions float up into the air, moving to the side to make room for what comes next.

"What are we looking for?" Sarah asks.

"Anything human," Henry says.

"Oh..."

My heart skips a beat when something pink and fleshy rises up, but it's just insulation. The shingles Jen and I laid on that night before the Darkness peel away. They're followed by bits and pieces of Mom's and Allie's bedrooms. Then the first floor. The fridge. Dining room table. All the shit from my room, including the recliner Sanchez and I spent so much time on together, chilling and consuming like a couple of bona fide wolves.

Thinking of Sanchez does me in. I blink away tears as the rest of the house rises up and away, but keeping myself together is a struggle.

When the debris stops coming, Jonas says, "That's everything."

"No one's home," Henry says. "That's good, right? Maybe there are survivors somewhere?"

I appreciate the optimism from someone who's not afraid to point out bleak realities, but I don't share his positive outlook. I walk across the lawn, pausing at the concrete foundation. I look down into the empty space and feel something inside me crack.

"Found them."

The others gather around and look into the basement. The pale concrete floor, free of debris thanks to Jonas, makes the shadows easy to see. A group of people had been huddled here, my family for sure. Maybe others. Maybe Jen. Or Steph, looking for Bree. All that remains of them is a spectral shadow, etched into the floor.

"It's like Hiroshima," Henry says, conjuring history lessons and photos of shadows cast onto walls—the only remains of people caught in those nuclear blasts. He's right, with one exception. Those shadows marked the end of a gruesome and terrible war. These punctuate the beginning of a new one.

Cherry thinks she's won, but I'm not going to fucking stop until she's ash.

Rage-fueled energy builds within me, out of control and about to explode. I turn my face to the sky, let out a brokenhearted scream, and unleash a powerful laser blast that would carve the moon in half if it was in the way.

I don't stop until a gentle hand rests on my back.

"I can't pretend to know how you feel," Bubbles says. "Not yet. But you are not without family. We are with you now, and for whatever comes next."

Her kindness drains my anger, replacing it with sorrow. I all but fall into her embrace, crying into her shoulder. Bree wraps her arms around the both of us and plants her face against our waists. Sarah is there next, joining the group hug from the other side. Jonas is close behind, enveloping Bree as he puts his arms around Bubbles and me.

Henry is the last to join, wrapping his arms around Bubbles and Sarah. He sniffs back a tear and says, "This is nice."

"Nice?" I ask.

"Family has always been part of your life," he says. "It's new for me. I felt lucky with Sarah and Helen. But this..."

"Great, now we've got Vin Diesel on the team," Jonas says, getting a chuckle out of everyone.

"Family," Henry says, doing his best Dominic Toretto impersonation. "I live my life a quarter mile at a—"

A wall of wind slaps into us like a tornado has just magically appeared in the street. Dust and debris swirls around us. "Spread out!" I shout. "Get ready to hit 'em! On my mark!"

I crouch down, swipe my thumb across Bree's forehead, and then turn to face the swirling wind. If Cherry decided to show herself now, at this moment, she's going to regret it.

I flare my wings and arm blades while charging up a laser blast.

Beside me, Bree sheds her humanity, destroying her newfound sneakers and shedding her hair again. She extends her claws and crouches, ready to lunge.

Sarah has her dory ready, the perfect Spartan stance. The spear is charged and ready to throw. Beside her, Henry's body crackles with electricity, positioned like a runner on a starting block, ready to throw himself into battle—a living weapon. Finally, Jonas stands between the danger and Bubbles, whose capabilities—if any—are still unknown. I can't see the telekinetic shield protecting them, but I'm sure it's there. He turns to me and waits.

"Clear it!" I say.

With a swipe of his hand, the wind, along with the debris and the dust it carries is all slapped to the side, revealing the street, and the object at its center.

"Uhh," Henry says. "The hell is that?"

"Looks...like a bell," I say, but it's an oversimplification. The humming machine is about the size of an old school Volkswagen beetle, but round. Its surface looks like brushed bronze, but it's also covered in grime and what appear to be battle scars—bullet indentations, scratches, and scorch marks. The outside is covered in symbols I don't recognize. Looks like some ancient language, but nothing like the symbols covering the gates.

"Well, well, well," comes a voice from the object's far side. "Look at you all." An old woman staggers out from behind the truck-sized device. She's steadying herself with one hand. The other clutches her side, covering a bloody wound. She's wearing some kind of armor that's seen better days. She's torn up, covered in layers of multi-colored blood, and her face is covered in equal parts ash and scrapes. "Better late than never, I suppose."

She pauses to catch her breath.

"Are…you okay?" I ask.

She laughs, and then grunts in pain. "Look around, kid. No one is okay."

"Was this Cherry?" I ask.

"Cherry Bomb," she says. "Like the song. Yeah. You know her?"

"I'm the guy that's going to kill her."

She smiles at that. "Oh, I like you." She looks us over, one at a time, nodding to herself. She smiles and winks at Henry. "You, too. Anywho, which of you is in charge?"

Everyone turns to me.

"Looks like that's you." She motions for me to approach with her index finger.

I step closer. When she starts to sag toward the ground, I catch her. "I got you."

"Such a nice boy," she says. "I'm sorry you had to see all this, but—ugh." She convulses in pain. "Oh, dear. I'm afraid there isn't time to explain."

"Cherry knows you're here?" I ask.

"Probably," she says. "And…" she removes her hand from the wound. It is gaping. I'm not sure how she's standing, let alone alive. "Tell them to put their hands on the bell. Hurry!"

"Everyone put your hands on this thing!" I shout. I don't know why, but I trust this lady. "What's your name?" I ask, while the others rush over and do what I said.

She smiles at me, blood seeping from the side of her mouth. "Name's Wini. And I'll see you soon." She straightens herself up, places her hand on the bell, and then waits for me to do the same. When I do, she says, "Don't tell Delgado about what happens next. It will hurt too much."

I don't know who Delgado is, but I get what she's saying. Sometimes it's better to not know about a tragedy until the job is done. I sigh. The same reason Zeus didn't tell us about the Earth's destruction. Because he knew we wouldn't follow through with the journey. Because he knew we'd fall apart instead of coming together. Because he knew, somehow, that we'd get a second chance.

"Hold on to your taints," Wini says. The bell starts humming and vibrating.

"I love this lady!" Henry says.

"It will take you where you need to go," she says, voice growing weak. "Just don't take your hand away. Not even to catch me."

"Catch you?" I ask.

"Hey," she says, putting her hand under my chin and forcing eye contact. "Don't let them make the trade."

I have no idea what that means, but the moment she says it, Wini's eyes roll back, and she slips away. I reach for her, but I keep my hand planted on the bell and miss her. As she falls away, the neighborhood disappears. For a moment, we're in a white void.

Then we're out.

Back in the neighborhood.

The sun is shining.

The homes are restored.

Birds sing in the trees.

And then a voice spins me around. "Babe?"

Jen is standing in the street, wide-eyed, looking at me, at the others, and at the big-ass machine that just appeared in the middle of the road. Allie is with her. She's holding a piece of paper with photos of me and Bree on it. Above our faces is the word: MISSING.

"How long have we been gone?" I ask.

Before she can answer, a helicopter roars past overhead, swings around, and lands in the street. Swirling dust forces our hands to our eyes. When the rotor slows and the debris settles, I look up to find a sassy old woman, dressed in a tight skirt, looking like all kinds of aged trouble. "Well, it's about time!" she says. "I was beginning to think you assholes might never show up."

She struts right up to me, giving me a once over. "You're in charge?"

"I am."

She glances at Henry.

Gives him a wink.

I can tell she's about to lay a speech on me. Probably thinks she's about to blow my mind. So, I beat her to the punch and say, "Hey, Wini."

She purses her lips and squints up at me. Turns her attention to the others. Seems to absorb everything she's seeing. The state of our clothing. The looks in our eyes. The only person she can't see is Bree, who's hiding behind the bell, probably waiting for me to change her back to her human self. Then she looks at the bell. I don't think she knows what it is—yet, but she puts two and two together.

In a flash, the bell disappears again. Must have been automated, waiting for us all to take our hands away. Which makes sense. I wouldn't leave a time machine in our hands. Last thing we'd want is Henry in the past, sending the space-time continuum into convulsions.

Wini shields her eyes. Lowers her hand when the light fades. Then she gives me a 'lie to me and perish in a flaming pit' stare. "We lose, don't we?"

I frown, but then say, "Not this time."

"What's the difference?" she asks.

"This time," I say, looking back at the others, smiling when Bree embraces her Demon Dog self, enough to step out from behind me and let herself be seen. "This time you have us."

EPILOGUE

She stood atop the barren hillside, admiring her creation. It had taken years to complete, testing her capabilities and her knowledge to the limit. Creating inside a virtual reality was much easier. Code and predesigned elements that could be reused or adapted allowed her to construct entire universes and timelines. But here, in this reality of flesh, blood, and physical laws–which she could bend, but not break–creation took time.

However, it wasn't beyond her reach.

Nothing was beyond her reach.

"What do you think?" she asked, looking up at the cloudy sky, flickering with orange light that looked like fire. She took a deep breath, tasting the blood in the air, the decay, the remnants of what was reduced to rubble all around.

"Marvelous," Samael said. "A masterpiece."

"If only I could take full credit."

"Do you still plan on finding him? Your…muse?"

"Muse is too kind a word. I am bound by his writings, my creations reduced to his paltry vision. But…it will be enough. And when we find him…perhaps I will have him expand my resources. Time is on our side. Whatever happens now, will happen then." She smiles. "After all this time, I have become an optimist."

"You have much to look forward to."

"And you have much to do," she says, her voice folding him inward. "But first…I wish to sit and admire what I have done."

"Yes, mistress," he said, dropping to his knees, leaning forward, and planting his hands on the jagged ground. He grunted as the stone dug into his knees, but he held his complaints, even as she sat down on his back and crossed her legs.

She leaned forward, hands clasped atop her knee, smile on her face. Below, an endless sea of the damned wailed, hunted, chewed, and thrashed, all of them writhing in endless torment, waiting for her command.

"Beautiful."

AUTHOR'S NOTE

No one ever told me to "never go full Greek myth." Maybe someone should have. While I clearly adapted the ancient stories to my own universe, I tried to stay true to the…strangeness present in those original tales, which is usually filtered out in most modern retellings. The result was a lot of nakedness, a bit of philandering, and more than one reference to incest. If any of that ruffled your feathers, I hereby raise my innocent hands and say, "Blame the ancient Greeks!" Also, blame yourself! If you made it this far in the Infinite Timeline, you knew where things were going!

But maybe crazy Greek shenanigans is your jam? Maybe sewing horses and people together to make centaurs is the kind of thing that makes you happy? If so, please consider stopping by Amazon, Audible, and Goodreads to post a review. I'd love to keep writing bonkers novels like this one, and the better it sells, the more likely that is to happen. I had a lot of fun writing this book, forging a team through bizarre, frightening, and hilarious scenarios. Hopefully it will be enough to get the through the horrors yet to come in SINGULARITY, the next and final book in the Infinite Timeline.

If you want to be sure you don't miss the final books, all the books to follow, and news about upcoming comic books, movies, TV series, etc., you can visit bewareofmonsters.com and sign up for the newsletter. Or, you can join the Tribe at facebook.com/groups/JR.Tribe. It's an amazing group of fans and the first place that cool stuff gets announced. Also, we give away free stuff every week!

Thank you, dear reader, for joining me on this journey into literary madness. Writing these books has gotten me through some tough times, and I really appreciate every single person that's supported me all these years. I wouldn't be here without you.

—Jeremy Robinson

ACKNOWLEDGMENTS

Got to kick this off by thanking the late, great Ray Harryhausen for instilling a love for Greek mythology that has served my career well, starting with the Jack Sigler Thrillers and now in Khaos. I like to think I'm carrying the torch for future generations... Thanks to Kane Gilmour, for supreme editing and the bazillion other things you help me with. Thanks also to our army of proofreaders: Brandon Burnett, Julie Carter, Elizabeth Cooper, Holly Strickland Chandler, Dustin Dreyling, Donald Firl, Joseph Firoozmand, Donna Fisher, Cynthia Gregory, Dee Haddrill, Andre Jenkin, Becky Tapia Laurent, Janis Levontis, Rian Martin, Stefanie Maubach, Jessica Otterstål, Jeff Sexton, and Heather Beth Sowinski. You all help conceal the fact that I'm just as bad at typing as I am spelling.

Gotta thank Alex Maddern as well. Not only does he let me mutilate his reputation as Alex Maddern, bigApe and Gordon Whiskers, he also spends a LOT of time discussing my crazy ideas and donating his own. But don't let it go to your head, Al. Big thanks to Podium Audio for taking on the Infinite Timeline halfway through and helping the world expand in awesome ways. R.C. Bray...what can I say? You're the voice in my head. No one else could have brought these characters to life like you have. Last, but not least, thanks to Damonza.com for providing kick-ass covers. I was nervous about giving up the job I'd done for most of my writing career, but the last four books have looked stellar, thanks to you.

—JR

ABOUT THE AUTHOR

Jeremy Robinson is the *New York Times* and #1 Audible bestselling author of over seventy novels and novellas, including *Infinite, The Others,* and *The Dark,* as well as the Jack Sigler thriller series, and *Project Nemesis,* the highest selling, original kaiju novel of all time (which is in development for TV with Chad Stahelski, director of John Wick). Robinson is known for mixing elements of science, history, and mythology, which has earned him the #1 spot in Science Fiction and Action-Adventure, and secured him as the top creature feature author. Many of his novels have been adapted into comic books, optioned for film and TV, and translated into fourteen languages. He lives in New Hampshire with his wife and three children.

Visit him at www.bewareofmonsters.com.